Something Blue

Something Blue

ALEX SARKIS

ultimo
press

Published in 2022 by Ultimo Press,
an imprint of Hardie Grant Publishing

Ultimo Press
Gadigal Country
7, 45 Jones Street
Ultimo, NSW 2007
ultimopress.com.au

Ultimo Press (London)
5th & 6th Floors
52–54 Southwark Street
London SE1 1UN

 A catalogue record for this
work is available from the
National Library of Australia

Something Blue
ISBN 978 1 76115 089 0 (paperback)

10 9 8 7 6 5 4 3 2 1

Cover design George Saad
Typesetting Kirby Jones | Typeset in 12/17.5 pt Adobe Garamond Pro
Copyeditor Ali Lavau
Proofreader Rebecca Hamilton

Printed in Australia by Griffin Press, part of Ovato, an Accredited ISO AS/NZS 14001
Environmental Management System printer.

 The paper this book is printed on is certified against the
Forest Stewardship Council® Standards. Griffin Press holds
FSC® chain of custody certification SGSHK-COC-005088.
FSC® promotes environmentally responsible, socially beneficial
and economically viable management of the world's forests.

Ultimo Press acknowledges the Traditional Owners of the country on which we work,
the Gadigal people of the Eora nation and the Wurundjeri people of the Kulin nation, and
recognises their continuing connection to the land, waters and culture. We pay our respects
to their Elders past and present.

For Dad, Mum and Tayta

and

In loving memory of my godmother,
Susan Sarkis

Chapter 1

'You still together? You and that idiot?'

My heart seizes at the mention of him. 'No, Tayta.'

'*Eh*, good. *Kess Emou*.'

My grandmother keeps watering the parsley, her left hand on her lower back, sundress billowing in a barely there breeze. I rest in my chair, but the damage is done. I'm thinking about him again and I feel sick from it. His face, the last thing he said to me. That nauseating betrayal. Tayta moves across the grass, stretching the hose to its limit with her arm raised like a stout ballerina in arabesque. I try to find a thought that doesn't hurt. But everything, *everything*, leads back to him.

'You no eating.' Tayta glares at me over her shoulder, a misty rainbow glistening at her feet. I'd worn a loose t-shirt today hoping she wouldn't notice how skinny I am, but of course she did. As soon as I came through the door, she saw it right away, grabbing my face and yelling, '*Yi, ya Adra!* What wrong with you?' Now the two of us are caught in a stand-off: her eyeing the plate of fruit in front of me, while I sip water, barely enough to wet my lips. '*Yallah!*'

The apples are turning brown in the heat. I force myself to take a slice when Ling appears over the back fence like a one-woman puppet show.

'Hi, Nada.' She waves at my grandmother.

'Hello, love.'

'Nice weather today. Very hot.' Ling fans herself from beneath a wide straw hat. It's always warmer out West by at least a few degrees, and even though it's only mid-September, I can hear the distant sound of an ice-cream truck, heralding the slow approach of summer. She spies me under the branches of Tayta's bottlebrush tree, its red flowers in full bloom like Christmas tinsel. 'You got visitor today?'

'Yeah, that my son daughter. Raymond daughter, Nicole.'

'Ohhh, very pretty.'

'Yeah, look like her dad.' Tayta says it proudly, still swaying the hose.

Ling nods. 'My granddaughter go America now. She doctor, and she marry doctor, too.'

God.

I watch as Tayta bends down to rip up a weed. 'That nice.'

Ling leans on the old wooden fence with a tentative look in her eye. 'You get letter from builder?'

Ah, so that's the reason for all this small talk.

Tayta keeps her back turned. 'Yeah, I see it.'

I take a small bite of apple while Ling makes her pitch. 'If we sell together, we get big dollar.'

My grandmother walks back to the tap and twists it tight. 'I no selling.'

'Jeffrey get one million dollar.'

I raise my eyebrow. *One million dollars for a red brick in Bankstown?* Well, that's Sydney for you.

'I no selling.' Tayta opens the back door and beckons me to follow. I grab my plate and cup and smile at Ling, who mutters something in Mandarin and then disappears.

'Why don't you sell and come live with us?'

Tayta slides the screen closed. '*Ma badi*,' she says. *I don't want to.* Her answer, though blunt, is unsurprising. There're too many memories here; she's too attached. How can you sell something that's a part of who you are? And it's not just her – it's all of us. You can see it on the walls: our baby photos and our school photos, all framed between rosaries and pictures of Jesus. This is where our childhoods were spent, swinging off the Hills hoist and climbing up the porch to pick sour grapes.

'I no leaving my home,' she says. 'Not for Ling, not for no one.'

Tayta dries her hands on her dress while I set myself up on the vinyl lounge next to Jidou's chair. It's a big brown recliner with worn-out arms and, even though my grandfather has been gone a while, no one's allowed to sit in it. He used to play cards against himself on a small square table, while his grandkids ran and yelled and hid behind doors to scare each other. Those were the days: simple, happy, unaffected. But I guess we all grew up.

Well, all but one.

My cousin Chadi kicks in his sleep on the opposite couch. The TV's on mute and one of his shoes is missing. He's here because he can't go home. His mother hates it when he drinks; if she saw him hungover, she'd lose it. So, they play this game every Sunday – their own version of hide-and-seek – with Chadi passed out at someone's house, and Aunty Faye calling around trying to find her son.

'*Yallah, oum!*' Tayta swats him with her bare hand. 'Get up.'

He opens his eyes and groans. 'Nic, I need water.'

I go to the kitchen and come back with a glass pitcher from the fridge. He pours it freefall into his mouth with surprising precision.

'What's the time?' he rasps.

'Twelve.'

He looks at the TV, sees the midday news and nods. 'I'm never drinking again.'

'*Ya Allah!* You saying this last week, *now you sick*!' Tayta yells while my cousin presses a pillow to his face. 'You same as you dad! *Jahesh!*' Donkey.

I sit watching them, chewing another slice of apple.

'When you gonna get marry?' our grandmother demands.

Chadi drops the cushion. 'Nic's older than me, she's not married.'

'By one day!' I snap.

'Nicole *very* good girl. *Inta jahesh!*' Tayta's standing feet apart with her hand pointed at the TV. 'Even this one get marry!'

We both turn to see footage of Salim Mehajer, pushing through a crowd of frenzied journalists.

'Yeah,' says Chadi, 'and he's getting divorced too.'

I take the TV off mute while they argue back and forth.

Salim, are you guilty? Salim, are you going to jail?

He's walking from Downing Centre Court wearing mirrored aviator sunglasses and a blue silk tie. A few months ago, no one knew who the fuck he was. But then he had that wedding – that *big Lebanese wedding* – where he'd paraded through the streets of Western Sydney like a real-life prince. And although for most around these parts it was little more than another colourful day in Lidcombe, the rest of Australia baulked. Because of course Salim wasn't a prince; he was a local councillor, a public servant.

'Why you have one shoe?' Tayta stares down at Chadi, but he ignores her. He leans back and lets loose a silent burp while I gradually raise the volume.

Salim Mehajer, seen here leaving court in June, is facing several investigations, including alleged electoral fraud.

'Yeah, that's what we need, Nic – *more noise.*'

The disgraced former deputy mayor continues to be the subject of an AVO, taken out on behalf of his estranged wife. The couple were married in the so-called 'wedding of the century' but separated less than ten months later.

The newsreader tilts her head. She reads the prompter with an arched brow and just the slightest hint of ridicule. But I don't blame Salim for the big wedding. Lebanese people talk so much about getting married that by the time you're in your twenties it's the only thing you can think about.

'Cuz, *turn it down!*'

I reluctantly lower the volume, while Tayta does just the opposite. '*You no baby anymore! You man!*'

'Okay, *okay!*' I watch as Chadi struggles to his feet. He puts his arms around our grandmother and kisses her face. 'I'm sorry, okay? I'm sorry.' I can see her body start to soften. She strokes his back, pacified by his childlike hug. Chadi, as the fates would have it, is her only grandson; the only boy on my father's side that can carry our name, *God help us.* They hold each other for a while, then he says, 'Can I have some fruit like Nic?'

Tayta starts laughing. '*Yi*, you big baby!' And she heads for the kitchen with a smile on her face.

'Fuck, the old girl's got a nag on her, hey?'

I fold my arms as he drops to the couch.

'What?' He twists his hand at me.

'Well, for starters, your shoe's in a bush out front.'

'Oh, nice of you to bring it in.'

'I wasn't sure it was yours.'

'*Cuz.*' He's propped up on his elbow now. 'Who else wears size eleven loafers in this fuckin' neighbourhood? *Ling?*'

I try not to laugh. 'Where were you last night, anyway?'

'Just went casino with my mates.' He lies down again. 'What'd you do?'

'Nothing, man. I stayed home.'

He rolls his eyes. 'Cuz, forget him, okay? The guy's a cunt – he's nothing special.'

'Well, maybe not to you.'

'Oh, come on, you can't be serious. He only cared about himself, Nic. About his hair and his shoes and his stupid fucking nipple ring.' He impersonates him now, lifting up his shirt and pulling a face like Johnny Bravo. 'What a loser.'

'Yeah, well, I didn't think much of that girl from Wenty Leagues, either, but you were smitten.'

'Wenty Leagues?'

'Yeah, the one with the septum piercing.'

'Oh, bro. Stop right there 'cos I won't be hearing a single bad word about Amy. You try find a girl that can drag-race down the M7 and roll a durrie at the same time.'

'I didn't realise those were positives.'

'You know something?' he muses. 'I would've married her. Like, if she was Lebanese and less of a druggo, I would've.'

'Right, so a completely different person, then?'

'Yeah' – he grins – 'but still called Amy.'

'Point is, Chadi, that just because you think someone's a cunt doesn't magically make things better for me. If anything, it's almost a character reference: *Chadi thinks so-and-so's a cunt*. Well then, he must actually be an upstanding gentleman.'

Chadi dismisses me with a wave of his hand. 'Yeah, well guess what? There's plenty of other cunts for you to date, so don't worry.'

'Okay, here your fruit!' Tayta brings a plate of freshly cut apples and oranges arranged in the shape of a smiley face and sets it on a wooden table in front of my cousin.

'Thanks, Tayta.'

'*Eh, sahten.*' They make love eyes at each other before she wanders back to the kitchen. All morning, the smell of *kafta ou rez* has wafted through the house, warming the air with its heady scent of onion and spice. Admittedly, it's not really the weather for it – a red-sauce casserole on a twenty-eight-degree day with only a single fan oscillating between us – but Chadi's already scoffed half his fruit.

'I'm fuckin' starved,' he says to me, taking a wedge of orange and chewing it whole. '*Hey Tayta!* When's lunch?'

She shouts from the kitchen, 'When you dad and you sister get here!'

'Yeah, hectic,' he mutters. 'So dinner, then.'

I reach for the remote and resume flicking channels. Tayta only has free-to-air TV, not counting the satellite on her roof that beams Al Jazeera from the other side of the globe. After a few routine laps of the five available English stations, Uncle Jimmy comes through the front door wearing the same Phuket t-shirt that he's worn since his Muay Thai trip in the late 1990s.

'Hi, sweetheart.'

I get up to kiss him. 'Hi, Amou.'

'How've you been?'

'Yeah, good.'

'Hey, I found this outside.' He tosses the missing loafer at his son. 'Big night, mate?' They're so alike, him and Chadi. Same blue eyes, same toothy smile.

'Always.'

'Yeah, well, good luck with your mum. She's fuckin' pissed.'

Poor Aunty Faye. I can imagine her keeping vigil till dawn.

'You should've sent her a text or something,' my uncle says.

'My fuckin' phone died. And when's she gonna relax?' Chadi looks to me for support. 'I mean, we're almost twenty-seven – when's the nagging gonna stop?'

I shrug and give the obvious answer. 'Never.'

'Mum, your garden's looking good!' Uncle Jimmy stands at the window, surveying the view.

'*Eh*, I just water all the flower,' Tayta answers him from the kitchen. '*Ana ou* Nicole, we both go out, it beautiful.'

'Oh yeah,' he looks some more before coming to sit beside me, his arm resting along the back of the couch. 'How's things anyway, love? How's Dad going?'

'He's good.'

'Work busy?'

I shrug. 'Yeah, you know how it is.'

Uncle Jimmy nods. 'Well, that's good,' he says. '*Allah awikoun*, busy is good.' He turns his attention to the TV. 'Oh, look at this one, poor bastard.' Another channel is running the same news story about Salim Mehajer.

'Dad, I swear his head's everywhere.'

Uncle Jimmy takes a slice of browned apple and bites it in half. 'That's what they do, son. They get their claws into someone, and they crucify 'em.'

We sit in silence for a moment, the three of us watching.

'You know the media? They're obsessed with Lebs,' my uncle continues. 'You do something wrong and you're Lebanese, you're fucked.' He turns to look at me now. 'Did you see in the papers the other day? A *two-page* write-up on the "culture crisis" out West. They've been banging on about some bikie war and the pork-free menu at Punchbowl KFC. And not in that order, mind you. It's the halal that's really got 'em howling.'

I'd seen the article, though I can't say I'd given it much attention. Lately, there's been a constant stream of news stories starring flashy, reckless Arabs, posted under headlines on the *Herald*'s front page.

Tayta's doorbell rings again, and my cousin Layla comes into the lounge room: a perfect, timely example of flashy and reckless. She has long, black hair like mine and a Leo tattoo that peeks above the waistband of her hipster jeans. '*Tfeh!* There's vomit on the grass,' she says. 'What scum would throw up in someone's yard?'

Chadi looks desperately at Uncle Jimmy, who stands from the couch and lies for his son. 'A dog must've done it.' He sidesteps his daughter. 'Go sit with your cousin, I'm gonna go check on lunch.'

Layla takes his empty seat, tossing her Versace bag on the vinyl between us.

'Hey, Lay.'

'Hey, babe. I miss you. Where've you been?'

Chadi answers for me: 'Hiding.'

He should talk.

'You've lost a lot of weight.' She eyes my legs.

'Yeah, too much.' Chadi again.

Layla gives her brother a look. 'I'm talking to *Nicole*, do you mind?' She's a year or so older than us and has always enjoyed the authority that comes with it. I watch as she flicks her hair, ready to impart some pearl of wisdom, older cousin to younger. 'Babe, when I broke up with my ex, I was fuckin' devastated.' She talks with her hands; her talon-like acrylics painted poison red. 'I lost five kilos, babe; I couldn't stop shitting.'

Chadi scrunches his face. 'Please, man, *yuck*.'

'Oh, shut up, Chadi. Girls *shit*. Get over it.'

'Wow,' he says. 'Classy.'

She kicks her feet off the couch. '*Classy?* Go fuck yourself! I had to step in your vomit just now!'

Chadi plays dead.

'Yeah, that's right,' Layla hisses. 'I know it was you.' She turns back to me, smoothing her hair. 'Anyway, babe, what were we saying? Oh yeah, I was *so* upset. I couldn't eat, I couldn't sleep, but you know what? He ended up with the biggest slut, she gave him chlamydia.' Layla pouts proudly and points to the sky. 'That's God.' The cross hanging from her neck is barely visible between her breasts. 'And *look*.' She puts a hand on her Versace bag. 'Now I'm with someone ten times better.'

'You mean ten times richer.'

'Fuck off, Chadi! *Gronk!*' She throws a cushion at him.

'Hey! Stop! *Fuckin' hell!* Watch some TV or something!' Uncle Jimmy yells at them from the kitchen, like they're both still kids playing pillow fights after school.

I grab the remote and switch channels. A cry comes out of Chadi.

'Oh, not this one again!'

And then from next to me, with a flourish of her hands, 'Is that Salim Mehajer? I don't know why, babe, but I find him so hot.'

I don't pretend to be special, but I know I'm *from* somewhere special. Nowhere in all the world is there a group of people quite like there is in Western Sydney. And the best way to meet them? Well, the same way we all met Salim.

At a wedding, of course.

Chapter 2

'The hair, babe, the dress. It's too much.' We stand between tables, looking at Instagram posts from earlier that day. 'And the crown? Like she's Miss World?' Elie puts his hand on his hip. 'Really babe, it's so *pageant*.' I look at Elie and realise that being single and Lebanese is probably much worse if you've just turned forty and you're gay as well – the type of gay that seems a lot more obvious to others than it does to Elie. He touches the brooch on his satin lapel, his nails more manicured than mine. 'When I get married, I want my wife wearing simple white. None of this woggy sparkle.'

God, the denial. I mean, it's one thing to be in the closet, but how far do you go before you end up in Narnia?

'Maybe she looks better in person?' I'd deliberately missed the 2 pm church service, not wanting to be caught in an hour-long Aramaic chant.

'Babe, there's three filters on this fucking photo. I can only *imagine* real life.' He turns from me now to study the reception. As Sydney's premier 'PR guru slash party planner', Elie has a frightening eye for detail, which he uses now to incinerate our surrounds. 'The flowers are fake, the cake table isn't centred, and whoever hung those chandeliers is completely unqualified, because the middle one is way too low.' He takes a glass of wine from a passing waiter and swirls it as if he were a sommelier. 'And God knows what this is. Probably poured from a bag of goon.' He's about to take a sip, his silver quiff tilted back, when we're interrupted by a brassy, unfamiliar voice.

'*Oh. My. God.* You look amazing!' I turn to see a woman standing beside us wearing enormous crystal earrings and a burgundy clip-on bun. I know she's married to one of my cousins – distant, on my father's side – but I can't quite remember her name. Tania? Therese?

'Oh, thanks,' I say, more confused than flattered.

'No, but really!' She takes a step closer, looking me over in genuine awe. 'Your body is *incredible*! I can't believe you just had a *baby*!'

Elie, who'd been watching on passively, chokes on a sip of wine.

'Oh, that's not me.' I try to stay light. 'You're thinking of my sister.'

'Oh!' She laughs awkwardly. 'Well, you're both so beautiful I can't tell you apart.'

I nod wordlessly, hoping she'll leave me alone, but she pushes on. 'How's the wedding planning, then? Not long till your big day!'

Jesus. 'No, that's my younger sister – she's the one who's engaged.' I don't look at Elie; I just can't.

'Oh … well, *aabelik,* gorgeous. You look great. You really do.' *Aabelik* is a way for smug marrieds to patronise hopeless singles. It translates roughly as, 'you're next', although I've never been next, and I'm not likely to be next this time either.

'Right,' says Elie, flagging down a waiter as she walks away. 'I think we'll be needing some more goon.'

'God, I hate weddings.'

He grabs me a glass from a proffered tray. 'Babe, forget it. You're a vision.'

'Yeah, for postnatal I look great.'

The two of us swig in unison as the MC moves to the centre of the dance floor and invites us all to sit. My family have been spread across two tables: Tayta and our parents on one, and us cousins on another. My sisters are already seated with their partners, and I realise on approach that in the suddenness of being dumped, I'd completely forgotten about the empty chair waiting next to mine. I part ways with Elie and pull out my seat, joining as a fifth wheel.

After a second announcement from the MC, the rest of our table starts to fill. Clockwise from where I'm sitting is my younger sister, Monica, and her fiancé, Luke, followed by my older sister, Jacqueline, and her husband, Mick. On Mick's other side is Layla – an eyesore in sequined fuchsia – with her bag resting on what should be Chadi's seat. The remaining few chairs are taken by Ainsley, a new Aussie addition to the family, followed by her husband, our distant cousin Fouad (aka Fred) who we all thought would die a bachelor, coming full circle to the vacant space at my right arm, now a pillory for public humiliation.

'Who's sitting here?' asks Fred. 'Is your boyfriend coming?'

'No. We broke up.'

'Oh.' Fred keeps his hand on his wife's thigh. 'Sorry to hear. I thought you guys were serious.'

It comes, of course, with the implication that we weren't. That the past few years were just a charade. But Fred doesn't know how hard I tried. He doesn't know about the pit in my gut or the silent panic attacks I've been having whenever I leave my house. So, I just stare at him and say, 'We were.'

'Hmm. Well, maybe you guys will work it out.'

'Hey, how was the honeymoon?' Monica brokers a change in subject, both of us knowing full well she couldn't give a fuck about Fred and Ainsley's two-day trip to Fiji.

'Yeah, it was good,' he says. 'Just something small before we do the States next year.' Ainsley nods along, leaning against his shoulder. They touch constantly, overcompensating for the fact that their families can't stand each other. Fred's mum has never approved of his Aussie bride (whose name she insists on mispronouncing, often as 'Ainsel' but sometimes as '*Ayri*') and Ainsley's dad, who used to work for Border Force, is still an outspoken advocate of the White Australia policy.

'Yeah, nice,' says Monica. 'Which parts?'

'Oh, just LA.'

'*Shou*, cuz.' Chadi comes from the bar, drink in hand, and sits between me and Fred, exorcising the ghost of my ex in one swift movement. 'How's it going, mate?' He squeezes Fred's shoulder and I stare at him, caught off guard but grateful. 'What?' He stares back at me. 'Can I sit here?'

'Yeah, of course.' I shift my chair to give him room. 'I just thought you'd be sitting next to Layla.'

'Fuck for? She's got her bag to keep her company, anyway.'

We watch from our seats as the bridal party begin entering through the double doors: first the parents of the groom, then the parents of the bride, then the flower girl and the page boy, followed by the groomsmen and a trio of bridesmaids who come to stand beside each other, smallest to largest, like a life-size set of babushka dolls. The maid of honour and the best man are next – dancing to LMFAO's 'Party Rock Anthem' and shooting dry ice extinguishers in the air. At the table over from ours, Elie rolls his eyes, his glass of wine near empty.

Then the lights are dimmed, and we're told to stand.

A troop of Lebanese drummers and men dressed in Bedouin garb take position along the aisle. We hear the first few tantalising notes of an Arabic flute, and then the MC – his bald head now sheened in sweat – bellows his biggest line of the night: 'Ladies and gentlemen, please welcome for the first time *Mr and Mrs Saab*!'

And, oh, the mayhem that follows.

The happy couple come dancing through the double doors, navigating an obstacle course of fire-breathers, and fireworks and overly aggressive drummers. Chadi and I move to linger on the outskirts, clapping in time to the music while the bride gets hoisted on a big man's shoulder – her two-tier crown almost knocked off by Elie's astutely observed 'low-hanging chandelier'.

'See?' The man himself comes up behind us. 'A few more inches and she could've sued.'

'Fuck, bro, I know.' Chadi looks back at him, his face wide with boyish amusement. 'It full took her out!'

Elie likes Chadi, I can tell. He casts aside his acerbic manner and laughs along with my cousin; a nervous giggle, spurred I'm sure by his second glass of goon. I'd first noticed this unlikely infatuation about three years ago, when I'd casually introduced them at a charity function for sick kids. Chadi had mentioned in passing his enthusiasm for a particular auction item – a football signed by the NSW State of Origin team – and we'd all watched on in shock as Elie outbid half the room, taking home the encased signatures for an 'absolute steal' of almost six thousand dollars, even though he'd never watched a game of League in his life.

In front of us, a *dabke* starts to form – a dance that, as a bystander, could get you stomped on or kicked in the shins. 'I'm going back to sit,' I say.

My cousin responds with an eager nod and the two of us inch past Layla, who's doing wrist twirls to the erratic pounding of a red-faced drummer kneeling at her feet.

'Fuck, what a circus,' says Chadi, and I guess for the most part it is. There are musicians leaping like acrobats, hundreds of cheering spectators, cousins clowning on the dance floor and – without being rude – the occasional bearded lady. I glance across at Ainsley, still stuck to her husband's side, and I wonder if she's used to it yet.

When the band finally stops, my sisters and Layla return to their seats.

'Babe, I'm starved,' says Layla, reaching for a plate of *kibbeh*. 'I didn't eat for three days to fit in this dress.' The meze before us is typical: an uninspired spread of hommous, tabouli and water-soaked carrots. Chadi pours me a glass of Coke from a plastic jug, then he tries to force some food on me. I take a piece of toasted bread to pacify him.

'Where's the baby, Jackie?' Fred shouts around the centrepiece separating him and my older sister. It's a styrofoam ball impaled with polyester roses that Elie described as inhumane.

'She's with Mick's mum.'

Fred gives my brother-in-law the thumbs-up. 'Night out, no kid.'

'Mate, it's not what it used to be.'

'Got that right,' says Jacqueline. 'My arse barely fits in this chair.'

To the left of me, Luke grins and nudges Monica, drawing her attention to the bride and groom. 'In a few months, Monnie, that's gonna be us.'

She follows his gaze, her dark eyes fixing on the newlyweds. It's supposed to be the most exciting time of her life, but for a homebody like Monica, the thought of being paraded in front of hundreds of people has begun to take its toll. Over the past month, her wedding preparations have descended into a gruelling game of extremes. She wavers between not wanting anything at all and then suddenly making major demands. Last week she wanted a horse and carriage, this week she wants to elope.

'Shit!' says Chadi. 'The footy's starting.'

I watch as he props his iPhone against the ice bucket, flicking between screens until the green grass of ANZ Stadium comes into view.

'Who's playing?' asks Fred.

'It's the semis, mate. Eels vs Cowboys.' He mutes the volume. 'Fuck, I hope Parra lose.'

'They probably will,' says Luke. 'I mean, I tipped them for an upset, but the Cowboys will win.'

Chadi stares at him in disgust. 'You tipped *Parra*?' He turns to Monica. 'Sorry, Mon, but I think you need to call off the wedding.' The Parramatta Eels are a blood rival of the Canterbury-Bankstown Bulldogs. Chadi, like the rest of my family, is a Bulldog: a devotion that goes far beyond wanting your team to win, but rather wanting your rival – regardless of who they're playing – to lose.

Monica takes the jug of Coke and pours some into a wineglass. 'Trust me, Chadi, at this point I'd call it off for a lot less.'

My cousin takes a handful of nuts from one of the bowls and leans back, readying himself for the game to start. It's almost time for kick-off, when a booming voice grabs my brother-in-law Mick from behind.

'HEY, BOYS!'

We all look up except for Mick, who's being held in an iron chokehold. He tries to twist out of it, quickly recognising the large hand splayed across his chest. 'Dave, ya dog!'

The giant behind him releases his grip with a laugh. 'How's it going, Mickey?'

Mick gets up and shakes his hand. 'Good, mate, good. The Rollie gave you away.'

Dave proudly brandishes his diamond watch. 'Always does. How's it going, Chads?' He slaps my cousin's back, before greeting Luke and Fred.

'You girls remember Dave?' We stare at Mick blank-faced. 'Dave. *Dave Dollaz.*'

DJ Dave Dollaz. *My God.*

The last time I saw Dave, he was spinning the decks at a nightclub called Heat. From what I've heard, he's since quit the club scene and become a builder, which, although lucrative, gets no points for originality. Almost every Leb I know is or was a 'builder', or lies and says they are. Mick invites him to join our table, and Layla, upon seeing a large man with a diamond Rolex, stops taking selfies and quickly gathers her bag.

'Yeah, babe,' she says. 'We got a spare seat.'

'You sure?' Dave moves to sit beside her, opposite to me. I think to myself that he's fair for a Leb: his greenish eyes and light brown hair making him look more … I don't know … Macedonian than Arab. But it's the way he speaks that gives him away – his burly Bankstown accent. 'Bro, what's wif this wedding?' he says to the table. 'I went to the bar, they reckon no vodka.'

Chadi laughs. 'Mate, what were you expecting? Bottles of Belvedere?' He swigs his Scotch. 'Did you let 'em drive your cars today?'

Dave pulls his phone from his pocket. 'Yeah, I did. The Rolls and the Lambo.' He flicks with his thumb and passes his phone to Chadi. 'We had the drummers wif us and everyfing.'

My cousin presses play on the video. 'Wow, bro! You shut four lanes!' I watch it over his shoulder: a shaky, ten-second clip, interspersed by a series of WhatsApp notifications from someone called 'Clare-tits' who calls Dave 'big boy' and asks if he wants to come over.

Chadi laughs. 'Hey, *big boy*! Clare's a bit keen!'

'What's this?' Mick smiles, wanting in on the joke. But Dave's not laughing. Instead, he's staring at me, his face now flushed with shame and panic.

I grab the phone from Chadi and pass it back to Dave. 'Stop it, you've embarrassed him. You're being rude.'

'Oh, come on,' says Chadi, still grinning. 'Dave's a single guy; there's nothing wrong with it.'

'Oh, so you're single?' Layla leans towards him, her cleavage bulging.

'Yeah, he is,' says Chadi. 'Are *you*?'

'Shut up, Chadi! I'm not asking for me.' Layla flicks her hair. 'I'm saying for *Nic*.' She points her hand in my direction.

'Why *me*?'

'Nic's newly single,' she says to Dave. 'You guys should go for a drink sometime.'

I'm still staring at her, my mouth slack. Dave's face is even redder than before, and all he can manage to muster is an awkward, 'Oh, yeah.'

'You know what?' Monica comes to my rescue again. 'I think it's a bit soon to be setting her up.' She shoots a look at Layla. 'And by the sounds of things, he's speaking to someone anyway.'

'Nah, nah.' Dave gets defensive. 'I'm not speaking to no one, she's just some Aussie.'

We all look at Ainsley.

Ainsley glares at Dave. 'What's *that* supposed to mean?'

'Shit, I didn't mean – I'm just saying she's not my girlfriend.'

Shock horror that 'Clare-tits' isn't his missus. *Jesus Christ.* I don't think I've ever sat at a worse table.

'Hey, Chadi, what's the score?' Luke runs a decoy to break the tension.

'Six–nil, Parra way. Their winger just landed a try.'

Ever since my cousin set his phone up, there's been a slowing of foot traffic behind our chairs, people loitering as they pass to check the points on the board or to curse the ref's mum.

'*Kess emou!*' Uncle Rashid croaks.

I look up to see him standing over me, staring at the game through his thick, black-rimmed glasses. He's dressed in his usual woollen turtleneck, same as he always wears even in summer. As kids we used to wonder why, and then we found out from Fred that he was almost decapitated in the Lebanese civil war. Everyone says he should have died, but Uncle Rashid's still here, yelling obscenities at Corey Norman and hiding the machete scar that curves across his throat.

He throws his hands up and storms off, irked by an unfair penalty.

'Don't worry, Amou,' Chadi calls out after him. 'It's only the first half. They won't win.'

Up on stage, the band resumes at a deafening volume. I reach for my phone on reflex and feel a sudden pang of grief. There are no calls and no texts. I tap my pin and stare at nothing, listlessly checking my apps the way a late-night snacker might peruse an empty fridge.

'You alright?' Chadi, though largely oblivious, has always had a radar when it comes to me.

'Yeah.'

'Watch the game with me,' he says. 'Just look here and focus on the game.' He angles his phone between us, his arm around the back of my chair, while The Cowboys and Parra score alternating tries. 'See what happened there,' he says. 'Fuck man! The Eels are making some runs. He scored that shit from 70 metres.' The two of us watch on until the bride and groom are presented with their second course.

'Don't eat the mains.' Elie appears behind us again. 'You'll seriously have *maghess* for the rest of your life.'

'Why?' I ask. 'What's wrong with them?'

Elie puts his hand on his hip. 'Well, *nothing*, if you like your chicken medium rare.'

Chadi looks down at his plate and promptly swaps it with my steak. 'What? Like you were gonna eat it anyway.'

True.

It's only now that I notice Dave Dollaz is still staring at me. I catch him watching, half-concealed behind the plastic petals of our table's centrepiece. His eyes immediately dart away, and so I do the same, focusing instead on the chicken à la salmonella in front of me. I wonder how long he's been watching. I think of how sad I was, staring at my phone, and I suddenly feel exposed.

'Aunty Mary says I'm going bald!' Layla, who'd left us to socialise, comes charging back to the table and I'm forced to look Dave's way again.

'What?'

She's standing by her chair, her bag flung wildly into Ainsley's lap. 'I went to the bathroom to fix my hair and Aunty Mary saw me in the mirror, and she said I'm going *bald*!'

Aunty Mary is Tayta's older, less likeable sister. She's the village spinster, and a trained sniper when it comes to people's weak spots. For Layla, it's always been her looks.

Monica frowns at her. 'You're not going bald; you've got hair to your arse.'

'But, babe, I've been shedding!'

'Mm … I wasn't going to say anything, but now that it's out in the open, you are looking a bit patchy.'

I turn to glare at Elie who gives me a boozy grin.

'Yeah, Lay,' Chadi joins in. 'Maybe you got alopecia.'

'What the fuck is that?'

'Oh my God, you don't have fucking alopecia!' Jackie silences the table. 'You'd be bald as the bloody MC. Or *Fred*.' Fred raises his glass in mock thanks. 'Just *sit down*, and everyone shut up! The speeches are about to start, anyway.'

Elie ambles off and the rest of us lapse into silence while the father of the groom and the father of the bride say their speeches. The former speaks purely in Arabic: a raucous toast to the newlywed couple with his hope that their union will produce many Saab sons. The second is delivered in English and sounds oddly like a eulogy: 'We will never see you walk down the stairs again. Our little girl has left us, our lives will never be the same.'

The bride and her mother begin to wail.

'Jesus, what a line-up.' Chadi pushes his chair out while the best man delivers a drunken ramble. 'Parra's getting smashed, by the way. Sorry, Luke, but you tipped the wrong team.'

'Fuck.'

'I'm going for a smoke, mate. Anyone wanna come?'

'Yeah, I'll come wif ya.' Dave gets to his feet and inches around Layla, who's still agonising over her hairline in a compact mirror.

The rest of us wait for the groom, and what follows – much to my amazement – is *perfect*. He talks about his bride: how beautiful she is, and how he couldn't bear to spend a single day without her. He says all the right things, but for me and my wounded heart, it's the worst speech of the night by far.

'I'm going to the toilet.'

Monica turns to me. 'Are you okay?'

'Yeah.' But I'm not okay, and I'm not going to the toilet either – I'm going home. Back to my bed, to where it's safe.

I'm almost at the door when the lights become dimmed for the bridal waltz, and I know now that I'm leaving at the right time, sparing myself the indignity of sitting alone while everyone joins for the couples' dance. Still, in a moment of morbid curiosity I turn to look back. And that's when I hear it: the one song I can't stand.

'Firestone'.

It brings back that summer: his smell, his taste. Dancing on the rooftop of a city bar; riding in the back of a cab, my legs across his lap. All those fleeting times I thought we were forever.

And it makes my stomach twist.

The bride and groom become blurred, swaying on a cloud of dry ice, and I imagine us dancing in their place.

My panic builds, my grief swells.

I turn my back and let it wash me out the door.

Chapter 3

They call my father the Car Yard King.

He owns six dealerships across Sydney that trade new and used vehicles, from European sports cars to second-hand work vans. When you drive along Church Street, you can see his name written on billboards, the largest being at his headquarters right in the middle of the strip.

I park my car beneath the bold lettering of NAJIM MOTORS on Monday morning, and walk through the showroom to the back stairs. I work on the top level, my desk pushed against a floor-to-ceiling tinted window in an open-plan office. From here I can see the whole of Parramatta; a skyline smattered with buildings and cranes and break-through towers. When I'm anxious, I play this game with myself where I stare out the window and try to find five things that are a certain colour. I read in a wellness magazine once, that concentrating on simple cognitive tasks helps you to detach from the onset of a mental spiral and aids in reducing stress.

Today, the colour is blue.

A blue bus.

A blue air dancer outside Ford.

A man in blue jeans.

'These are for you. Last month's deals, ready to be paid.'

Shivani, my father's long-serving, long-suffering executive assistant, places a stack of manilla folders on the edge of my desk. She's worn the same warm smile and the same braided bun for the past fifteen years, though lately it's started salting at the roots.

'Thanks.'

I push my chair out and power up the photocopier with my first batch of papers in hand. Each folder has been loaded with loose forms: contracts signed by customers, vehicle specs, licence plate registrations and lease agreements. By the time I'm done scanning them all, my computer has finally booted, so I return to my desk to check my emails. There are one hundred and four new messages since Friday at 5 pm.

I can breathe, but I can't swallow.

Blue sky.

Blue sky.

Blue sky.

'Hi, sweetheart.' My dad comes up behind me and rests a heavy hand on the back of my chair.

'Hi, Dad.'

'How's it going?'

'Good.'

'Anything happening?'

'No.'

He nods, staring down at me. Then he says, 'Okay, well, we got some new cars next door – we'll need you to get some photos later. For Facebook and that.'

It's his way of humouring my 'hobby'. Of keeping me here, piled to the teeth with paperwork, and not feeling so bad about it. I glance at the Nikon camera on my desk, and it makes me feel pathetic. I'd bought it years ago with my first few paycheques, intending to use it in far off cities, 'capturing ordinary people in extraordinary places'. That was my mission back then: to go to Paris or to Rome and just immerse myself in the local culture. Imagine being a bus driver, I'd thought, whose route revolved around the Colosseum. Imagine living in its shadow. I'd wondered if, after years of riding around it, that bus driver would even see it anymore. Probably not. He'd be too busy thinking about himself; about his kids and his tired wife, and the *bella donna* in the black dress sitting three rows back. Those were the stories I wanted to know; the ones that make you see a person as more than just an outline of the space around them. But instead, I've been here: crouched by the tyres of a ute, shooting the 2017 HiLux at forty-five-degree angles.

There is, of course, the obvious solution: that I fuck off overseas and stop martyring myself. But something about it feels like mutiny – there's an unspoken debt that I owe to my dad. He's spent his whole life building a 'family business', and you can't have one of those without steamrolling the dreams of your kids. So, I start from the top, checking each email with my father still lingering at my arm.

'Are you hungry? Have you eaten today?' He perches himself beside me, my desk creaking beneath the weight of him.

'No. I just got here.'

'Well, why don't we go for a walk to the corner? Get a muffin or something.'

'No, thanks.'

'What about a coffee, then?'

'I'll make a tea later.'

He glances around my desk, searching for signs of dysfunction, but everything is organised and neatly in its place. The only hint that I might be bordering on rock bottom, comes from the pale crest of my collarbones, peeking from my crisp white shirt.

'I really think you should eat,' he says.

I keep my eyes on my screen. 'Dad, I'm busy.'

He sits a bit longer, then he says, 'Okay, sorry.' He pats my shoulder and returns to his glass-walled office, resuming play on an old Western that's been paused mid-shootout on his flatscreen TV. Aside from his love of cars, my dad has always had a fondness for black-and-white movies. When he and Uncle Jimmy were kids, Tayta used to work long hours at a whitegoods factory in Belfield. She'd wake them at dawn to clean the house, and then at midday, they were allowed to sit and watch a movie in between chores. I think that's how they both learned English: by mimicking the Three Stooges, who barely spoke English at all. In any case, the habit stuck, because all these years later, Dad still watches the classics to take his mind off work. Today it's John Wayne in *Stagecoach*, and all I can hear from his open door is the sound of random gunfire, and him calling out to Shivani for another cup of coffee.

Moments later, Monica comes winding up the stairs, her phone pressed to her ear.

'What, this Saturday?' There's a pause while she listens. 'Yeah, but, Luke, we've got two open homes to go to. No point getting married if we haven't got a house.' As usual, she's conferring with her fiancé, always about some newly listed three-bedder or their upcoming Mediterranean honeymoon.

She walks over to the desk beside mine, dumping her bag and a black folder marked WEDDING with a loud thud. 'God, I know, I'm so over it. I can't wait until we're on that plane flying out of here. No more headaches, no more *work*.'

Blue.

Blue.

Something blue.

'Hey, cuz.' Chadi, who's been working here almost as long as me, struts across the floor and drops a thick wad of paperwork by my elbow.

'Hi.'

'I signed this guy last week; do you reckon you can advance me my commission? It's urgent.'

'Urgent in what regard?'

'In that I have a hotel booked on Friday.'

'Right. Well, you might want to cancel that, then.'

'Oh, come on, Nic,' he says. 'It's my only sale this month.'

'Chadi, see this pile?' I point at the just-scanned manilla folders. 'I got all these commissions to pay, and all your mates from downstairs have said the exact same thing. They're all *urgent*.'

'Yeah, but they're not your cousin.'

I swivel to face him. 'Did you hear what I just said? I'm *busy*. And I can't pay a deal that hasn't settled. You know that!'

'Okay, *relax*. You got your periods or something?'

I can't find blue anymore. All I can see is red. 'Oh, fuck off, Chadi! You finally do your job, for what? The first time in a month, and now it's *my* problem?'

Monica wheels her chair out, worried that things will escalate, but my cousin just waves me off and walks downstairs.

'*Nicole!*'

It's Dad.

My hands are shaking. 'I'm busy.'

'I know,' he says. 'But I want you to come here.'

I get up and go to his office.

He motions for me to shut the door and take a seat. 'What's wrong?'

'Nothing Dad, I'm just really busy.'

'Yeah, you keep saying that,' he says. 'But you've been staring out your window all morning.'

We're sitting opposite each other with the rest of the office watching, save for a strip of frosted glass that runs the length of his walls at eye level. He has his hands clasped on the desk between us and his movie on mute. I feel small in my chair, dwarfed by a man who's become deified for his size. When my dad was born, he weighed a freakish fourteen pounds, and while still in the crib he pulled a bee sting from his face with his bare little hand. He's never been back to Lebanon, but they still talk about him in the village; Raymond Najim: The Goliath child with bee immunity.

He leans forward, his eyes locked on mine. 'Why were you yelling?'

'Chadi was pissing me off.'

He nods, then he says, 'A lot of people have been pissing you off lately.'

'Well, a lot of people have been *a pain in the arse.*'

Dad sighs. 'I don't know, Nic. Maybe you should take some time off.'

'How, Dad? Who's gonna cover for me? *Mon?* She's too busy planning her bloody honeymoon.' As soon as I say it, I know I've shown too much.

'Is this about that jerk?'

I keep my arms folded and my face blank. Hanging on the wall behind him is a framed photo of Al Pacino and Terry Lamb's Bulldogs jersey. My dad's a man's man, but God has a sense of humour, and being father to three daughters has taught him a lot about women.

'*No.*'

'I think it is.'

I don't say anything else. Dad relaxes in his chair, inviting me to settle in mine. 'You know what marriage is like?' He looks out his window, trying to think of what to say. 'Marriage is like eating your favourite food every night.' He turns to me. 'What's your favourite food?' When I don't answer, he says, 'Mine's *kibbeh nayyeh*. Do you like *kibbeh nayyeh*?'

I nod. He nods back.

'You have it for dinner the first night, you love it. You have it for dinner the second, it's good. The third night you don't finish your plate. A week later you start saying, "This *kibbeh nayyeh*'s alright, but I wouldn't mind a bit of tabouli with it." You get what I'm saying?'

I nod again, wondering what my mother would think.

'You need a man that can stick to his diet, Nic. Otherwise he's just a pig.'

I look at my hands, still not willing to lay blame on my ex. For some reason – even now – I get defensive over him.

'Why don't you get the girls together and have a night out? Dress up, go to the city. You used to love doing that.'

Men – especially dads – are always looking for a quick fix. But heartbreak doesn't heal like the movies. It isn't a two-minute montage where you cry, and drink wine, and binge-eat.

He leans in, reading me. 'Be patient, Nic. The right man will come along.'

'And what if he doesn't?' I can hear the tremor in my voice, and I'm embarrassed by it. 'What if I'm alone forever, like Aunty Mary?'

Dad looks at me, his mouth set in a smirk like John Wayne in those bloody Westerns.

'Sweetheart,' he says, 'you're not that lucky.'

* * *

I take my break at twelve and sit outside in the heat. There's a low brick wall that borders the lot and I perch there, people-watching. Our sales manager, Linda – who moonlights as a personal trainer – is showing an Asian couple the ins and outs of a Porsche Cayenne. The man sits in the driver's seat barking questions, while the woman watches on, her face stoic beneath the brim of a visor hat.

A few cars over, there's a young guy – younger than me – circling a second-hand Ferrari. There's a chance he's only here for the free bottled water, but my dad always tells his sales staff to *'never judge a customer'*. People with real money often never show it and even if a customer can't afford a car today, that might not be the case next year. He says everyone has a dream, and a lot of the time driving a nice car is a part of that vision.

But it's never been a part of mine.

Half an hour later, I push against the glass doors and into the showroom; the cold air blowing through the open pane and pulling me into a clinical stillness. When I get to the stairs they look like ladders. I climb them with my hand on the railing until I'm back at my desk, confronted by another stack of folders. I check my emails: 33 new messages. I try to read them, but I can't.

Monica comes from the kitchenette with a cup of coffee. 'Hey, are you okay? I got worried when you left last night, but Mum kept telling us to leave you alone.'

Small mercies. Nothing worse than a family intervention, especially one involving my mother.

'Yeah, I'm fine – I just had to get out of there. It was too depressing being told *aabelik* every five seconds.' I grab the mouse and tap it around. 'I don't know, Mon … I wish I could just get over it.'

'Nic, it's still pretty fresh.'

'Not for him.'

'Well, he had a three-month head start, the cheating dog. I can't stand him. I couldn't stand him from day one.'

'Who you guys talking about?' Chadi again. He's followed me up from the showroom, already recovered from our morning spat.

My sister shoots him a look. 'Judas.' That's her name for my ex; a comparison that in some ways seems unfair, since at least Judas Iscariot had shown a sense of remorse. 'I'll never get my head around it,' she says. 'How he waited for the ink to dry on his new Audi before dumping you. Three years of stringing you along, but hey – at least he got his car at cost.'

I swallow back bile and the acrid taste of humiliation.

'Fuck him,' says Chadi. 'I got someone better.'

Monica folds her arms. 'Who?'

'My friend Dave.'

I turn from my emails. 'Dave Dollaz?'

'Yeah. He called me this morning; he's heaps keen.'

Monica answers for me. 'Can't you see she's depressed? And now you want to set her up with a DJ?'

'Oh my God, he's not a DJ anymore, okay? He's a good guy. And he drives a *Lambo*.'

I look at Chadi. 'What do I care what car he drives? If there's one thing I'm clearly not short on, it's a fucking car.'

Shivani's pretending not to listen, but she's shifted her headset to the side.

'I'm just saying the guy's loaded, and he really likes you.'

'Who gives a fuck? Do you think I care about money?'

He shrugs. 'I don't know. I'm used to Layla, I guess.'

I turn back to my emails, not reading a word. Every few seconds, a new message comes through, my total unread bordering again on triple digits. In my head, my thoughts are white. Each louder than the last, in a blinding, deafening panic.

I'll never meet someone, not like my ex.

I'll be stuck here forever.

No one wants me.

I'll have to marry Dave.

Dollaz. Dollaz. DJ Dollaz.

Hi, how are you, I'm Nicole Dollaz.

Heart like a drum; back wet with sweat.

'Ah, cuz … are you okay?'

I stand. The room spins. I grab my desk and say, 'Shit.'

The floor is falling.

There's no way to stop it and the pit is black.

Chapter 4

I come from a long line of hypochondriacs.

This family flaw can be traced as far back as my great-great-uncle Habib, who used to sleep with his hand on his heart every night, so he could feel if it suddenly stopped beating. Sure, we laugh about it now, but I can't say the rest of us have evolved much, since most of our family barbecues are usually spent comparing imaginary cancer symptoms and consoling each other.

So, when I'm finally carried from the office that afternoon – half-concussed with one of Linda's frozen protein meals held to my head – the tension around me is high. Dad, Monica, Chadi and Layla (who happened to be dropping off her brother's lunch) all come with me to the medical centre up the road, each shouting their own diagnosis.

'She's had a fuckin' stroke, babe! Look at her face!'

'What's wrong with my face?'

'Nothing!' Monica shoves Layla out of the way. 'What's wrong with *yours*?'

'Babe, what? I just had my cheeks done, is it bad?'

'*Can youse all shut up?* She's fuckin' sick!' Chadi guides me to a plastic chair while my father bellows my basic information to the woman at front desk, who's barely raised an eyebrow since the five of us barged in. It seems the staff at Westbrook Medical Centre are used to our 'emergencies'.

'You got a little knot, cuz.'

'Huh?'

Chadi's taken the frozen curry from my face. 'A lump. You hit your head on the desk. Does it hurt?'

I nod.

'Lay, get her some Panadol. Go ask the lady.'

Layla stalks off, just as Dad comes back, hands on hips. 'Okay, Dr Roberts is seeing you next. You alright, Nic?'

'Yeah, Dad, I'm fine. It was just a head spin; I think we should go.'

'*No*. We're not leaving until you speak to him. You could've brained yourself Nic; we don't know.'

Minutes pass. Monica stares impatiently at the back of Layla, still standing at the receptionist's desk, before finally going to check on her.

'She's booking herself an appointment,' Monica tells us on her return. 'Wants to ask about treatment options for alopecia.'

'Oh, for fuck's sake,' says Chadi. 'I'm gonna rip her hair out myself!'

Eventually a nurse approaches with two Panadol and a plastic cup. 'We're going to move Nicole in to one of the rooms for a bit of privacy.'

I stand up on my own, with Chadi's arm cautiously hovering around my back, while Dad and the nurse lead the rest of us through an open door. The other people in the waiting area watch as we pass, not having bargained for this level of lunacy on a quiet Monday.

'Just in here,' says the woman. 'On the bed, love.'

I make slow progress towards a white gurney in the corner of the room.

'And give me that box – I'll get you a proper icepack.' She takes Linda's now partially defrosted lunch and looks at the label. 'Chicken korma. Well, that sounds yummy.'

My stomach churns in response.

'The doctor will be with you soon,' she assures me. 'He's just in the middle of a rectal exam.'

Jesus, what an overshare. Chadi looks at me like *what the fuck*.

'Well, let's fuckin' hope he's washed his hands,' says Layla.

'Okay, how about you and Monnie go wait outside?' Dad's had enough. 'In fact, everyone get out – this room's not big enough for all of us. The doctor won't know who to help first.'

Monica, now insulted at being paired with Layla, throws open the door to reveal Dr Roberts.

'Well, hello, Mon,' he says, before peering into the room. 'Oh, we've got everyone here today. The whole family.' Dr Roberts has been our family GP for almost twenty-five years, and as such has seen it all: moles we thought were melanomas, reflux that Uncle Jimmy thought was acute angina, and a photo of a 'strange shit' that Chadi once did.

'Yeah, sorry, doc,' says Dad. 'We've had a bit of a faint at work. Nic's not feeling well.'

Dr Roberts holds the door aside for the others to leave. 'That's unfortunate,' he says. 'And how's she feeling now?'

'I think a little better.'

Monica and Chadi walk past him, followed closely by Layla, who presses up against the doorframe, not wanting even the slightest contact with someone who's just come from fingering a stranger's arse.

'So, tell me what happened today, Nicole.' It's just me and Dad and Dr Roberts.

'I fainted.'

'Right.' He pushes my hair back to look at the lump on my head.

There's a knock on the door and it opens.

'Ah, thank you, yes. We'll be needing that.' He takes the icepack from the nurse and closes the door again.

'And this is from what?' He asks. 'What did you fall on?'

'Her desk,' says Dad.

'And has it happened before?'

'No.'

Dr Roberts passes me the icepack. 'Here, keep this on your head.' He reaches for a blood pressure cuff. 'Well, why do you think it happened today?'

I shrug.

'Have you been under any stress?'

'She has,' says Dad. 'She's been very upset. Now, I keep telling her she's gotta eat, but she won't listen. Everything I gotta deal with at work, and now *this*!'

Dr Roberts signals for calm. 'You do look a bit underweight, Nicole. And you're probably very dehydrated. Have you had anything to drink today?'

'Some water,' I lie.

'And what about food?'

My stomach groans; a loud betrayal.

'Food?' scoffs Dad. 'She hasn't had anything since bloody yesterday.'

'Yeah, I didn't have breakfast – so what?'

'*So what?* So what is that we're here because you fainted! Now, it's not right, Nic. We've all been really worried – it's time for you to snap out of it!'

Snap out of it?

Dr Roberts clears his throat. 'Do you mind if I speak to Nicole alone?'

'Sure,' says Dad. 'Maybe you can make some sense of it: why my daughter, who has *everything*, is so fuckin' miserable it's making her sick.'

My throat goes dry, but my eyes are not. I stare at my lap until I hear him leave.

'Right,' says Dr Roberts, unwrapping the cuff from my arm and handing me a box of tissues. 'Let's start with a simple question. How much do you think you weigh?'

'I don't know,' I say, and then I lowball, 'Fifty kilos.'

'Can you stand?' He helps me off the bed and onto the scales. The needle stops at forty-eight. 'So, you've not been eating, and you've definitely lost some weight. Can we agree on that?'

'Yes.'

'Have you been sick? Vomiting, diarrhoea?'

I shake my head.

'Are you sure?'

'I'm not bulimic, if that's what you're asking. If anything, I'm backed up. I hardly go to the toilet at all.'

Dr Roberts takes the icepack from my head and asks me to lie flat on the gurney. He presses the cold metal of his stethoscope against my abdomen. 'Any pain?'

I shake my head.

He nods, then sits me up, talking to me in simple terms as if I were child. 'Your body,' he says, 'is like a car. You'd know all about cars, thanks to your dad.' I watch as he gathers my used tissues and tosses them into the bin. 'Your body needs *fuel*. It cannot run unless you're feeding it the proper things.'

'I know, but I haven't been hungry.'

'Well, unfortunately that's irrelevant. Your body needs *petrol*. Something needs to go in, and something needs to come out. Do you understand?'

I nod, yes.

'Now, you're a smart girl, Nicole. Smart enough to know that your gut and your brain are connected.' He puts his hand on his round belly. 'All our strongest thoughts and emotions, we feel them *here*. That's why they call it a "gut feeling".'

I think about the butterflies I used to get with my ex, and now the nausea, the cramps.

'If you're *depressed*, if you're holding on to things, your body will likely do the same.' He speaks again, this time softly. 'Your father said you've been upset. And after seeing you today, I'm inclined to agree.'

I bite my lip.

'Would you consider seeing a therapist?'

'*No*. I'm just tired, that's all.'

Dr Roberts sighs, the both of us knowing I definitely do need therapy, but for whatever reason – pride, apathy, fear – I'm not going to go. He leans on the edge of the bed now, icepack in hand. 'Are you sure you don't want to talk to me about anything? I know I'm old, but I'm a good listener.'

The love of my life left me for a blonde teenager.

Dr Roberts stares at me. I stare back.

'Alright then.' He shakes his head. 'Lots of fluids, lots of rest … And two weeks stress leave.'

Chapter 5

'You didn't finish your juice.' Arab mothers are a mystery. They smother you into adulthood, and then wonder out loud why their children grow up to be so pathetic.

'Mum, I'm fine.'

'You're *dehydrated*.'

'I *was* dehydrated. I'm not anymore.'

But she won't let it go, so I reach for the juice and drink it.

Then she starts.

'See what he's done to you? I always said break up with him, but you wouldn't listen. Now look!' She paces the kitchen, her dark brown hair in a tight twist. 'No one ever listens to their mother!'

I stare at my hands, hoping to induce some sort of open-eyed coma.

'You were too soft! You always loved him more, and he *knew* it!' She walks to the dishwasher then back again, throwing plates around like Zorba the Greek. 'Now he's gone off with that *girl*. I bet she's not like *you*! What a waste! *What a waste of your life!*'

I sit and think – and not for the first time – about what his new missus is like. She'd be sexier than me, that's for sure. She'd know how to bribe him with her body and pout and play the game.

Those were the lessons I missed somewhere along the byways of becoming a woman. In my mind's eye I see myself at fifteen years old, wearing flared jeans and FILA sneakers to the school dance. I was never popular with the boys, though I imagine it would've been easier to flirt if I didn't have the austere face of St Charbel glaring over my shoulder.

'And the nerve of him!' Mum bellows. 'Coming here and meeting your father, and pretending he was serious about you! I always knew he comes from a bad family. He's *no good*.' She's standing at the toaster now, hand on hip with a ready plate.

'There's nothing wrong with his family.'

'Who'd raise a son like that?' She cuts my toast in half, her hand weighed down by a two-tone Rolex and a double diamond band. 'Trash! That's what he is: *trash*!'

'Mum, it's over, he's gone. You don't have to worry about him anymore.'

'My daughter concusses herself and I'm not supposed to worry.'

I'd parted my hair this morning to hide the purple lump on my forehead.

She looks at the ceiling, talking to God. 'What did I do to deserve this?'

'*Jesus*, Mum.'

'*Don't say the Lord's name!*' She crosses the kitchen in a single stride. 'And eat your toast!' It's wholegrain bread with the slightest smear of Vegemite. 'You don't eat, and you don't *drink*! That's why you're not *shitting*!' She refills my glass and slams it down on the vast marble benchtop between us. '*Yallah!*'

I take a few bites of blackened crust and then I clear my plate, sidestepping around her while she gapes at me in furious disbelief.

'*Where are you going?*' She follows me into the hall yelling in Arabic. '*Nicole, come back here!*'

I open the garage door.

'Your father said you're supposed to rest!'

But I can't rest here.

I've got a fortnight's worth of stress leave, and there're only a few people I know who don't work a full week.

One of them is waiting for me in Greenacre.

* * *

My car idles on the M4 off-ramp beside the exit for Sydney Olympic Park. I glance at the road signs with my music on low, waiting for the lights to go green. It makes sense that they built it here – the stadium, and all those other arenas – because Homebush sits right at the centre of Sydney's map. It's been seventeen years since the world watched Cathy Freeman win gold in her green-and-yellow bodysuit. She was twenty-seven at the time – same as I'll be in a month and a half – but instead of drifting aimlessly through life without purpose or a plan, she'd already reached the pinnacle of her career and was preparing for retirement.

I think of her running that race, and of all the people who came to witness it: hundreds of thousands of tourists from almost every country in the world, all brought *here*, to the humble streets of Sydney's West. And I wonder what they thought about the suburbs around them. I'm sure they came with the harbour in mind – a beachside city for surfers and marsupials – but most of us don't look like Lara Bingle, or live by the water, or have pet kangaroos.

The arrow turns green and I join the overpass, switching lanes along Centenary Drive. I try to think of how I'd explain it, all the different faces of our city, to one of those visiting tourists. And I realise that, like the points of a compass, Sydney has four distinct quadrants: The North, The South, The East and The West.

The North is a leafy haven lined with heritage-listed houses. It has a cluster of elitist private schools named as if they teach wizardry, and lots of rich, white families who really give a fuck about rugby union. It also has a lot of Asians – but, to be fair, Sydney has a lot of Asians everywhere.

On the other side of the city, there's The South – better known as the Shire – which spans all the way from Georges River to world's end. Again, mostly Anglos, but nothing like The North. Far removed from the rest of Sydney, it's known for its beaches – in particular Cronulla, where about ten years ago the good people of 'God's Country' started a race riot that made international news: thousands of beer-fuelled men chanting, '*Fuck off, Lebs!*' and bashing random Arabs in the street.

Then there's the city and The East: that part of Sydney seen on postcards and airport billboards. The Opera House, Bondi; sun-kissed people eating smashed avo. Two extremes of resident: the filthy rich, or backpackers and creatives who are into the arts and surfing. The rich of the Eastern Suburbs are their own blond breed and shouldn't be confused with the elitist North Shore. They're not as worried about wearing the right uniform.

And finally, beyond all that – way out where the sun sets – there's The West.

It's here that Australian TV finds its ethnic stereotypes: the gym junkies, the drug dealers, the dodgy tradesmen, the divas, the imports, the bikies. A dreamscape for Pauline Hanson's worst nightmare, and a constant backdrop for the five o'clock news. But mostly, The West is just a stronghold for the working class. The largest, most diverse region of Sydney, it spans a monstrous six thousand square kilometres and is home to over two million people.

I drive along Waterloo Road, straight through the guts of it – that patch of postcodes known by locals as 'The Area'. When I get to the intersection at Juno Parade, I ease through the lights, passing a new boutique selling sequined hijabs and a fruit shop where you can buy Lebanese cucumbers by the crate. I look out my window at the foot traffic: kids riding bikes, scarfed women pushing prams and an errant pet goat. Once I'm past the shops, the homes here start to tell a story. Some are still from the seventies, red-brick with yellow glass windows. Some are just four fibro walls with suspiciously expensive cars parked in the driveway. And some are big and brand-new: cement-rendered mansions built by people who could've moved elsewhere but chose not to. It's the trees, though, that have always stood out to me the most. Almost every street in The West is lined with native Aussie flora: golden wattle, towering eucalypts and, of course, red bottlebrush. In other parts of Sydney, the sidewalks are more refined. There are flowerbeds and green lawns cared for by rich councils. But here in The West, there's only the wild. It's like nature's way of reminding all the immigrants that this is *Australia*. That we've all, as the song's called, found a *Home Among the Gum Trees*.

I park my car at the kerb. I know he can see me already. There are cameras above the driveway and on the roof of his two-storey house. Across the road, an old man sits on his porch, smoking a cigarette. He bows his head in my direction; a silent, mystical greeting. I don't know his name, but I've come here enough that he's used to me, and I sometimes wonder if everyone who visits Acacia Avenue has to get his nod of approval.

I lock my car and make my way to the path, where I'm greeted by a barking pit bull. I can see his pink jowls and bared teeth protruding through the metal bars of a large gate attached to a tall brick wall.

'Hi, Bruiser.'

He softens at the sound of my voice. When I ease into the yard he starts whimpering and wagging his tail. I crouch to the ground and rub his ears. 'Where's Danny?'

'Hey, Nic. He's inside.' Danny's cousin George comes striding from the porch with two other boys. He's a big man with bear-like features, his eyes too small for his face and his cheeks made fuller by a thick brown beard.

I smile up at him. 'Are you heading out?'

'Yeah, you know how it is. Always on the move.'

'Back to the garage?'

He comes to stand beside me, his white Nike sneakers roughly the size of two space boots. 'Nah, we got a, ah, call-out in Campsie.'

I don't ask anything more, I just say, 'Okay, well I guess I'll see you later.'

He gives me a nod before climbing into the driver's side of a battered cargo van, while the third guy mounts a motorbike that makes the whole street sound like a war zone. I hike up the front stairs with Bruiser trailing me as far as his chain will allow. The door's been left unlocked, so I make my way in without knocking.

'Hey, Nicky.' Danny's voice sounds from the shadows, gruff and warm. As the glare begins to fade, his broad shoulders start to take shape. He's sitting on the couch with his iPhone in one hand and a TV remote in the other. There's a second phone – a burner – on the table in front of him, and an open can of Coke.

I smile back at him. 'Hey.'

'Haven't seen you in a while.'

'Yeah, I know.'

'So, we bludging today?' He's grinning at me like a kid; like we've both skipped school to hang out.

'Yeah, apparently I have mental problems.'

'*Eh, wallah?*' he jokes. 'What a shock. Who's the genius that told you that?'

I go sit beside him, the two of us in our usual positions: me curled up in the corner, him stretched out on the lounge. At just over six foot, he takes up most of the sofa, though he's leaner than his 'roided associates. There's a soccer game on TV and, above that, a split-screen monitor showing vision from all his cameras. I can see his house from every angle: my car parked on the kerb, Bruiser pacing at the gate, the birds in his backyard. Everything. 'You know, I can't figure out if this is the safest place on earth, or the most dangerous.'

He's still smiling. 'Bit of both.'

He gets up, stretches, then walks to the kitchen, returning with a pack of KitKats and another can of Coke.

I put my hand in the open bag. 'Just like the old days.'

'Yeah, well, make sure you eat it. You look like a fuckin' sponsor child.'

I turn and tuck my hair back, realising a second too late that I've exposed myself.

He towers above me, gaping at the bruise on my head. 'What the *fuck* is that?'

I'm too embarrassed to tell him I fainted.

'Who did that to you!'

'No one! It wasn't anyone. I'm just – I haven't been feeling well, and I blacked out the other day. I hit my head.'

'You *hit your head*?' He parrots it back at me like I'm lying.

'Yes! On my desk at work.'

Danny leans in to get a closer look. Then he stands and stares at me some more. 'Say swear to God.'

'I swear.'

'Nah, say it.'

'I said it already – *I swear to God*.'

He glares again at the offending lump, before dropping to the couch, his right leg crooked and the other straight. 'What do you wanna watch?' He's still angry.

'I don't know. Anything.'

He raises the remote and starts flicking channels. I sit quietly, seeing flashes of talk shows and sitcoms, while he searches for something good. There're certain things we like to watch: the cooking channel, *Catfish*, and a few cartoons like *The Simpsons*. One of his favourites is the episode where Moe teaches a class called 'Funk Dancing for Self-Defense'. Homer watches through an open door while Moe fires three shots from a double-barrelled gun to the beat of some rap music. It always makes Danny laugh, because he actually knows a guy called Moe who shot six live rounds at a nightclub in Bexley. And because, as Danny once pointed out, you can't fire three shots from a double-barrelled gun; it can only shoot twice. After that, you have to reload.

Danny does another browse before giving up, turning to his phones instead. Every now and then they vibrate, but he doesn't answer. It's as if all that buzzing is a message in itself – each call and text a sort of Morse code that he monitors between sips of Coke.

'It's not right, what he did.' He doesn't look at me; he just says it. 'Fucking off without even checking on ya. If someone did that to my sister …' His voice trails off and he shakes his head. 'You just don't do that to your missus, you know? Not someone like you. He's a fuckin' low-life.'

I shrug. 'Sometimes it's better just to have a clean break.'

'How the fuck's this better?' He gestures at the state of me. 'What an absolute piece of shit. You shoulda let me talk to him.'

'Yeah, well, we all know you're not big on words.'

He cocks his brow. *'Come on.'*

But I give him a look. 'The last time you "talked" to someone, they went missing for three days.'

'Who?' He stares at me, all innocent.

'What do you mean, *who*? The guy with the fuckin' stutter.'

'Oh, well, fuck. It took the cunt three days to spit it out.'

I start laughing, even though I shouldn't.

'Fuck me dead, all I needed was a simple yes or no.'

I shake my head. 'Jesus, honestly. If you weren't my friend, I'd run.'

Another call comes through on his phone. It's a private number. He lets it ring, then he switches it to silent. There's a woman on TV cooking quiche in a country villa. I look back at Danny. He's not really watching, just resting, with his hand an inch from my foot. Then he says, 'Gab gets out next week.'

I sit up at the sound of his name. 'Really?'

Danny flicks through his phone; a wordless nod.

'What's it been – six years?'

'Think so.'

I lean back, mulling it over. 'I thought he'd be in for longer.'

'Me too. Reckons he got early release. Good behaviour or some shit.'

I pull a face. 'Doesn't sound like him.'

'Well, he's off the drugs, thank God. I went to see him, and he's different now. More like before, you know?'

We all grew up in the same street, me, Danny and Gab. It was a cul-de-sac called Amber Way not far from here. We used to play together under the sprinklers outside. All us kids running around in our undies while our mums watched on, gossiping in Arabic and wearing the latest designer knock-offs. Gab's mum had a pair of 'Versace' sunglasses with half the rhinestones missing, and an 'LV' bag that she'd bought from a market in Bangkok. It was a happy childhood, living side by side in our little commune, but just before I started high school my father opened his second dealership and Mum started wearing store-bought Chanel. He moved us all to Kenthurst after that, a semi-rural suburb in Sydney's north-west with big houses and high fences. Danny would send me letters sometimes – long ones about school and his family – but eventually he stopped.

'We're gonna have a barbecue for him. I'll let you know what night.'

He taps my foot with the back of his hand and rests it again, still with an inch between us. When I ask for the remote, he stretches his arm towards me, baring for a second the full extent of his sleeve tattoo. There are images of saints, his father's name, rosary beads and a spiral of Arabic writing that twists around his elbow, each letter like a leaping flame.

Years ago, when his father died, I went to the funeral with my family. It was the last time that everyone from Amber Way had gathered together in the same place. Even Gab had been there, only a few months shy of being busted with a boot full of pills. I remember watching from the aisle as Danny laboured past me carrying the coffin. He was only twenty-one at the time and the two of us had drifted; a long-coming casualty of living so far apart and going to different schools. But after that day, we started speaking again. He was just a boy when he became the head of his household, but he could still be a kid around me and not feel guilty about it.

'You alright?' He's caught me staring.

'Yeah, just thinking.'

'About?'

'I don't know. Life, I guess. How strange it is.'

'You reckon yours is strange? Come live a day in mine. It's like fuckin' *Fat Pizza*.'

On the wall behind him there's a large wooden cross, with a photo of his father enshrined on a glass table beneath it. Some heartbreaks are just for a time, and some you wear like a scar. Danny loved his dad more than anything.

'Hey, what about this?' He nods towards the TV at a rally in Martin Place, where a reporter in a rainbow tie interviews an androgynous, blue-haired activist about marriage equality. 'You think they'll get it?'

I listen for a while, then I say, 'Yeah, why not? Everyone's getting married except me.'

'Well, I'm not married.'

'Maybe there's something wrong with me. You'd tell me, right?'

He considers this with a level of seriousness I didn't expect. 'Listen, you're a pain in the arse, and you really are fuckin' mental. But there's no one like you, so you're worth it.'

I've known Danny a long time; long enough to know he has his demons. There's a reason he can sit here at 11 am on a Wednesday in socks and slides with nothing to do, but he's got a money counter in the back room. Danny doesn't do life by the book, but he isn't a fuckwit either. He doesn't show off or make empty threats or pretend to be better than he is. His yes means yes, and his no means no. So, whenever he says something to me, I believe it.

His burner rings again and this time he answers. 'Yeah. Put 'em in the garage. Automatic or manual? Okay, park it near the truck.'

I wait for him to hang up. 'Was that work?'

He rubs his beard and nods. Aside from whatever else he does, Danny owns a body shop that's known throughout The Area for doing special mods. I've been there a few times, mostly with Chadi, who cares more about primping his car than he does his own personal hygiene. I'm about to reach for my Coke when one of the cameras outside signals some movement. The two of us watch in suspense as a dark sedan pulls up slowly alongside mine.

Danny narrows his eyes. 'I think that's my mum.'

'Fuck's sake.' I sigh, relieved. 'All these cameras just to spy your mum?'

He laughs. 'Mate, she's worse than a drive-by.'

We sit grinning at the monitor, while his mother threatens her way through the gate, swinging her bag in wild circles to keep Bruiser away. I'm straightening the cushions when Danny leans across the couch and says, 'Nicky, I gotta tell you something.' His voice is different; lower, less himself.

'What's wrong?' I ask it, knowing something is.

'Nah, it's nothing,' he says. 'But I might be going away.'

I stare at him. 'Away? Like on a holiday?'

'Yeah. Hawaii.' He rolls his eyes. 'I mean to jail.'

'How's that *nothing*? What do you mean "might be"?'

'Nic, relax. It's not for sure; I'm just letting you know.'

'Just letting me know? This whole time I've been here, we talked about *Gab*, we talked about *jail*, you didn't say shit.'

He turns mute.

I try again. *'Danny?'*

Outside, the screen door shudders open, and he gets to his feet. I know he's said this now so we can't keep talking about it. He never tells me too much, only what he has to.

Always choosing his moment.

He's smart like that.

Chapter 6

It's 2 am.

I can't sleep.

My camera is sitting on the edge of my bed, staring at me like a cyclops. When I came back from Danny's I found it here and I haven't touched it since. I know it was my father who brought it home. He's been agonising over me these past few days, always asking how I am and really *looking* at me. Last night, he watched me eat a bowl of Maggi noodles until I finished the whole thing. It's an embarrassing regression, having to be fed and supervised by your parents – especially when you're old enough to be one.

After a while, I lean across the quilt and drag my camera over by its strap. It feels heavy in my hands. I can see my face in the lens – a black reflection on dark glass – and I remember how my interest in photos first began. I was sixteen years old, on a school excursion to the Museum of Contemporary Art. It was mind-numbing overall, and most of what I saw was shit. A plain white canvas, a scrap metal sculpture, a screen-print of a blue dot, each with a long-winded blurb, forcing depth and meaning on minimalism.

But on the top floor, inside the Aboriginal exhibit, I saw a massive portrait. A raw photograph of a young Indigenous woman enlarged to cover a whole wall. I stood there staring; the picture so clear I could see her pores. And she stared back. Her light brown eyes studying my own face with equal awe. She was beautiful but frayed: a small scar on her top lip, and a mole high on her cheek. I looked around to read its plaque, hoping for a lengthy explanation – wanting to know her name, her background, her job – but there was none. The photo, simply called *Mirror*, was meant to reflect the viewer's curiosity, the longing for human connection, and the wonder of never really knowing anyone at all.

I come back to myself, my face in the lens, and I feel empty.

Photos aren't special anymore. They used to be, back when you'd buy film and take pictures on occasions. But the camera phone has killed the art. Think of all the photos in the world, all the snaps being taken right now. The filters and the photoshopping; the endless stream of selfies.

These days, people only want to look at themselves.

I get up and go to my laptop. It sits open but idle on a study desk in the corner of my room; a remnant of my senior year, now predominantly used as a clothes horse. There's a Google tab already loaded, and I sit to search her name – just as I've done many times before, ever since that day at the museum.

Bronwyn Farley.

When I click on her website, *Mirror* is the banner image. She's done other work since then, other award-winning portraits and whole exhibitions, but it's the course link at the bottom of the page that I always come to revisit. I know the terms already. She offers a six-month mentorship for novice photographers at her studio in Paddington. But you have to be selected – you have to submit a body of work that, in her words, 'captures who you are, without showing yourself'.

It's the ultimate anti-selfie.

I go back to bed and press the power button on my camera. There on the screen is my last photo: a wide-angle shot of a red convertible. I keep scrolling through the images: door open, door closed. Roof up, roof down. The console. The steering wheel. The front bumper, the boot, the back seat. Then another car, and another. Hundreds of photos, all taken in the same, depressing sequence.

This isn't why I started.

I stare a moment, my thumb lingers, and then I do it. I clear the card. The screen in my hands turns bright black, and a sudden fear comes over me. It's a small step, but there's no undo.

How will I fill the space?

I lean against my pillow, waiting for rest. And as I drift, I remember:

Ordinary people, in an extraordinary place.

Chapter 7

'We want the best. Everything, the best.' My mother sits opposite Elie. She's wearing a full face of make-up and a silk blouse, ruffled at the collar like a frill-necked lizard. We've all been positioned around the formal lounge drinking Arabic coffee out of gold cups: me, my sisters, my cousin Layla and Tayta. There's a forced sense of civility, even though Elie was here two days ago, watching *The Bachelor* and eating Cheezels out of the box.

Of all the rooms in our house, I like this one the least. The tables are made of white marble and the couches are upholstered in white suede. In fact, everything, from carpet to curtains is completely albino – a colour scheme so stain-prone, I'm scared to sit.

We all look at Elie, his eyes fixed on a stone sculpture of a near-naked man wearing a Roman laurel. My mother had it imported from a gallery in Milan, and even though she too has an appreciation of art, her tastes are very different from mine.

I cue him in. 'Elie?'

'Right! *The best*. Well, when it comes to weddings, what else is there?' He gives a shallow laugh and taps the iPad resting on his lap. 'So, you've got the venue, the church, the DJ and the florist. The MC, the drummers, the cars and the cake. All confirmed?'

Monica answers, 'That's correct.'

'Hair, make-up – have you locked those in?'

'Yeah, I booked them ages ago.'

Monica, being the control freak she is, had refused the help of a wedding planner from the start, but has agreed to meet with Elie as a 'last-minute consultant', since the stress of her encroaching nuptials is becoming too much. Today marks two months out from the wedding – a crucial turning point in the countdown. The invitations have been sent out and we're starting to get some numbers back. There's been a buzz around our house; handymen doing minor renovations, and my mother – always on the phone to caterers or relatives in Lebanon – shouting with the call on speaker. I've tried to stay on the fringe of it, mostly for my own miserable sake, but partly for everyone else's. Still, some things are mandatory, and today's meeting is one of them.

'Good. That's all the groundwork done.' Elie puts the tablet down and crosses his legs. 'What we need to do now is really *hone* your vision.'

'My vision?'

'Yes. You need a theme.'

Monica looks around at the rest of us, then back at Elie. 'What?'

'*You need a theme.* It's the latest craze in Lebanon. There was a wedding there last week; the theme was "Winter". *Babe.* They had *ice sculptures*, they had fake snow *falling* from the ceiling. And the bride? She arrived on a sleigh. She wore a fucking *mink!*'

When it comes to weddings, nothing has ever compared to the absolute lavishness of mother country Lebanon. Their cakes alone are 20-tiered; so tall and wide, they have to be cut with an Arab sword.

Tayta sips her coffee and agrees. *'Eh*, very nice *bi Libnan.'*

'I still don't get it. Like, why would I need a theme? It's a wedding, Elie, not a perfume launch.'

'It's all the same shit, babe,' he says. 'That's mostly what I do in my industry; I party-plan. I take a mundane product – in this case, your standard Sydney wedding – and I turn it into an *experience*.'

'I wish someone asked me if *I* wanted a theme.' Jackie cradles her newborn daughter Ava, swaddled and asleep. 'No one gave a shit.'

My mother receives her daggered look. 'You didn't need a theme.'

'And Monica does? I got the wog wedding special, and now we're all sitting around drawing up a mood board.' Firstborn children always suffer the brunt of their parents. They are usually the first to get married, too – and the first to get married has the '*wejbet*' or 'duty' wedding. This means inviting every single person who has ever invited your parents to a wedding, so that all the proper respects are paid. At Jackie's wedding there were nearly six hundred guests – some of whom were strangers to us all – but Monica will only be burdened by half that number. '*You didn't need a theme.* Who the hell does?'

'Everyone! Everyone needs a theme!' Elie yells the room into silence. 'Now *think*! We need something *special*.'

'You know what, babe?' Layla looks up from her phone for the first time today. 'I have the maddest idea. Let's do *Versace* theme. Versace *everything*. Plates, chairs. All us bridesmaids in Versace. *Wow*.'

Elie nods along, pretending to consider. Then he says, 'Absolutely not.'

'We've already ordered your dresses anyway.' Monica brings them up on her phone.

'Yeah, thanks by the way,' says Jackie, 'for putting us all in figure-hugging satin when I've just had a baby.'

'They're not *satin*, they're *silk*. With a beaded lace overlay, so shut up!'

'Oh, wow. And in black! Divine.' Elie swipes at the pictures. 'Who's making them?'

'Yasmine.'

'Ah, of course. I saw Selena Gomez wearing one of her dresses on Instagram the other day. It's amazing how well she's been doing. And to think she got started making hijabs for her aunts.' He sips some more coffee. 'Are you still close with her, Nic?'

'Yeah, we talk all the time. She's busy in London, but she's coming for the wedding.'

Layla cuts us off, pitching another theme. 'You know what else I love? *Red*. Red roses, red carpet, red tables. *Red*.'

Elie snorts a laugh. 'Sounds Chinese.'

'Well fuck, I'm the only one helping!' Layla points a claw at him. 'Isn't this *your* job, anyway?'

Elie falls back in his seat with a mischievous look in his eye, and I realise that the last five minutes were just a courtesy – a pretence of open discussion – leading us to this moment; to a theme he had chosen long before we all sat down.

He steeples his fingers and says it proudly. *'Midsummer Night's Dream.'*

The room falls silent.

'*Shou?*' Tayta looks at Mum.

Layla says, 'What the fuck is that?'

And from next to me, my sister. 'I don't. Want. A theme.'

'Well, what *do* you want?' Elie snaps. 'Another boring, *woggy* reception, with a smoke machine?'

'Yeah, thanks. That sounds *exactly* like the woggy reception *I* had.' Jackie rocks her baby and stares at Mum. 'Did you hear that? Boring. I had a boring, *woggy* wedding.'

Elie flusters. '*Look*. The problem with Sydney weddings is that everyone does *the same thing*. They get the same event planners, the same florists, the same dressmakers. But if you do the same, you get the same, and it's all forgotten in a week. That's why we need to be extra; *Beirut* extra.'

'Yeah, but what's the summer dream?'

'*Midsummer Night's Dream*, Lay. It's a Shakespeare play. About a fairy queen who falls in love with a donkey.' I give as concise an explanation as I can, noticing that the crux of the plot is the perfect summation of most relationships.

'*Yi! Ou* who the donkey? *Luke?*' Tayta's losing patience. She'd rather be watering her parsley, but instead she's been forced to attend this meeting, headed by a man who, in her opinion, needs to be prayed for.

Elie rolls his eyes and smooths his silver quiff. 'Babe, look. Do you want my help or not?'

My mother answers, 'Yes. Yes, she does. You're the best; we only want the best.'

He puts his iPad down and elaborates. 'I like the idea of doing something seasonal. They did it in Lebanon with that winter wedding, so why can't we? You've got a beautiful garden at the venue. We need to work with that space. I'm talking grandiose florals; I'm talking *fairy lights*. I'm talking love potion cocktails at the door.'

'I'm talking a budget.' Dad walks past our sit-down in shorts and thongs, barely breaking his stride on the way to the fridge. It's a much-needed reality check, but Elie, by some miracle, has made the right pitch.

Monica has always loved fairy lights.

'What do you think, Nic?'

Everyone turns to me. I look between their faces, my mother glaring towards the kitchen. There's no real motive for what I say next, except that I want this meeting to be over and, despite his inflated ideas, I have full confidence in my friend. If anyone can pull off an eleventh-hour revamp, it's Elie.

'I think we should leave it to the expert.'

Chapter 8

Every girl in The West knows that the best place to be on a Saturday is at the salon. What appears to be a beauty shop is in actual fact peddling the most powerful commodity on the streets: information. And nowhere in all The Area has a better live feed than Houda's in Punchbowl.

I managed to excuse myself from the bridal meeting by explaining to my family that I was off to get my hair done. You can always tell a person's mental stability by the state of their hair, and mine has never looked worse. As I come down the stairs of our front porch, I hear the welcome sound of wheel-crushed gravel from the top of our drive. My friend Rita – who is actually Jackie's best friend, but whom I seem to have inherited now that Jackie has to breastfeed ten times a day – pulls to a stop in her pearl-white Lexus. I watch as she rolls her window down, her face half-covered by black glasses, like a mob wife arriving at her husband's arraignment.

'Get in, dickhead, we're going to Punchbowl.'

I smile to myself and pull the door open. 'Yeah, I missed you, too.'

'Fuck, my roots are bad.' She checks her regrowth in the visor mirror before snapping it shut. 'It's all your fault, you know. This spiral you've been on. Now we both look like shit.'

'How's it my fault? Can't you get your hair done without me?'

'What's the point,' she says, 'when there's no one to sit and bitch with?' Rita is a third-generation, full-blooded Italian who runs a cafe and a catering business – which means she knows people in both the literal and intrinsic sense.

'Well, it's only been a couple of weeks.'

'It's been over a month, mate.' She measures from her scalp to the start of her brassy blonde highlights, showing me an inch between her finger and her thumb. 'See? Maybe even more. The hair doesn't lie.' She rolls down the window and lights a cigarette, speaking without her lips. 'How've you been, anyway? Are you okay?'

'Yeah, getting there, I guess.'

It's all I can muster: the mild assurance that I'm somewhat better than yesterday. Not great, but no longer lying unconscious on my father's office floor. And Rita, in her wisdom, senses this, so she doesn't push. Sometimes, the best therapy you can get from a friend is not to talk about your problems at all. Instead, she asks about Monica's wedding, and I tell her about the meeting I've just fled.

'A theme?'

'Yeah.'

She takes a pensive drag. 'My cousin Catalina had a theme. Positano or some shit.'

'Was it good?'

'I think it would've been, but it rained. Anyway, they got divorced. He cheated on her with a girl from work, which to be honest I already knew, because a friend of mine saw them at the casino.' She ashes out her window. 'Point is, she had a theme and she got divorced. So, take from that what you will.'

'I just hope it's not woggy, you know? Like, Elie is a genius at what he does, but what if his flair for throwing parties at nightclubs doesn't exactly translate?'

'I'm gonna let you in on a little secret,' says Rita. 'Anything you do for this wedding is gonna be woggy. You know why?'

'Why?'

''Cos we're *wogs*. Doesn't matter how nice or classy something is, you still got all your woggy cousins showing up, dancing to woggy music and eating woggy food. So, you might as well just go with it.'

True.

We're almost on Silverwater Road when a text comes through on my phone. It rests on the console between us, and Rita picks it up, thinking it's hers. 'Oh, it's yours,' she says. 'It's Danny.'

I stare at his name.

'How's he going, anyway?' she asks.

'Yeah, good. Same old.'

I've been worried about him since we last spoke. For the past few days, I've replayed his words in my head.

I might be going away.

He was so calm, the way he said it. Sitting there in his footy socks, while I stared at him, eyes wide. I've wanted to call, but I know he won't talk on the phone. Anything important – anything to do with his other life – he only ever says in person. And even then, it's always in code. Half stories hinting at whole truths. Like the time he said there was 'a bit of a problem with Gab', and then we all saw Gab on the nightly news, strapped to a gurney.

I slide the screen to see the message.

Nicky Nic 😊 *BBQ for Gab next Saturday*

I tap out a reply: *Is it still at yours?* And then: *you ok?*

He writes back: *Yeah.*

But I don't know which it's the answer to.

When we get to Punchbowl, Rita parks her car on The Boulevard and the two of us cross the road, jaywalking to a pedestrian island, and then crossing again in front of an old-model Corolla with platinum rims.

'Bloody Lebs,' say Rita. 'Look how they park.' She points to a van mounted on the kerb while its driver eats a wrapped kebab. He nods and winks at Rita, and she rolls her eyes in return. *'God.'*

If you've ever been to Tripoli, you'll understand why Punchbowl looks the way it does: a muddled market, where shopkeepers spend more time socialising in the street than they do at the till. Everything here is foreign – the food, the faces, even the conversations; some in Arabic, some in languages I've never heard. But when we finally get to Houda's salon, it feels like home.

'Hey, girls!' Our hairdresser, Nat, smiles at us from one of the basins. 'I'll be a minute, come sit.' She nods towards two empty chairs, both her hands entangled on a soapy scalp.

We venture in, past the resident Vietnamese nail lady who's arranging bottles of polish at a table by the window. She keeps company with a golden lucky cat that fist-pumps to a nineties dance mix blaring from a small red speaker.

'Hey, Nat, you mind if I get my nails done too?' I ask.

'Yeah, sure, girl,' she says. 'Jenny can do it later while we're drying your hair.'

I look back at Jenny, who grins at me from behind a white mask. 'Pick a colour.' She makes a sweeping motion with her hand the way a fortune teller might invite you to pick a card. I go to the basket beside her and start rifling through ready-painted plastic nails, pretending to consider a cherry red. That's the kind of thing that Layla would do. She goes with what she feels: a neon pink to match her lipstick, or long, jewel-encrusted claws that reduce her practical skills to flipping people off and one-finger texting. Jenny humours me, both her and her golden cat watching with knowing eyes as I idly place a purple swatch above my own chipped nail. But I can't live like Layla. I can't just choose some God-awful colour and suffer with it for weeks on end. So I reach for what I know: a nude-pink polish with a subtle shimmer.

Jenny smiles at me. 'Same colour. Always pick same colour.'

'I know, I'm sorry. Very boring.' I'm speaking back at her in broken English; a ridiculous reflex.

'No, no,' she says. 'Don't sorry. Look good on you, very pretty. I wear, too.' She wheels out from the table and shows me her toes. 'See?'

'Oh, cool.' I smile. 'We're matching.'

'Yeah. This colour, nice colour. You pick same all time, mean you peaceful.'

Peaceful? God. I couldn't be more the opposite.

I put the basket down and take my seat again beside Rita. There's some yelling from out back and then Nat's aunt Houda appears, stony-faced and wearing a t-shirt that says *Houda's* in cursive. She stands at the counter, mixing a bowl of colour with a half-smoked cigarette hanging out of her mouth.

'You know this lady before?' she says to Nat. 'Maybe I kill her if she coming back.' It's loud enough that the rest of us can hear.

Nat looks at her aunt, confused. 'The priest's wife?'

'*Eh*,' says Houda. 'From the Orthodox church. She a bitch.'

Aside from Aunty Mary, Houda is one of the most menacing women I've ever met. She's from a village in North Lebanon that's famed for producing militants and psychos. Sometimes, when I look at Houda, I can see she's a frustrated warmonger, and that instead of being on the front line of a clan feud, she's now stuck here, wearing slogan t-shirts and mixing hair dye for infidels. I watch from the mirror as she casts a narrow glare around the room, before flinging aside a curtained recess, where her Muslim clients are waiting with their scarves off.

'Where my brush?' Houda bellows from behind the partition, punctuated by the sound of a slamming drawer. '*Who take my brush?*'

An apprentice with tattooed eyebrows rushes to help her, while the rest of the salon – customers included – search tables and trolleys as if looking for a live grenade. Houda yells louder now, cursing the brush in Arabic and calling its mother a whore.

'Aunty, check the kitchen! Did you leave it near the sink?'

There's the sound of heavy steps and then, a moment later, the conceding roar of a hair dryer. It's normal this, the yelling and the chaos. Some days it's even worse. But getting my hair done in Punchbowl is one of the few ways I stay connected to The Area, to that feeling of belonging and of being a local. My sisters go to nicer salons now – ones that serve tea and are closer to home – but I don't mind the drive out West, and despite the lies they tell themselves, nowhere in all of Sydney does a blow-out quite like Houda's.

Jenny turns the volume up on 'Mr. Vain', which elicits a smirk from Rita. 'The original fuckboy anthem. Every dickhead I've ever dated, this song is about him.'

I listen for a while, thinking of Judas. He was, upon reflection, the type of boyfriend who never did anything seriously wrong but, if I'm honest, never did anything especially right either. On the rare occasion he'd take me out, he spent most of the night staring around the restaurant hoping to be seen. He was the beautiful one – the prize – and I needed to be perfect too.

On our last, ill-fated date, he'd leaned across the table and showed me a photo of Blondie on his phone. He told me she was 'desperate' and that she wouldn't stop messaging him. Days later, when I told Rita about it, she'd looked at me like I was brain-dead and said she 'would've ripped his dick off, then and there'.

What's she doing messaging him, anyway? was the repeated, obvious question. But of course, I never asked, so I didn't know.

Between the dryers and the music and the shouting around us, Rita and I sit side by side, lost in thought.

'Fuck, I'm fat,' she finally says. She's staring at herself in the mirror, same as she did in the car, always finding fault with what she sees.

'You are *not*.'

'I ate a whole ricotta cake last night. I couldn't stop.' She reaches for a magazine on the ledge in front of her and reads the headline out loud. '*Kim Kardashian's ten-kilo weight loss.*' She stares at the cover. 'What a bitch.'

I lean across to see the latest smouldering photos of Kim, who's earned herself a devout following out West, thanks to her dark, Arab-like features.

Rita looks again at her reflection. 'I think I need lipo.'

'*God*, man. Enough.' I try to snatch the magazine away, when a voice sounds from behind us, deep and deadly.

'Hi, Nicole.'

I look into the mirror to see Sydney's biggest arsehole staring down at me. It's the risk I run by coming here: crossing paths with people I can't be fucked for. 'Hi, Zena.'

She sidles between our chairs, her left hand raised to her chest, making sure I have full view of her diamond ring. It winks at me once, catching the light against her linen blouse. 'Ugh, *yuck*.' She looks at Rita's magazine with loathing. 'I can't stand Kim. Her face is so fake. And has everyone forgotten she made a porno? Why do people even like her?'

'Well,' says Rita, 'no one ever won friends by being a frigid bitch.'

Zena frowns at this, her mouth a hard line. 'Mmm,' she says. 'But I hear it's how you win *husbands*.' Zena is a type of anti-feminist. She spends her life wearing Zimmermann and abstaining from almost anything cosmetic, not because it's her honest choice, but because it gives her an added edge of superiority. She thinks that by being a 'natural beauty' it somehow makes her godlier than others, as if Jesus had spent his time on earth preaching against the perils of rhinoplasty. This abstinence, of course, also extends to any touching below the waist of her full-brief undies, which would normally be fine by me, except for the fact that Zena wears her hymen like a sheriff's badge. I don't consider myself a raging advocate for women's rights – not to the extent that I would grow my armpit hair and picket for abortion – but I also don't go around slut-shaming other girls.

Well, not often, anyway.

'And yet Kim has been married *three* times.' Rita turns back to the article, leaving Zena to focus on what she really came for: me. Our rivalry has been a long one, beginning the day we met in Arabic school as kids. She was already fluent and had seemed to be enrolled just to make the rest of us look like idiots. Later that year, when it was time to do our Arabic-speaking Christmas play, Zena won the starring role of Mother Mary – a performance which, to this day, was a high point for her and a low point for me, since I was cast as the donkey.

She puts her hand on the back of my seat. 'So, *Nicole*. I haven't seen you at church in a while.' She eyes my reflection. 'Have you been sick?'

'No, just busy.'

'Mmm.' She smiles at me like I'm going to hell. Then she says, 'By the way, I heard about your break-up.' Just the mention of it chokes me. 'I couldn't believe it when I found out; I thought he was going to propose.'

Rita turns to us again, watching while I try to play it down. 'Yeah, well, these things happen.'

'Mmm.' Zena thumbs the band of her diamond ring. 'But do they? I mean, he met your parents and then he just leaves you for someone else? Anyway, I'm sure God will bring you to the right person. Look at me and Joey. When it's meant to be, you just *know*.' Their Instagram announcement had been unmissable: a video via drone of the actual proposal, followed by an onslaught of professional photos captioned *I said yes*, as if it all weren't obvious enough. Just for once, I'd like someone to upload a picture of their partner on bended knee with the caption, *I said no*. Now that'd be something worth posting about. 'We got engaged on my birthday after less than a year of dating. I was *so* surprised.'

'Yeah,' says Rita. 'I'm sure you were.'

Zena, who'd been gazing beatifically into her mind's eye, glares at her. 'What's that supposed to mean?'

'What?' Rita keeps her cool, the very image of innocence. 'You said you were *so* surprised, and I can only *imagine* how surprised you were.'

I take my cue to douse them out. '*Mabrouk*, Zena. We're both really happy for you.'

She purses her lips, her arms crossed. 'Yeah, well, *aabelkoun*, girls. Hopefully one day it'll happen for you.'

I watch as she paces away to the basins, like a jungle cat after a big kill.

'Fuckin' bitch.' Rita tosses the magazine back onto the shelf. 'I bet she's still telling people she's a virgin.'

'Is she not?'

'*No.* That's the only reason she's marrying that dickhead, and now she's out here pretending it's ordained. You know her proposal? She planned the whole thing herself. The whole bloody thing!'

I look at her. 'Really?'

'She picked the ring; she booked the boat. It wasn't a fuckin' surprise.'

'How do you know?'

'My friend Julie works at the jeweller. Reckons she was there with her dud fiancé every week, making sure the ring was perfect. Have you seen the video, the way she gasps?' Rita mimics her, mouth wide. 'What a fuckin' loser.'

God. How gross.

Houda comes out from the back again, reeking of smoke and yelling orders. She stands behind the woman seated next to me and sprays half a can of hair lacquer like it's a high-pressure hose. 'Mm,' she grunts. '*Ktir* wow. Like movie star.' We all sit in a cloud of grey mist, while the woman with the updo struggles to breathe. 'This one nice. This classy.'

Jesus, I think to myself, *it's a fire hazard at best.* I cough and wave my hand, unwittingly drawing her attention.

'You need wash.' She pulls the elastic from my hair, and it falls in twisted tendrils, aching at the root.

'Yeah, I think a treatment.'

'*Eh*,' says Houda, her nostrils flared. 'And *trim*.'

She sends me to the basins, where the girl with the tattooed eyebrows starts washing my hair, in the same unruly way that one might scrub a toilet. By the time she ushers me back to my seat, Rita is recounting her latest Tinder date to Nat. 'So, this dickhead shows up in a lowered Subaru and asks if I give head.'

Nat, who's preparing Rita's foils, stops to gape at her. 'No he didn't.'

'I know, can you believe it? I mean it's 2017,' says Rita. 'What grown man drives a lowered Rexy?'

The girl with the eyebrows puts me in a cape and starts combing out my knots. I turn towards Rita, straining against the pull of the brush. 'Um, what *grown man* asks a girl he's just met if she goes down?'

Nat's still shaking her head, her long, grey-blonde hair skimming her waist. 'What was he? Was he Lebanese?'

'Nah, Greek.'

'Oh, well there you go.' She scoots towards Rita on her stool. 'I dated a Greek guy once.' She looks over her shoulder, making sure that Houda can't hear. 'Only cared about his car and his ...' She gestures south, not saying the word.

'Cock?' Rita smirks. 'You can say it, you know. Anyway, at least he entertained me for a night. God, it's been boring. It was better than sitting at home.'

No offence to Rita, but I'd honestly rather die than waste a single night with some random wanker. I can't think of anything worse than starting again, of having to relearn another human, especially if it involves a rating system. 'I don't know why you bother with Tinder and all that. The men on there are fucked.'

Rita scoffs at this. 'Men in general, *everywhere*, are fucked. And anyway, you get some good ones. I met that guy on Bumble once – what was his name?' She looks at Nat. 'Joe? John? The one who left his wife 'cos they couldn't have kids.'

I reach for my phone. 'Sounds dreamy.'

'Yeah well, we can't all be picky like you. I'm older than you, for starters.'

'So? It doesn't mean you have to settle.'

'Mate, I know. I'm just saying, I can't expect to find someone at this stage of life with no baggage. I mean, think about it. Who do you know that's single and that ticks all the boxes?'

Nat and I look skyward, the both of us reaching for a name.

'*Exactly*. And if you think it's bad now, God help you in a couple of years. You know what dating in your thirties is like? It's like pairing odd socks. You're what's left after the laundry, and instead of being put with your "perfect partner", you get dumped in the singles pile. Or even worse, folded by mistake with the wrong match.' Rita turns to the mirror, her hair now doubled back between bits of foil. 'Believe me when I tell you, the good ones are married.'

'Or gay,' I add.

'Or Muslim.' Nat whispers this under her breath, worried again that her aunty might hear. She's been dating a Muslim guy named Ahmed for the past few months, but neither of them has had the cherries to tell their families. Arab parents are notoriously strict when it comes to their children marrying their own religion, and because of this there are countless miserable couples all over Western Sydney who cannot be together.

The three of us fall silent, our dating pool now whittled down to an impossible sliver of the population: the unmarried, Christian man who likes women. I sit with my arms crossed, silently mourning all the men who would've made great husbands were they not already married, or Muslim, or looking for husbands of their own.

'That's why you have to keep an open mind,' says Rita. 'With any luck, in a few years everyone will get divorced and then we can marry the dregs.'

'She's right,' says Nat. 'Not about the divorcees; about keeping an open mind. I know it's a bit soon, Nic, but you need to take some chances. Like, maybe Tinder's not your thing, but who knows? It could be a way to get yourself out there again. I mean, what if your *soulmate* is waiting, *ready to meet you*, and all you have to do is sign up?'

'Nat, my soulmate's not on Tinder.'

She gives me a look, her tint brush poised in the air. 'And why's that?'

'Because if he was, I wouldn't date him.'

Thanks to my many years of watching *Catfish* with Danny, I've come to realise that some things in life are better kept offline. People these days have whole relationships based on Instagram bios. But where's the romance in a rose emoji? Or the mystery in seeing someone's nuts before you've even met?

My phone vibrates on the ledge in front of me. When I reach to check it, I see two texts from an unsaved number.

Hi gorjus its Dave. Got ur number of chadi.

Was finkn me n u could go 4 dinna?

I look at the mirror, then back at my phone.

Finkn? 4 dinna? Who the hell writes like that? And why would Chadi give my number out? He saw me *faint*, I told him *no*.

Jenny brings her manicure kit over and crouches beside me, preparing to paint my nails a 'peaceful' pink, just as I'm plotting to kill my cousin. She says, 'You want long or short?' And my mouth says, 'Okay,' because my brain is still trying to decode Dave's texts.

I'm on my third go of the second message, when Zena comes prowling back from the basin, her hair wrapped high in a towel turban. The lady with the updo left a while ago, and so she takes the seat beside me, her purse tucked neatly at her arm.

'By the way' – she leans across and touches my chair, flaunting her three carats again – 'I saw your ex the other night. He was holding hands with his new girlfriend. I can't be sure, but I think they were having dinner with her family.'

I go cold. I go blind. I try to move but my thighs are stuck to the seat.

'She's not very pretty, *harram*, but he must be happy. I saw on Instagram he sent her this massive bunch of roses; a *hundred* at least.' Zena sighs and shakes her head. 'You poor thing. It's all so public – and so *soon*.'

Rita and Nat are watching now, with Jenny still squatting between us, looking worriedly at my face. But there's nothing they can do. I've tried so hard to protect myself; to avoid knowing anything about him. And now I know it all.

He's met her family.

He sends her roses.

They hold hands.

It's enough to spawn my own disgusting scenarios. The two of them sharing dessert; him kissing her forehead, the way he did with me. I imagine them in every happy moment, but the thing that hurts most, what really cuts me deep, is that he never gave me flowers.

Not even once.

Zena checks her teeth in the mirror, blissfully aware that I'm spiralling. I feel queasy; I feel used. All the time I spent worrying about him and trying to fix us only ended in a bunch of roses for someone else.

I grab my phone. I'm sick of it.

Sick enough to press reply.

Sick enough to say yes to Dave Dollaz.

Chapter 9

Dave Dollaz is almost half an hour late, despite driving his Lamborghini Aventador, with its roaring V12 engine. I watch from the restaurant bar as he inches over a speed bump and parks across two spaces, his driver door gliding upward like a flag at full mast.

Yesterday, Zena left the salon with a fresh blow-dry and a piece of my soul. I waited until she was gone and then I cried behind the curtained partition while a Muslim lady stared at me from one of the hidden chairs. When she asked me what was wrong, I said, 'Sorry, I'm just going through a break-up.' And she nodded to herself and said, '*Eh, ahsan*. Better he go. It's better for you.'

The minute I'd replied to Dave, I wished I hadn't, but I promised Rita and Nat that I'd give him a proper chance. Between the two of them, they knew more about his business dealings than the ATO. Rita estimated his personal net worth at $53 million, based on two sources: her uncle Lorenzo, who used to do formwork for Dave, and the girl with the tattooed brows who reckoned her friend had 'rooted' him once. Nat, in turn, was able to offer some slightly less vulgar intel: that he owned a small shopping centre up the street, and that he often helped his tenants with rent relief.

All in all, they both agreed that going on a date would help me 'move on', and I listened while the two of them touted his credentials. *He's tall*, they said. *He's successful and self-made, and he's friends with your cousin.* But men are never the cure for man troubles – they just bring more of their own – and the longer I've sat here churning my thoughts, the more I've realised,

I'm not ready.

I don't know why I'm still here or why I agreed to come at all, and now I'm too far in to leave.

'Hi, gorgeous.'

My chest tightens as he comes towards me. He fills the space around us with his size, and the sound of his voice, and his heavy cologne. I don't remember him being so bombastic, and for a moment I can't move; I just stare at him as if he were a demon I had accidentally summoned.

'How's it goin'?'

'Yeah, good.' I slide off the stool, standing half a head shorter than him in heels.

He leans in to kiss my cheek, holding me by the waist and then leaving his hand there.

'Did ya get yourself a drink?'

'No, not yet.'

He says nothing about being late, but instead looks to the bar. 'Well, where the fuck's the waiter? We wanna sit.'

There's another couple sitting by the window, and they look us over: Dave's velvet-embossed blazer and collared shirt, my miniskirt and flowy top. I can see them whispering to each other and I know they're judging us; not just Dave, but me as well. They think I fell for his car; for his flashy clothes and his cocky mouth.

They think I'm a stupid girl.

The host walks us past a glass partition and into a larger dining area behind the bar. It's a modern waterfront restaurant, where the lighting's so low you need the menus in braille. We're seated near the terrace doors for what I imagine would've been a beautiful sunset view, *half an hour ago*. Now it's pitch-black.

'You been here before?' Dave sits in his chair while the waiter pulls out mine.

'Once, but a while ago.'

He nods. 'It's good.'

I watch as he glances around the room the way my ex used to do; searching in the dimness, wanting to be noticed by anyone. He cranes his neck to look behind him, eventually spotting a bald-headed man on the far side of the restaurant. They nod and wave at each other. 'That's my plumber,' he says. 'He works for me.'

'Oh, okay.'

'Yeah, I always see people when I'm out.'

Well, when you look that hard, who wouldn't?

'Any drinks to start?' The waiter stands between us with two menus.

'Yeah, I'll get a vodka soda.' Dave nods at me. 'How 'bout you, gorgeous?'

I decide I need proper drink too. 'I'll get a wine. A pinot gris.'

'And water? Still or sparkling?'

'We'll have still.' Dave doesn't ask, he just orders.

I haven't been on a first date in three years, and I'd forgotten how awkward it could be; sitting across from someone you barely know and watching each other eat. The more I think about it, the more wrong it feels; like a weird social experiment, where you sit with a napkin on your lap and try to figure out if someone likes you enough to look at you naked.

Dave leans back in his chair, eyeing me in silence. Then he says, 'I'm ready to order the entrees, too.'

'Okay, sure.' The waiter pulls a notepad from his apron pocket.

'I wanna get that risotto I like, the grilled prawns, and them deep-fried zucchinis.'

'Certainly, sir. Is that to share?'

'Yeah, it is.' Dave reaches for my menu. 'Don't worry, beautiful – I got us the best stuff.'

'Um, okay.'

'It'll be good,' he says. 'You can just pick.'

The waiter repeats our order before leaving to get our drinks. I'm completely stranded now. It's just me and Dave and the faint sound of a slow instrumental.

'Nice watch,' I say. It's the same one he wore to the wedding: the diamond-encrusted Rolex that could end poverty.

'Yeah, thanks,' he says. 'I got a few.'

'Can it tell the time?'

He smirks at me, amused. 'I'm sorry I was late. I was at the gym.' He says it like it's an actual excuse. Like jury duty or hospitalisation.

'The gym?'

'Yeah.'

'Well, you said seven.'

'I know, I know. I like eating early, but I had to go look at some land and I ran late. Then I rushed for the gym and now I'm here.'

'Right.'

'It's one of those things, I can't miss it. I gotta go every day. It's good for stress. Even just a bit of cardio.' He scans me, assessing what little he can see of my figure. 'How about you – do ya work out?'

'No.'

'Come train with me, you'll like it.' Why do men always say this? As if that's our idea of romance: sharing a weight machine.

'I like walks and fresh air. I get bored at the gym.'

'Fair enough.' Another silence. 'Did you have fun at the wedding last week?'

'No, not really.'

He smiles. 'I saw you left early.'

'Yeah, weddings aren't really my thing.'

'Oh, come on,' he says. 'All girls like weddings.'

'That's like saying all men like football.'

'We do.'

'Well I don't. I don't like weddings.'

He grins. 'Better for me, I guess. You won't be some bridezilla.' God, the *presumption*.

'What do you mean "better for you"? Who said we're getting married, anyway?'

He gives me a wink. 'You never know.'

'Dave, at this point I don't even know your real name.'

'It's David Abdallah.'

I frown. 'Abdallah?'

'Yeah,' he says. 'Don't worry, it's Christian.'

'Nah, it's just … I don't know. It's weird you have an actual name.' I've only ever thought of him as DJ Dollaz; a cringey kid who used to kiss his biceps between spins. But now he's *someone*. He's a person with parents who gave him two names, and for some stupid reason it makes me look at him differently.

I mull it over a bit more.

'Makes sense, I guess. Abdallah, *Dollaz*. It's got the same ring.'

'Yeah, growing up they used to call me Dave 'Dallah. Then it became Dollaz.'

I concede a smile. 'Catchy.'

He nods to himself, then he says, 'You know, I didn't fink you'd come here tonight.'

'Why's that?'

'I dunno,' he says. 'I didn't fink I was your type.' Dave talks the way he texts, fumbling his words in shorthand.

'And what'd be my type?'

He shrugs. 'Maybe an Aussie.'

'An Aussie?'

'Yeah, you know. Someone from up your way.' He takes a roll from the breadbasket and tears it in two with his Hulk-like hands. 'Where d'you live again?'

'Kenthurst.'

'*Ooft*, that's far. Nice houses, but not many Lebs.'

'There are actually. There's a lot of Lebs that live in my area.'

Dave snorts. 'Meaning what? One every fifteen acres?'

'I don't know, there just is. But yeah, I get what you're saying, it's not like The West. It's a different demographic.'

'*Demographic?*' he echoes. 'Fuck, you even talk like an Aussie.'

It's a predictable dig, and something I've got used to since moving from The Area. But the way he says it pisses me off – as if I'm a fraud or a poser.

'Why? 'Cos I can string a sentence together?'

'Relax,' he says. 'It was just an observation.'

'An *observation?*' I pretend to be impressed. 'Well, that's a big word.'

He leans back, grinning. 'I fink I'm right,' he says. 'I fink you're used to boys that are a bit soft.'

'My ex was from Guildford and a tradie like you, so I'm not really sure what you mean.'

Rita and Nat had given me strict instructions *not* to mention my ex, the discussion of previous partners being an obvious faux pas. But I figure I'm allowed at least one, and thanks to Dave, I'd say it's the absolute least of tonight's evils. Still, I can see by his face that it's bothered him, although not in the way I'd expect.

'A tradie like me?' He cocks his brow. 'First of all, I'm not a tradie, I'm a *developer*. And second, there's no one like me; no one's done what I done.'

The waiter returns with our drinks and I take a deep swig, bracing myself for the bullshit to follow. It's the Sydney builder syndrome: a sort of ego disorder brought about by spending six days a week on a job site, surrounded by nothing but testosterone. Dave raises his glass in a toast, and I awkwardly return suit with a mouth full of wine. He then goes on to describe his latest projects, including 'the tallest tower in Burwood': a high-rise apartment block that conveniently doubles as a phallic monument to his own success.

'It's forty-five storeys, it's fuckin' massive. I won Young Builder of the Year 'cos of that. No one done that except me.' He shows me a photo of him on stage, shaking hands with a man in a tux. 'I got heaps of awards – from council, from government. Anything I done, I done it the best.'

I nod along, quietly recalling the time he won the prestigious title of 'Sydney's Worst DJ' in a 2009 Facebook poll.

'And what about your music – are you still into that?'

He scoffs. 'No.'

'Why not?'

'Got no time.'

Valid enough. Between building dick-shaped towers and talking out of his arse, I doubt Dave has time for anything else.

'All I care about is work and making money. Been that way since I was a kid.' He takes a sip of his vodka, his eyes watching for my reaction. I give none. 'I made my first million at twenty-three. You know that? Twenty-three years old. Most builders at that age, they don't even have their licence.'

A call comes through on his phone, his ringer set to loud. He puts his finger up, indicating that I should be quiet.

'Hey, bro. *Hahahaha*, you're a sick cunt, cuz. *Hahahaha*, fuck off, *ayri*! I'm at dinner, bro. Huh? A friend. I'll talk to you later. *Hahahaha*, just fuck off – I'll talk to you later. Okay, bye. Bye, cuz, bye.' He hangs up, still smiling. 'Sorry, that was work.'

I'm staring at him over the rim of my wineglass, drinking enough to get a refill. Dave locks his phone with a loud click, then he leans on the table, his heavy arms forcing us into a tilt.

'So, what else?' he says. 'Do you like tattoos?'

For fuck's sake.

I sit back, glass in hand. 'The one on your neck's a bit of a worry.' It's a dollar sign, large enough to cover the right side of his throat.

He pulls at his collar, baring it all. 'Really? It's my favourite.'

'I'm sure it is.'

'I got it done when I was DJ'ing. You know, as part of my persona.'

On the table next to me, my own phone lights up. I normally wouldn't check it, but since he took that call, who gives a shit? I raise a finger the same way he did to me.

It's a message from Rita. *How's it going???*

I write back: *I'm in hell.*

Why what's wrong – are you being nice??

I reply, *No.*

Why not!

Because, I type, *he's an arsehole and he's wearing red shoes.*
Red shoes? Fkn nightmare.

When I look up again, Dave's waiting on me with his arms crossed. I order myself another glass of wine, and the waiter says, 'Certainly,' in a way that denotes a shared gut-full of the evening's proceedings.

Dave reaches for his vodka. 'You know, I'm really a nice guy. A lot of people get the wrong idea.'

I play dumb. 'What do you mean?'

'Well, what do ya fink of me?'

Guys like Dave love to ask this question – not because they give a shit about your opinion, but because they like hearing about themselves. I don't want to humour him, so I lie and say, 'I'm really not sure.'

'I fink you fink I'm a wanker.'

To the point. 'A bit. But most men are.'

He nods and looks down at his diamond watch. 'It's hard to enjoy what I've earned wifout getting the wrong attention.' He stops, then finds my eyes. 'People see me and they fink I got it all. But I did it myself. I had no help; not from my dad, not from no one. So, why shouldn't I, you know, enjoy it? And then you get these jealous cunts, they fink you owe 'em – but for what? Because you went to school together, or 'cos they're your fuckin' third cousin?' He shakes his head. 'I don' have much mates. Chadi and Mick, I like 'em a lot, but I'm always busy. And wif other people, I gotta be careful, you know? They say they're your friend but they're not.'

If it were anyone else, I'd sympathise. But for some reason, I can't bring myself to feel bad for him. 'Well, that's life, I guess.'

'Yeah,' he says, raising his vodka. 'It's the same with women too. A lot of girls just want me for my money.'

Poor Dave. I stare back at him, bored. 'No offence, but you don't show much of anything else.'

'What do you mean?'

I try to choose my words. 'You're very … overwhelming. The car, the watch. The dollar-sign tattoo.'

He puts a hand to his neck defensively.

'It's a lot to take in.'

'I was broke when I got this tatt.'

Even worse. 'I'm just saying, you can still have money and be cool about it. You don't have to go around wearing it on your neck.'

'Well, maybe I want to. Maybe I'm proud of myself. What's wrong wif that?'

I reach for my refilled glass, my patience starting to wear thin. 'Nothing, really. But let's put it this way: I've got a pretty good rack, and yet I didn't come here topless.'

Dave's eyes instinctively drop to my chest. He begins to stammer but is interrupted by a plate of grilled prawns. The other starters follow, the zucchini flowers and a mushroom risotto. Dave reaches for the tongs with his pinkie in the air; an attempt at being delicate. I smile to myself, but he thinks I'm flirting.

'I don't get it,' he says. 'How are ya still single?'

It's one of the shittiest questions you can ask a woman, but the worst is still to come.

'I mean, you must be wanting to settle down. Girls and their clocks, ya know.'

There's a seafood fork beside my plate and I imagine stabbing him with it. 'Too much time on the wrong guy, I guess.'

'Sounds like a real cunt.' It's the first endearing thing he's said. 'Who wouldn't be happy wif a girl like you?'

Now it's my turn. 'A girl like me?'

'Yeah. Smart, *beautiful*, ejucated.' He smiles at me. 'What's the catch?'

I take a prawn out of politeness and peel it from its shell. 'Does there have to be a catch?'

'Guess not,' he says. 'But I fink wif you there might be.'

There's a piece of orange flesh impaled on my fork, and I hold it high as a precaution. 'I think men pretend to like those things – smart, beautiful women. *Worldly* women. But they don't. They just like the idea of it.'

He considers this a moment, his face paused mid-chew. 'Well, what do we like then?'

'Men like easy.'

'Easy?' He shakes his head. 'That's not true. I've always liked a challenge.'

I watch as he serves himself another zucchini flower, leaving me just the one, and even though I've barely been eating, the assumption that I'd only need a single portion pisses me off anew. 'Men aren't what they used to be, Dave. That's why so many girls have given up.'

'Oh, here we go,' he says. 'You know that's women's fault, don't ya? Youse are the ones that wanted equal rights, and now all of a sudden it's a problem.'

'What?'

'Yeah, you're one of them feminists, aren't ya? I bet you are.'

'Well, that depends.' I put my fork down. 'Sometimes yes, sometimes no.'

'Typical woman. Always wanting the best of both.' He shakes his head and smirks. 'Listen, you either want your door held in life or you don't.'

'Oh, I want my door held. Doesn't mean I'm regressive; I just like good manners.'

He shrugs at this, then he says, 'A man should be a man, and a woman should be a woman. There's nuffin' wrong wif it, but these days, the girls wanna wear the pants and the boys let 'em. Not me, though.' He reaches for his vodka. 'I'm a man's man. *Khay rjel.*'

'Yeah, well. Your eyebrows are telling me a different story.'

He draws them together, the pair of them perfectly waxed. 'What?'

'Nothing. I think I need more wine.' I wave the waiter over and order my third glass.

'You like a drink, hey?'

I say it dry: 'Only on special occasions.'

Dave keeps eating. He takes the bowl of risotto for himself and forks one of the mushrooms into his gaping mouth. 'You're upset,' he says between chews.

I take a bite of prawn as if to prove otherwise. 'No, not at all.'

'You sure? 'Cos I fink you are.' He grins. 'Don't worry, I'm used to women and their moods.'

'Yes, I imagine you would be.'

'Look, I'm just being honest. You said that men these days are no good, but I'm telling you, the women are worse. They lie, they cheat, they fuck around. They love money – they fuckin' *love* it. And they're all on rack.' He eats some more. 'Can't cook, can't clean. They just sit around and spend our money.'

'That's a bit broad, don't you think?'

'Not from what I've seen.'

I fake a contemplative nod. 'Yeah, it's a shame "Clare-tits" isn't wifey material.'

He flushes red. 'What?'

'The woman that messaged your phone. Where's she tonight?'

'I don't know. I didn't ask.'

'Mmm. Well, don't worry, I'm sure she's somewhere waiting for you.'

'Sounds like you're jealous.'

'Of what?'

'I don't know, it just does.'

'Well, I'm not. I'm making a point.'

'And that's what? That I fuck around, too?'

I lift my glass. 'You know, you're probably the rudest person I've ever met.'

Dave laughs at this. 'Really?'

I watch as he reaches across the table and takes the remaining half of my prawn.

'Here,' he says. 'I'll finish that for ya.'

I lower the wine from my lips. I'm stunned. 'Are you trying to be funny?'

'No, why would I?'

We both sit staring at each other. He has my prawn on his plate and the table still tilted towards him like the deck of a sinking ship.

'Then why'd you do that?'

'I don't know,' he says. 'I just thought you didn't want it.'

I nod as if it's fine, but from all the thoughts I have, there's only one that comes out clear:

I want to leave.

I want to leave.

I want to leave.

Dave's still watching me. He tries to pass the prawn back but it's too late. I put my napkin on the table and I reach for my bag. You can tell a lot about a man by his table manners, and as my father so rightly put it, *This one's a pig.*

'You know what, Dave?' I push my chair out. 'I think I've had enough.'

He looks around nervously and laughs. 'You serious?'

'Yeah, I am.' I take a last sip of wine and look him dead in the eye. 'And just so you know, *David*. Your money? It doesn't faze me. This act you've put on, all of this *bullshit*, maybe some moron would be okay with it, but I'm not.'

Dave listens now with a look of amusement on his face. I watch as he puts his cutlery down, giving me his full attention. 'Well, what fazes you, sweetheart?'

'Turning up on time. Letting me order my own food. Shit like that.'

He nods, taking it in.

'See, Dave, the truth is, you *like* dating dumb girls that are after your money. Know why? 'Cos it means you can be an *arsehole* and get away with it.'

He holds my stare for a moment, the two of us caught in a silent reckoning. Then he gets up, takes a menu from the table next to us and hands it to me.

'I like you,' he says. 'I like you a lot.'

Chapter 10

Gud mornin gorjus.

I squint at the text with one eye. *Jesus, what a start to the day.* I should've left him at the table with his fake teeth and his fancy shoes, but I wasn't sober enough to drive. Three glasses of wine on a very empty stomach had turned my legs limp, so I sat there guzzling water and eating French fries (the main course of my choosing), while Dave watched on entranced. He really tried towards the end, but for me, there was just no saving it.

Maybe I should block his number.

'NICOLE!'

I roll onto my back. *'YEAH, MUM?'*

'Time to wake up – it's almost lunch!'

Wake up for what?

I stretch and sit, forcing myself from bed. It's my last week of leave. In six days, I'll be back at my desk filing paperwork and watching the world outside my window in single colours.

I'm running out of time.

The door to my bathroom is only a few feet away. I stumble to the toilet and sit with my eyes closed, savouring the numbness of sleep. After showering and brushing my teeth, I walk to my wardrobe naked and catch my reflection in the full-length mirror. I stand there staring at myself, trying to understand the woman before me. She's thin, but her hair falls long and thick. There's a darkness under her eyes that never used to be there, and her skin, normally almond, seems pallid and grey. The bump on her head is almost gone, but the bruise has predictably jaundiced. I look a little longer, not knowing myself. And then I reach for my camera and tuck it in my bag.

The beach, I think. That's the cure for almost anything chronic, not least a faded tan.

'*NICOLE!*'

'YEAH?'

'*YALLAH.*'

When I get downstairs, my mother's sitting at the kitchen bench talking on the phone. Behind her, I can see our garden through our big bay windows. There's a large jacaranda tree just beyond the porch, its purple flowers rejoicing in the mid-morning sun.

'*Eh, lakken*, I'll send her down. *Badik shi? Eh*, okay, bye.'

'Who was that?' I ask.

Mum eyes my shorts and my orange bikini. 'Go change. Tayta needs a lift to church.'

'What?'

'You heard me.'

I try to find an out. 'Can't Layla do it?' If there's anyone as jobless as me, it's bloody Layla.

'No. She's asked for you.'

Fuck this life.

I wasn't even bothered getting out of bed. Now I've got to drive all the way to Bankstown, just to take Tayta five minutes up the road. I walk to the fridge, my thongs slapping against the tiles, and reach for a can of Coke.

'That's not breakfast.'

I crack it open. 'Well, like you said, it's almost lunch.'

My mother glares at me from across the marble benchtop. 'When are you going to *grow up*?' She watches as I sip from the can. 'When are you going to settle down and mature like your sisters? They've both found decent men, they're happy – but you! You find an *idiot* and you bring him home!'

'Yeah, do you mind? I'm already quite upset about it.'

'I don't care! I'm sick of biting my tongue in my own house!'

When the fuck?

'You know, when I was your age, I had two kids and a husband! I didn't have *time* to sit around and be sad. I had *responsibilities*!'

And even though I can't stand her, I know she's right. I know there are heaps of women going through worse problems, who can't take a two-week break, or talk to someone, or even cry about it. And it makes me feel like shit.

But I don't show it.

I look at Mum, and I say, 'Good for you.'

Because sometimes I think, if it wasn't for her and all her criticism, I'd be married with two kids too.

* * *

Tayta's waiting for me on her front porch. I watch as she ambles down the driveway, followed laboriously by Aunty Mary, whom no one saw fit to warn me about. The two of them bicker on approach, only stopping when Tayta bends to check her letterbox. She leans against its little roof and takes a wad of envelopes from inside the hatch. Then she says, '*Khay!* Beautiful day!'

Aunty Mary grunts in response, '*Shou?*'

Tayta yells it over her shoulder: 'Nice weather!'

'Ahh. *Eh, helou lal bahr.*' *Yeah, nice for the beach.*

There's a lone kookaburra sitting atop a telegraph pole laughing with an open beak and I inwardly curse it, knowing already that the joke's on me.

Tayta shuffles the letters, sorting through the pile. The first few envelopes get stuffed in her bag, but the last she scrunches in her fist.

'This 'nother letter from builder.'

I talk to her through my open window. 'Did Ling end up selling?'

She shrugs and purses her lips. 'I no moving. I staying here.'

Tayta is the last resistance on what's fast becoming a turf war. The houses on either side of hers have been bought by the same builder, and now have SOLD signs pitched on their lawns like flags over conquered territory. Ling's house backs on to Tayta's, and from what I've seen, Ling's pretty keen to cash in. The only problem – the only missing piece to this perfect parcel of land – is Tayta. Her house sits right in the middle; without it, they're fucked. There can be no apartment block, no big development. *And no pay day.* I watch as she heads for the bin, her stout legs stomping across the grass, and a small part of me starts to feel really sorry for that builder.

I'm still smirking to myself when Aunty Mary reaches the car. She yanks the door open, and I stiffen as she climbs in behind me. She smells of smoke and bitterness and, as usual, is dressed in black. I've often mused that she has all the calling cards of a recent widow, but since she was never married, I can only assume she is in perpetual mourning for the crucified Christ. She coughs and clears her throat, her piercing blue eyes glaring at me in my rear-view mirror.

'Hi, Aunty.'

'Put AC.' She says it like I'm a hired driver.

I set the aircon to max and check the vents. We wait in silence while Tayta waddles around the front of the car. She lowers herself in beside me; right foot first, holding tight to the handle.

'You okay?'

'*Eh, yallah*,' she says, before crossing herself. '*Ya Rab.*' It's a small, impassioned prayer uttered at the start of every drive, as if the three of us were setting sail to Bermuda. I reverse onto the road and immediately take the left lane. Anything over sixty will send the oldies into a panic.

'So, what's happening at church today?'

Tayta answers me. 'We doing the feast.'

'Oh, nice. Like with the *saj* and that?'

'*Eh*. We making the bread for the people.'

There's always something going on; a Saint Day or a prayer night, or a food run for the homeless. Tayta makes the best *sambousik* in Sydney and she donates whole trays to the mission group. That's how she is; always working with her hands and helping others. Most women of her generation seem to run on kinetic energy, and I sometimes wonder if I have that same drive lying dormant in my bones. But every time I look in the mirror, I see my own worst fear staring back at me.

Aunty Mary, the miserable spinster.

'*Ahk! Ya ekhteh*, my back. Very bad today.' She sits hunched over, burdened by life.

Tayta turns to her. 'You taking you medicine?'

'*Ma badi*. I no liking this doctor, he fuckin' idiot.' God, what a mouth. She's seventy-eight years old and she's worse than Chadi.

'*Eh*, well.' Tayta shrugs. 'You no help yourself, you no getting better. I'm right, Nicole?'

I'm too scared to agree, but by the way she looks at me, I get the feeling she's not just talking about Aunty Mary.

I turn off Stacey Street and keep driving until I see St Maroun's church. It spans a whole block; white-bricked with a sandstone belltower. There's a car park on the corner and a school on the other side. As far as Lebanese Catholics go, St Maroun's is ground zero. It sits right on the borderlines of Bankstown, Punchbowl and Greenacre like a tripoint on a map and has a parish of thousands. A few years ago, the prime minister came here for Easter mass, and it was all over the news. Things like that don't really happen out West; the country's top official coming to have communion at an Arab church. I remember thinking how nice it was – although to be fair, you never really know the motive. Maronite churches in Sydney have treasuries like the Vatican and a devout following. What better way to inspire voters and funding than by coming to The Area and kissing our Bishop's ring?

But the oldies don't care about any of that; the politics and the grinning handshakes. They're just here to make the bread.

'*Eh*, park here,' says Tayta. 'I see my friend.'

I pull up near the gates. Behind me, Aunty Mary struggles with her door, but when I get out to help, she waves me away with a bony hand. 'Too late!' I watch as she agonises to her feet, her thin legs riddled with varicose veins, and inches her way past the boot.

On the other side of the car, there's a group of old women gathered at the kerb, squawking at each other like buzzards. When they see us, they come pecking up the path as if we'd scattered crumbs. They're all dressed alike: dark skirts, leather sandals and layered necklaces, each with a large cross or a blue evil eye, or the talisman of a Catholic saint. A few of them have scarves tied around their heads, ready to prepare the food.

'*Kifik, ya Nada?*'

'*Eh, mnieha*, thanks God.'

They come to kiss Tayta and then their eyes turn to me. '*Ou min hal sabiyeh? Bint Ebni?*'

'*Eh, Bint Ebni.* Raymond daughter.' Tayta presents me proudly, and I'm met with a chorus of blessings and praise:

'*Issmissalib!*'

'*Shou helwi!*'

'*Smallah, smallah!*'

Their eyes trace the length of my figure, and I fold my arms, suddenly conscious of my gym tights and baggy tee. Then the smallest of them – a wrinkled woman with a wooden cane – comes forward. '*M'jawazi?*'

Tayta shakes her head. 'She no marry.'

'*Ahh.*' It's a collective sigh of sympathy. An unmarried twenty-something; they'll be matchmaking all day. I give them an awkward smile and retreat towards my car. Danny's house is only a few minutes down the road, and I've been meaning to check in on him.

'Okay, well, have fun. Call me when you're ready, I won't be far.'

I'm about to slip behind the wheel when Tayta stops me.

'No,' she says, 'you staying here.'

Everyone looks at me.

I stare back. 'Why?'

''Cos *we* making the bread.' She points between the two of us, and I suddenly realise what this is. Tayta didn't need a lift; she just wanted to get me to church. Mum must've told her what happened last week, and now I'm in the midst of a spiritual intervention. I look past the women to the statue of St Maroun, his right hand raised in the air, and I'm annoyed I didn't catch on sooner. Tayta often used to preach that depression comes from the devil; she experienced it herself when her daughter died. I remember she'd point to her head and say, '*Hayda shaytan*' – *This is the devil* – and now she's lured me here for some sort of exorcism.

Aunty Mary puts her hand on her hip. '*Shou?* We standing here all day?'

I can't think of a reason to leave, but I'm also not bothered to roll dough with a bunch of widows. 'Tell you what, you go make the bread, and I'll go pray.'

No one can argue with that.

They all head off to the community hall, while I take sanctuary in the church like Quasimodo. I climb the stairs with my bag on my shoulder, still weighed down by my camera and a bottle of coconut oil. St Maroun's has a high timber ceiling and a long nave. I bow and cross myself, before walking the length of its red carpet, coming to sit in one of the pews, third from the front. I can't remember the last time I was here; the last time I came to mass or said confession. I guess it all became too draining; standing and chanting when I just didn't *feel* it.

Truth is, I've never been a real Catholic. Not like the 'churchies' – like Zena – who come here every week. They never ask questions, or think, or doubt. They just take whatever's said at the altar and use it against each other. But the more I sit here in the calm of its cavernous space, the more I miss it. I rest against the pew, quietly absorbing the incense, when Father Boutros passes me in the aisle, his long robes skimming his feet.

'Nicole! How are you?'

I'm surprised he still knows me. 'Good, Father, and you?'

'I'm good, thank God. Did you come here with your *tayta*?'

'Yeah, she's busy making bread or something.'

He gives a little chuckle. 'Yes, she's very good. I hope you're staying for the feast.'

'I think it's looking that way.'

'Well, I'll leave you be. You can call out if you need me.'

He disappears into the sacristy, and I'm left on my own again. I look around at the walls, the floors, the ceiling. There's a giant wooden crucifix above the gilded tabernacle, and paintings of saints hung high on either side. I've been coming here my whole life, not really seeing any of it; the yellow glass windows, the timber railings, the faux flowers offered at the shrine. But more than anything, it's the muted smile of St Rafqa – a Lebanese patron saint – that draws me in. She gazes at me from a golden frame, her fingers entwined with a simple black rosary.

As someone who comes from a family of raging hypochondriacs, her story is, in my opinion, the most terrifying tale of canonisation ever told. See, St Rafqa, bless her name, prayed for sickness. She asked God to afflict her, in the hopes that through her suffering she'd be more like Christ. And God answered her prayer. The very next night, she became blind and paralysed; one of her eyes had to be removed and the socket started haemorrhaging. But she never once complained. Even without her sight, and with crippled legs, she would crawl to chapel.

I sit, staring at her serene expression, wondering why anyone would wish that upon themselves. Surely there are other, less gruesome ways to get closer to God. But then I start thinking; I start looking at my own life, and all the times I've *really* prayed.

Like when my aunty died. Or when I thought I had bowel cancer. Or whenever I'm in Chadi's car. The sad reality is that people only reach for God when they're suffering or scared shitless.

Outside, a school bell rings. I can hear kids running between classes, laughing at each other. I fold my hands, and I wait. *Maybe there's a point to what I'm going through.* Maybe all this heartache is for a higher calling. But I'm not strong like St Rafqa; I want to find God in something good.

I keep my eyes on her portrait, and when the noise dies down, I bow my head, and I breathe. I don't say fancy words; I don't recite the rosary or try to think the right thoughts.

I just *breathe.*

And then slowly, through the incense, you know what I start to smell?

Baking bread.

* * *

I cross the courtyard, and for the first time in months I feel the dull ache of hunger in my gut. The sun glares off the white brick walls and the light is blinding. I blink and follow my nose; that warm aroma willing me forward.

When I reach the hall, I see the old woman with the wooden cane crouched beside a smoking *saj.* She places flattened dough on its black metal dome, and I watch as it bubbles and bakes.

'Is my *tayta* inside?' I ask.

'*Eh.* She inside. *Badik manoush?*' She pinches a browned edge, dragging the flatbread onto a paper plate and folding it in half. It feels hot in my hands. I pull at the dough with my teeth, tasting the tangy *za'atar* and the subtle flavour of sesame.

'*Tayib?*'

I nod. 'Very good.'

She smiles. '*Eh, sahten.*'

'*Aa albik.*'

I move to the shade and eat it all, watching from beneath the awning as people start to gather for the feast. They come through the gates in the afternoon sun: schoolkids, families and neighbours from across the street. Behind me, I can hear Tayta yelling orders through an open door. I throw my empty plate away and peek around the threshold, curious to see the 'kitchen'.

There are ten or so old ladies seated along a foldout table with Tayta at its head. Some roll and cut the pastry into circles, others add the filling (either meat or spinach), and another group pinches the pastry into triangle pies. The rest of the dough is sent to the *saj*. In the far corner there's a smaller group of women gathered around a large pot of soup simmering on a portable stove. It's a meat and wheat stew called *hrisi*, and it's so thick it has to be stirred with a wooden paddle.

I'm too shy to join them, so I call out over the noise. 'Tayta? *Tayta!*'

The room stops. Tayta looks up at me, elbow deep in flour. '*Ayni.*'

'I finished praying.'

'*Eh*, good.' She smiles up at me, waiting for more.

'Do you need any help?'

'*Eh*. Come sit here, next to me.'

One of the women hands me a hairnet and a pair of rubber gloves. I take a chair from against the wall and bring it to the table. A low murmur rolls through the room and then everyone starts working again: cutting, kneading, plating and cleaning. They chat as they go, gasping at village gossip and making jokes about their senile husbands. I sit idle until Tayta trusts me enough to spoon spinach onto the centre of the circle-cut dough. I do this over and over, sliding my finished work to Aunty Mary who, having been forced down the line to make room for me, finds issue with everything.

'This no good. Not 'nuff.' She takes the smallest amount of spinach from the metal bowl and adds it to my attempt.

I nod and try again.

'Too much.' And she deducts the same amount.

We work this way for a while, until she pushes back her chair and announces to the table, 'I going for smoke.'

No one answers, though among their faces I see a shared look of relief.

She shuffles out the door, holding her lower back and groaning loudly. From the show she puts on, I can tell she'll be gone a while.

'Here, Nicole.' Tayta leans down and picks up my bag from the floor. 'Put on the chair, better.' She points to Aunty Mary's empty seat. '*Yi*, very heavy.'

'Yeah, I know. I got my camera with me.'

'Oh, that nice. You taking photo today?' She starts rolling the dough again.

'No, not today. I was in a rush getting here; I should've left it at home.'

She shrugs. 'You can take photo here. It nice for the people.' I glance around the room. 'Father Boutros love it. He love picture. Maybe he put in paper.' She smiles at the idea and keeps rolling. 'I like picture too.'

I bite my lip and think it over. I've been looking for something to photograph ever since I re-read Bronwyn Farley's course criteria.

It's proving to be more of a challenge than I thought – putting together an abstract self-portrait, when I have absolutely no idea who I am anymore. My life at the moment seems so far off track, not even my own reflection rings true. Still, I have to find a way to tell my story, and what better place to start than by taking photos of someone I love?

'Okay. But just of you.' I peel the rubber gloves off my hands and pull my camera from my bag. When I stand and raise the lens, Tayta smiles and talks through her teeth.

'Like this?'

'Yeah, that's perfect.' I press down on the shutter. 'Okay, one more.' And I go again. 'Okay, this time just roll the dough.'

She adjusts her hairnet then moves the rolling pin back and forth while I snap away.

'These are good.'

'*Eh*, let me see.' We look together at the little screen. She's youthful, my *tayta*; she could easily pass for a decade younger than her seventy-five years. She has highlights in her hair and her skin is still smooth. Even her eyes have stayed bright; light brown – almost amber – just like mine. I wait while she stares at herself. Finally, she approves. '*Eh*, good. Nice photo.'

I'm about to lift the strap from my neck, when a raspy voice whisper-shouts from behind me. 'What 'bout us?' One of the old ladies has an arm around her friend, already posed.

'Do you want a photo?'

'*Eh*, why not. We working too.'

I take their photo, and then after that the whole table wants in. I thought they'd be camera shy, but they're smiling and posing with their rolling pins in the air, and I start to realise, old people are just the opposite. They *love* having their photo taken. They love being *looked at*. Because no one ever does anymore. They walk around unnoticed and undesirable; hidden in halls, making pies. And it's not fair. Because even though they're old, they're still *here*. They still wake up every morning and do their hair and choose their clothes. Some of them are even wearing lipstick. So, I take my time; I do my best to make them feel beautiful. A few ask for portraits and I start to learn their names: Martha with the thick glasses, Salma with the rosy cheeks. Hayet and Jamila who live across the road, and Amira who has mild dementia. I'm halfway through a photo shoot of a 90-year-old with missing teeth when we hear a shout from the opposite end of the table.

'Who put this here!' Aunty Mary has come back from her break and she's not happy about my bag being on her chair. She knows it's mine and she scowls at me from the other side of the room.

'*Me.*' Tayta keeps kneading, her voice firm.

Aunty Mary turns to her. 'This *my* chair.'

'*Eh*, so?'

She takes my bag and drops it on the floor. 'So, move.'

Tayta stops what she's doing and glares at her sister. 'Put *here*.' She points to the chair beside her.

There's a mounting tension in the room. We all watch as they face each other – both too proud to back down – and I don't know what comes over me, but I call out just to fill the silence.

'Aunty. *Badik soura?*' I hold my camera up for her to see.

She looks at me like I'm fucked in the head. '*Shou?*'

'Come get a photo. Everyone's had one.'

'*Eh, helwi bitkoun,*' lisps the 90-year-old with missing teeth. 'It for the church.'

'*La*. I no want.'

She turns back to Tayta, so I call out again. 'They need them for the paper!'

'For the paper?' Now I've really got her attention.

'*Eh.*' Tayta joins in on the ruse. 'To say *special* thank you.'

Aunty Mary glares around the table. In her mind, she's the hardest working pie-maker here – despite taking a forty-five-minute smoke break – and she's not the type of woman who likes to be overlooked. If anyone deserves to be acknowledged in the *Maronite Monthly*, it's Aunty Mary.

She draws herself up and walks to where I'm standing, giving silent consent. I pull a chair over to the window. She sits with her back straight and her hands in her lap like royalty. I say, 'Turn more towards me,' and, shockingly, she cooperates. There's a hush around the room; a collective intake of breath. I bend to her level, camera raised, and for a moment I think we might really connect. 'Okay, Aunty, smile on three.'

But when I look through my lens, all I see are those angry, piercing eyes.

'I no fuckin' smile,' she says.

Chapter 11

I'm hungry. I'm starving.

Ever since I had that *manoush*, I can't stop eating. When I got home from church last night, I sat at my computer editing all the photos I took and snacking on whatever I could find. I stayed up until 2 am, experimenting with different filters and slowly formulating an idea for a body of work.

There were over a hundred images and the more I browsed, the more I realised the type of story I want to tell.

I can show who I am,

by showing where I'm from.

Once I was done with Aunty Mary, I started taking pictures of my own – candid photos of old hands working at the table. I took a few more of Tayta laughing with her friends, and then I ventured outside to the woman at the *saj*. Her eyes were milky in the setting sun, and she taught me how to bake the bread, kneading it flat with her three crooked fingers. I took pictures of the bubbling dough, and her ancient, innocent smile, and I filtered them all in black and white.

Yesterday morning, when I looked in the mirror, I saw a blank space; someone unwell and alien. But today I feel different. Not better, or brand new – just more myself. And instead of being plagued by bad thoughts, I get these respites now where I imagine all the photos I could take. I think of the ways I could show The West: all the little landmarks around our neighbourhoods and the scores of people who live there.

An unsung cast of thousands.

I know what Bronwyn will be looking for. I know because I saw it that day at the museum. She wants to see what *reflects* us; what I do on a Sunday, and where I got my amber coloured eyes from. Those are things that can only be found out West, and if I want to capture them, I have to be ready for those moments all the time. And that means taking my camera everywhere.

Even to lunch with Chadi.

He comes through the car yard with his sleeves rolled up. We haven't seen each other since I fainted last week. I look beyond him at the sign, NAJIM MOTORS, and something inside me immediately constricts. I can't go back to taking photos of front bumpers and dashboards – not when I've finally been inspired. But for now, there's a more pressing issue.

Chadi opens the car door and dumps himself on the seat beside me. 'You missed me, hey?'

I give him a sweet smile, and then I pinch his shoulder as hard as I can with my pink-polished nails.

'Aghh! *Fuck!*' He rears back, rubbing his arm. 'What the fuck's that for?!'

'Don't *ever* give my number out again.'

'Fuck, it stings!'

I honk the horn. '*Ever!*'

'Okay, okay!' He puts his hands up.

'Because of you, I went on the worst date of my *life!*'

'Yeah,' he says, 'but you *went.*'

I narrow my eyes at him. 'What's that supposed to mean?'

He shrugs as if to say, *You tell me.*

'In case you haven't noticed, *cuz*, I'm not really in my right mind. And your friend DJ Dickhead has made it worse.'

He smothers a laugh. 'Look, I know it was wrong. But Dave *really* likes you. *Haroum*, man, I felt bad for the bloke.'

'Feel bad for *me*. I've still got a migraine from the smell of him!'

Chadi sits forward, hand on heart, giving me one of his well-practiced apologies. 'Okay, I'm sorry. Alright? I'm *really sorry.* I won't do it again.'

'You better not.'

I can see him smiling from the corner of my eye; he reaches across to tickle me.

'Stop it! Fuck, you're annoying!'

He pulls away, grinning. 'So, where we going?'

'Granville. I'm craving chicken.'

'You, Nicole Najim, are craving chicken?'

'Yeah, I'm hungry.' I shift the gear into drive.

'Since *when*?'

'Since Tayta took me to church. I prayed a bit, and then I ate this magic *manoush*, and now I can't stop eating.'

He doesn't even bother asking what I'm talking about; he just shrugs and says, 'Okay.'

When we get to the M4 overpass, I make a left onto Parramatta Road, but as I come around the bend we almost get swiped by a drifting Camry. I slam on the brakes and reach for Chadi, who's yelling out the window from his seat. 'Fuck me dead, this fuckin' idiot! *Pick a lane, bro!*' He glares at the driver as we overtake. 'Can you explain how a dickhead like that can drive, but they take my fuckin' licence?'

I straighten the wheel and slide his window shut. 'I think the cops did a pretty good job of explaining why.'

Chadi had his licence suspended for a year. Thanks to anti-hoon legislation, he got done for doing burnouts – or, as the arresting officer put it, 'a deliberate loss of traction'. To be honest, getting him off the roads was a relief, although driving him around for the past eleven months has been a real pain in the arse.

He folds his arms. 'Fuckin' gronks. Anyway, who cares, I get it back soon. And my car will be finished, too.'

'What do you mean?'

'I'm dropping it at Danny's next week. It needs a lift, you know. A bit of a buff, some new rims. I'm even getting new plates.'

When Chadi and I turned twenty-five, my father got us matching BMWs. Not the usual car for people our age, but a welcome perk nonetheless. Almost two years later, mine is still in its original condition but Chadi's has been a constant work-in-progress. He adds something new to it every few months – like coloured lights on the dash or a louder exhaust – and it's all done courtesy of Danny, whose garage fit the mods for cheap.

'What'd you get on the plates?'

He gives me a devilish grin. 'You'll see.'

I turn right onto Bold Street and drive up over the train tracks, stopping at the lights.

After circling the block, we find a park near Habibi's Patisserie. The smell of butter-sugar and orange blossom water seeps from the back of the building and it makes my stomach groan. Chadi leads the way along the footpath, the road beside us loud and dusty. A van drives past blaring Arabic music, a train rattles into the station. At the chicken shop, the line moves quick: a mix of students, tradies, cops from up the street and mums with man-faced kids.

When we get to the counter, I order a quarter chicken with tabouli and a side of falafel. Chadi gets a wrap and a bowl of chips.

We take our number and head outside. 'Can you see any tables?'

'Umm … yeah, over there.' He points towards a family of Islanders in patterned skirts, who've left behind a plate of chicken bones piled high like a mass grave. We wait until the table is wiped, trapped between the wash trolley and group of Indian men who're eating with their hands and speaking Hindi.

I look around. 'You know, you really get all types in Granville.'

'I swear to God,' says Chadi. 'There's not one normal head.'

Minutes later, our food comes out. First the chicken with bright-pink pickles, then the salads and the chips. Chadi reaches for the *toum*. 'So, how's your break been?'

'Pretty shit.'

'Get up to much?'

'Not really. But I've started taking photos again. I'm applying for a course.'

'Oh, that's cute, Nic.' He says it the way a distracted parent might appease a dancing child.

'Yeah, thanks.'

'What? I mean it.' He takes a bite of his wrap, his mouth full. 'I think it's really cool. You were always good at shit like that.'

'Well, let's hope I still am.'

'What's the course?'

'It's a mentoring thing with a woman in Paddington. But I have to get selected first.'

'Oh yeah, like how?'

I bring up the terms, now saved on my phone. 'She wants six original photos that show who I am without, you know, just taking a selfie. And I have to hand them in by October twentieth.'

He swallows and looks at his watch. 'So that's in, what? Three weeks?'

'Yeah, three weeks exactly.'

'Well, how many you got?'

'What, photos? None so far. I mean I took a few at church but nothing since.' I lean across the table, letting him in on my plan. 'I've got this idea to take, like, photos of The West and all the places we grew up around.'

'What?' he asks. 'Like this dump?'

'It's not a *dump*, Chadi. It's actually really interesting, if you have the right eye for it. I mean, you said so yourself: there's not one normal head.'

'Oh, well, yeah. If you put it like that.'

'I just think that's the best way to show it: who me and you and all of us are. By taking photos of where we're from, and our family too.'

'Ahhh, I get it,' he says. 'You want me to model for ya.' He gives me a big, dumb grin. There's a piece of parsley stuck in his teeth. 'Make sure you get me from my good side, yeah?'

'And what side is that?'

He laughs and gives me the finger. 'You know I'd be alright if I didn't break my nose.' He pinches the bridge, conscious of how it bulges in the middle. The day he broke it, we were all at Tayta's playing cricket in her front yard. She still talks about it with tears in her eyes: her precious grandson, disfigured in full view of the whole street.

'Yeah, you'd be a god.'

'Oh, shut up,' he says. 'Like you're looking much better.'

'I've been sick, you jerk.'

Chadi looks down at his plate. 'Yeah, I know. And if I *ever* see your dumb fuck of an ex, I'm gonna give him a nose just like mine.'

I raise an eyebrow.

'What? You think I won't? I've learned Muay Thai off Dad, okay? I'll fuckin' tiger claw his face off.'

'Tiger claw?'

'Yeah.' He puts his hand up and stiffens his fingers. 'Right in the kisser.'

'Are you sure that's Muay Thai? I thought they wear gloves.'

'Listen, you think when people are punching on, they'll stop and say, *Oh, sorry, bruv, you've used a bit of karate there, that's not allowed*? Like, fuck me, Nic, I'll kick him in the nuts if I have to.'

'Jesus, whatever, okay? I don't want to talk about him anymore; I just wanna focus on these photos.'

'Yeah, well, you haven't got much time. We shoulda took some today.'

I tap my bag. 'Good thing I brought my camera.'

'Aha! So that's what we're doing here. Are we going for a walk?'

'Yeah, but only if you're bothered. I don't want to drag you around.'

'Cuz, no offence,' he says, 'but you've been dragging me around since birth.'

When the two of us have finished eating, he follows me down the street, past a displaced flock of seagulls who've rehomed here for the hot chips. 'So, what are we looking for exactly?' he asks.

'I don't know. Anything … familiar.'

'Cuz, it's *all* familiar. It's like looking at your own arsehole.'

'Are you alright? You're supposed to be helping.'

He shrugs an apology.

'I need something that stands out. Like something that seems normal to us 'cos we grew up here, but to somebody else it wouldn't.'

'Well, what about that guy?' He points to an Asian man on a bicycle selling a bag of oranges for five dollars.

'What about him?'

'Bro, I don't know, but what a bargain.'

'You're really not getting the brief.'

'Nah, come on, I'll go ask him. I reckon he'd be good.' Chadi steps lightly from the kerb but I clutch at his sleeve to stop him.

'No! *Jesus*.' I glance around at all the stony-faced locals, realising now that I didn't think this through. 'It's way too busy today, anyway. I'll come back later; let's just go.'

Chadi frowns at me. 'Well, did you want to try the other side?'

'Of what, the tracks?'

'Yeah.'

'Nah, it's too far.'

'Cuz, to be honest, that lunch is sitting like a brick, and I could really use the walk.'

I follow my cousin now, back past the chicken shop and up through the station. We shoulder our way to the opposite exit and come down the stairs to a less chaotic Granville. There's a pub on the corner advertising Topless Tuesdays and a tattoo parlour near the roundabout that seems to specialise in the art of blasphemy. Chadi stands expectantly with his arms crossed, and I tell myself to take photos of bloody anything just so we can get out of here. I'm about to make a big deal of a graffitied bin, when something across the road catches my eye. It's a massive black billboard with the words VOTE NO written in white: a protest against the upcoming vote for gay marriage.

I stand still, staring at it. The whole of Sydney has been littered with rainbow flyers for the Yes campaign. But not Granville.

Not The West.

I step back to survey the bigger picture: there's a shopfront two doors down filled with religious icons; statues of saints and a large crucifix framed in neon light. Further up – underneath the billboard – a group of scarfed women examine fruit at the local greengrocer. I wait until their faces are turned and then I raise my camera, getting as much of the street and the sign as I can.

Chadi watches on, amused. 'Yeah, I'm not sure your photographer friend in *Paddington* is gonna like this one. I hear they're pro-poof on Oxford Street.'

'Yeah, exactly.' I press the shutter. 'Anyone who lives in The East would be shocked by this. I mean, it's even shocked me. Can you imagine seeing this in the city? You just wouldn't.'

'Yeah, hectic,' he says, 'but we're starting to get some looks.'

Across the way, a man drinking beer from a paper bag stares at us.

'He probably thinks we're cops.'

'Well, wouldn't you?' Chadi shifts uncomfortably. 'Hurry up before he legs it back to the titty bar and calls his digger mates.'

'You know, for someone that talks a big game you really are the most chicken-shit person. What happened to Muay Thai and your tiger claw?'

'Cuz, it's called *the discipline of restraint*. I can't just go around unleashing myself on randoms. And anyway,' he concedes, 'I'm a Leb. We're only brave in packs.'

I take a few more photos of the billboard and then I hunch above my camera, making sure I got the right shot.

'Happy?'

I nod. 'Yeah.'

'Good.' Chadi slaps his hands together. 'Let's go before we get bashed.'

Chapter 12

The barbecue for Gab is bigger than I expected. Music pumps from the party, alternating between Arabic and rap, loud enough that I can hear 2Pac's 'Hit 'Em Up' from halfway down the street.

As I inch along the road, I see a group of men stationed on Danny's driveway, smoking. I've never seen them before and the realisation that I'm at a welcome-home party for an ex-con starts to take a hold. The largest of them prowls towards my headlights, his face and neck scrawled with tribal tattoos like an angry Māori god.

'*Nic!*' Danny's cousin George comes jogging over from the porch, and I think, *Thank you, Jesus.* He waves me up the drive, and when I've parked and turned the engine off he opens my door.

'Who're they?' I glance in my rear-view mirror at the men behind me.

'Oh, don't worry about them.' George grins. 'They're harmless.'

'Are you sure it's okay I park here?'

'Yeah, of course. Danny told me to save it for ya. He's inside; he'll be out in a minute.'

I reach for my bag and follow George along a darkened path to the backyard. There are plastic tables and chairs, and the air is thick with smoke. He clears a way for me, holding out his arm as I sidestep the flaming coals of a motorised spit.

'Gab'll be happy to see ya.'

I wave at one of Danny's aunts. 'Yeah, me too. How's he going?'

'Mate, he's been with us five seconds, we wanna send him back.'

I laugh. 'Well, where is he?'

George points to the far side of the yard where I see Gab, leaning against the washing line, shirtless, sculling whisky.

'Classy.'

We continue onwards, squeezing between people and greeting them as we go. There're a few female relatives, but otherwise it's mostly men – older uncles, cousins and compatriots from around The Area. Some I recognise, some I don't. When we get close enough, George calls out to Gab.

He turns to face us with his gut hanging over his jeans. There's a moment of bleary-eyed static and then, like a monster, he's running through tables and chairs to get to me.

'*NICKY NAJIM!*' He puts his arms around my neck and presses my face against the MEOC tattoo on his sweaty chest. His breath smells sour: the telltale stench of a recent vomit.

'Gab! Gross!'

'Fuck, sorry, Nic! Haven't seen a good-looking girl in a while!' He grins at his own joke. 'They got me at this party, you think there'd be some gangas. Six years, Nic. Six fuckin' years.'

There's something different about his face. He's still the same – still short and stocky and energetic – but his eyes are empty. Gab used to be the best boy; the type of kid that would give you all the red Skittles from his mini pack. But when he got older, he started using. I've seen his mum at the salon sometimes, colouring the greys that her son has given her. Years ago, before Gab got jailed, she tried weaning him off meth. She locked him in a room for a week and listened to him scream and cry. She cleaned his piss-stained sheets and held him through a four-day fever. She even got a priest to come and pray over him – an attempted exorcism, to draw the devil out of her son. But it was all for nothing. A month later he was back on it, and when she tried to help him again, he beat her so badly he broke her jaw.

I think about my old friend, the one who always gave us first dibs, and I say, 'Well, we all missed you.'

He rubs his nose with the back of his fist and takes another swig. 'Me too, man. I missed everyone. You, Dan – even this big bastard.' He grabs George by the shoulder, slaps him on the back. 'What about you – you been good?'

I nod. 'Yeah. Same old.'

'How come no one's married you yet? Thought you'd be long gone by now.'

Already he's a nuisance. 'I don't know, Gab. There's really not much to choose from.'

'Ah,' he says, stifling a belch. 'You're fussy like me.'

Jesus.

George's phone starts ringing, and he walks away to answer it. I turn to look for Danny, but he's nowhere in sight. As I'm texting him, I can feel Gab watching me, studying my face the same way I did his; trying to patch together the past six years.

'You haven't changed,' he sniggers. 'You're still pretty. Maybe even prettier.'

'Thanks, I guess.'

'Still snobby, too.'

'Oh, fuck off, Gab.' I say it like I used to, and his face lights up. 'I'm here, aren't I?'

He laughs and raises his hand. 'There she is! You can take the girl outta Greenacre, but you can't take Greenacre outta the girl.'

I roll my eyes and reluctantly meet his high five. I'm about to ask him where Danny is, when one of his cousins calls out from the barbecue. '*Yallah, khaye! Ash badak?*'

Gab slaps his belly. 'About fuckin' time!'

He staggers away to the spit, leaving me on my own, so I go and say hi to the women.

They're sitting at a table near the shed: Danny's mum and his sister Sarah, Gab's mum, two of his aunties and a few of Gab's cousins. We all exchange kisses before I circle back to Sarah. She watches as I approach, her eyes half-hidden beneath a long brown fringe.

'Is anyone sitting here?' I point at the empty seat beside her, and she shakes her head.

Over my shoulder, Bruiser barks and bashes his paws against the shed door. Danny always locks him away when he has people over. Much like his owner, Bruiser doesn't do well around strangers.

'Where's Dan?' I ask.

'He's inside. I think he's on the phone.' Sarah doesn't look at me. She mumbles and plays with her hands when she speaks. I glance around at the rest of the group. The older women are chatting in Arabic; the younger ones are staring at their phones. Danny's mum smiles at me from across the table and says, '*Khalili albik. Badik* barbecue? *Fi lahem, ou djej ou kafta.*'

'Thanks, Aunty, I'll go get a plate soon.' I turn back to Sarah. 'I'm gonna go find him. Wanna come?'

She shakes her head. 'I'm not allowed; I have to stay with my mum.'

It's a strange thing to say. Sarah's almost eighteen; she doesn't need babysitting. I look towards the house. There are people coming from the back door with platters of food, and through the kitchen window I can see a group of women laughing at the sink.

'But it's okay if I go in?'

She nods wordlessly. I stare at her a minute, but she doesn't say anything else. Sarah wasn't always like this – as a kid, you couldn't shut her up – but ever since her father died, she's been a different girl. It was a slow and laboured death, their dad, until one morning it wasn't, and they awoke to find him dead on the couch, his coffee cold. He'd migrated here with his wife and son in the early 1990s, after surviving a bomb blast in Beirut. The doctors there had given him a dodgy blood transfusion and this, combined with his injuries, meant that Sarah had only ever known her father to be sick, and Danny was forced to become the breadwinner of his family as soon as he was old enough to ride a bike.

I take my phone from my bag and stand. 'Want me to bring you anything?'

Sarah shakes her head again, and I walk away from her feeling heavy. I don't know if I said enough, or if I should've stayed.

I'm almost at the stairs when I finally get a text from Danny: *I'm inside where are you??*

I reach the back door, holding the screen open for one of his aunties. She's carrying a tray of skewered onions and shouting over her shoulder for more bread.

'Nicky!' Danny comes striding down the hall, shirtless. 'Fuck, man, I'm so sorry.'

'What's with this party? Doesn't anyone own a shirt?'

'Gab spewed on mine.' He ducks into a room and emerges with a fresh tee. 'I had to have a shower. I sent George out to get you. Are you okay?' There's a scar above his hip and three large crosses tatted on his chest; a homage, in part, to the penitent thief who died beside Christ at Golgotha.

'Yeah, I'm fine. I thought you said he was sober now?'

He stretches the t-shirt over his torso. 'Nah, I said he was *clean*. Sober's a different story.'

'Well, it's your fault he's this fucked up. You said a barbecue, not a *hafla*.'

'You think I wanted a party this big? I fuckin' hate having people at my house.'

'Then you should've just said no.'

'I felt bad! The poor cunt's done six years.'

'Yeah, and he's complaining there's not enough women.'

Danny sighs. *'Ayreb* his head. I'll get him a girl later.'

'Oh, how *lovely*. Maybe get yourself one too.'

Danny's got the type of face that can flip like a coin. Most of the time it's stony and still – a permanent mugshot, made worse by a monk-like beard. But when he laughs, he becomes a boy again. He puts me in a playful headlock, and when I try to twist out of it, I see the women in the kitchen are smiling at us.

Danny reaches for the door. 'You hungry?'

'Yeah, I am, actually.'

'Eh, yallah.' He pinches my side. 'You could do with a bit of *lahem*.'

He walks to the head of the queue and serves me first, upselling every dish. After the salads, I follow him to the barbecue, where one of his uncles chooses our skewers fresh from the coals. *'This one good. This one special for you.'* The old man holds up a stick of blackened chicken like it's a culinary masterpiece.

'You want a drink?' Danny asks.

'Yeah, just anything.'

He goes to the ice buckets and comes back with two cans of Coke. I get some napkins and some cutlery, and the two of us move to the end of a long trestle table and sit alone.

'So, when you back at work?' He stabs his salad with a fork.

'Monday.'

'Have you been feeling any better?'

'Yeah, I think so. I've been eating more.' I put some lamb in a piece of bread and eat it like a wrap.

'I can tell. *Sahten.*'

I nod in response, my mouth full.

'You seem better, anyway. A little less mental.'

'Yes, thank you. I love that I can come to you with anything and not be laughed at.'

'Oh, don't make me feel bad.' He grins. 'You know I take all your problems very seriously.'

'Well, *good*. Because this sort of thing – this sort of quarter-life crisis – it's very common.'

'A quarter-life crisis? You make that up?'

'*No*. It's an actual thing. It's like a fear that hits you in your late twenties when you realise you don't have a fuckin' clue what's going on.'

'That's a bit delayed for that – late twenties.'

I look at him.

'We're all in the same boat, Nic. You just been huddled below deck a little longer.'

'Right. So, you're saying that I've been sheltered, then?'

'I mean, a bit.' He can't stop smiling.

'Oh, you're enjoying this, are you?' I reach to pull his beard.

'*Oi!* Okay, okay!' He's laughing. 'Tell me more about this crisis. Maybe I can help.'

'I don't need your help. I'll get through it the way everyone does – with alcohol. And by doing something random. Like, I don't know – getting a tattoo.' I say it just to bait him.

Danny, choking on his salad, says, 'Don't you dare.'

'Why not? Maybe it'll make me less "sheltered". Less boring and "below deck".'

'Hey, I never said you were boring. But a tattoo? It just wouldn't suit you.'

'Oh, come on, Dan, it'll be cute. We can get something matching.'

He seems almost tempted, then he shakes his head. 'Nah, no more for me. I got my tatts when I was younger. And, you know, I got 'em 'cos I thought they would show things. But really they just cover you up.' He leans back in his chair, his ink-mottled arm resting beside him. 'That's why it wouldn't suit you. There's nothing about you that needs to be covered.' The way he says it makes me pause.

I peel some bread and change the subject. 'So, do you actually know all these people?' I look around the yard.

He keeps his eyes on me. 'Yeah.'

'Like every single one of them?'

He smirks now. 'Yeah, why?'

'I don't know, it's just funny. Like, I figured you must, but I didn't realise you had so many friends.'

'Fuckin' hell – thanks.'

'I'm serious: I'm shocked.' I look over his shoulder. 'Who's that guy over there? The one with the matching tracksuit?'

He turns and follows my gaze. 'That's Paulie. We play poker together.'

'Ah. And what about that one over there? The bald guy with the Angry Bird eyebrows?'

He laughs. 'That's Roy. Went to school with me and Gab. Used to be a boxer, now he owns his own gym.' Danny watches while I look some more. 'Are you asking for yourself, or just testing me?'

'Neither.' I shrug. 'It's just … you've got all these mates I've never heard of. I thought I was special.'

'Well, there's mates,' says Danny, 'and then there's best mates. But you already know that; you're just fishing.'

'Hmm. Am I really, though?'

'Really what?'

'Your best mate. I mean the competition's pretty thick.'

'Let's put it this way,' says Danny. 'You're by far the most fuckin' annoying person at this party, but I'm still sitting here next to you.'

'Wow. Way to make a girl feel loved.'

'Well, you know me, Nic,' he says. 'I'm all about the romance, babe.'

I give him a look and the two of us laugh.

'So, what else? What've you been up to with all your time off?'

'Oh, not much. I was actually gonna come see you the other day, but I got stuck at church.'

'At church?'

'Yeah, with Tayta.'

He gives an encouraging nod. 'That's new.'

'Well, don't get too excited. I'm not gonna make a thing of it.'

'Why not?' Danny goes to St Maroun's every Monday night. He doesn't go to mass; he just prays in the furthest pew.

'I don't know. Not all of us are devout Catholics like you.'

He laughs at this. 'Yeah, I'm a fuckin' saint.'

'You know, you're really not as bad as you think you are.'

'Maybe.' He shrugs. 'I might be worse.'

'What's that supposed to mean?'

Instead of answering, Danny busies himself with the food on his plate. But I need to know if he's okay; if what he said the other day was just a scare. It's been playing on my mind since last week, and even though I keep telling myself nothing's going to happen, I can't shake the fear that it might.

'Dan, have you heard any –'

'*NICKY, NICKY, NICKY!*' Gab comes over with a glass of *arak* and a *kafta* skewer. 'Fuck I missed youse!' He bends down and kisses Danny's head.

'Us too, brother. Come sit.'

Gab pulls out the chair across from mine and collapses into it. 'The old Amber Way crew! Fuckin' *heavy*!'

I grimace as he takes a swig of his drink.

'Hey, Nicky, how long we known each other now?'

'I don't know, Gab. Twenty-four years?'

'Fuck, that's blood.' He raises his now-empty glass in a toast.

'Here.' I push my drink across the table. 'Have a bit of this.'

He pours it into his mouth, belches, then says, 'Pardon me.'

Danny gets up and fetches us a few more cans. We sit there, the three of us watching, while a chopper circles overhead. I can see its spotlight dancing over the neighbourhood, its red and blue tail-lights pulsing against the night sky.

'Is that the cops?'

Danny shrugs it off. 'Don't worry, it's normal.'

But I wonder what they're looking for. With this crowd, it could be us.

'It's those Raptor cunts, fuckin' pigs!' Gab lifts up his arm and gives them the finger. 'Six years in hell. Fuckin' scums.'

I look at Danny, but I don't say anything. He reads my face and grabs my hand under the table. It's something he's never done before, and the feeling of it both warms and worries me. 'Well, Gab,' he says. 'You're out now, brother.'

The helicopter slowly drifts away. Greenacre's native nocturnal bird.

Gab takes another sip of Coke. 'You know what's the worst thing about jail?'

I look over at him, really wishing he'd shut up.

'No pussy.'

I roll my eyes; I should've guessed.

He pulls at the *kafta* with his teeth and mauls it with an open mouth. 'Nicky Naj, you got any friends for me?'

I sit back in my chair, pretending to think. 'No, they're all pretty decent.'

He swallows. 'Too bad'.

The music transitions from Fetty Wap's 'Trap Queen' to a classic Arabic ballad and a few of Gab's uncles gather on the porch to sing. They serenade each other with their hands in the air, spurred on by claps and yelps from the rest of the party. Gab stands on his chair to join them, wailing each word with his eyes closed, while Paulie in the matching tracksuit steadies him from behind. They're almost at the chorus when Danny leans into me, our arms touching.

'Hey, Nicky, I need a favour.' He seems shy about it, his eyes straying for a second to the women by the shed. 'Sarah's formal's coming up. I gotta take her shopping for a dress. Can you come?'

I look across the yard at Sarah, still sitting with her mum, still staring at her hands.

'Yeah, sure,' I say. 'I'd love to.'

Chapter 13

The next morning, I wake up with a gentle rumble in my gut. I walk to the bathroom, and for the first time in months I go to the toilet without stress or strain. My dad told me once that Elvis Presley died from constipation. He'd been suffering with it for years when they found him on the bathroom floor. I think about how depressed I've been, and how depressed Elvis was, and I come to the humbling realisation that it doesn't matter who you are, there's nothing more debilitating than a broken heart and a stagnant bowel.

When I got home last night, I sat on my bed for an hour just thinking about the barbecue and Gab. He was right when he said we were blood; not in the literal sense, but in the way that we are joined by time and the tenacious bond of childhood. People say you can't choose your family, but a lot of the time you can't choose your friends either. They come to you young, and they stay. Even when you've both stopped liking each other.

And that's Gab.

He was my first friend at Amber Way; my only friend. He and his family moved to the neighbourhood when I was three years old, and then a year or so later came Danny. I lived between the two of them at the top of our cul-de-sac, and somehow – on the commons of my driveway – the three of us became best friends. Growing up, Gab was always my favourite out of everyone on our block. He was funnier than Danny for starters, and I'd known him for longer, too.

But now it's all changed.

That's the thing about a group of three: there's always someone on the outs. And after last night, I know it's me. Because even though I grew up in Greenacre – even though I started at the centre of our street – I sometimes feel like a visitor, as if the people there are living in another world. I think about Sarah, about her sad eyes and her twisted fingers. I wonder why she sat alone. I think about the women at the table, and the men by the grill, and the helicopter circling on high. But more than anything I think about Danny; how I never got to ask if he was okay, and why, hours later in the quiet of my room, I can still feel the touch of his hand.

I check my phone; it's 8 am.

The rest of my family are still asleep, so I pull my sneakers on and jog along our pebbled drive, hoping to clear my head. There are properties on either side of ours: sprawling estates and farms with stables. I keep to the path with my headphones in, when through the reggae notes of Rihanna's 'Work', I hear a muffled shout from up ahead.

'G'day, Nic!'

Our neighbour, Gary, has come to the fence with one of his prize-winning fillies. They stand between tufts of grass, his horse chewing a piece of hay like a cartoon yokel. Gary's what you'd call a 'real' Aussie; the type of person that'd help a stranger – the type that would run to the centre of a crisis in a pair of thongs. The first time I saw him, he reminded me of John Farnham, and his wife Tess looked like Kylie Minogue. Whenever something big happens – in politics or with the economy – I'll always catch Dad on Gary's driveway, getting his opinion on things. It's as if he thinks Gary has the inside word from Canberra, just because he's white and wears an akubra. But Gary doesn't care much for politics, especially since the Liberal Party's 'gone to shit', and 'that drongo' Malcolm Turnbull started running things. Gary's a fourth-generation farmer from Dubbo, and so the only thing he really gives a fuck about is the drought.

I pull out my headphones and slow to a stroll. 'Hey, Gary. How's it going?'

'Oh, not bad,' he says. 'Could do with a bit of rain, though.'

'I checked the weather this morning. There might be some next week.'

'Yeah, there always is, but it's never in the bloody dams.'

I nod as if I know.

'You're up early for a Sunday.' He leans against a wooden post, holding the reins of his horse with one hand.

'Yeah, thought I'd get some exercise.'

'That's the way, love. Look, I just wanted to thank your mum for those delicious baklavas she sent for me and Tess.'

'Oh yeah, sure, I'll pass it on.'

Mum and Gary have developed this little barter system, where they trade fresh fruit for *baklawa*. Last week, Gary brought us a box of mangoes, picked from one of his partner plantations up north.

He pats his horse. 'Nice lady, your mum. But Jezza in heaven, she can yell.'

I have to stop myself from laughing. Only a true-blue bogan would abbreviate the name of our Lord and Saviour to 'Jezza', as if he were a mate from up the pub.

'She was rippin' in the other day. I heard her from the stables; she spooked me horses.'

'Sorry, that was probably my fault. I've been getting on her bad side lately.'

He chuckles. 'Ah well. Mums will be mums, I guess.' He waves me off. 'Enjoy your walk, love.'

I wave back and start again, striding past a rose farm and the high hedges of a hidden mansion. The houses here all have names, and as I jog my usual circuit, I take my time to peer at them all. When I first moved here as a kid, I remember thinking it felt lonely. It's always been beautiful, but it took me some time to make it my own. My friends weren't waiting on my doorstep anymore, and our closest neighbours were almost an acre away. Still, I've come to love it now – the fresh air, the quiet; that feeling of being burrowed in a secret place.

When I get back to my driveway, my phone dings with a message from Danny.

Hey Nickyy what you doin?

I write back, *Just went for a walk* 😊

What, out there in the sticks?

I send him an eye roll emoji. *Sorry I don't have helicopters flying over my house*

Lolll

Then he adds, *Thanks for coming last night* ♥

I smile to myself and reply with three hearts.

Up on the porch, I take my sneakers off before entering the cool of the house. 'Mum!' I shout. 'Gary said thanks for the sweets!'

I'd heard some chatter in the kitchen, but when I call out it stops.

'Mum?'

There's still no answer.

'*SURPRISE!*'

'Oh my God! *Yasmine?*'

She laughs and comes towards me, her long, thin arms outstretched. 'Babe, the look on your face!'

'What are you *doing* here? I thought you were in London working on your range!'

'Well, I was. But I missed my high school sweetheart.'

The two of us had met on the first day of year seven, befriending each other purely on the basis that we were both new and Lebanese. Being the only Arabs at an Anglo school, we became immediate allies against our pre-pubescent Aryan peers, who teased us constantly for having C-cup tits.

'You look good, Nic.'

I huff a laugh and lead her back through the house. 'Not as good as you.'

She shrugs. 'Well, it's my job.'

I notice that she doesn't disagree, but then again, modesty was never her strong point. After graduating as dux of our year, Yasmine went on to design school and launched a clothing label: a high-end, international fashion house that she herself is the face of. She has four boutiques – one in Sydney, one in Melbourne, and two in London – as well as a network of luxury stockists. Today, she's wearing one of her signature designs: a rose-gold maxi dress, ruched at the waist. It's an outfit better suited to a Parisian runway than a casual Sunday at a mate's place, though as Yasmine once said, 'You can never be too dressed up, or too thin.'

When we get to the kitchen, Monica is waiting. She's eating a bowl of cornflakes and grinning at us.

'Were you in on this?' I ask.

She takes another spoonful of cereal. 'Yeah, I thought you could use a fresh face.'

'And what fresher face than mine?' Yasmine adds.

I roll my eyes. 'You want breakfast? We got Coco Pops or Crunchy Nut.'

She shakes her head. 'I'm paleo, babe. Do you know how *bad* dairy is for your skin?' She shoots a look at Monica, who's stopped eating her cereal mid-mouthful. 'Seriously. You're a *bride.* Those breakouts on your cheeks? I wouldn't be having milk.'

My sister pushes her bowl away.

'Okay … well, we've got fresh fruit,' I offer.

Yasmine leans forward on one of the bar stools. '*Oui, merci.*' Since moving overseas, she's adopted a mixed accent. I'd forgotten how annoying it was, this Euro-Arab-American dialect, from someone who is essentially as homegrown as Gary's mangoes.

I take one from the fridge and serve it to her cold, still in its skin but sliced into squares.

'*Mmm,*' she moans. 'They don't have fruit like this in London.'

I cut my own and take a bite of its dewy pulp. 'How is it over there, anyway? Have you met the Queen yet?'

I say it as a joke, but she swallows and says, 'I didn't meet *her*, but I went to a ball and saw Kate.'

I raise my eyebrows, impressed. 'Wow.'

'Kate was a beautiful bride.' Monica stares glumly at her abandoned breakfast.

Yasmine nods. 'She was, wasn't she? A real princess.'

'Yeah, I don't know. I thought her dress was boring.' I try to give my sister some encouragement. 'I think Monnie will put her to shame.'

'Me too.' Yasmine takes the hint. 'No one does a wedding like the Lebanese. Not even the British monarchy.' She starts on the second half of her mango. 'How's Elie, anyway? He sent me an email about your bridesmaid dresses. Apparently there's a theme now?'

Monica looks at her. 'Yeah. It's called, *fuck what the bride wants*.'

Yasmine nods. 'The theme of every wog wedding.'

I move away from the sink so my sister can rinse her bowl. She scrapes the remains of her cornflakes into the bin, talking over her shoulder at Yas. 'Don't change the dresses, yeah? I still want them black; I don't care what he says.'

'Okay, babe, I won't. I guess the colour goes with his "midnight dream".'

'It's *Midsummer Night's Dream*, not that anyone gives a shit.' Monica grabs her bag and turns to leave. 'I'm meeting him now, anyway. We're going to look at place cards.' She sighs and heads for the hall. 'He says they need to be *ethereal*.'

'Meaning what?'

'Meaning seven dollars each.'

I hear the garage door close behind her and I'm left alone with Yas. She eyes me from her side of the bench, watching while I clear our plates.

'So,' she says. 'What's been happening?'

I look up at her. 'With what?'

'Your life.'

'Nothing really. I got dumped. That's about it.'

Yasmine reaches for some almonds in a bowl beside her. 'Have you heard from him?'

'No.' Not a word, not a peep. Not even a whisper.

'Mm. Well, I've missed you. You haven't been online for a while. I saw your Instagram's gone.'

'Yeah, I know. I just needed a break.'

She nods again, quietly assessing me. Then she says, 'You know what else we don't have in London? *Sun.*' She glances outside. 'Why don't we go lay out? I brought my bikini; we can work on our tans.'

She's off her seat already, opening the big bay doors that lead to our deck. I hurry upstairs and put on the orange bikini from my derailed trip to the beach. Then I grab two towels and meet her by the pool. She's laid out in Missoni Mare with an uncorked bottle of rosé from our cabana fridge. I watch while she pours me a glass – almost to the brim – before taking a sip of her own.

'*Voilà!* What could be better than this? Back at home, with my oldest friend.' She raises her glass and I'm forced to do the same. '*Salut!*'

'We say "cheers" in Australia.'

She laughs. 'I know, babe. Honestly, you don't realise how *uncultured* this country is until you live overseas.'

Here we go.

'I mean, seriously. What sort of country doesn't have, like, a Musée d'Orsay?'

'A country that's not France?'

'Sydney has its perks, babe, its beaches and the like. But really, it's just a small town with too many Lebs. Driving around in their financed cars and pretending they've made it.'

'Yeah, some of us actually sell those cars, so take it easy.'

'Yes, but you don't *have to*. I've told you a million times: come stay with me. Come travel the world! You don't belong in this city, it's so ... *limited.*' She sits up and looks around the yard. 'Babe, can you get a pic of me near those hedges? *NetStyle* sent me this one-piece and I need to do a post.'

Fuck's sake.

I climb off the sun lounge and grab her phone, preparing for an hour-long shoot. Aside from being a fashion designer, Yasmine also runs a lifestyle blog for the modern Muslim woman, which has a following of almost a million. I take at least sixty frames of her fake laughing, while she flicks her hair back and forth.

'Wow, I love them, Nic! You really know my angles. Okay,' she says, 'one more.'

But it isn't one more, and eventually I give her phone back, threatening to throw it in the pool.

'Oh, come on,' she says. 'It's all good practice.'

I watch as she walks to the shade, scrolling through her camera roll and favouriting the ones she likes.

'Monica says you've started taking photos again.'

'Yeah, I have. But I'm being a bit more ... I don't know ... *journalistic*. Nothing to do with fashion.'

'Hmm.' She comes to lie down, and by the way she moves her hand – carefully touching the screen – I can tell she's probably cinching her waist. 'You know, I think it's time you got your Instagram back.'

'Nah, I'm over it, Yas. Everything on Instagram is a lie.'

'It's not a lie; it's good marketing.' A fitting response from a public relations expert.

'Sounds like something Elie would say.'

'And he'd be right.'

'Well, in that case, what's my pitch, then?'

She stares at me over her mirrored sunnies, and I see myself in their reflection. 'That you're young. And you're beautiful. No lies there.'

'But I don't feel young. And I definitely don't feel beautiful.'

'Well, that's *your* fault.' She shrugs. 'It's true what they say: no one's going to love you unless you love yourself. It's the same with business. People like my clothes because *I* like my clothes. I didn't go to London and say, "Please, please, buy my dresses." I went to London, upped my prices and made them pay for the privilege.'

'I guess.'

'How are you planning on showing your photos, anyway? Or are you going to hide them in your room, like last time?'

'*No.*'

'Well?'

'I'm working on something. I want to do a course.'

'What course?'

'The one with Bronwyn Farley.'

'Ah, yes. The one you've been fantasising about since high school.' She stretches out. 'You know she shot that cover I did for *Mogul* magazine? It was the influencer's edition, and she had this ridiculous idea that we should all pose "sans make-up", to, like, "connect" with the public. I hated her.'

'Oh.'

'She might be good for you, though. But you still haven't answered my question.'

'What question?'

'About showing your work. A course is great and all, but photos are meant to be *seen*. By actual people. With eyes.'

'Bronwyn's got two.'

'Yeah, but what if you don't get in? Or what if you do, and you don't like it? What are you going to do after that?' She's up on her elbow now. 'You shouldn't bank all your hopes and dreams on just one person. On whether or not Bronwyn likes you. You should be out doing things for yourself and building a bit of momentum.'

'Like what?'

'Like starting a photo blog? There's a special app for it – I forget what it's called.' She clicks her fingers. 'Oh yeah: *Instagram.*'

I concede a smile. 'Yeah, I've heard of it.'

'Just set up an anonymous account and start posting.' She takes another sip of wine. 'I'll even give you a shout-out.'

'I'm not sure you'll want to.'

This gets her attention. 'Why not?'

'Well, you know those "small town" Sydney Lebs you were talking about? I'm doing a photo series on them. A sort of homage to The West.'

'What happened to Paris, and wanting to take photos of beautiful places?'

I shrug. 'Sometimes, you've got to work with what you've got.'

She considers this with a pout, then she says, 'The West. It's provocative. It's edgy. I like it. And you know what?' She slips her feet into a pair of Hermès slides. 'It might be good for my followers to, like, *see* my humble beginnings.'

Though not exactly raised in The Area, Yas used to live in Arncliffe near the mosque, a completely unchronicled point of fact.

She walks to the pool and readies herself for a dip. 'We need a name.'

'For what, my page?'

'Yeah. Something catchy, something cool.' She wades into the water. 'That's your homework; I want you to think of a name and start an account. You can keep it anonymous, but just *start*.'

I nod. 'Okay.' It seems harmless enough.

'The best thing you can do is focus on your work.' She bounces towards me on her toes. 'I learned early on, *never* trust a man. You'll spend the best years of your life building him up, so he can go spend his money on someone else.' She stops at the shallow end, spreads her arms and grins. 'So don't waste your time, Nic. Make your own money, and spend it on yourself.'

I'm smiling back at her. I can't tell if she's dangerously jaded or a champion feminist. It's rare in our community – almost too rare – to find someone like Yasmine, who has completely freed herself from the patriarchy. Even the most forward-thinking girls still have an inexplicable need to fulfil the role of 'wife'. We date and work, and wear sexy clothes and go out at night, but the minute a guy pays us any attention, we cast those freedoms aside as if they were burdens.

'Yas?'

'Yeah?'

I peel back my bikini bottoms to check my tan. 'Do you ever wish you were a boy?'

She looks at me like I'm an idiot. 'What for?'

'I don't know. They just pick and choose their women; they can say and do whatever they want.'

'And you can't?'

'No, I can, but it's different for us. We've got rules.'

'Says who? Your *tayta*?'

'Says everyone. Maybe it's different overseas. But it's still a boy's club most places.'

She props her sunglasses on top of her head. I can tell that she's on the verge of saying something harsh, because she comes to the edge of the pool, right at my feet, and stares at me. 'You know why you're so upset about your ex?'

I don't answer. I didn't want to get into it and now she's throwing it in my face.

'It's because you feel like you *failed*. You thought being married to him was your life's calling, but you couldn't make it work. He *humiliated* you. The one thing you thought was right turned out to be wrong. *Why?*'

She's got me in a corner. 'I don't know.'

'Yes, you do.' She holds my gaze. 'The truth is, it didn't work because you didn't want it to.'

I sit up. 'No, you're wrong.'

'Am I? If you really wanted it to work, Nicole, you would've got on your hands and knees like he asked. You would've done *anything* to be his wife. But you didn't want to. I remember when we were kids, all the dreams you had, all those art awards you won. You want something *more*.'

I don't say anything. She swims to the stairs, leaving her words to bob along the water like ducks. Then she says, 'I'm doing a media launch on Friday night. Some cocktails and a fashion show. You're coming.'

'Ah,' I say. 'So, you're not *just* here to see me. For a minute there, I thought this trip home was a holiday.'

She gives me a smirk. 'I'm always working, Nic. And anyway, it'll be good for you to get out. You should bring your camera, too.'

'I told you already, I'm not doing fashion shoots.'

'Mm, what was it that you said? "Sometimes you've got to work with what you got"?' She reaches for her towel. 'Besides, it's not a photo shoot. It's an exclusive social event – only the crème de la crème – and there'll be plenty of "journalists" there. So, stop making excuses.'

I lie back, unsure. 'I don't know, Yas; I haven't been going out much.' Even the thought of it makes me tight in the chest – all those strangers, and me on my own. 'I don't know why, but I've been scared to.'

Yasmine stretches out on the sun lounge, soaking up the heat, and for the first time today her Aussie accent comes out clear.

'Well, mate,' she says. 'It's time to get your balls back.'

Chapter 14

'*Sell, sell, sell*, you bastards! You're here for one reason: to SELL!'

Coming up the stairs, I catch the end of Dad's monthly sales meeting, run by him and Leg-day Linda. All the boys from the showroom are seated in our open-plan office, while my father points at a line chart, circling a slight dip in September revenue.

'For fuck's sake, it's not quantum physics! *Car. Customer.* You're all fuckin' useless!' He spies me edging around the back of the room, and his face brightens. 'Oh, hi, sweetheart! Welcome back. I got you a muffin – it's on your desk.'

Everyone turns to look at me. I give him a small wave and then I slink to my chair.

'And *another thing*! I've noticed that some of you are looking a bit slack.' Dad stares pointedly at Chadi. 'Everyone is to wear a suit and a tie, and some bloody deodorant. We're selling luxury cars, lads, so for fuck's sake smell the part.'

I power up my computer while the salesmen behind me start to disperse. After spending yesterday with Yasmine, listening to her talk about corporate slavery and quoting Maya Angelou, I came to work this morning with the full intention of quitting my job. But now, having just witnessed my father rip shreds off half his workers, I'm starting to lose my nerve.

'Hey, Uncle! Did you watch the grand final?' Chadi struts up to Dad with his tie loose. 'I can't believe the Cowboys lost.'

'Yeah.' Dad reaches out, tightening the knot around my cousin's neck. 'Another bunch of useless bastards.'

'Don't worry, Uncle.' Chadi coughs. 'Next year the Dogs will win it.'

'Mate, I admire your confidence, but the fact is they're shit. The coach, the captain, the lot of them. And now Reynolds is gone, the one bastard I could stand ...'

'I know.' Chadi shakes his head. 'He was a real Bulldog. Lived in Belmore and everything.'

'Yeah, well, he's gone now. For that fuckwit Foran.' They both stand together, arms folded. 'Thank God the season's over. I'm sick of watching 'em.'

Chadi looks worried. 'But you're still gonna get the box for us next year, yeah? All us boys would love it.'

'Fuck for?' Dad scoffs. 'Sell some bloody cars and maybe I will.'

I draw away from them, back to my computer. Shivani's been checking my messages while I've been gone, and so today, there are only a few unread emails. I lean back, relieved, when, like a mounting storm cloud, the server starts to refresh. I watch the grey bar at the bottom of my screen glitch and load, bringing with it a downpour of those dreaded yellow envelopes. Another six come through; another five. My throat goes tight, same as it used to – like it's me that's being noosed with a knotted tie.

I turn back to Dad, still standing with Chadi – the two of them disputing a high tackle charge – and I say, 'Hey, can I talk to you for a minute?'

They both stare at me.

'Yeah, sure. Everything okay, *hayeti*?' Dad looks me over, assessing the risk of another faint. 'Did you eat your muffin? I got you the raspberry one you like.'

I glance at the brown paper bag on my desk. 'Not yet – I just need to talk to you first.'

'Okay.'

I head into his office while Chadi backs away to the stairs. Dad closes the door behind us. 'What's going on?'

I take the chair across from him, my heart hammering. 'Nothing, Dad. I just …' *God, what do I say?* 'I've just been thinking these past few weeks, you know. About whether it's right for me to stay here.'

He doesn't say anything.

'It's not you, Dad. I know I'm really lucky to have you. And I don't want to upset you, or let you down, but I've been here since high school and, you know, I just don't think I should work here anymore.'

I stare at my hands; the silence sits. A call comes through on his phone. It rings and rings, but he doesn't answer it.

After a while, Dad sighs. Then he gazes out his window. 'You know, when I was a boy, we used to live in a little two-bedroom house with a tin roof. Right near the train tracks at Belmore.'

I glance at the framed Bulldogs jersey mounted on the wall behind him and ready myself for the coming lecture: the ones where parents make their childhoods sound like wartime atrocities. It's not that I'm not empathetic, but the problem with these lectures, is that they always seem to happen when we're supposed to be to talking about me.

'We were poor, Nic. And I don't mean "poor" – I mean *poor*. We had our arses hanging out of our pants.' He points his thumbs towards himself. 'I never had new clothes, or new toys. All we ate was rice and *loubyeh*. It was rough.' I feel a spasm of second-generation guilt, picturing my dad eating bowls of bean stew for dinner. A decade later they moved houses to Tayta's red-brick in Bankstown, but for families like ours, Belmore will always be the heartland: a suburb built on blue-collar migrants and team spirit. Whenever I think of it, I imagine my father watching Bulldogs games from the grassy side of Belmore Sports Ground, where the houso kids could sit for free. He clasps his hands then he says, 'When I got a bit older, I started to rebel. I *hated* being poor. I hated it so much that, one night, me and your Uncle Jimmy, we climbed the roof at church and we stole a bunch of tiles.'

I raise my eyebrows. Who robs a *church*?

'Yeah,' says Dad. 'We ripped them off the roof, and then I sold them to a tradie for cash.' He does a slow nod, really owning what he did. 'But, Nic, the next night, I lay in bed and I couldn't stop shaking.' He shows me how with his brawny arms, holding them from his body and trembling. 'I was so upset about what I'd done, and I prayed to God, *Please forgive me. Please calm me down, God, I'm so afraid.* I thought He was going to punish me. I'd taken something from His house, and I'd sold it. That's a sin; it's a *big* sin.' He looks at me, his eyes wide. 'But you know what? As soon as I prayed, I felt this peace come over me. I was in bed, but my body felt lifted. I'd never had that before, and I haven't felt it since.' He leans on his desk again. 'It was the first time, that I really knew God existed. That He was my *friend*, and He was *real*.

'After that, I decided I was going to work hard. I didn't want to be poor anymore. I wanted to wear a suit and a tie and *be somebody*. So, I started making plans. I worked at the markets packing fruit, and then I got a job selling vacuums to businesses.' He smiles to himself, remembering. 'I used to go doorknocking in the rain, but my car was so old, it'd flood. I had to drive barefoot up and down Canterbury Road so my socks wouldn't get wet.'

It sounds horrible, but he's laughing.

'I was so afraid, I had no idea what the fuck I was doing, but I kept praying. Every day I said to God, *I trust in you*. And look what He did! I walked into a car dealership one day with a Hoover tucked under my arm, and the rest is history.' He gestures at a trophy table of local business awards: the stuff of miracles. 'I've come so far. But still, out of everything, my biggest achievement in life, my pride and joy, is you. You and your sisters, and the women you've become.'

I look at my hands, and I don't know if I should feel flattered or really sorry for him.

'That's nice, Dad, but it's not true. Especially with me. I haven't done anything to make you proud.'

'Maybe not in the ways that you think, but you will. Life takes you from one small thing to another, until you're doing great things. That's God's way of guiding you; of building you up. You keep thinking you should be ahead of yourself, but maybe you're right where you need to be – just like I was, driving barefoot in the rain.'

I don't say anything. I feel like he's trapping me again, bending me to suit himself, and I hate it.

'Listen,' he says. 'I didn't work this long, and this hard, for you to be miserable. *Look at me.*'

I lift my head to meet his gaze.

'You can do what you like, Nic. But I tell you what, I won't let you leave here just so you can lay in bed all day and get more depressed. Do you really want to sit at home with your mother?'

It's another clever tactic, but I ignore it. 'Dad, I want to start working on my photos. I know you think it's just a hobby, but I'm good at it. I've got all these ideas, and I can't make them happen from here. I need to be on my feet, *chasing it*. That's what you were doing in the rain. You weren't sitting at a desk; you were out there doing things.'

I've used his story against him, and it seems to do the trick. If there's anything my dad understands, it's having a dream.

He leans back in his chair, tapping his mouth with his finger. Then he says, 'Okay, how about this? We'll keep you working here part-time, so you're still getting some extra money, and then on your days off you can do your photos.'

I look at my dad, doing what he does best: negotiating a good deal. 'How many days?'

'Well, three days here and two days off.'

I think about it, then I say, 'What days? Like, what if a job comes up and I can't come in?'

'Let's say Monday, Tuesday, Thursday. And then if something comes up, you can swap 'em around.'

I nod. 'Okay.' It's not the total liberation I was hoping for, but given the guilt I felt about leaving, and the glaring reality that I have no other income, it may just be the best-case scenario.

'Alright, good. Well go on, then.' Dad waves me away before pressing play on a Cary Grant movie. 'I got work to do.'

* * *

Two am.

I'm staring at the open browser on my laptop and that infamous ombré icon.

Instagram.

It used to be fun for me. A way to share memes and occasionally fan the flames of my ego. But ever since my break-up I've started seeing it as a torture tool. I got sick of browsing people and their endless propaganda: the fitness models, filtered and fixed, who never swallow food. The mummy blogger who posts her baby in Versace Bambino but never mentions her tummy tuck or the fact that her husband is fucking an intern. The influencer who travels to far-off places but has to put out for the plane ticket. The wellness coach with hidden anxiety. The smiling socialites with suicidal thoughts. The entrepreneur who's up to his neck in debt posing on a parked Ferrari that belongs to someone else. All these sad, sorry souls, photoshopping who they really are, and for what?

It's almost enough to turn me off; to make me close my laptop and go to bed. But then I think,

I could do something different.

I could show people that the things we were taught to be ashamed of – like coming from a rough neighbourhood or having an ageing face – aren't ugly at all. They're the truth. And as the Lord Christ Jezza once said,

The truth will set you free.

The sign-up form sits to the right of my screen. I could hide behind an alias like Yasmine suggested, but it wouldn't be brave. If I want to change my life – if I want to reclaim myself – I have to put my name to it. And so that's what I do. I reactivate my old account. There are twenty-two photos, and twelve of them are of Us. Him holding me by the waist, Him beside me in the car. Him on the couch, Him at the beach. *Him.*

I breathe through it, and I delete them all. Every trace of him, gone. And then I find his name and I block him, too. It feels freeing to have done it first, unpressured and on my own. After everything – after all the highs and heartache – I'm literally back at square one on an empty grid. The same as when I cleared my camera, but this time the blankness beckons; a cross within two circles, telling me to 'share'.

I shrink the tab and start browsing all the photos I've taken: Tayta and her friends at church, the Vote No billboard, and some random ones I took of half-built apartment blocks lining the banks of Parramatta River. Already, I can see the fine threads of a burgeoning narrative, and even though my approach so far has been rudderless, it seems that every step I take to further myself is rewarded with an opportunity. Like today, for example. Father Boutros called Tayta – right around the time I was having my sit-down with Dad – and asked for the photos I took at the feast. Turns out, he really does want to use them in the *Maronite Monthly*, and despite the fact that it's little more than a two-page pamphlet, printed on stapled A4 paper, I feel a sense of validation. In less than a week from starting, I've managed to get a few of my photos published for an entire parish to see, and I take it as a sign from God that I'm on the right track.

An hour later, I've prepared my first post: a carousel of photos from the feast day, that I caption HELP YOURSELF // @StMarounsPunchbowl.

There's nothing left for me to do.

I'm a click away from going live, when I get that familiar panic in my chest. That cold grip of doubt. It's the same whisper all those bloggers must hear every time they pass a mirror.

I fight it off and force my hand.

Share.

Chapter 15

The day of Yasmine's media launch, I ready myself with an early morning blow-dry and a sheet mask from Sephora that makes me look like I'm suffocating inside a plastic bag. It's a Thursday, which means it's my second consecutive day off work this week.

Well, sort of.

Yesterday I'd planned to go exploring with my camera, but a thunderstorm hit Sydney – the way they only do in Australia – where the sky goes green and the lightening cracks, and the heat from the bitumen sizzles like a sausage at the first drops of rain. I took some photos of the storm from our porch, but then – as Dad had predicted – I found myself trapped at home with nothing to do. My mother suggested the two of us should rearrange the pantry, 'starting with the spices', so I ran to my car in the pouring rain and drove my arse to work.

It was hardly the start that I'd wanted, but today, I'm hoping, will be different. Yasmine has assured me that her fashion show will be going ahead, rain, hail or shine. There's only one problem, and it glints at me from my wardrobe door, hung high on a black velvet hanger. I sit on my bed in a pair of nude seamless underwear – the only type of knickers suitable for a dress as minimal as this.

Yasmine had it delivered this morning, along with the promise of a hire car to pick up me and Elie at precisely 6 pm.

'NICOLE!' my mother yells from the stairs. 'ELIE'S HERE.'

Fuck.

I walk over to my wardrobe and stare at the black embossed swing tag pinned to the dress's inner label: *Yasmine Ali*

God, I lament. *There's always a catch.*

The dress feels heavy in my hands. I hold it against myself, appraising its thigh-high split. The material, though sheer, is embellished with thousands of gold beads that seem to converge around the peaks and valleys of my privates. When I finally pull it on, it clings to my body like a desperate lover. My breasts sit like two half-moons, accentuated by the plunging neckline that almost reaches my navel. Objectively speaking, it's a beautiful dress. But it belongs on someone else; a Hollywood starlet, or a kohl-eyed Egyptian queen.

Mum and Elie are waiting for me, swapping pleasantries in the hall. In a last, feeble attempt at modesty, I part my hair and push it forward to cover my cleavage. Then I come around the banister and slowly step into view.

Elie ceases fake-laughing and gapes at me from the bottom of the stairs. '*Babe.*'

I look from him to my mother, who seems equally stunned.

'*What. A fucking. Dress.*'

My mother says nothing. I had planned on getting past her by acting as cool as possible. She's never liked her daughters leaving the house 'half naked', and so I figured my only hope was to feign an air of self-confidence. But, like most predatory beasts, my mum can smell fear. She quickly regains her composure, casting a critical eye from the crown of my head to my gold strappy heels. Then she says, 'Why've you got your hair like that?'

I stall beneath her narrowed gaze. 'Like what?'

'Like how it is.' She points at me with an open palm. 'Push it back.'

I sweep my hair behind my shoulders, revealing the full extent of the plunging neckline.

'*Amazing*,' Elie breathes.

And to my surprise, my mother agrees. '*Much* better,' she says. 'You can't be shy in a dress like that.'

* * *

'So, talk to me about your Instagram.' Elie sits beside me in the limo, legs crossed, holding a flute of champagne in one hand and lightly scrolling his phone with the other.

'Oh, yeah. I got it back.'

'Yeah, but why did you delete everything? And what's with the church ones in black and white?'

'It's for that course I was telling you about. That's the whole reason I'm going tonight. To try and get some photos.' My camera sits between us, along with a crystal-covered clutch I'd borrowed from my mum.

'Mm.'

'I only did that one post. It didn't get many likes.'

'Well, you put it up at 3 am, for starters. Only the Lord God is awake at that hour. And you didn't hashtag, babe. It's important you pick the right ones.'

Elie, like Yasmine, has a large following on his Instagram profile, @eliaskarampr. When Yasmine told me yesterday that I could bring a plus one, it came with the proviso that it was Elie, purely for the fact that he could blog about her dresses to a hundred thousand prospective partygoers.

'Hashtags? Isn't that a bit lame?' I readjust my seatbelt to keep my chest in place.

'Lame?' Elie looks at me. 'You're posting photos of your *tayta* at church. No offence, Nic, but you need to be a bit more provocative. Like, I get the premise, but if you want new followers you have to chase them.' He checks my profile again. 'You've got seven hundred and fifty-six from before, which I guess is a start, but until you get that magic K you're a nobody.' He opens his own Instagram now and flips to selfie mode. 'Come here.'

'What are you doing?'

'Just sit here and smile and pretend you're normal for two minutes.' He grins at the screen, smoothing his already perfect quiff, before holding the white record button. 'Hi, guys! So, I'm on my way to Yasmine Ali's media night; amazing, *amazing* couture designer. And I'm here with my favourite photographer in the whole world, *literally my favourite*, Nicole Najim.' He pans the camera towards me, and I smile and tilt my head like I've been lobotomised. 'Isn't she gorg? I'm actually *her* plus one tonight, *and* I'll be taking over her Instagram for the whole event! So, if you want to see all the action, make sure you follow *her page*. It's stories only, guys, so tune in!' He ends his broadcast with a little wave, and I sit stunned as he swipes a filter over our faces and tags my account. 'That's the type of shit you've got to do.'

'But I'm not a photographer,' I say. 'Not really. I don't have any work.'

'Well, you do now, my darling. And if you don't, you better fake it.'

* * *

By the time we arrive at Carriageworks, Elie has commandeered my phone and my mother's crystal clutch, which he now wears tucked under his arm so I can take photos 'unhindered'. We'd travelled through Redfern to get here, past the train station and the brown snake mural on Eveleigh Street. With The Block to our right, Elie had paused his lecture about the magic of editing apps – that, in his words, 'could make a donkey look like Kylie Jenner' – to quickly check the doors were locked. 'I don't want to get robbed by the Dingo clan,' he said. 'My shoes alone are a thousand dollars.' Growing up, there'd been news reports of occasional riots, and aggressive photos of Anthony Mundine posing with his fists up in front of The Block. But like everywhere else in Sydney, Redfern is changing, slowly conceding ground to the relentless spread of hipster cafes and urban gentrification. The railway workshops where we've just arrived, have been cleverly converted into a sprawling arts centre. The two of us come down a flight of stairs that lead from the road to a long, open courtyard.

'*Nicole!*' Yasmine calls to me from a Moët & Chandon kiosk. She's wearing a long, satin jumpsuit with a delicate silver belt – an outfit much more understated than mine – and is flanked by three assistants. I wave at her, keeping one hand on the railing with Elie beside me, blogging our arrival. When we get to the bottom of the stairs, she greets us each with a kiss, before standing back to appraise me. '*Yes*, bitch!' I notice that her accent today is purely American – inspired, I assume, by the gaudy red carpet and the waiting media throng.

I steady myself against an old brick wall. 'You didn't have anything else for me? A fuckin' jacket, maybe?'

Yasmine grins. 'It looks *exactly* how I thought it would. I mean, *wow*! Who knew you had boobs?'

'It's too much.'

'No, it's not; it's my favourite piece.'

'*Yas.*'

'It's a low neck with a split. Stop dressing like a boy!'

'I don't dress like a boy.'

'I mean, sometimes you do.' Elie relaxes his recording hand. 'And not like *me*, either. Like a jobless boy who only wears gym gear but doesn't work out.'

'Yeah, thanks.'

'Nic, come and stand here.' Yasmine takes my arm and pulls me to the edge of a media wall: a broad white backdrop with the words YASMINE ALI X MOËT & CHANDON printed in gold. 'Give me that.' She takes my camera and hands it to one of her assistants. 'Okay, act candid.'

'Act candid?'

'Yeah, like, just be cool.'

I stand awkwardly while she takes rapid photos on her iPhone, before I seize up completely at the sight of a group of photographers swarming towards us. 'Okay, I can't do this,' I say. 'There're too many people.'

Yasmine looks around, annoyed. 'Elie, go get your photo taken.' She waves him to the middle of the wall. '*Elias Karam!*' she calls to the photographers. '*Major PR guru!*' Then back to Elie, 'Hurry up, we need a diversion.'

'Well, someone better hold this,' he says, passing me my mother's crystal clutch. 'I don't want people thinking I'm gay.'

We watch as he struts to the centre of the carpet, his shiny, thousand-dollar loafers setting his walk ablaze. The photographers follow, and Elie strikes at least five consecutive poses flawlessly. Front, side, hand-in-pocket, one-leg-out, smile, pout. Then he does a little spin, and it makes me laugh. When I turn back to Yasmine, my face still wide with delight, I realise she's been taking photos of me the whole time. Elie's 'diversion', it seems, was just as much for my sake as it was for the cameras.

'Look, Nic! Look how hot you are.' She shows me her photo reel, and to my relief I actually look good. I look bronze and slim, and my long black hair is just right for the gold dress. But more than anything, I look *happy*. It's an expression I haven't seen on myself in a while, and I stare at it, remembering something dormant. Yasmine favourites one photo in particular: a mid-length shot of me smiling with my hand up, tucking my hair. 'I'm posting this,' she says. 'With the right filter, it'll really pop.'

'Okay, I'm back.' Elie reclaims the crystal clutch. 'Where to now?'

'They need me inside,' says Yas. 'You guys stay and enjoy the drinks. Oh, there's food as well – canapés and doughnuts. Mingle; have *fun*.' She strides away, trailed by her trio of assistants. I can tell she's back in business mode by the way she abuses a hapless usher. Friendly Yas is gone – although considering the scale of this event, I'm surprised she made an appearance at all.

Elie and I spend the next half-hour taking photos: me on my Nikon and him blogging from my phone. He bitches between takes about various 'influencers' as they arrive – one of whom he refers to as 'a chronic *sharmouta*'.

'I don't know why she's here,' he says. 'And who the hell wears leopard anymore?'

I agree that leopard is over, but when said *'sharmouta'* crosses the courtyard to greet Elie, he kisses her thrice before asking me to take their photo. 'You look amazing, babe,' he says. 'I love the leopard – it's so wild.' I have to take their photo six times, while the 'influencer' on his arm trials varying degrees of sucking her gut in. By our last attempt she looks concave.

'Thanks, hun, I love it. And I love your dress, wow!'

I wait for her to leave before giving Elie a look. '*It's so wild*? What's wrong with you?!'

'Babe,' he says, 'that's the way this shit works. Everyone hates each other, but I'll tag her, and she'll tag me, and by the end of it we'll both have, like, fifty new followers.'

'You better not be posting anything dicky on my page. I'm serious.'

'Oh, stop it,' he scolds. 'Remember what you said to your sister? Just *leave it to the expert*. Those were your words, babe, not mine.'

When it's almost showtime, Elie and I find our seats, front and centre along a wide concrete catwalk. There are waiters dressed in white handing out bottles of sparkling iced tea from silver trays, and I take one. At the end of the runway the photographers have gathered, perched side by side on a set of black bleachers. I look around at the fashion critics and glitterati and I can't believe this is all for my friend: my schoolmate who used to tailor both our uniforms with her second-hand sewing machine.

I think about what she said the other day, about wanting something more in life, and I know she's right.

The room goes dark, Yas's name comes up in lights, and for the first time in a long time, I forget about myself.

* * *

'Babe, *wow.*' Layla sits opposite me in the boardroom at work, with Jacqueline to my right and Monica at the head of the table. She holds her phone out for my sisters to see. 'The photo of you that Yasmine posted, it's full viral, babe. Almost ten K likes since last night.'

Jackie leans across the table for a closer look. 'Hot, Nic. Tits look great.'

'Babe, do you know how many people have screenshot this and sent it to me? Like, at least five people. When my girlfriends saw it, they almost choked.'

I almost choke myself, imagining how my picture may have circulated and to *whom.* I think of it surfacing in group chats and being laughed at.

'Don't you think I look a bit keen?'

'*Keen?*' Layla looks around at the table. 'Babe, no offence, but before last night no one even knew you existed.'

Though I'm loath to admit it, Elie did a great job funnelling followers to my page. After the fashion show, I posted a carousel of images from Yasmine's red carpet, which I captioned JUST BE COOL //. The views on my stories had more than tripled.

'Yeah, great. I'm glad Nic's famous now, but can we all stay focused on the hens'?' Monica flips open her wedding folder with a thud. 'It's only two weeks away, and by the sounds of things, no one's done shit.' She's called Layla and Jacqueline here for this lunchtime meeting as a punitive measure. 'Have the three of you even spoken about it?'

'You literally decided *four days ago* that you wanted one.' Jackie comes through with an easy defence. 'Maybe if you weren't such an *arsehole* we would've organised it by now.'

'Well, I didn't think I wanted one, but now I do!' Monica fumbles for her puffer. It's the latest in a string of increasingly random prescriptions. She's developed a cough that Dr Roberts diagnosed as a sort of nervous twitch but that my sister maintains is terminal lung cancer. I'd caught her googling the symptoms this morning.

'Oh, for God's sake!' Jackie snaps. 'Great fun you're gonna be, sucking on your puffer all night!'

'Swear, babe. Like, what a downer.'

'Guys, come on.' I try to refocus them. 'Mon's right. We've left it really late. What about a club or something?'

'No clubs,' says Monica. 'And *no strippers.*'

'Babe, why no strippers?'

'I'm getting *married*, okay? It's not appropriate.'

Even I roll my eyes at this. Navigating the crossroads between eastern and western wedding traditions is always a pain in the arse, especially when the bride wants both but nothing at all. In my experience, there are two types of Lebanese hen: the one who pretends she's never seen a dick in her life, and the one that pretends she has.

'Well, what do you suggest then, Monica?'

'I don't know, I just don't want anything tacky.' My sister sips a cup of tea which, after Yasmine's advice, she's made without milk. 'Maybe, like, a girls' night in, with a grazing table?'

Layla scoffs. 'Babe, I'm not showing up to a hens' party where the only salami we're getting is on a fuckin' plate.'

'Same.' Jacqueline folds her arms. 'All I do is breastfeed my kid and wipe her arse. I want a proper night out.'

'What about a strip club?'

Monica turns to Layla. 'Did you not hear what I just said?'

'Yeah, it'll be classy, babe. Girls only.'

'Look, I'll consider doing a boat.'

'A boat!' Layla hoots. 'Good luck finding anything but a fuckin' dinghy at this short notice. And by the way, babe: hair doesn't do well on the high seas.'

'The high seas? Who are we, Captain Cook?'

'Well, you'll be looking like a convict by the end of it, babe, that's for fuckin' sure.'

'I thought you'd like a boat,' says Monica. 'Isn't that what you and your mates are into?'

'What we're into?'

'Yeah, boat parties and shit.'

Layla looks around the room, a dawning. 'What, you think 'cos I'm hot and I got hot friends, we go slut it up on boats?'

Silence.

'First of all, babe, I doubt your "boat party" will be anywhere near the *calibre* of Moey's thirtieth aboard the *Southern Star*. And secondly, I resent being stereotyped. Here I am, trying to minimise your frizz factor, and you're putting it on me like I'm some sort of gronk.'

'Jesus, no one's having a go, alright?' I hold my hands up between them. 'And no offence, but for the good of the group, I'm gonna veto this whole boat thing. Can you imagine the four of us stuck together in the middle of the harbour?'

'Yeah, babe,' says Layla. 'We'd probably sink it.'

'Well, that was my only compromise.' Mon shrugs. 'I prefer the night in and the grazing table, anyway.'

'Yeah, of course you do, babe. You'd prefer a fuckin' prayer circle.'

Jacqueline interjects now, her arms still folded. 'Look, are we having a hens' or what? I'm sick of these bullshit events. Why does everything have to be so *fancy*?'

'Yeah, babe, and *boring*.'

'Mon, why don't you go get some lunch or something?' I decide to rid the room of one lunatic. 'You're not even supposed to be here, it's for *us* to organise and you to show up.'

'Okay, fine.' She closes her folder reluctantly. 'But I'm serious: *no strippers.*'

The three of us watch as she leaves, waiting for the boardroom door to close behind her. 'So, I think we should get some strippers.' Layla starts tapping on her phone. 'I've got a really good contact, babe. The guys are hot.'

'No way – she'll kill us.'

'Babe, what else is there?'

'I don't know. Maybe a weekend away – up the coast or something?'

'A weekend away? I got a kid, you idiot.'

'Well, we can't keep catering to everyone's shit.'

'I'm not "everyone", *Nicole*, I'm the maid of bloody honour. In fact, *I'm* the one who should be running this, not the two of you!'

'And how are you planning on doing that? While you're breast-pumping between feeds?'

'You know what –'

'Okay, *stop!*' Layla gets up and commandeers Monica's empty seat. 'Babes, let's be honest: the only person at this table actually fuckin' qualified to organise a hens' is *me*.' She points at Jacqueline with one of her talons. '*You* haven't been out since you got knocked up. And Nic, babe, no offence, but *Tayta* goes clubbing more often than you.'

'Maybe so. But anything *you* organise, Monica's gonna *hate*.'

'Okay, tell you what' – Layla leans towards me – 'why don't you come out with me and the girls this weekend? You know, get some ideas. Think of it as research, babe.'

I laugh. 'Research?'

'Yeah, babe. I mean, unless you've got another bright idea you'd like to share?' She spreads her arms, giving me the floor.

I glance at Jackie, who shrugs. 'She's right, Nic. I wouldn't have a clue where to go and neither would you.'

I used to, I think. I used to go out all the time before I met Judas. And I remember loving it. 'Okay, fine.' But even as I say it, my anxiety flares.

What if I see him?

What if he sees me?

This isn't like yesterday: a closed event, hosted by a friend. This is going out to the city on a Saturday night with a group of women I hardly know. In camera speak, it's *high exposure*.

Layla taps her hands on the table triumphantly. 'Tomorrow night, babe. I'll pick you up.'

Chapter 16

Within thirty-six hours, my newfound popularity on Instagram takes an abrupt turn, and I learn what it's like to be cancelled. Yesterday, I'd been inundated with likes and over-inflated compliments.

But then I uploaded the photo from Granville, the one I took on Good Street of the Vote No billboard, which I'd captioned THE OTHER SIDE OF THE TRACKS //

In hindsight, it was the worst time for me to post it: a day and a half after Yasmine's event, when my page was still being visited by the fashion industry's elite. The photo got reported, and instead of being praised for my work, I found myself at the centre of an equal rights debate.

Delete this photo now!

SO sad to still see this level of homophobia. Unfollowing.

100% VOTE NO, if you don't like it fk off!

Reported! This is hate speech!

It's FREE SPEECH you gronk

LOVE IS LOVE!!!!

God said marriage is for a MAN and a WOMAN.
Not two blokes!

It's just a photo! Calm down!

I'd watched the comments all day in a sort of paralytic panic. But despite suffering some of the worst anxiety I'd felt in weeks, I couldn't bring myself to delete it. Because the billboard I photographed was actually in Granville, and a lot of the people there *will actually vote no*. That's not to say it's right or progressive – it just *is*. And as much as others might disagree, you cannot change the doctrines of dead men, or their friends, or a whole generation of war-hardened immigrants.

Not even for someone as wonderful as Elie.

I think about how he's lived his whole life in hiding. I think about how funny and talented and generous he is, and how all of it seems eclipsed by the fact that he can't accept himself. The church, his family – everyone closest to him: that's who he's scared of the most.

I'm sitting on my bed, scrolling my phone by lamplight, when Layla pulls up ready for our night out. She rounds my mother's rose garden, spraying gravel and blasting Migos's 'Bad and Boujee'. She honks her horn twice and then my phone dings.

Babe I'm here

And don't wear fkn jeans

I look down at myself, at my jeans and my heels, and I yank them off. I try to think of some alternative, but nothing I own would be 'cool' enough for Layla's crowd. My cousin and her friends have a habit of dressing like high-class escorts – something they would take as a compliment. I'm standing at my wardrobe in a G-string when another two texts come through.

Something short something black

Hurry up im fkn starved

I shove each hanger aside, finally grabbing a mini dress that fits the brief. I put my heels back on and trade my wallet for a YSL clutch. Then I triple-check that my curling iron is off, before finally unplugging it altogether, and rushing downstairs to the now ceaseless sound of Layla's horn.

'Okay, *okay*! I'm *here*!' I pull the door open and slide into the passenger seat.

'Fuck me dead, did you wear something nice at least?'

I quickly compare our outfits: she's in tiny black shorts and a sheer, shimmery crop that only thinly veils her cleavage.

'Good.' She shifts the gear to drive. 'Let's go, we're running late.'

We take the M2 to the city. She speeds along the motorway entrance, the evil eye on her rear-view swinging wildly at the turn. When we finally hit the open road, she crosses three lanes without looking and lights a cigarette.

'You heard this song? It's a fuckin' track.'

I listen to Nicki Minaj rap a verse about money and dick. 'Yeah, it's good.'

Layla sings the chorus, then she lowers the volume. 'You know, you should really start coming to the gym, babe. I swear, you'll love it. I met this guy the other day, he owns a concrete pump, and babe, *every time* I get to the gym, he'll stop what he's doing to spot me.'

'What do you mean "spot" you?'

'You know, get behind me and help me with my squats.'

'Yeah, I'm pretty sure he's just copping a feel.'

'And what? You think I'm not?' She grins and licks her teeth. 'Babe, he's *big*. Like *really* big.' I can just imagine my cousin pushing her arse up against some guy and disguising it as a workout. 'I swear, babe, the gym is *the best* place to pick up. You do a circuit, it's like speed dating. Every machine, there's some new guy there just *waiting* to have a grab.'

'Right,' I say. 'Sounds a lot like sexual assault.'

Layla rolls her eyes. 'Seriously, babe, you need to loosen up. Have a bit of fun in life.'

'What happened to your boyfriend? The one you told me about at Tayta's?'

'Oh yeah, Steve. We're on a break, babe. I was getting bored.'

'I thought you really liked him.'

She blows a stream of smoke out her open window. 'I did, babe, but I'm over it. And anyway, it's almost summer. Do you think I wanna be stuck with some dud all summer?'

'I guess not.'

'Dating is like doing the stocks, babe. People's values go up and down, and you gotta trade while the market's hot. And it's *hot* in summer. Everyone'll be out, tanned, *drunk*. That's the time to sell. Like right now, your stock price is stable. You're a fresh face, but the problem is you're frigid. So, unless you wanna marry a churchie, you gotta start putting out.'

I fold my arms, only mildly surprised at her grasp of basic economics. 'Well, what about you? What's your market value?'

She leans against the armrest, one hand on the wheel. 'Stocks are up, babe. And now that the two of us are *both* single. *Wow*. It's like double the attention. Everyone's been talking about you since you wore that dress for Yas; heaps of guys been asking what your story is. Now if you're smart, babe, you'll make the most of it. We'll take some pics of you tonight, and we got Monnie's hens' too. We'll get some real slutty ones at that.'

I roll my eyes in the dark. 'Elie said he's coming, by the way.'

She frowns at me. 'To what? The hens'?'

'Yeah.'

'Oh good,' she says. 'We can all compare pussies.'

I try not to laugh. 'He's only coming past. Just to make sure the night goes well.'

'Babe, *please*. You'd think he'd just come out already. No one would care, no one would treat him different.'

'Well, *we* wouldn't.'

'Yeah, exactly. I mean he's gay to me either way.'

'You know, sometimes I think, imagine he's not? Like, imagine we've all got it wrong, and he's just one of those guys that's really fuckin' metro.'

'Listen, babe, I know you've been attacked by lesbians all day – I mean, that would scare me too – but there's nothing wrong with just saying it how it is, and Elie is as gay as can be. I mean, you know he's in love with Chadi, right? And fuck knows why, babe. There are so many god-like gays, and he's fallen for my idiot brother.'

'Yeah, I kind of picked up on that.'

'He full loves him, babe. Thank God Chadi hasn't noticed; if he did, he'd fuckin' freak.'

But I don't think he would. If anything, it'd only fan his ego.

'Where's Chadi tonight, anyway?' I ask. 'Is he out?'

'Yeah, babe. He said he's going Cross. If you want, we can meet him later.'

The Harbour Bridge comes up in front of us, its steel arches lit by an ethereal glow. Layla's got the sunroof open, and I can see the silver gulls flying over the flags. We pass the yellow signage of the Shangri-La, and James Packer's half-built Crown hotel at Barangaroo, towering to our right. The road winds down around Darling Harbour, all the way to the red lanterns of Chinatown and into the waterside streets of Pyrmont.

'God, I haven't been here in ages.'

Layla hears the worry in my voice. 'Babe, you're with *me*. No one's gonna bother you. And if they *do*, I'll rip his face off.'

She leaves her car with the valet, then drags me past the casino's main entrance and into the blackened den of a dimly lit sushi restaurant. 'So, listen,' she says. 'The girls know about your break-up. Dee wants to talk to you.'

I slow down to stare at her. From what I've gathered over the years, Dee is the leader of Layla's group. Her requesting a sit-down is the equivalent of a summons from Don Corleone.

'Why?'

'Dee likes you babe. She cares.'

'Lay, I've met Dee *twice*. And I thought the whole point of tonight was "research".'

Layla flicks her hair and looks at me like I'm a burden. 'Yeah, babe,' she says. 'It is.'

They've already started eating when we arrive at the table. Everyone stands to greet us, and we do our rounds, finally ending with Deanne 'Dee' Zaia. She eyes me the way one would a potential recruit, before nodding at the YSL purse hanging from my hand. 'Nice bag.'

'Thanks.'

'Come sit.' Her voice is deep like a man's, made stranger by the fact that she's a meagre five foot tall. All her features are extreme: big lips, thick brows, long lashes and a silken black bob. With a wave of her tiny hands, the rest of the table moves down so that Layla and I can sit nearer the head.

After we order, one of the other girls – who's draining the last of a lychee martini – makes a slurred attempt at conversation.

'Babe, I love your nose – where'd you get it done?'

I glance at Layla before answering. 'It's mine.'

'No way, babe, it's so straight!'

'Oh, thanks.'

She tries to speak again but is quickly silenced.

'So, Nicole …' Dee's eyes – dark and dangerous, and winged with black liner – are fixed on mine. 'I heard about your ex.' She says it like the stench of my situation has reached her on high. 'I'm sorry for what happened to you, but everyone knows he's a scum dog.'

I nod, not sure what to say.

'And you know the nightclub upstairs?' She points towards the gaming floor, her arm stacked with Cartier bangles, each a medal from her litany of lovers. 'That's the pound, babe. Only scum dogs go there.'

I nod again, reaching for a sip of wine.

'Your ex was always leeching, babe. Always on my boyfriend's table, never paid for shit.' Dee's boyfriend, who, according to her own logic, must also be a scum dog, is a plumber and a drug dealer too. 'And his new missus? What a *rat*. I said to Layla, how can you go from Nicole to that ugly bitch?'

Everyone agrees.

'Well, he's happy, I guess.'

'He's using her, babe. Her and her family, she's got the right connections.' She rubs her fingers together to indicate cash. 'They're bankers, babe. Bankers and politicians. He'd be fucking her every day just to get his loans approved.'

I sit back, silent.

'She's right, Nic.' Layla reaches for some nigiri. 'It's not just us girls that can be gold-diggers. It's men too.'

I look around the table, each of them patched in designer like a gang of thieves.

'All men are dogs, babe.' Dee taps her glass, and the waiter refills it. 'Some are poodles, and some are pitties, but they're all fuckin' dogs.'

Layla chews. '*Haroum*, poor Nic. She copped fuckin' Clifford.'

Dee laughs at this. 'The biggest dog of all!' She reaches out with her chopsticks. 'Don't worry, babe. All men are cheating scums. Just find a *rich* one. The rich ones are fuckin' ugly, but at least when they cheat, you can take 'em for half.' She passes me a plate of yellowtail sashimi with jalapeño. '*Yallah*,' she says, 'have some. It's good, babe. A bit spicy. Like us.'

I serve myself a piece, relieved at last when the conversation stops being about me. They begin to discuss some recently jailed fraudster who, according to Dee, committed the 'lowest of low acts' by buying his girlfriend a splurge of designer handbags with a series of bad cheques. They all hang their heads in silent mourning upon hearing that a rare croc Birkin had been repossessed.

'But, babe, how did this happen?' asks a stricken-faced girl at the end of the table.

'Yeah,' says another. 'I thought he was a dealer, babe. I thought he was rich.'

'Babes, *no*. He was always a flop. And anyway, dealers only pay cash.' Dee leans forward on her little arm. 'I've never seen *my* boyfriend write a cheque in his life.' She talks about drug dealing as if it were a respected profession; the same way other women might boast about their partner being a doctor or a lawyer. I sit there, listening quietly, until a waiter interrupts us.

'Excuse me, miss, but the gentlemen at the bar sent these over.'

He offers Dee a tray of six peach-coloured shots and, after

glancing back at a group of grinning forty-year-olds, she accepts them with a wave of her hand.

'You know what you need, babe?' Dee pulls at an edamame with her porcelain teeth. 'You need a few new guys. Not just one – *a few*. Even if they're flops, babe, they'll keep you busy. They'll text, they'll call, they'll take you out. And you just keep them on rotation.' She drops the empty bean pod in a bowl. Then she says to me, 'You know this pain you're feeling? You only feel it once. You'll never be this hurt again. It's a one-time thing, babe, and then you become heartless.' She spreads her arms, and the other girls laugh.

'She's right, babe,' says Layla. 'But anyway, you've been good; you've been going on dates. Chadi told me you been talking to Dave.'

I recoil. 'It was one date. And no, we're not "talking".'

Dee looks at me sidelong. 'Dave who?'

'Dave Dollaz.' Layla talks with her mouth full. 'You know, the builder.'

'Babe, he's *cashed*.'

'Yeah,' says Layla. 'And she's been hanging out with Danny more, too.'

I glare at her.

Dee grins. 'Danny Lahood?'

The mention of his name sends a hush around the table. I notice that the girl with the lychee martini has turned a pretty shade of pink. Dee leans towards me and whispers, 'Him and Angie had a thing.'

I look again at Angie, who won't look at me, and I don't know why, but I get this sickening wave of jealousy.

'Was it recent?' I ask.

Dee shrugs. 'Start of the year. It wasn't serious.' She leans back in her chair and takes another sip of wine. 'Anyway, Danny, Dave – you've got a lot of "D" to choose from.'

Layla laughs. 'I swear.'

After the mains, the waiters bring dessert. They serve it down the centre of the table: alternating plates of Mochi ice cream and mango pudding. I take a spoonful of each while Dee eyes me in the dim light. 'You ever get that girl?'

I look up at her. 'Who?'

She stares at me like I'm wasting her time. 'That bitch – Blondie.'

I shake my head. 'What for?'

'She *stole* something from you. In my country, if someone steals something, we cut off their hand.'

She's gone from throwing back shots to advocating sharia law. I'm about to make a joke of it, when Layla interrupts us with some truly shocking wisdom.

'Yeah, babe,' she says. 'But that's the thing about stealing a man. You gotta fight your whole life to keep him.'

This seems to pacify Dee. She nods, thinking it over. Then she raises one of her chopsticks and appraises it in the shadows.

'Maybe, babe,' she says. 'But I'd take a fuckin' finger at least.'

* * *

Somewhere between dessert and my third glass of wine, I agree to go to the Cross for further 'research'. Layla leaves her car and her friends at the casino, and the two of us take a taxi across town to meet Chadi. We ride through the city in silence, our cabbie smelling of sweat and spice, while Layla texts a 'hot guy' who happens to be going to the same place. 'He's got a table, babe,' she says. 'Free drinks for us.'

'Oh, thank God,' I say. 'We could've never afforded our own.'

Once we pass the gothic peaks of St Mary's Cathedral, the iconic Coke sign comes flashing into view. It hangs above the off-ramp on

William Street like a Las Vegas billboard: a fitting neon welcome to Sydney's infamous red-light district.

'Just turn here and drop us where you can,' Layla gives directions, while touching up her make-up in the visor mirror.

I watch while our driver taps the wheel, stealing the occasional glance at my cousin's unavoidable cleavage.

'Are you Indian?' he asks, pausing the Punjabi music wailing from his radio.

Layla looks at him like it's the worst insult of her life. '*No.*' She snaps the visor shut. 'I swear, babe I *never* get Lebanese. It's always something random. Indian or Assyrian or Persian.'

As he pulls over, she tosses him a twenty, before dragging me out of the taxi by my arm. 'Hurry, babe, Chadi's waiting.'

I follow her across two lanes of traffic until we're safely on the other side. For many here, the night has just begun. There are young men wearing collared shirts and chinos, girls in bandage dresses, and a homeless person sitting on the stoop of a 7-Eleven, yelling at me and my cousin as we pass.

'Jesus wept, what a fuckin' disgrace! You're a shame to your parents, the lot of youse!'

I give him a wide berth, wary of the ancient-looking cane at his side and his total lack of self-awareness. I mean, it's one thing to be chastised by some bespectacled member of society, but it's another to be copping it from a junkie.

'Always on your phone! Get off your fuckin' phone!'

Two more steps and we're in the clear.

'Ya think yer so good, don't ya! You and your fuckin' mate! But yer all fucked! The lot of youse are fucked!' He spits this last part at a drunken teen, who staggers around him like newborn foal in her Windsor Smith heels.

'Look at this one, worse and worse!' He lets out a crackled laugh. 'I can see up yer skirt, ya stupid slut!'

I cling to Layla while she carries on texting with one hand. 'Fuck, babe,' she says. 'The weirdos are really out tonight. I can't believe that cabbie thought I was Indian.'

I can tell this could turn into another ongoing issue, much like her non-existent alopecia, and so I decide to kill two birds. 'Who cares if he did? Indian girls are gorgeous, and they've got the best hair in the world.'

She runs a pensive hand through her flowing locks. 'True, babe,' she says. 'They got good eyebrows too.'

'*Hey, Nic!*'

We're standing at the entrance of a large courtyard opening on Bayswater Road, when I see Chadi waving at me from a line of clubgoers. The two of us hurry to join him, skirting the metal bollard of a burgundy velvet rope. 'Fuck, bro. Just in time. Got worried youse wouldn't make it.'

Potion nightclub is guarded by four Tongan bouncers and a white-blonde door bitch who, as a collective, appear to be a no-frills version of Khaleesi the dragon queen and her Dothraki muscle. Khaleesi stands on the stairs and peers at us.

'Just you three tonight?'

Chadi answers, 'Yeah, we got a table.'

'What's the name?'

'Najim. Chadi Najim.'

She flips the pages on her clipboard. 'I don't see you.'

Of course.

Layla pushes me out of the way. 'Check again.' Thanks to her eight-inch stripper heels, she's the only one of us who can look Daenerys dead in the eye. 'Last name *Najim*, first name Chadi.'

The door bitch glares back at her. 'Can you *spell* it?' It seems more a dig at our ethnicity, or at Layla's intellect, than a genuine question.

'Yeah, *sure*. C for cu—'

'That's me, bro! I'm right there.' Chadi taps the clipboard.

We wait while the door bitch eyes the list. 'Ah yes, there you are.' She makes a mark next to Chadi's name, before casting a final critical look at Layla. 'Tori will take you through.'

One of the Tongans checks our IDs and then the three of us are greeted by a waiting redhead in a black corset. She guides us up two flights of stairs and into the pink-tinged shadows of Potion. There's a mural of a naked woman drinking from a crystal vial on the far wall, and a dark, carpeted corridor that branches off into two separate wings.

'Babe, Robbie's table's this way.' Layla shoves a stick of gum in her mouth and motions to the other side of the club.

'Who's Robbie?'

'The hot guy I was telling you about!' she shouts over The Weeknd's 'Starboy'. 'He's got a table, babe – him and his mates and a few of the girls! Come!'

I turn to see Chadi arriving at his own table to hoots and high fives from his misfit friends. I weigh my options, watching them. 'You go, I'm gonna stay here.'

Layla looks at me. 'With these gronks?'

'Yeah, just for a bit.' I give her an encouraging nod. 'Go – I'll find you later.'

Layla shakes her head, disappointed but unsurprised. 'See, babe,' she says. 'This is what I mean. *Frigid*.' She flicks her hair and stalks away, just as Chadi comes up behind me.

'Fuck's she going?'

'I don't know – to see some friends.'

'Yeah, right.' He stares after her. 'Come on, cuz. Let's get you a drink.'

I follow him back to his table, where Tori the redheaded barmaid is serving vodka under lock and key. 'You boys remember Nic?'

I give a small wave as he reminds me of each of their names. 'You can have the couch,' he says. 'Us boys, we like to stand.' The group of them move aside, giving me the entire booth, before merging again to form a fortuitous human barrier between me and the rest of the club.

'Cuz, vodka?' Chadi raises his glass and points to it.

'Yeah, vodka soda!'

'You want lime?'

I nod.

Tori pours it. First the ice, then the latchkey Belvedere, then a dash of soda and a wedge of lime.

I sip it and sit back, absently checking my phone, as if anyone would have the fucks to message me.

'You okay, cuz?' Chadi dumps himself beside me on the lounge.

'Yeah, I'm good. Just enjoying my drink.'

'Feels like the old days, hey?'

I shrug. 'It does a bit. But nothing'll ever beat it.' When me and Chadi first turned eighteen, Kings Cross was a twenty-four-hour party hub, overlorded by Lebanese gangsters. Those were the glory days of the Golden Mile, and looking back, I consider us to have lived a piece of history.

'Yeah, you're right,' he says. 'I miss when Johnny Ibz was running the doors.' He nods at the booth beside us. 'Now look at the crowd. Fuckin' ugliest heads.'

I glance beyond the partition to see a group of tattooed men being presented with a giant bottle of Belvedere. One of them has an angry, ragged scar running from his ear to the corner of his mouth, like a road map marred by life's wrong turns. He glares around the club while his stony-faced mates pose for a photo, their man bags and diamond watches bared for all to see. The girls with them are equally as typical. I watch from the safety of our corner booth as they lick each other's tongues and laugh at nothing.

'Hey, why aren't you smiling for?'

Good Lord, was there ever a worse question? It comes from one of Chadi's friends – whose name I've forgotten already – and whose face has the strange, asinine look of a wild donkey. He stares at me cross-eyed, sniffing and blinking and bucking on the spot.

'I don't know,' I say. 'Is there something I should be smiling about?'

He wipes at the smattering of white powder stuck to the end of his nose. 'Guess not,' he says. 'But I like to smile anyway.' He gives me a toothy grin and takes the seat beside me. 'Your cousin's run to the toilet. He said to keep an eye on you.'

I look to my left, annoyed to see that Chadi's vanished.

'Thanks, but I think I'll be alright.'

'Hey, what d'ya think of that girl?' He points at one of the bikie molls, grinding against a bald man in a thick Versace chain. 'You think she's cute?'

'I think she's taken.'

He shrugs and reaches for a shot. Tori's brought a tray of them and she offers one to me. 'It's called Potion,' she explains. 'It's our house specialty.' The drink she gives me looks exactly like the mural in the hallway; a cloudy pink shooter with a sugar-dusted rim. I wait a beat, and then throw it back.

'Hey, you're alright!' says Donkey Boy. 'I didn't think you were, but you are.'

I gag at the poison-berry aftertaste. 'Thanks.'

He looks again at the girl in the other booth. 'I don't know why,' he says, 'but the girls I like, they never like me.'

She's getting her own drink poured into her mouth by Scarface and his mates.

'It's probably for the best. Girls like that come with a lot of problems.'

My minder shrugs. 'All girls come with a lot of problems.' He turns to me. 'How about you? Are you with someone?'

There's a slow warmth spreading through my chest. 'No, not anymore.'

'Don't worry,' he says. 'The wrong one will come along sooner or later.'

'What? I don't get it. What do you mean?'

He rubs his nose. 'They always do. It goes round and round. You never get the one you want, because the right one wants the wrong one, and the wrong one wants you.'

The room tilts as I turn away. It feels like I've been staring at the sun. I close my eyes, but when I open them again, the boys in the booth are gone.

And then I see Chadi.

He's standing on the table with his feet apart. There's a bottle of Dom in his hands and he thrusts it back and forth in a manic wanking motion with his tongue out. Tori yells and ducks for cover. I try to tell him *no*. I try to grab him by the shirt, but I can't reach.

And that's when I feel it explode.

My cousin takes his thumb from the open bottle, and showers everyone with champagne. And I mean everyone. The men in the booth beside us are drenched.

'YOU FUCKIN' CUNT!'

Scarface glares at us with gritted teeth. Things happen quickly after that. One minute my cousin is on his feet, the next he's in a headlock, his body bridging the space between our booth and theirs. I jump onto the couch and grab hold of him.

'*Let him go!*'

Scarface looks up at me; the rest of the boys are gridlocked like a scrum. He's frothing spit and wrenching Chadi's neck. I shout it again, clawing at his corded arms. 'LET GO OF MY COUSIN!'

There's a moment of hesitation; a widening of his eyes, barely visible in the dark. Scarface stops and stares at me. 'You Danny's girl?'

'*What?*'

'*Danny.* Danny Lahood. You're his missus.'

'No, I'm not!' I'm still pulling at Chadi, trying to free him.

'Yeah, I saw youse together. At the barbecue for Gab.' He reluctantly loosens his grip, the veins on his face still bulging. Everyone around us eases up. Scarface shoves Chadi away, before reaching over and grabbing him again. 'You're lucky, you little *fuck.* Any other cunt, I would've killed 'em.'

The bikies are allowed to stay, but Chadi and I are escorted to the stairs by two Tongan bouncers and an Eastern Suburbs twenty-something with a walkie-talkie.

'You fucking idiot!' I push through the courtyard ahead of my cousin.

'I can't believe they kicked us out,' he rasps. 'We still had half a bottle.'

'Half a bottle?' I turn on him; I'm shaking. 'You're lucky that bottle isn't up your arse!'

'Cuz, *relax.*'

'God, man! This is *exactly* why I don't go out with you. You're a fucking menace!'

Chadi starts laughing. 'I can't believe you jumped that bloke. You were on him like a fuckin' ninja.' He doubles over, coughing and clutching his throat.

'Shut up, Chadi! I mean it! I should've left you there to get your arse kicked!'

'*Babe!*'

We both look up to see Layla, calling down to us from the verandah. Her lipstick, that last I saw had been perfectly applied, is now smudged around her mouth in the telltale sign of a drunken pash. There's a boy standing beside her – Robbie I presume – and he leans on the railing, drink in hand.

'Are youse okay?' she slurs.

I shout back, 'No!'

'Babe, I'm gonna stay. Get Chadi to take you home.'

Chadi rolls his eyes. 'Yeah, no worries, Lay. You look a bit busy.'

'Oh, fuck off, gronk!'

By now the entire courtyard is watching us, with Layla bellowing her lines from the balcony, a belligerent prima donna. I wave and turn on my heel, striding to the street with my bag gripped firmly in my hand. I'm almost at the kerb when I feel my phone start to vibrate. Long, intermittent buzzing, followed by the final quiver of a missed call.

Danny.

I stare at the screen, he's ringing again. Scarface must've got word to him, and for the first time in my life, my stomach twists at the sight of his name.

'Hey.' I do my best to sound casual.

'Where are you.' He says it without asking.

'I'm outside. I'm okay.'

'Did anyone touch you?'

'No.'

'What the *fuck* happened?' He's breathing now, his anger giving way to worry.

'Nothing – it was dumb.'

'Put me on the phone with your *fuckin'* cousin.'

'I told you already: it's okay.'

'You know how ugly that could've got?' There's a tremor is his voice, and it makes me feel like shit. 'I'm leaving now; I'm coming to get you.'

'No, *don't.*' I pace the gutter; him coming here would make a bad night even worse. 'I'm getting a taxi, it's quicker. I'm going home.'

'Good. Message me when you're in the car.'

I hang up and turn to Chadi, the sight of him pissing me off afresh. 'Well, can you do something useful and get us an Uber?'

'Yeah, I would,' he says, 'but my phone's dead.'

'Well, that's just *classic*, isn't it? Honest to God, I don't know how you get through a day. It's like you're fuckin' stunted. You're the man of the family, you know that? *The man.* And yet here we are, stranded on a Saturday night, because *you* wanna *piss* champagne on some fuckin' –'

'SHUT. THE FUCK. UP!'

I stop dead, wondering where this third voice has come from. I look at Chadi; Chadi looks at me. And then, over his shoulder, I spy the homeless man outside 7-Eleven, boring into me with his beady, bloodshot eyes.

'Do you ever shut up? All ya do is fuckin' bitch! It's always me, me, me – and for what? You can barely fuckin' stand yourself, anyway!'

I'm stunned silent by the accuracy.

'And you! Ya fuckin' dickhead wog. GROW UP!' He hurls a half-cup of Slurpee at Chadi but misses by a metre. 'You're a fuckin' disgrace!'

Chadi turns to me, wide-eyed. 'Who's this cunt now?'

'How the fuck should I know?'

He shakes his head and starts to laugh. 'This fuckin' night.'

'It's not funny! None of this shit is funny!'

'Come on, cuz, it is a bit.'

I pull him towards me by the arm, keeping my voice low, so as not to further provoke our toothless spirit guide at the 7-Eleven. 'I'm sick of this fucking night, okay? All I want to do is go home and forget it ever happened. But I swear to you now, if you piss me off again, I'm gonna call both our parents and tell them what a *dickhead* you are!'

It's the oldest threat in the book, but it seems to work. He pockets his hands and waits in silence while I stalk along Bayswater Road, tapping my Uber app and pinning our location, which I figure as somewhere between Hump's hostel and hell itself.

'You get one?'

'It's *loading*, Chadi.'

He comes to stand beside me.

'Sheng in a silver Camry,' I say.

'*Eh, yallah*, Sheng.'

'Fuck, I'm thirsty. I think I'm gonna be sick.' With Scarface still safely in the club and Sheng now on his way, I can feel my adrenaline starting to wane. 'What the fuck was in those shots?'

'I don't know. But I'm fuckin' wrecked from that fight, hey?' Chadi rubs his neck, stretching it both ways and wincing.

'What *fight*? He had you like a fish on deck!'

I'm still mouthing off at him when a black Rolls-Royce pulls up alongside us, flashing its headlights.

I squint against the glare, waiting to see what new lunatic this night might bring. Everyone around us is watching too, including a group of caked-face girls who seem to be mesmerised by the silver badge fixed atop the Phantom's bonnet.

My cousin leans forward, bent in suspense at the slow opening of its passenger window.

'Dave, you beautiful bastard!' Chadi is beaming. 'Can you give us a lift?'

Jesus, what a saga. I haven't seen Dave Dollaz since our dinner date, and I've ignored his last few texts.

He ducks his head to the window and speaks to Chadi, his diamond watch glinting at the wheel. '*Wallah*, bro, I was just coming past to see ya! Where youse headed?'

'Kenthurst, mate. She wants to go home.' Chadi gestures at me with his thumb and Dave darts a quick glance, the both of us avoiding eye contact. I use his hesitancy to grab Chadi's arm.

'We don't need a lift – we've got an Uber.'

Dave unlocks his doors. 'Yeah, so?' he says. 'Just cancel it.'

'No, it's fine, it'll be here soon.'

Chadi snatches my phone. 'Cuz, *ayreb* Sheng.'

'No, leave it! I live too far.'

'*Yallah*, it's fine,' says Dave. 'I like a drive – it'll be good to get some country air.' There's a grin in his voice; a dig meant just for me.

Chadi cancels our Uber, then he opens the Phantom's rear-hinged door and pushes me inside. 'Wait with Dave,' he says. 'I'm gonna go get us some water.'

Before I can protest, he's sprinted off – back up the road to the 7-Eleven – leaving me and Dave Dollaz in a silence so pressing it's almost physical. There's cold air coming from the vents and the faint scent of leather cleaner – mixed, of course, with Dave's unmistakable cologne.

'So …' He taps the wheel. 'Youse have a good night?'

'No, not really.'

He nods, putting his car in park. 'I never liked the Cross, to be honest. Too many heads, hey? I used to work here in my DJ days, back when Heat was still open.'

'Mm.' I quickly send Danny a text.

'You looked good the other night. I saw a pic. You went to a party or something.'

I glance up at him. 'I didn't know you followed me.'

'Nah, I don't. It got sent around.'

God.

'I seen your other photos, too.'

'Oh, yeah?'

'The ones of your *tayta* and that. They're nice.'

'Thanks.'

'I didn't fink you'd be into stuff like that – artsy stuff. Didn't fink you was the type.'

I stare at him from the back seat, his heavy arm resting on the centre console. 'What's that supposed to mean?'

'Why does it have to mean something? It's a good thing. It's a *compliment.*'

The silence between us thickens from before. I lower my window, needing relief.

'You okay?' Dave looks over his shoulder. 'You gonna be sick?'

'Don't worry.' I roll my eyes. 'I won't spew on your seats.'

He turns away, his frown visible in the rear-view mirror. 'You know, I'll be honest wif ya. Your face, your body. Boys must fuckin' die for you. But your attitude? It's a *big* turn-off.'

I'm too nauseous and too tired to bother with a comeback – the obvious being that I was never trying to turn him on in the first place. Instead, I rest back in my seat, taking deep, measured breaths of the cool night air and wishing I was anywhere else.

He keeps watching me, restlessly jigging his leg and redirecting the air vents flush at his face. 'You know, it's a bit rude, not replying to my messages.'

'Look, Dave, it sounds like you're having some really deep thoughts, but can we save this talk for another time? I'm really not up for the drama.'

He nods to himself, as if affirming some long-held suspicion. 'Wow,' he says. 'That ex of yours must've really fucked you over.'

This rouses me enough to raise my head. 'You know what, Dave? It's late. Don't fuckin' mention him and mind your own business.'

'See how rude you are? You're fuckin' rude.'

'You should talk! Where the hell is Chadi, anyway?' I lean forward to look out my window but he's nowhere in sight. I consider getting out of the car to go and find him, quietly weighing what little energy I have left against the probability of having to pry him from another headlock.

'You fink you're better than me, don't ya?' Dave's voice pulls me back. He's still staring at me in the rear-view; his face red-lit by the tail-lights of a waiting taxi.

'What?'

'Yeah. You fink 'cos you went private school, you're classy or something?'

I look around in the dark, bewildered.

'You fink I'm dumb, right? But you see all this?' He waves his hands at the dash and the starlit ceiling. 'I *earned* it. Maybe you don't know what that's like, 'cos daddy gives you everything. But some of us came from *dirt*.'

I sit with my arms crossed, glaring at the back of his head. '*First of all*, you can leave my father out of it.'

'Oh, fuck me,' says Dave. 'Don't put words in my mouth, okay? I'm talking about *you*. Not your old man – *you*.'

'Well, if you've got such a problem, I'll get out!'

'And go *where*? I'm tryna be nice, Nicole! I'm tryna take you home and help you – just like I did the other night – and you're givin' me nothing but shit!'

I realise, now, that this is the second time Dave has seen me drunk.

He doesn't say anything else. He just sits there with his hazards on, not wanting to make things worse. And the more I stare at the back of him – at his big arms and his broad silhouette, hunched hopelessly at the wheel – the more I taste those two little words building in my throat like bile. I need to get them out.

'Dave, I'm –'

'Sorry, mate.' Chadi opens the front passenger door, surprising us both. 'There's your water, cuz.' He passes me a cold bottle from a plastic bag and then, on second thoughts, he passes me the plastic bag as well. 'That bum at the shop is fuckin' losing it. The cops came picked him up – took three of 'em just to cuff him.'

Dave pulls out from the kerb, inching between two taxis. We glide again past Potion, back towards the traffic lights, and as I take a sip of water, I see him: the homeless guy, slumped in the back of a paddy wagon.

Drunk and disorderly.

Just like me.

Chapter 17

What Dave said in the car bothers me for the rest of the night and most of the next day. Mainly because he's right. I have been a bit of an arsehole, and as far as 'the struggle' goes, well, I've never really known it. That's not to say I don't appreciate the value of a dollar – of course I do. I have a job and wage, like everyone else. But people like Dave and my dad have a different perspective; one that comes from desperation – from having to dig ditches on a job site, or from doorknocking in the rain with wet feet.

I only stop thinking about it when I meet Danny at Roberts Park, a footy field in Greenacre just around the corner from his house. I watch from my car as he kicks a football clean between the posts, while Bruiser sits stoically at his feet. There are two kids standing on the try line and they run to high-five him. When he sees me crossing the grass, he sends them for the ball and then waves them away.

'Hey.' I say it tentatively, noticing he hasn't smiled. 'Making friends?'

'Nah,' he says. 'I know their dad.' He looks at the ground. 'Wasn't supposed to see you till Thursday.' We'd finally locked in our shopping trip with Sarah.

'Yeah, well. I guess I missed you.'

It's meant to break the ice, but it doesn't work. He keeps his distance.

'Danny?'

He looks at me.

'I'm really sorry about last night.'

He doesn't say anything; he just nods.

'I mean it: I'm really sorry. That fight came from nowhere. We had no idea who they were.'

'You're not the one who should be sorry. I'm not angry at you; I just hate not being there if you're in trouble. It really fucks with me.'

'I know, but I'm fine.' I stand with my arms outstretched. 'See? Not a scratch.' Aside from the dull throb of a hangover, and the blister burn on my foot, I managed to escape my first drunken fracas relatively unscathed.

He raises his eyebrows, his gaze catching on my bare midriff. 'Yeah, you're looking well.'

'I am. I even came here for a walk. That's how well I am.'

'Mm.' He looks at his dog, a smile tucked away at the corner of his mouth. Then he says, 'My mate called me today.'

'Which mate?'

'The one from last night.'

'Who, Scarface?'

Danny grins. 'Yeah, "Scarface". He says you're a little staunch.' He's smiling at me now like it's the proudest moment of his life.

I shoot him a look and start walking.

'He says you're cute, too.'

I roll my eyes. 'I'm flattered.'

Danny picks up Bruiser's chain and follows, the three of us strolling around the oval.

'How'd he get that scar, anyway?'

'Samurai sword.' He says it like it's the most normal thing in the world.

'Doing *what*?'

'I don't know,' he says. 'Just mucking around.'

'Yeah, with who? Bruce Lee?'

Danny pulls at the hood of my jacket, bringing me back to him, his arm around my neck in mock seriousness. 'I think he likes you, Nic. Should I hook you up?'

I shrug him off. 'I'm glad you find this so funny, you and your ugly mate.'

'Oh, come on.' He laughs. 'He's not that bad.'

'Thanks, *Daniel*, but he's really not my type.'

Danny keeps smiling but a small, dark shadow crosses his face. He clicks his tongue at Bruiser, then he says, 'Yeah, but, you know, some people are nicer than they look.'

I glare at him sidelong. 'Sure. He seemed real nice, choking my cousin to death.'

I'm expecting him to laugh but he doesn't. Instead, he becomes irritated, his face heavy at the brow.

'You know, Chadi starts a lot of shit. He's too fuckin' cocky – and it's worse when you're around.'

'Why's it worse?'

'Because you're the one that's spoiling him! Who paid for that champagne he sprayed like he was in fuckin' Ibiza?'

'Well, not me, for once. We got kicked out before the bill came.'

'Yeah, but who *would've*?'

I bite my lip; we both know the answer. 'So now you're saying it was my fault?'

'No. I'm saying if you got hurt, I would've killed those boys and your cousin too.' He tugs the lead and Bruiser comes trotting back to us, licking his pitty jowls.

'You know what? First you try set me up with Scarface –'

'I was joking, man.'

'– and now I've gotta listen to your death threats as well.' I put a finger to my chest. 'That's *my* cousin, okay? He might be a dick, but he's *my* dick' – Danny's face widens at this – 'and if anyone's gonna kill him, it's *me*.'

'Okay, okay.' He smiles. 'I'm sorry.' He nods towards a kiosk on the other side of the track. 'I'll buy you an ice cream.' It's a peace offering that's been working its charm between us since the late 1990s.

'And a KitKat?'

'Fuck, okay,' he says. 'I'll get you a KitKat, too.'

We start walking again, but the further I follow him, the less at ease I feel. Even the park – that was once bright with sun and patched with cotton clouds – slowly becomes grey. I steal a look at Danny. Ever since that day at his house, I've been waiting for bad news, knowing he wouldn't have said what he said unless it was real. But I've heard nothing since; no talk of any charges, *nothing*. And I couldn't bring it up again – not on the phone and not around people. I've had to wait. And now, today, we're finally alone. I know it's the right time.

He knows it too.

'Danny, what you said about going to jail, I'm really worried.'

He rubs the back of his neck. 'I know, I'm sorry.' We've slowed down now, enough that Bruiser has to circle back. 'Maybe I shouldn't have told you.'

I stop walking and I turn on him. 'Well, you *did*. And you can't say something like that and expect me not to give a shit.'

He stays quiet.

'I wanna know what's going on.'

He wraps Bruiser's chain around his palm, clenching his fist to form a knuckle duster. I can see him thinking; weighing what little he's willing to say against the look on my face and trying to find a middle-ground. He sighs. 'They've opened an old case, Nic.'

'An old case?'

'Yeah,' he says. 'Someone must've flipped.'

I come closer. 'Like someone's ratted on you?'

He nods.

'Well, who do you think it was?'

'If I knew who it was, we wouldn't have a problem.'

'Yeah, but how do you even know about it?'

'I know some people, some mates of mine. They only told me what, they didn't say who.' He stalls, staring at Bruiser. 'Cops haven't got enough yet, but they're building something. I can feel it.'

My whole life with him, I've always known my limit. It's how we've survived – how our friendship has kept its innocence – by staying separate from the truth. All the times I've seen him with stitches on his face, or scars on his body, I've never asked what I'm about to ask him right now. 'Well, what did you do?'

He shakes his head. 'Nic.'

'I'm really worried, I need to know.'

'I don't want none of this coming back on you.'

He tries to walk on, but I stop him. 'I'd rather hear it now, than from someone else.'

There's the distant sound of a bike bell, and the all-consuming roar of nothingness. When he finally speaks again, he measures each word in exactly the right portion.

'I hurt someone.' It's the truth, but only part of it.

'Why?'

He shakes his head. 'It was a long time ago.'

'So?'

'So, it's a long story.'

Bruiser ambles around us, sniffing at our feet.

'Was it over money?'

'*No.*'

'Then what?'

He pulls at his beard. I'm trying to read his face, but he looks away. 'Years ago, after my dad died, we had a lotta people in the house. Lotta boys come to pay respects.'

I don't speak, I don't move; I just stand there and let him tell it.

'I wasn't paying attention. I was … my mind just wasn't there.' He closes his eyes, and when he opens them again, his pupils are the size of pinpoints. 'One of the boys, the sick fuck, he snuck upstairs and he … he touched Sarah.'

I can't feel my face. I don't know which of my emotions has surfaced first; anger, shock, disgust – it's like they've all come to a bottleneck and forced a blank.

How could someone do that? How could they hurt a grieving child in her own home?

'He was there because of me.'

I look at Danny; both his fists are balled.

'We done business; I should've known. *I* brought that scum around my sister – it was *me.*'

I will myself to reach for his hand, the one bound in chain. 'It's not your fault.'

'I couldn't let that go. Someone like me, we don't let that go.'

'I know. No one would blame you.' I try to loosen his grip, but he shakes his head and pulls away.

'The cops don't care what I did. You think they care about some pedo? It's bigger than that. It's to do with what I used, and where I got it.'

Guns. That's what this is about. It's all just bait for a bigger fish.

Danny's jaw is set and he keeps a tight grip on his dog. Everything inside me wants to reach for him, and so I do; I put my arms around his neck, and I pull him in.

'It's okay,' I say. 'It'll be okay.'

He rests against me, his heart beating like a drum. I cling to him, to his tired shoulders, and I think about Sarah; about how timid she is. How she wouldn't leave her mum's side at that barbecue, not even for a second. I squeeze my eyes against the thought of her face, and it makes me hug Danny even tighter, wishing I had been there for them more.

'What are you gonna do?' I'm stroking his neck, soothing us both.

'Whatever I have to.'

But 'whatever' is what got us here in the first place.

When I pull away, he looks down at me, his eyes like dark water. I say, 'How about that ice cream?'

And he smiles again. I've never been so anxious to see it.

We walk the rest of the way in silence, listening to birds and bike bells and shouts from the footy field. I still don't know the extent of it; how much he 'hurt' the low-life that molested Sarah. What Danny says is always veiled, but I know he used a gun. And I doubt he would've have spared his sister's rapist. There's a word for what he did: it's black and white, and it gets printed in headlines, to be feared and frowned upon over a morning coffee. I see the word in my head, and even though some small treacherous part of me starts to look at him different, the rest of me doesn't. And I don't know what's worse – the thought of him taking someone's life, or the fact that it doesn't bother me half as much as it should.

When we get to the kiosk, there's a blue cardboard menu on the wall. It has pictures of different ice creams: those suburban summer delicacies like the classic Cornetto and a green-nosed Bubble O'Bill. I pretend to study it, but instead I'm trying to remember what I can from the weeks that followed Danny's father's funeral.

Had he done it by then?

Did he even know about it?

Or was he still just grieving his dad?

The lady at the till – a middle-aged woman wearing lorikeet earrings – asks, 'What can I get you?'

Danny speaks first. 'Umm, I'll get a rainbow Paddle Pop. Nic, what you want?' He looks at me over his shoulder.

'Yeah, I'll get a Paddle Pop too.'

Danny digs in his trackpants and pulls a fifty-dollar note from a wad of cash. 'So that's two Paddle Pops and two KitKats. Can't forget the KitKats.' He winks and pinches my side.

The woman buries it in the till and hands him his change. 'You're a cute couple,' she says, and she smiles at us. But when Danny turns to look at me, I see that same, small shadow from when we spoke about Scarface. He leaves her the coins and pockets the rest.

'She's not my missus,' he says. 'I'm not her type.'

Chapter 18

For the next two days I sit at my desk at work, thinking about Danny. But I don't hear from him, and I don't message him either. It feels like we've both shied away; that what he said at the park was so heartbreaking and burdensome, the two of us needed to recover. I know I should call. He's probably on his couch at home, thinking I want nothing to do with him. That somewhere between eating our ice creams and waving goodbye, I had a sudden change of heart.

But I haven't.

If anything, I'm bound to him even more. When someone tells you the darkest thing about themselves, unless you're made of pure light, like Christ, it darkens you a little bit too. And Danny knew it would; that's why he kept it from me for so long.

The last few years I lived at Amber Way, were in many ways a revelation. When you're all raised playing on the same street – sharing toys, and going to the same school, and eating Maccas for dinner – it honestly never occurs to you, that between your house and your neighbour's house, there's any real difference. But of course there was. I was ten years old when I realised that Danny and his family were doing it tough. Sarah had just been born, healthy and whole – a sort of miracle baby given the state of their dad – and we all went around to visit. I remember my sisters and I being excited, because despite living side by side for nearly six years, none of us had ever been invited over to the Lahood's. And it didn't take long to figure out why.

Inside, their house was empty.

It had nothing useless; none of the usual bits and pieces that would normally fill a home. Just a couch and second-hand crib, and a small TV. I know now that my father helped them as much as he could without infringing on the pride of Danny's old man. But seeing Danny that day, standing in the corner of his lounge with his fists balled, staring at his shoes, was enough to silence the lot of us. And even though it's not unique – this brush with relative poverty that preambles most immigrant stories – once my eyes were opened to it, they've been sorry for him ever since.

It's almost closing time on Tuesday afternoon and I'm typing my last email when my phone lights up and my heart jumps, because at first glance, I think it's Danny. But it's not.

It's Dave.

'Hello?'

He clears his throat. 'Hey.'

I haven't heard from him since Saturday, and after the way we spoke to each other, I have no idea why he'd be calling me at all.

'Are you okay?' I ask.

'Yeah,' he says. 'All good. Just calling to check on ya.'

'Oh. Well, I'm good too. I'm just finishing up at work.'

'Did you have a good day?'

'Yeah, I guess.' *What the fuck does he want?* 'How was yours?'

'Yeah, good – just been onsite today. Did a bit of digging.'

'Oh.'

'Listen, I'm sorry for what I said the other night. I didn't realise youse had been kicked out. I woulda been shitty too.'

I'm surprised he's apologising – especially since most of what he said was valid – and so I decide to meet him halfway.

'Look, I'm sorry too. I shouldn't have talked to you like that, and it was nice of you to drive us home. All the way to the sticks. It's a long way.'

He laughs a little at this, then he says, 'So what're you up to?'

I look around at my desk. I don't know if he's asking in general, or if he's trying to see me. 'Um, still at the office. You?'

'Oh, just driving back through Parra. I wanted to show ya somefin'.'

I hesitate, and he hears it.

'It's not a date or nuffin'; just as friends. It's somewhere close, and I'll drop you back.'

'Yeah, but where are we going?'

'Up into the sky,' he says. 'Bring your camera.'

* * *

Dave Dollaz pulls up in a dirty ute. I'm standing on the lot with my camera around my neck and a bottle of water in each hand. He parks alongside me, but before I can step from the kerb he gets out and opens my door.

I watch him warily. 'No Rolls tonight?'

'Nah, not wif these boots.'

I look him over. He's wearing a bright orange worker's tee with its collar turned up, and some Hard Yakka pants that are caked in mud.

'I've never seen you in work clothes.'

'Same,' he says. 'Is that what you wear to the office?'

I'm in a hoodie and sneakers.

I shrug. 'I've started working casual.'

He laughs at this. 'And dressing to match.'

I hand him one of the bottles. 'This is for you. Thought you might need it after your day of digging.'

'You know what?' he says. 'I'm actually fuckin' thirsty. Thanks.' He looks at the label and twists it open. 'You guys got your own water. Fancy.'

I open my own. 'Well, it's the least we can do when someone's buying a Ferrari.'

'True.' He swigs from the bottle then says, 'You ready to go?'

'Yeah, I guess.'

I slide into my seat, and he closes the door behind me. There's a rosary on his rear-view and a picture of Mother Mary tucked against the dash.

We make small talk in the car, driving past Rosehill Racecourse before merging onto the M4.

'So, are you gonna tell me where we're going?'

He shakes his head. 'It's a surprise.'

'I told Chadi I'm with you.'

He almost laughs. 'Yeah, I'm not gonna kill ya.'

'Are we going to the city or something?'

'Nah,' he says. 'I told you it was close.'

We take the motorway to Burwood. He turns right onto Shaftsbury and parks his ute outside a massive construction site. It's a multistorey apartment block, newly finished but vacant. When I crane my neck from the window, I recognise it immediately as Dave's dick-shaped tower. There's still some scaffolding around the footpath and hoardings that say DOLLAZ DEVELOPMENT. I look at him. 'What's this?'

'It's my site.'

'Yeah, I got that from the signage. I mean why are we here?'

"Cos I wanna show ya what I do.'

Great. Another wank for Dave. Maybe he wants me to take some photos of the inside or something.

He gets out of the car and opens my door. 'Come on.'

I sit staring at him.

'We won't be long, trust me.'

He unlocks the main entrance with a swipe card and we walk through the lobby to the lifts. It's eerily quiet. There's no one around, not even a night guard or a cleaner.

I stop short while he presses up. 'Are we the only ones here?'

Dave grins to himself. Then he gets out his phone, dials Chadi and puts the call on speaker.

'Dave, ya dog!'

'Hey, mate.'

'What's up, brother?'

'I'm wif ya cousin at my Burwood site. If ya don't hear from her in twenty minutes, call the cops.'

Chadi laughs. 'You got fifteen, ya bastard.' And they hang up.

The elevator dings, and once we're inside Dave hits the button for the roof. I stay quiet all the way up, convinced he's going to throw me off the edge.

When the doors finally open, we step out onto a large, paved terrace with wooden benches and box hedges. It's not as windy as I expected, and the lights are on. For a moment, I hesitate.

And then I see the view.

Everywhere, for miles around us, I can see Sydney's Inner West. It's lit up under the muted light of dusk. There are houses and highways and peak hour traffic. I can see Burwood below us and, beyond that, my dad's old neighbourhood. I go to the railing and I breathe it in. The world is full of beautiful places, bigger buildings, maybe even better people. But this, right here, is my heart. I stand there for ages, just looking at the lights. The Westfield, Parramatta Road, the dark patch of park. There are other apartments, and I can see people coming home from a long day's work. It's easy to get caught in your head when you're down there on the street. Everything seems so important and so crushing; the mistakes you make, the posts you post, the opinions of others. You need answers and closure and a calling. But up here, the whole world rolls out before you – like a roadmap to nowhere – and you realise that everyone around you is just trying to find their way home.

Dave comes to stand beside me.

'It's beautiful,' I say.

'I wanted to show ya what I done. And I know you been doing those photos about The West and that. I thought you'd get some good ones from up here.'

I smile at him. 'It's amazing.'

I raise my camera and start taking pictures of the skyline, using the light while I can. Dave watches as I work my way around the railing, getting whole suburbs in one snap, and then finally aiming my lens towards Belmore and the rest of The Area. I think about my dad and how hard he worked, coming to this country with nothing and starting over. People were racist back then, much more than they are now, and he had to prove himself to everyone. And then I think about Dave, how he built this skyscraper from the ground up, how hard he would've laboured – the stress and the money he would've spent.

And I respect it; I respect it so much.

'Thanks for this,' I say. 'I really did think you were gonna kill me, but it turned out alright.'

He smiles, then he faces me fully. 'That time I took ya to dinner, I was testing ya. I shoulda been nicer. I'm sorry.'

I fold my arms, half joking, half not. 'You ate my prawn.'

Dave cringes. 'Your dumb cousin told me you had a fuckin' eating disorder! I didn't know what to do. Fuck, I got so nervous, I just ate all the food. I didn't want ya feeling pressured.'

God, I'm going to kill *Chadi.*

I look at Dave again, and this time I notice the faint markings of a burn on the right side of his neck. 'What's that?'

He holds his collar up and backs away. 'Nothing.'

I walk over to him and stand on my tiptoes, batting his hands away to pull it down. 'What happened to the dollar sign?'

He grapples against my arms. 'I'm getting rid of it. I got it lasered.'

We look at each other. I can't believe it. 'Why?'

''Cos it's dumb. And 'cos you didn't like it.'

I stare up at him, trying to read him right. Is this the real Dave, or is this just another act? He's still got his hands wrapped around my wrists, the two of us stopped mid-struggle.

'You know I like ya,' he says. 'And I'll do anyfin' for ya. Anyfin' ya want, I'll get it.'

I stare at him a moment. When I drop my hands, he lets me go.

The wind's picking up; I look out at the view again, and I think about the final temptation: *All this I will give you, if you bow down and worship me.* Maybe that's his offer. Maybe it's the best I'll get. And I don't know what to say, but he's looking at me, waiting, so I go for honesty.

'You're a good guy, Dave. But it's the wrong time.'

He nods. 'I know. Like I said, just friends.'

And it puts me at ease, because he's not angry or sad or proud. He just says it, happy with what it is, not reaching for more.

I feel my phone ringing in my hand. It's Chadi.

I say, 'Hey.'

'You still alive?'

'Yeah, but you're dead.'

I take a last, longing look at the suburbs. Dave's watching me, his collar still up to hide the burn. And I remember something my grandfather used to say. He said if you put money above you, it will weigh you down. It'll make you small in the eyes of others. But if you put it beneath you, if you put it under your feet, it'll build you up, bigger than you ever imagined.

Chapter 19

When I get home from Burwood at about 8pm, Mum, Monica and Jacqueline are all seated around the dining room table, tabulating wedding RSVPs. Dozens of little white cards have been arriving on a daily basis since last month, and now they're being sorted into piles, one on each side of Monica's laptop. I sit with them to help.

'Who's Walid and Roula Youssef?' Monica looks up from her spreadsheet. 'Walid and Roula Youssef *and family* – there's six of them.'

'Oh,' says Mum. 'That's my cousin's son. The one with the crooked leg.'

'The crooked leg?'

'Yeah, from birth, *harram*.'

'Right.' Monica punches the number 6 next to their names. 'And what about … Roni and Yvette Khoury?'

'You know Roni and Yvette,' says Mum.

'No, I don't.'

'Yes, you do. Amou RoRo *ou* Aunty Eve. Tayta's cousins.'

'God,' says Mon. 'I thought they were dead.'

Mum stands from the table, my niece cradled in her arms. 'Here, take your daughter.' She passes Ava to Jackie, who, judging by the stains on her shirt, has endured another evening of breast-pumping and cleaning up baby vomit.

'Is she asleep?'

Mum nods. 'Just now.'

I watch as my sister reaches for Ava. 'Oh, my darling.'

'*Issmissalib*,' says Mum. 'She's growing so fast.'

'I know, almost four months already.'

'Time flies, huh? Soon you'll have two or three. *Inshallah* your next one is a boy.'

We all fall quiet. Jacqueline keeps her head down, only glaring up at us once Mum has left the room. 'You see that?' she whispers. 'That's Lebs for you. They're *never* happy.' She shifts in her seat. 'You think getting married will shut 'em up, but it's just the beginning. As soon as you're back from your honeymoon, they'll start asking if you're pregnant. And if you don't have a baby right away, they'll gossip about how there's something wrong.' She shakes her head and looks at Ava. 'And even when you *do* fall pregnant, even when you give birth to a beautiful baby girl, it's *still* not good enough. They'll want a boy. Then they'll want another. They're a pain in the fucking arse.'

Monica stares at her over her laptop. 'Yeah, thanks,' she says. 'As if I wasn't dreading this wedding enough, now I got that to look forward to, too.'

'Well, it's the truth, isn't it? Better you know now.'

'People always say stupid shit, especially the oldies.' I lean back in my chair. 'Worst thing you can do is listen.'

'Yeah, but coming from Mum? She's copped it her whole life for having three daughters. Now she's doing the same to me. You'd think she'd be a bit more sensitive.'

Monica scoffs. 'Mum, *sensitive*? When's that ever happened?'

'Mon, I've sorted your hens' by the way,' I say. 'I didn't get much from my night out with Layla – except that you were right: a club is absolutely out of the question.'

'Thank you.'

'But it's still going to be fun. I booked a penthouse in the city and we're doing a costume party: "Leather and Lace". Layla picked the theme.'

'Great, another theme.'

'Well, it was the only way we could reach a compromise. The good news is there'll be no strippers. The bad news is you'll be dressed like one. Everyone has to wear lingerie – but don't panic; you can pair it with a robe, or even a nightie or a negligée.' I say this last part to Jackie, who sends me daily Snapchats of her stretchmarks.

'Oh, I'll be wearing a bra,' she says. 'My boobs are looking great.'

'Righto. Well, everything's been organised, so that's that off the list.'

'Good, because I really need to focus on this wedding. I've got so much to do; I'm so stressed out.'

Jacqueline rolls her eyes. 'You've got Elie helping you. That's more than I had.'

'Oh my God. *Yes*, Jackie, okay? You had it *so* hard.' Monica throws her arms up. 'Like, fuck me dead, how many times do we have to hear it!'

'*Keep your voice down.*' Jacqueline points at the bassinette. 'She's sleeping!'

'*I don't give a shit!*' Monica spits. 'You're supposed to be here to *help*. If you don't want to help, then fuck off!'

'You know what's going to suck?' I raise a random card in an effort to distract them. It's the RSVP for Fred and Ainsley, the latter being both allergic to tomatoes and a pescatarian. '*Table seatings*. What a punish.' There's no greater challenge than trying to divide hundreds of relatives into tables of ten. Many a feud has been born from this: from seating the wrong people at the same table, or from putting certain families too close to the toilets or certain uncles too far from the bar.

'That's Mum's problem,' says Monica. 'I don't know half these bloody people anyway.'

'*Shou hal hakki?*' Mum returns from the kitchen, a cup of tea in hand. 'Stop saying you don't know them; you know them all.'

Monica taps in another number. 'Yeah, I could probably pick 'em out in a line-up, if that's what you mean.'

'Listen,' says Mum, putting down her cup as she prepares to deploy that fail-proof, wog-parent response. 'When *you* pay for the wedding, you can invite who you like.'

Chapter 20

The next day, Wednesday, is my day off. When I venture downstairs that morning there are two men outside inspecting the backyard while my mother watches on from the terrace. I can see her pointing longways, before gesturing ahead with both hands, like an air traffic controller at Kingsford Smith. The men nod in agreement, before trudging across the grass while Mum comes back inside.

'Who're they?' I ask.

'They're the marquee people. For Monica's *laylieh*.'

'Oh, right.'

'I tried to get your father to have it in a hall, but he says we have to have it here.'

Mum, unlike most Arab mothers, hates having people in her house. She likes things done and kept a certain way, and large parties of people tend to ruin that – especially when the party is a *laylieh*, arguably the most raucous of all wedding events. It is based on an old village tradition in which, the night before the wedding, the groom and his family would stage an ambush and abduct the bride.

'So, that's it,' she says. 'I just got the garden looking good, and now the grass, the roses, it'll all be trashed.'

One of the marquee men knocks against the window and she steps outside. After a quick discussion, she sends them away.

'Five thousand dollars for a tent,' she says, coming back indoors. 'Let's see how *that* fits in your father's "budget"!'

I take a glass from the cupboard and pour myself some juice.

'Alright, I'm off.' Mum grabs her bag. 'I need to go to the butcher; your dad wants *kibbeh nayyeh* again.' She looks at me, still in my pyjamas. 'What are you doing today? Are you staying in or going out?'

I take a swig of juice and shock us both. 'I don't know,' I say. 'Maybe I'll come with.'

* * *

Mum's butcher is in Merrylands, a suburb that sounds like a theme park but that at one point had the highest rate of drive-by shootings in Sydney. Even though we live in Kenthurst, we still have to come out West for our meat and our Lebanese groceries. An Aussie sausage is one thing, but if you're looking for *makanek*, you're not going to find it at McGinty's Fine Meats in Cherrybrook.

My mother drives exactly to the limit. What should've been a thirty-minute trip is drawn out to almost an hour, made longer still by the silence in the car, and the looks she keeps giving my camera.

We lumber along Hilltop Road, before she parks her Mercedes bumper to kerb in front of a row of three shops. Out on the footpath, Mum takes the lead; her purse tucked neatly to her arm as she struts along the pavement in a pair of crocheted espadrilles. I always forget how short she is. I don't know why, but in her own home, she towers.

'Alright, I'm going to get the meat. Are you sure you'll be okay?' Her question comes with two implicit warnings: first, that

I'm to do what I need to do *away from her*, and second, that much like Granville, the locals here may not appreciate a camera in their face.

'Yeah, Mum, I'll be fine.'

I wait for her to leave before surveying the potential around me. The shop beside the butcher is a Lebanese mixed business. There are two women loitering outside, chatting in Arabic and choosing bags of bread from big plastic crates. I move into the shade of the store, absorbing what I can with all my senses. The shelves beneath the register are stacked with retro candy and chewing gum labelled in Arabic. Several gilded hookahs sit high atop a wooden ledge, and the glass case beneath them is filled with roasted nuts – brown almonds, golden cashews and mixed *fistouk* – piled alongside each other like rolling desert dunes.

The till is typically abandoned, but as I move down the aisle I see an old man crouched beside a box of baby eggplants. He rubs his head, caught in a heated exchange with his wife, who yells abuse at him from out back. *'I told you to put them out yesterday! And now we've ordered double, who's going to buy it all?'*

He stands and raises his hand, putting his index and middle finger to his thumb in the shape of a teardrop – a well-worn Arab gesture, entreating her to shut up. *'Ya Ami*, I am begging you, please shut up.'

'Shut up? Shut up? Maybe if you listened I would!'

I look around – plotting to sneak a photo while he's distracted – but by the time I turn back, he's staring at me. *'Marhaba.'*

'Hello.' The two of us stand in silence. 'I was, ah, hoping to take some pictures. Of your shop.'

'I no like. Bad for customer.' He points to the women out front with a bony hand.

'Are you sure? I can do it quickly. I promise I won't get them in.'

He seems to soften, but he's not convinced. 'Also … I, ah, need some *batinjen*.' I point to the box of baby eggplants. 'As many as I can get.'

The old man raises his wrinkled brow. '*Eh*, okay,' he says, limping past me in his leather slides. 'You take the photo, then come to me.'

I capture what I can of this cave of wonders, from the backgammon boards stacked upright like books to the haphazard pile of *raqweh* pots that seem to have stilled in time, mid-avalanche. When I get to the counter, I grab two packs of Juicy Fruit gum, a loaf of Afghan bread and a bag of sugar-coated chickpeas, marked down by a handwritten sign to $11.99 a kilo. He already has the eggplants waiting for me.

'You want any fruit? Fresh today.'

'No, thanks.' *Not necessary when you've got Gary for a neighbour.*

The old man starts ringing up my purchases using a till from the 1990s with plastic-covered buttons and an Aussie flag taped to its side.

I ask, 'How long have you been living here? Living in Australia?'

He shrugs and says, 'Maybe thirty-five year. I come from the war, a refugee.' The Lebanese civil war, he means. The one that turned beautiful Beirut into a burning crater.

'Have you ever been back?'

He shrugs again. 'A few time, but better here in Australia. More money. More safe.' He shifts his wife-beater to show me a deep purple scar in the middle of his chest. 'I get shot. In the war, in the fighting. Here, and in my leg.' He points to his knee, explaining the limp.

'*Salamtak*,' I say; a prayer for his peace.

'It long time, now.' He weighs the chickpeas and punches in another number. 'War, very bad for the people. I see the young man here; they think they tough.' He nods towards the street and shakes his head. 'They no tough. No war, no tough.'

I think of Danny. I think of his dad. I think of Gab and Dave and Chadi, and the privilege of our generation compared with people like Uncle Rashid.

'*Shou issmik?*' he asks.

I answer, 'Nicole.'

'*Ana,* Badwi,' he tells me.

'*Eh, tcharruffna.*'

He gives a half-bow, receiving the honour, and smiles. I notice the gleam of a gold tooth. It glints in his mouth among stained and broken bone like a hidden treasure.

'Would you let me take your picture?' I ask. 'Just you, no customers.'

He thinks for a moment, then he points to the hookahs on the shelf behind him. '*Argileh* on sale. Thirty per cent off.'

I roll my eyes and choose a bronze one with a red glass bottom. Badwi sets it on the counter and grins.

'Okay,' he says. 'I ready.'

* * *

Later that afternoon, I sit at my laptop and look out my bedroom window. Last night I posted the view from Dave's apartment block, and I captioned it UP IN THE SKY //. He liked it and commented 'nice work ☺'.

I scroll now through the photos I took in Merrylands, and then I upload the picture of Badwi with his gold tooth and his battle scar peeking from his open shirt.

NO WAR, NO TOUGH //

It's my fifth post.

Outside, one of Gary's horses gallops across his property at full pelt. It's a black Arabian stallion with a braided mane. I watch as it races around the field, turning down the slope and then eventually slowing, its coat iridescent like oil. I reach for my phone and, for the first time in three days, I open Danny's chat. I haven't been avoiding him; I'm just unsure of what to say. I think on this some more, and when I still can't find the right words, I send him a red heart emoji. Not the tacky, shiny one that comes in different colours. I send him the heart that sits below the club.

It's a deeper red, and it suits us.

After a while he sends me the same one back.

Then I say, *Are we still on for shopping tomorrow?*

Thought you might not want to.

I reply, *Why?*

He types, then stops. The tick's left blue.

I say, *Danny*

He says, *Yeah?*

I reply, *You're my best friend*

He looks at it a while. Then he says,

You're my best friend too

Chapter 21

The next afternoon, I rush home from work to get ready. I shower and straighten my hair, and then I pull on a pair of high-waisted jeans and some white leather sneakers. I turn my wardrobe upside down trying to find the right top, finally settling on a fitted singlet.

When I come downstairs, Mum's waiting at the kitchen bench. She sits on one of the bar stools flicking through the glossy pages of *Home & Garden* magazine. There's a large tray of *sheikh mehshi* that she's made begrudgingly, using the fifteen baby eggplants I'd bought as a bribe.

'Dinner's ready.' She flicks another page.

I check the time. If I don't have a bowl, she'll kill me.

'Where are you going?'

'To the shops.' I quickly scoop some of the casserole, then I blow on my fork and brave it.

'Mm.' She pauses for a moment, turns a page. 'I don't want you seeing Danny anymore.'

I speak with my mouth full. 'What?'

'You were at the park with him on Sunday.' She keeps browsing the article in front of her like we're talking about the weather.

'So? He's my friend.'

'Someone saw you together. I don't want my daughter being seen with trash like that.'

Trash? I'm on my second forkful, and I'm starting to sweat. 'Mum, I'm not a kid, yeah? I'm almost twenty-seven – I'll be friends with who I like.'

'As long as you're living under *my* roof, you'll be friends with who *I* say.'

'It's *Dad's* roof. And before we lived under *this* roof, we were living at Amber Way. Don't think you're so above it.'

My mother slams her hand on the counter. 'He's a *criminal!* Or are you the only *idiot* that doesn't know?'

I take my bowl and tip it in the bin. 'He's the kid that used to mow our lawns. Back when we didn't have *fucking* acreage. Or did you forget?'

Mum stands from her chair, incensed. 'How *dare* you speak to me like that! Come back here! *Nicole!*' She follows me out to the hall, and I quicken my pace, half-expecting her to throw a shoe at the back of my head. Surely I'm too old for that now; the impending airstrike of a flying slipper. But then I'm also too old for what she says next: 'Wait till your father gets home, what I'm going to tell him! That his daughter is dating a *thug!*'

'He's not my bloody boyfriend!' I yell. 'I had one of those, and you hated him, too!' I turn to face her now, almost at the door. 'For three years straight, all you did was put him down, and point out all our problems. You never helped, you never *listened.* And now you're doing it again! Everything has to be *perfect;* everything has to fit in with what *you* think is right. And if it doesn't, God help us!'

'That's my job!' she counters. 'I'm your mother!'

'Well, I'm done with being mothered! So just *leave me alone!*' I pull the door open. 'Danny's a good man, Mum!' I shout it from somewhere deep. 'He's a *good man*, and he's had a hard life! And no one should judge him for it – not even *you*!'

My words ring out. I didn't realise how much I needed to hear them from my own mouth.

Danny is a good man.

'Mum, I'm going.'

She glares at me like I'm leaving for good. But she doesn't try to stop me.

* * *

The Westfield in the city sits at the base of Sydney Tower, as if some giant deity had marked it on a map with a golden pin. It's almost 6 pm when I finally get to Pitt Street, and the roads and sidewalks are still heaving with peak hour traffic. I've always loved driving through the city, even at this time of night. Most people find it stressful, but the truth is I've never felt more at ease than I am right now, sitting at the wheel of my car. It takes a lifetime to learn a city. You can't just move in; you have to marry it. And Sydney's been mine since birth.

I leave my car at valet parking and ride the lift to level four. Danny and Sarah are waiting for me on the couches outside David Jones, surrounded by a dozen sleeping Asians.

'Sorry I'm late.' I kiss them both.

'Nah, don't worry. I would've picked you up but she had tutoring.'

I imagine my mother seeing Danny in our driveway, and I silently thank God that he didn't.

'You get here okay?'

'Yeah, yeah. Just parked downstairs. It's busy, hey?'

'Packed.'

The three of us stand in the midst of it, none really knowing how to read the other. There's a predictable tension between me and Danny; a quietness on his part, more so than usual.

'Well, I'm excited to do some shopping.' I turn my attention to Sarah. 'Where do you want to go?'

She shrugs. It's the first time I've seen her since the barbecue, and when I look at her now, I feel an ache. She stands apart from us, with her school uniform buttoned to her neck, and I wish I could tell her how sorry I am. But I'm careful – so careful – to treat her the same.

'Do you know what kind of dress you want?'

She shakes her head.

'That's okay. We'll have a good look around, and if we don't find anything you like, you can always get something made.'

Danny and Sarah glance at each other awkwardly.

'Well, not really,' he says. 'Her formal's next week.'

'*Next week?* This isn't like picking a suit, mate. It takes time.'

He laughs a little at this. 'Then you better get to work.'

I lead them up through David Jones, realising now that I only have a few hours to find a dress for someone who is essentially mute. I tell myself I'm up for the task, but as hard as I try, I can't imagine her in anything beyond that bloody awful uniform. When we get to the top of the escalator, we're met by two white mannequins wearing feathered hats, and a kaleidoscope of spring fashion spanning an entire city block. 'Okay, so I think we'll start here. It's got everything in one place, and we can figure out what you like.'

Sarah nods. Danny says, 'Sounds good.'

I lead the way around the perimeter, browsing each section, while the two of them lag behind. For the most part, I'm talking to myself, holding up dresses that Sarah reluctantly endorses with either a nod or a shrug. It always happens that when you're shopping for someone else, you see a thousand things you desperately want – like the perfect pinstripe blazer, or a pair of satin shorts.

'You like anything, Nic?' Danny loiters next to me with his hands in his pockets, two fists bulging from his black trackies. 'If you see something you want, just tell me. You too.' He nudges his sister. 'Get whatever you want.' He puts his tatted arm around her, and she rests against him like a wary pup. The image of it; the fact that this street-hardened mechanic is out here on a Thursday night, hugging his sister and helping her pick a dress, somehow makes him ten times the man he already was.

We continue around the store together until Danny gets a phone call and wanders away, leaving Sarah and I alone to shop.

'What about this one?' I reach for a pink dress with a cowl neck.

She mumbles, 'Yeah, it's pretty.'

'Or this one?' It's mid-length and black.

She nods. 'It's nice.'

I start collecting them on my arm, randomly pulling out colours and styles and hoping to God that one of them fits. A green one, a long one. A short red dress with a puffy skirt. A taffeta gown with a detachable train. Sarah nods at each of them with the same, unreadable expression, and as the minutes roll on our silences start to stretch. I don't know what I expected; that we could come here tonight and cure seven years of repressed trauma with a bit of retail therapy?

How dumb.

But then I start to think, *Maybe Sarah's not the problem. Maybe it's me.*

I look at her now, absently touching a folded sweater, and I realise that I never even asked her if she wanted me here.

Maybe she didn't.

Maybe she wanted to come on her own, and a part of me doesn't blame her. When I was seventeen, I wanted to do things on my own, too.

'I remember my formal.' It's the first time tonight that I've said something without shoving a dress in her face, and it lures her attention. She stares at me from the other side of a low-standing rack with the same brown eyes as her brother. 'I wore this, like, bright blue dress with a silver sash. It was the biggest fail. I looked like a Bulldogs cheerleader.'

Sarah smiles; it's miniscule, but it's there.

'And you know what? I thought I was so hot. I mean, I actually thought I looked like J.Lo. I think I wore her perfume, too.' I cringe as I recall my silver eyeshadow and matching blue mascara. 'Wait,' I say. 'I think I've got a pic.'

We stand together while I sift through Facebook. '*God*, there it is. Worse than I remember.'

Sarah leans in to look, smiling an actual smile, and then withdrawing again. When I turn to put it away, she shocks me by asking a question. 'Did you take someone?'

Did I take someone?

'Um, yeah. I did.' I'm suddenly conscious that my answer might be uncool. 'I had to take my cousin Chadi. My parents were pretty strict.'

She nods and looks at her feet. 'Me too. Danny won't let me.'

I stare at her now, seeing a small opening that wasn't there before. 'Well, do you have someone that you want to take?'

'Maybe,' she says. 'But I'm not allowed.'

I shift the dresses to my other arm. 'So, you've already asked Danny, then?'

She shakes her head. No.

Sarah isn't the type of person who just says what she wants, as I've experienced first-hand over the past half-hour. My arms are starting to ache, and I know if I want to make this work, I'll have to be forward enough for the both of us.

'You don't like these dresses, do you?'

Sarah reddens.

'It's okay, just tell me.'

'No, I like them, but …'

'But you'd prefer something else?'

She nods.

I dump what I've been holding on an empty chair. 'Do you have a picture?'

She nods again.

'Well, where is it?'

Sarah reaches for her phone, and I almost laugh when she shows it to me.

It's a beautiful dress – backless and white – and I've seen it before. On a runway, about a week ago.

'Come with me.'

* * *

Yasmine Ali's Sydney store is in the Strand Arcade. I find Danny near the escalators, and the three of us head down to ground level. There's a busker playing his guitar in the Pitt Street Mall, and he sings James Arthur's 'Say You Won't Let Go' as we pass.

When we get to the Strand, we climb the stairs to the top floor. It's an old Victorian-style building with stained-glass windows and several wooden elevators that I always try to avoid. Right at the end of the upper level, leaning against the railing beneath a sign with her name on it, stands Yasmine. 'You know we're closed.' She grins at me, hand on hip.

'Yeah, well, this is an emergency.' When I reach her, we hug.

'So, your formal, how exciting.' She smiles at Sarah. 'Me and Nic wore matching dresses to ours. Mine was green and hers was –'

'Blue. I've already traumatised her with the photos.'

Yasmine laughs. 'Well, *entrez-vous*. It's only me and Erica today. You're lucky we're still here; we've been unboxing the new range.' She holds the door open, and we step inside. Erica – who I recognise as one of Yas's assistants from Carriageworks – is crouched on the carpet, steaming the skirt of an embellished gown. Yasmine gestures for Sarah and me to take a seat, while Danny watches on from the door.

'So, what are you after?' Yasmine asks.

'She wants a dress from your show: the white one with the low back.'

'*Low back?*'

We all look at Danny. I roll my eyes. 'Reasons I never wanted a brother.'

'Yeah, but how low are we talking?'

I turn to him fully now. 'Mate, do you want to wait outside? It's girls-only in here.'

He stifles a grin. 'Okay, fine. Just call me when you're done.' The bell over the door dings as he leaves.

'So, the dress she wants, I'm actually not releasing till next month.' Yasmine sits behind a sleek black desk and clicks around on her laptop, probably at nothing. Her accent today has a strong French flavour, meaning she's in the right mood to be an arsehole.

'Yas, her formal's next week. Can't she have the sample or something?'

She purses her lips and thinks. 'I mean, I guess she could.' She looks across at Sarah. 'But we'd have to take it in.'

'Yeah, that's –'

'*Erica!*'

'Yes?'

'Can you fetch the Nicky gown for Sarah? Pin it to fit, please.'

I look at Yasmine. 'The Nicky gown?'

She swivels her laptop. 'It had a last-minute name change.' There on the screen is a photo I took from her fashion show. It's the banner image on her website: a wide-lens shot of a dark-skinned model parading down the runway in Sarah's white dress. 'Don't you just love it?'

'No way!'

'You did good,' she says. And I know she means it. Because even though we're friends, Yasmine's never been one for charity. She wouldn't use anything for her business – especially on the homepage of her website – if she didn't really like it.

Sarah leaves us for the change room, and I look around to check for Danny. He's pacing along the balcony outside the shop, talking on the phone. When he sees me, we give each other the thumbs-up. Yasmine sits back in her chair, her dark nails drumming on the desktop. 'You never said he was hot.'

I look back at her. 'What?'

'*Danny.* All these years you've talked about him, you never said he was hot.' It's like I've been hiding something from her.

'Is he?'

'Yes, you bitch! And the way he looks at you? *My God.*'

We both turn to stare at him. His gait, his shoulders, the fresh lines of his fade. I think when you know someone so long, you get used to the way they look. It's such a rapid evolution from boy to man that, when it happens, your brain can barely keep up. Sometimes when I look at him, I still see that kid snapping his KitKats in two. But he *is* – from the eyes of stranger, from anyone really – he's handsome.

We're so absorbed in watching him that when he suddenly opens the door the pair of us jump.

'You alright?' he asks, smiling. 'Did I scare ya?'

'Yeah, man, *Jesus*. Knock next time.'

He gestures at the window, still teasing me. 'You couldn't see me coming?'

I tuck my hair behind my ear. '*No*. Anyway, Sarah's getting fitted.'

Erica draws the curtain aside and guides Sarah towards a gilded mirror.

Danny stares at his sister in awe. 'Wow, Sare. You look like an angel.'

She gleams at him; she's glowing like an angel, too.

Once the alterations are properly pinned, Sarah and Danny say goodbye to Yasmine, while I linger behind to thank her.

'I really owe you one, Yas.'

She kisses my cheek, then looks through the window at Danny. 'Get yourself a date, and we'll call it even.'

But I need to get someone else a date first.

* * *

It's late by the time we get to Danny's.

He took us for Chinese after we finished shopping; one of those seafood restaurants where they pull your dinner from a tank. I probably should've gone home once we'd been served our complimentary mooncakes, but when I thought about facing my mother again, I decided it was best to stay out.

Danny sets us up on his couch with three cups of peppermint tea. Sarah follows him into the kitchen, and they return with a plate of Tim Tams and a bowl of party mix. Normally Danny would call dibs on all the pineapples, but tonight he doesn't reach for them once. He just sits on his side of the lounge, watching while the two of us talk.

'What shoes should I wear?' Sarah browses on her phone, flicking between sites. It's her second question of the evening, and even though she still mumbles, I can tell she's warming to me.

'I don't know.' I lean over. 'Maybe a silver or a gold? Those look nice.' I point to a picture of a high-heeled sandal with a crystal strap. 'They're hot.'

'Yeah, I like them too.' She saves them to Favourites and we keep browsing. We talk about her hair, the make-up she wants, and whether or not she should wear a jewelled earring. The more we chat, the nearer she draws to me, and by the end of the night we're curled up close, eating lollies and liking pictures on Kylie Jenner's Instagram.

At about 11:30, I reach for my bag. With Danny so quiet, I figure I should leave him to sleep. Sarah hugs me at the door, she says, 'Thanks, Nic. Thanks for helping me.'

And I hug her back, careful not to show too much emotion or to hold her too tight.

When I turn to leave, Danny follows. We cross the road together and he rests his arm on the roof of my car. 'Thanks for tonight.'

'Thanks for inviting me, I had fun.' I open the door and throw my bag on the seat.

'Nah, I mean it. I think it's good for her, being around you. I think it helps.'

'Yeah, she's a good girl. I'm really happy we found her that dress.'

We stand together, his face like moonstone in the streetlight. There's an energy between us; it flickers and pulls. He inches closer, but the feeling of it overwhelms me.

I panic and cut him off.

'Listen, I think she wants to take someone. To her formal.'

He looks at me like I'm crazy. *'No.'*

'Danny.'

'No, Nic. She's not ready for that.'

'She's almost eighteen! It's a school dance, Danny, not a rave.'

He shakes his head.

'I know you're worried. I know you want to protect her. But she needs to feel normal. Otherwise, she'll never get over it. *And neither will you.'*

He won't look at me.

'Hey.' I put my hand on his chest.

He touches my hip to keep me away.

'It's too soon,' he says.

Too soon for who? 'Danny, it's been seven years.'

He looks at his feet, head bowed beneath the weight of it. And I don't know what to say; what words there are that might bring him back. So, I do what I did at the park. I put my arms around his neck, and I breathe him in.

He smells holy.

A mix of faded cologne and warm skin and pheromones that I inhale like incense. I press myself closer, feeling his hands against my bare waist. Then he says, 'Okay.'

I pull away. 'What?'

'I said, *okay.'*

'Okay, like she can take someone?'

He nods. 'Yeah.'

I smile at him, surprised by the win.

'But if something goes wrong,' he adds, 'it's *your arse.*'

'Yeah, you'd like that wouldn't you?'

He grins. 'You know, when I didn't hear from you after the park, I thought you got scared. Like it was too heavy or something.'

I tilt my head to his, the both of us illuminated by white light. 'You could never be too heavy. Not for me.'

He bites his lip and looks away. 'Yeah, well, you're not too heavy for me either.'

I see it coming a second too late. He drops his shoulder and lifts me off the ground.

'*Danny!*' The world spins; a rapid, unbreachable vortex with us at its centre.

'Fuck, you're tiny.' He laughs.

'Okay, *enough*, put me down!'

He lowers me against his body, and the feeling of it makes my stomach clench. I push my hair back and hold his arms, waiting for the road beneath us to flatten again.

'*Yallah*,' he breathes. 'Message me when you get home.'

He kisses my forehead and closes my door. I'm driving away before I even realise that I'm at the wheel, and I don't know why, but I can't stop smiling. I just think about his laugh – the sound of it, the creases around his eyes – and it triggers a joy in me. His face is a face I've known forever.

A mirror that'll never break.

A compass that'll always point me home.

The road both ways is clear, but before I turn out, I look back.

And that's when I see him in my rear-view, standing in the middle of the street, smiling too.

Chapter 22

'Mate, you're doing it wrong. There's too much water.' Rita moves around me in my cabana, her honey-coloured hair in a large, claw-clipped bun. I haven't seen her since our trip to the salon, and even though we'd normally keep our catch-ups for the car ride down to Punchbowl, I've been missing her particular brand of 'no bullshit' advice. 'I don't know how you're Lebanese and you don't know how to do this. It's like me needing tips on boiling pasta.' I watch as she pours some of the water out, screwing the bronze *argileh* into its red glass base. 'You got the coals?'

'Yeah, here.'

Rita reaches for the *fahem*, before piercing the foil with a toothpick until it looks like the head of a lotus pod. Then she places the embers on top. 'See?' she says. 'There's a science to this shit.'

'Clearly.'

She takes a few long drags from the pipe to get the water bubbling. 'The heat, the water, the smoke. It's like the perfect combination of chemistry and physics.'

Chemistry and physics. The words cling. I've been thinking about them ever since Thursday night: the primal pull of physical attraction, and the complicated layers of personal chemistry. With

Danny, I've realised, I have both. And I don't know when it started. Was it at the park? Or at his house? Or was it years ago, silenced and suppressed for the sake of friendship?

'God, what an absolute waste of a weekend.' Rita exhales a column of smoke. 'You know, I spent all of last night just lying in bed, looking at my phone. One app to the next: Tinder, Bumble, Plenty of Fish.' She talks over her shoulder now, crab-walking along the tiles to put the hookah poolside. 'Man, I miss my single days with Jackie. Just the two of us out on the town, picking up guys.'

It was a sad inevitability, the fork in the road of their friendship. My sister met and married Mick in under a year, and then cemented it by falling pregnant just a few months later. Suffice to say, Jackie's progression from being a single girl to a stay-at-home mum was, unfortunately for Rita, quite rapid. 'Well, we can always go out, me and you. Although I can't say I'm overly keen after last weekend.'

'Mate, who are you kidding?' She kicks off her thongs. 'Half the clubs are closed, anyway. And after yesterday's abysmal trawl of Tinder profiles, I'm ready to die old and alone.'

'So, I'm guessing there's been no new dates, then?'

'Nah, can't be arsed. I started talking to this Portuguese guy, but I found out he works as a PT.'

'Oh, nightmare.'

'Imagine the pressure. I just want a *normal guy* that wants to go somewhere and *eat*. I work in catering, for God's sake. The only meal prep I'll be doing is a bain-marie of *boscaiola*.'

Rita passes me the pipe, the two of us now reclined on a pair of sunbeds, swathed in grape-flavoured smoke and the purple light of dusk. 'How's Jackie been, anyway? She good?'

'Yeah. I asked her to join, but it's hard with the baby.'

Rita nods to herself, her hand resting on a full belly. We'd eaten pizza together for dinner, which she'd critiqued as only Italians do, before swearing off carbs for the rest of the month. 'I got my eggs counted the other day.'

I raise my head to look at her. 'Really? Have you been worried about it or something?'

'I mean, yeah. I guess most women my age are. I might freeze them, I don't know. It's very expensive, though. Very full-on.'

'Well, did they tell you there's a problem?'

'No, no. I've got a normal egg count, thank God. I'm just ... planning.'

'I think Linda at our work had it done. But she's older than you by a few years. I reckon almost forty.'

'Well, the more you wait the worse it is. Fertility when you're forty is a whole different ball game.'

I hand her back the pipe.

'Hey, how was shopping the other day?' she asks. 'Did you find anything nice for Sarah?'

'Yeah, we ended up getting her a dress from Yas.'

'Perfect.' She puffs. 'And how was Danny?'

'Yeah, good. Really quite patient, considering.'

'You ever think' – the shisha bubbles as she inhales – 'that something might happen there? You know, between you and him?'

I play it cool, as if the notion had never occurred to me. 'Why?'

She passes me the pipe again. 'Well, why not?'

'I don't know,' I say. 'I just ... you know, maybe he doesn't look at me that way.'

Rita does an eye roll that could orbit the sun. 'Do you honestly believe that? Like, fuck, bro, the poor bastard probably has blue balls from being around you.'

'Rita, come on. And anyway, my mother would disown me if I ever brought him home.'

'*So?*'

'So, have you met my mum?'

Rita swings her legs off the lounge and sits up. 'Let me explain something to you, since maybe you haven't caught on. Wog mums don't believe in happiness – mainly because most of them have never had it. So, if something makes you *happy*, you should give it a chance. You were never happy with your ex, *that's a fact*. Maybe you thought you were once or twice, when he stopped being a cunt for two seconds. But overall, you were fucking miserable. So, if Danny can make you happy, then bloody let him. What's so wrong with him, anyway? Yeah, he's a bit rough, but who isn't? At the end of the day, he's tall, he's Lebanese and he's *Christian* – which is more than we can say for Nat and Ahmed.'

'God, I forgot about Nat. How's she going?'

'Well, it's looking like she'll have to elope.'

'Fuckin' hell.'

'I know, right? It's like Punchbowl's version of *Romeo and Juliet*.' She reaches for the pipe now, using it to punctuate her point. 'So, yeah. Think about *that* for a bit of perspective. Some people,' she says, 'are put in front of you for a reason. A good-looking man who cares about you and is cut from the same cloth, that's like winning lotto: it's one-in-a-million odds, and you're set for life. Don't sabotage yourself by overthinking it, or you'll end up like me. Counting the eggs in your basket.'

The irony isn't lost on me that Rita's advice, though delivered with equal passion, is almost the exact opposite of what I'd received from Yasmine on these very same sun lounges just a fortnight ago.

I watch as Rita reclines again and, feeling that I should, I offer her up a window of potential. 'Well, Sarah's got her formal next week. She asked me to come round, so I guess I'll see Danny again then.'

'Good.' She gives a satisfied nod. 'And how's your other mate, Dave Dollaz?'

We both grin. 'He's a real character, that one. I mean I started out hating him, but now … I don't know. He's alright.'

Rita nods and puffs. 'A good plan B.'

'God, I wouldn't go that far.'

'Well, whoever you choose,' she says, 'don't complicate things. Just do what makes you happy.'

But when was life ever that simple?

We stay like that for the rest of the night, passing the pipe back and forth. And I think about the web around me. Danny, Dave, my ex. Nat and Ahmed. Even Elie's secret crush on my cousin. I think of all the bleeding hearts in bed right now, beside the wrong person. And all the people who love someone who will never love them back.

So many moths, tangled and trapped.

And I wonder when I'll stop being one of them.

Chapter 23

That night, I dream it's the summer I met my ex. He has his arms wrapped around me and I can smell him.

The dream is so real *I can smell him*.

I know we don't have long, so I cling to him the way you would if your soulmate came to visit you from another world. We stand together in the waning light of dusk, waiting for space and time to shift, pulling us aeons apart.

And by sundown, he is gone.

* * *

I wake in the morning and check my phone. There's a message from Chadi sent half an hour ago.

Cuz you coming to work today? I need a favour

I write back: *What*

Can you take me to Danny's. Like at lunch or something. I wanna check my car and pay for rims

I stretch and groan, pushing back the covers and getting to my feet.

This fucking car. It was supposed to be finished a week ago; what's taking so long?

I stumble to the bathroom, consoled by the knowledge that in just a few days Chadi's licence will be returned, and I won't have to drive him around anymore.

* * *

It takes me almost fifty minutes to get to Parramatta. The traffic today is worse than usual, and even with all my windows down I'm still dogged by the scent of my ex. When I finally pull up at work, I message Chadi.

Come down now I wanna get this over with

A minute later, I see him bounding across the lot. 'Hey, cuz!'

'Yeah, hey. Get in.'

He walks around my car and gets in beside me, bringing with him a fresh wave of potent nostalgia.

I pull him in. 'What cologne are you wearing?'

'Nothing, just Lynx. Why?' He sniffs his pits. 'What's wrong?'

'Nothing. Nothing's wrong, let's just go.'

I take the M4 to The Area, while Chadi sits next to me singing at the top of his lungs. Between the sound of his voice and Judas's lingering aroma, I can barely function. I turn into Waterloo Road and we join the end of a slow-moving convoy; five or six cars, all banked up behind a police wagon.

'Can this cunt move?'

'He's doing the limit,' I say.

'Actually,' says Chadi, 'he's doing fifty-five in a sixty.'

'Well, why don't you get out and tell him?'

I turn the radio down and we both fall silent. I get a whole nine seconds of Chadi staring whimsically into the distance before he speaks again.

'Hey, Nic, remember those guys in Parra? The ones that yelled at us?'

I look at him.

'The ones that called me a rapist?' he prompts.

'Jesus, yeah.' How could I forget? We were only fourteen at the time, and the Bulldogs were in the midst of a major off-field scandal. I was walking along Church Street with Chadi when some Aussie guys pulled up alongside us and called my cousin a 'fucking rapist'. I'll never forget the look on Chadi's face. I remember he was wearing his Bulldogs jersey – his favourite one, signed by Hazem – and instead of going to the shops, we ran back to the safety of the car yard, him shirtless, hiding his Bankstown colours.

'Fuck, that was slack. I didn't wear that jersey for a whole year.'

'What made you think of it now?'

'Oh, I don't know.' He grins. 'Just after the other night, I guess. Me and you, always in some drama. Always copping abuse.'

'Chadi, it's you that's always copping abuse. I'm just collateral damage.'

He laughs. 'Oh, come on, Nic,' he says. 'Be honest. How bored would you be without me? I mean, who else gives you this same sense of adventure? The two of us back-to-back, fighting our way through life.'

I don't answer. Even through my brain fog, I can sense the inklings of a master manipulation.

He drums his hands against the dash. 'Fuck, I'm just so excited for these rims. They've ordered them from America. Like what Snoop Dogg would drive around with. Real gangster shit.'

'You've wasted so much money on that stupid car. Why don't you try and save for once?'

'I do save,' he says. 'It's a company car.'

A company car. I pull to a stop at the lights, slowly making sense of it all. 'You're telling me that all this bullshit you've been doing – the new exhaust and the speakers, and now the rims and your fuckin' mystery plates – are a *company expense*?'

'Oh, come on, cuz, it's almost done. We just need to pay.'

We?! Now I understand why I'm here: because I've got a company credit card.

'Does Dad know?'

Chadi shifts in his seat. 'Yeah, he said it's fine. *Swear to God*, he said it's fine.'

I take my eyes off him and turn onto Juno Parade, finally free of the cop car convoy. There's an ad break on the radio; a weather update, followed by a guy and a girl role-playing the woes of erectile dysfunction.

'See, now that's one medical problem us Najim men have never had.'

'Chadi, do you mind? I'm sick as it is.'

He reaches to change the station, but I swat his hand away.

'What's wrong with you today?'

'What's wrong with *me*?'

'*Yeah.*' He folds his arms. 'Like, did I do something? You've been spazzing this whole time. Smelling me and being weird.'

'I'm just tired, okay? And I don't want to bloody talk about it! I'm not like *you*, who has to fill every second of silence with your lunatic train of thought.'

He narrows his eyes. 'So, there *is* a problem,' he says. 'A problem you are reluctant to discuss.'

'Correct, Chadi. *Correct.*'

'Well, I think you should tell me about it. It's healthy to say what's bothering you. It might save us another trip to the doc.'

'Yeah, funny.'

'I'm serious, Nic. It's like what they say: a problem shared is a problem halved.'

I look at him sidelong. 'Man, not in this fuckin' family. A problem shared is a problem doubled, more like.'

'Yeah, true.' He laughs. 'The other day I showed Dad a lump I found on my neck. And then guess what? He found one on *his* neck, too.'

'Well, maybe it's a gland or something. *Jesus*. Like, if you've both got the same lump in the same spot, it's probably meant to be there.'

'Yeah, that's what they said at the hospital.'

'Oh, fuck's sake.'

'Anyway, listen. Tell me what's wrong.'

'Nothing, man. I just had a bad dream.'

'So?' he says. 'It's not real.'

'Well, it felt real.'

'What was it about?'

'It was … I don't know. It was about my ex. He hugged me and I could smell him, and it's been stuck in my head ever since.'

Chadi groans; an obnoxious roar that makes me wish I never told him.

'You know what fuckin' burns me?' He sits forward, opening his window for air. 'That after all the shit this gronk did to you – the way he *left*, the way he's thrown that fucking girl in your face – you still sit there thinking he's God's gift. How sad! What a fuckin' sad girl you are!'

'Why are you being such an arsehole?'

'Because you need it, man! How long can this go on? You gotta let it go!'

'It's only been two months!'

He sits back, counting the weeks in his head. 'Fuck. Feels like longer.'

'Well, it's not! And I don't need love advice from someone who cares more about their fucking car than whatever girl they've got in the back seat!'

'*Wow.* Can you relax? Maybe you should aim some of that anger at your dog-arse ex.'

I wipe the tears from my face.

'Think of all the times he never showed up. Think of all the shitty things he did! He's a *dog*. He's a *fucking* dog! Stop being sad and *say it*! He's. A. DOG!'

But I can't. I just *can't.*

There's a minute of stony silence; the type that makes even the indicator seem loud. Then Chadi puts his hand on my arm, his breathing slowed. 'You know I love you, Nic. And you've been doing so good. Working on your photos and that.' He hands me a tissue, a little white flag. 'Don't let that dickhead pull you back.'

* * *

When we get to Danny's garage, I see Danny himself standing out front. He's not normally here, but today he's got a new apprentice.

Gab.

I park across the lot and watch them work; Danny laughing with a customer and Gab bent behind him, waxing an Audi R8 with a yellow rag. He rubs the polish in circles, sweating through his shirt in the mid-morning sun.

'Yo, Dan!' Chadi calls out from his open window.

I turn the engine off and follow him, fixing myself in the mirror before I do.

Danny smiles when he sees us, but it fades as I approach.

He shakes Chadi's hand, then he reaches for me. 'You okay, Nic?'

'Yeah, I'm fine.' I turn away. 'You got Gab here now?'

He looks at me some more. 'Yeah. Just doing some small stuff. I didn't know you were coming.'

'Yeah, same.' Gab's by the tyres now, pumping them with air. 'Hey, Gab.'

'Oh, hey, Nic.' He pretends he didn't see me.

'You have fun the other night?'

'Yeah, it was good.' He's a lot more subdued than when I saw him last. He moves around the car, no time to stand and chat. I eye him a little longer, watching while he labours, but some small, jaded part of me doesn't believe it. With him there's always a phase. A sober phase, a *functional* phase. And then it all goes to shit. I don't know if he's better now; I hope to God he is. I just don't want Danny to get used.

'Is George around?' Chadi slaps his hands and rubs them together. 'He said he ordered my rims.'

'Yeah.' Danny gestures towards the office. 'He's inside.'

I watch my cousin as he goes. 'So, is it finished yet or what?'

'His car? Are you joking?'

'Why? What's taking so long?'

'Well, we've been busy.' Danny points at the cars double-parked. 'Plus, your cousin keeps adding shit. We gotta keep it another week for the rims and the paint.'

'The paint?'

'You wanna see?'

'I don't know. Do I?'

He leads me into the warehouse. There are cars suspended on jacks and hoists, and men in matching t-shirts working beneath them. It's louder in here than it was outside; the sound of drills and shouts made worse by the aggressive rap blaring from an unseen radio. My eyes catch on a poster of a naked woman tacked to one of the walls. There's a bumper sticker stuck between her open legs, a surprising act of chivalry. I scrunch my face and follow Danny until we reach the bi-fold doors of the paint booth, where I peer through one of its windows, seeing my cousin's BMW in pieces.

'You've got to be kidding me.'

Chadi's car is in the process of being painted candy blue – a colour choice made even worse by his shiny new number plates, set aside on a nearby table: BULDOG.

Danny talks loudly over the noise. 'We've only done the first two coats. He wants a white "V" on the bonnet as well. And the rims won't be in for another week.'

I'm still staring at it, taking it in. The last time I saw Chadi's car, it was black like mine. I try to imagine it with those white stripes painted on the hood, just like his old Bulldogs' Jersey. And I think,

There'll be no hiding these Bankstown colours.

'Anyway,' he says, 'if he doesn't ask for anything else, it'll be done by Monday.'

'Well, it's a company car, Daniel. So send us the bill when you're done.'

'Are you fuckin' serious? He could've bought a Rolls with what he's spent.'

I shrug.

'You know I'm not charging you shit.'

We're on the brink of an argument when one of the boys in the warehouse shouts for Danny. He directs us back through the garage and into the glaring light. There's a tow truck easing up the drive with a grey sedan chained to its back. It has a bullet hole in its driver door and another through its broken windshield.

I look up at Danny. 'What's happened here?'

He walks over to the towie, grabs the job log and signs the form. 'Remember that bloke who got shot up the road?'

'Yeah, what, at the start of the year?'

'Yeah. It's his car. They only just released it from impound.'

I remember seeing his funeral on the news and feeling bad about it. It's funny who we choose to feel sorry for; the death that causes a pang, when another doesn't. Sometimes I'll hear stories about mass murders, or a plane falling out of the sky, and I'll barely flinch. But when I saw this man's wife on TV it made me realise that even the most wayward people have someone who loves them. Someone who wishes they'd done different, or been different, or never changed. I look around; the lot is quiet. And what I say next, I normally would've kept to myself. 'Why would anyone want to live that life?'

Danny tenses but he doesn't look at me. Then he says, 'It was a drug debt,' as if somehow distancing himself from the carnage in front of us.

'It's all the same,' I say. 'How's it any diff—'

'Nic, don't.'

We stand together, the grey sedan looming over us like a bad omen. Danny grits his jaw; his shoulders squared against an unspoken truth.

'You ever lived without rules?' He looks at me, his voice low. 'You ever had that?'

I shake my head and he turns away.

'That's the real drug. Making money off of nothing. And you can't quit. You can't go back to being normal; to getting a wage and working shifts. You just can't. So, you keep running; you keep dealing.' I know he's talking about himself. Him and his guns and whatever the fuck else they're doing in the back of this garage.

But the person I'm looking at, the person I'm really thinking about, is Gab. The ex-con, the recovering junkie. Still bent beside the Audi, with a dirty yellow rag.

* * *

The following evening, I decide to go to church and pray. I couldn't sleep after seeing that car wreck at Danny's. I keep worrying about him and wanting to help, but the truth is, I can't. Because I'll always be on the periphery of his secret inner circle. Never consulted; only called upon for shopping trips or walks around the park. And it frustrates me – it makes me desperate and resentful. Because the thing he'll never own to, the thing he only hinted at yesterday, is that deep down he *loves* what he does. He was wired for it. Strong and stealthy, with the mental agility to calculate the street value of anything, and the boldness to get away with it. Lately, I've been feeling a hollowness in my gut whenever I'm around him; a confusing mix of desire and dread. Rita said I should do what makes me happy.

But what if the person who makes me happy,

could actually turn my life on its head?

I park my car on Catherine Street and walk to St Maroun's. When I come through the gates, I hear people in the hall. Not the expected murmuring of mid-week condolences, but an excitable chatter. I hurry across the courtyard, hoping to pass unseen, but of course nothing ever goes to plan, and I run into Lucifer on the front stairs.

'Hi, Nicole.'

'Hi, Zena.' She's wearing an embroidered knee-length dress, and a pair of round-toe kitten heels.

'What are *you* doing here?'

I tuck my hair behind my ear. 'Just in the area. Thought I'd come past.'

She looks down at me from the top of the landing. 'On a Tuesday? Poor you; you must be having the hardest time.'

Oh, fuck off.

'There's no set time to talk to God, Zena. And anyway, what are *you* doing here?'

She raises her hand, always eager to show her ring. 'We had marriage class.' She waves over my shoulder at another couple who are leaving the hall arm in arm. 'Joey's gone to get the car.'

Of course.

The Catholic church runs mandatory marriage classes for all engaged couples. Monica and Luke have been going as well, and they always come back with a story. Last week, a priest told an evening class of Arab fiancés that a man should love his wife more than his own mother, and it almost caused a riot. I personally find it funny that celibate clergymen have been burdened with the role of lecturing young couples about the mechanics of marriage and sex. And what's even funnier is that half its parish have been fornicating since high school. I'm not saying there aren't any virgins; I'm just saying that at least ninety per cent of every class could probably skip the slide titled *What an Erection Looks Like*.

I stare at Zena. 'Learning much?'

She smiles at me soullessly. 'Mm, lots. It's a shame single people can't come. It might help them be better.' We hear a car horn from the street. 'That's for me.' She descends the stairs like royalty, placing her hand pityingly on my arm. 'I'll pray for you.'

I watch as she saunters to her fiancé's Merc, pocketing another win, and I don't know if I'll ever be that smug in my life. But then, as my father once said, *only idiots are happy*.

The lights in the church are dim and the pews are empty. I walk down the aisle and sit in the first row. I'd thought that just by coming here I'd experience another miracle like I did that day with the magic *manoush*. But despite how deeply I breathe, I can only smell *bakhour*. I've started asking God for guidance when Father Boutros comes grumbling from the backroom.

'Hello, Father.'

'Nicole. How are you?'

'I'm good, Father. How're you?'

I'm expecting the same response, but instead he points to the pew I'm sitting on. 'Is it okay?'

'Yeah, sure.' I shift to the side even though there's plenty of room. I've never sat with a priest before – not casually like this, as if the two of us were chatting by a pond.

He lowers himself beside me and sighs.

'Long day?' I ask.

Father Boutros puts his feet out. 'Yes. I just did another marriage class.'

I nod sympathetically. 'I've heard they're rough.'

He raises a hand as if it's all too much. 'Some people,' he says, 'shouldn't get married.'

I laugh a little, surprised by his honesty. But then I decide to test him. 'It's important, though, isn't it? Getting married?'

He nods indifferently, worn out by the last few hours. 'It's a holy sacrament. But we all have different callings.' He gestures to himself as an example; an old man, unmarried, his life spent serving God. It's a noble vocation, but what about the rest of us?

'In the Bible it's important,' I remind him. 'It says it's what we're made for. God told Adam and Eve, *be fruitful and multiply*. It's the first thing he said.'

He looks at me curiously. 'Yes, God gave us many commandments.' There's a long pause; the creak of wood.

'I had someone.' The words come to the surface, an unplanned confession. 'I didn't do my best and now he's gone. And I know I should trust God. That maybe I'll find someone better. But what if I don't?' My voice catches and I look away. 'I know it's my fault what happened; it has to be. Because he's happy now. He's happy with someone else and I'm not.' I wipe my cheek with the back of my hand, suddenly feeling sorry for Father Boutros. He's spent the better part of the evening explaining wifely virtues to Zena – a task that should see him to sainthood – and now, instead of resting, he's out here dealing with me.

He reaches into his robes, retrieves a folded tissue and hands it to me. 'I know it's hard,' he says, 'but we must always trust in God's plan.'

I shake my head. 'Not everything's God's plan. I hear that all the time. Every time something goes wrong, people hide behind God. But where's the accountability? Isn't it possible, Father, for us to lose something not because it's God's will, but because of our own ignorance or imperfection?'

Father Boutros nods. 'Maybe you're right,' he says. 'Maybe you weren't perfect in your relationship. But what about forgiveness?'

Forgiveness?

I look around at the walls; at the life-size body of Christ, hung high on a replica cross.

'Nicole, do you know what love is?'

I say the obvious: 'Corinthians.' *Love is patient, love is kind …*

He smiles. 'Yes, that's a good list. It's a good start.' He shifts towards me. 'But what did Jesus say?'

I shrug. I don't know.

'Jesus said that love, *true* love, is laying down one's life for another. That's what he did for his church. That's why he's called the *bridegroom*. Because he laid down his life for his bride.'

I look over at him, trying to imagine that love, wondering if men like that even exist.

'You are the bride, Nicole. *You* are the bride. It's the man who needs to win *you*, just like Christ won his church.'

I feel something inside me lift; an anchor that's been sitting in my soul. I think about Danny and Dave and Judas, and in the dim light of St Maroun's I start to let go.

'If you made mistakes, it's okay. We can all be wrong from time to time. It didn't stop Christ from loving his church, and it shouldn't stop a man from loving you.'

I nod, wanting to cry again, but this time for different reasons. I inhale against it, ready for my reparation. 'Well, what should I do?'

Every time I've confessed to a priest, it ends in penance. A prayer, a promise. *Something.* I've poured my heart out; now I need to pay.

But Father Boutros stands to leave. I watch as he rises from the pew, and then he says one word – so strange, but so obvious at the same time.

He says, 'Nothing.'

Chapter 24

Be still and know that I am.

I thought it was a pardon, but it turns out that 'nothing' is the hardest penance to pay. Because it means you have to wait. You have to wait on God, or the universe, or whatever you believe in, to bring you out of wherever you are. It's about trust, and patience and humility – three things I've never been good at.

People often say that true faith is tested during hard times. That your belief in God wavers most when you're faced with one of life's major catastrophes, like the death of someone you love or a terminal illness. But that's not always true. Like the blessed St Rafqa, when the human spirit suffers most, it clings ever more to its invisible God. And it certainly isn't tested in the good times either, like when the person you love loves you back, or when you're drunk at a party and your song comes on.

No, the times that faith is *really* tested is when nothing is happening at all. When everyone around you seems to have found their path, their partner, their purpose. When their prayers have been answered. When, through karmic intervention, the people who hurt them have been made to pay. And instead of you enjoying even the slightest taste of the same momentum, you are *stuck* –

maybe for years – without any sign that heaven is still above you, *working*.

The next day I drive to Bankstown with my camera on the seat beside me, and Bachelor Girl's 'Buses and Trains' blasting from the radio. My photos for Bronwyn Farley's course are due on Friday, and even though I've taken more than enough to choose a decent six, I still feel something is lacking. A secret or a sentiment specific to me. I just don't know where to find it. Some things can't be condensed into a single frame – a feeling or a smell or a sound. Here's what Tayta's porch is like: the warble of a magpie, the scent of gardenia, the thrum of mid-morning crickets. The sound of Arabic music wafting through her open door. A photo could never show it.

I ring the doorbell, hearing heavy footsteps and the sound of jangling keys. '*Ahlan!*' Tayta pushes the screen open and starts dancing around me on the slate. '*Habibi Tayta!*' She takes me in her arms and kisses my face. '*Shtaktelik!*'

'I missed you too, Tayta.'

She's surprised to see me on a weekday. 'You still no workin'?'

'I've started part-time. I get Wednesdays and Fridays off.'

'*Eh*, good.' She waves me into the house. 'How everybody?'

'Yeah, not bad. Busy, I guess.'

'*Eh*, everybody busy. And 'specially with wedding, too.'

'Yeah, not long now. Another month.'

'You bring you camera again?'

'Yeah, I've been working on a project. It's due on Friday.'

'*Eh, aafeki ya Tayta*. Good on you, good luck.'

I'm already looking around for things I can photograph. There's a shrine set up in Tayta's hall – not unlike the one for Danny's dad – and I pause a moment to look at it. It has a photo of my aunt draped in rosary beads, surrounded by saints and electric candles.

But today there's something different. I watch as a little column of smoke rises from a dish of incense; an offering only lit on special occasions.

Tayta follows my gaze. 'It her birthday today.'

'*Allah yerhama*. I'm sorry, Tayta.'

'It okay. She happy in heaven, she no in pain.'

I was thirteen years old when Aunty Louise died of ovarian cancer. She fought it for three years, but in the end we had to put her in a hospice in Lidcombe that had cots for beds and ceiling fans. It was as if my family's worst fears had manifested inside of her; a seven-inch tumour that grew so big it blocked her bowels.

Looking back, I see her as an oddity. A real nineties girl, despite being the daughter of two conservative immigrants. She liked reading and cooking and travelling. She worked at a publishing house in the city, and from what I've heard she had three proposals of marriage, all of which she turned down. It was a colourful life, ended so unfittingly in a white-washed room at St John's palliative care. Visiting her at the hospice made the hairs on my arms stand straight. I'd walk past beds of half-dead people – a purgatory of balding, bloated patients – all the way to the end of the hall, where my aunt would be waiting; for me and for God, and for her next dose of Endone.

After she died, the old wives of our family disgraced her memory. Even though I was young, I remember them sitting at Tayta's house dressed in black, and they shamed her. They said that she had died such a horrible death because she hadn't used her ovaries in the way God intended. A single, childless woman with a stagnant womb. What could be worse? A life so devoid of maternal duty, that she'd ended up carrying a tumour in her belly roughly the size of a small foetus, instead of being pregnant with a baby.

I look at the incense again, burning for my aunt, and even though I doubt I'll find anything more secret or sentimental, I can't bring myself to photograph it.

'That life,' says Tayta, tearing up. 'Only God know what happen.'

I follow her into the lounge room, where I'm once again met by the steely, black figure of Aunty Mary.

Tayta sits beside her sister with a bowl of raw zucchinis on a table between them.

'Oh, hi, Aunty,' I say. 'You making *kousa?*'

She grunts and keeps her eyes on the TV. There's a talent show on the Arabic channel; some guy standing centre stage with ten watermelons. God knows what he's about to do.

I take a seat on the opposite couch, my camera tucked back in my bag, watching as they deftly gut the zucchinis.

'I buy beautiful dress for Monica wedding,' says Tayta.

'Oh good, what's it look like?' I realise my mistake as I say it.

'I show you.' She stands and wipes her hands on her apron, and for the next two minutes I'm left alone with Aunty Mary. We sit in silence watching the talent show and ignoring each other. At one point, she glares across the space between us, and I'd honestly rather smash a watermelon with my face like the guy on TV than make any attempt at conversation.

'This the one I buy.' Tayta comes from the hall, revealing a silver midi dress with a matching bolero.

'Wow, I love it!'

She smiles proudly. 'This designer, no cheap. I buy from Greek lady in Lakemba she know me thirty years. She say it nice for me, it cover my arms.'

'Yeah, beautiful, Tayta. *Mabrouk.*'

She nods her appreciation, then she says, '*Aabelik ya Tayta*. I hope you gettin' marry before I die.'

God, what a guilt trip. 'Tayta, at this stage I hope I get married before *I* die.'

Aunty Mary laughs at this; an ugly choking noise that makes me and Tayta turn. We watch as she guts another zucchini, dropping its hollowed body in a separate bowl. Then she says, 'You know you problem?'

I stiffen in my chair, preparing myself for a criticism that might scar me for the rest of my life.

'You like boy.'

I glance between her and Tayta. 'I like boys?'

'No, *you* is like a boy. This your father mistake. He no having the son, now *you* the son.'

Tayta comes to my defence. 'Nicole very good girl.'

'*Heye awiyi*,' says Aunty Mary. '*Metl* Lou.' *She's too strong, like Lou.*

The mention of my Aunty Louise drains the energy from the room. No one says anything more because no one can.

Tayta leaves us again to put her dress away, and I'm back in a stare off with the Wicked Witch of The West.

Maybe she's right.

> *Maybe there's something wrong with me.*

I'm halfway to thinking that I, too, might be struck down by some womb-related cancer, when my phone vibrates once in my hand. It's Danny.

Hey nicky what's doing

I write back, *Just at Tayta's being traumatised by Aunty Mary Standard. You still coming tomorrow?*

It's Sarah's formal. *Yeah I'll be there. I'm excited :)*

Fuck I'm not. Can't believe I said yes to this shit
I type, *You better be nice and not ruin it for her*
I'll be on my best behaviour 😈

'Quick! It start!' Tayta runs in from the hall and ups the volume on an Arabic soap. 'This my favourite; I been waiting all week.'

I put my phone down and we sit in silence, watching a show that in my opinion is the worst excuse for acting since Zena's portrayal of the Holy Mother. The love triangles, the longing looks, the *eyebrows* – I've never seen anything so overdone in my life. Aunty Mary hates it too. She keeps digging at the *kousa* and groaning under her breath. But when the brother of the evil businessman tells the pregnant pianist that he loves her – my *tayta* literally gasps. I sit there, watching her face more than I'm watching the actual show, and when the credits finally roll, I say, 'Tayta?'

'*Eh?*'

'Have you ever been in love?'

To my surprise she answers, 'No.'

No? 'So, you didn't love Jidou?' I glance at Aunty Mary, but she doesn't even blink.

'No, I love him, but not in love.'

My grandfather, *Allah yerhamou*, passed away ten years ago. I remember Tayta telling us that she and Jidou had been neighbours in their village, and that she'd married him when she was just fifteen. I sit quietly, picturing myself at that age, and I know that even though it was normal for them back then, there would've been nothing romantic about it. I imagine getting pulled out of school and given to a man twice my age. I imagine their wedding night; how awkward and painful it would've been. And then my mind flashes to Sarah; how she suffered something even worse – something *soul-destroying* – and yet her longing for love had miraculously prevailed. Because all Sarah wanted was a date for the dance.

'So, you've never been in love with anyone – not even someone else?'

Tayta shakes her head, 'No.'

A wave of sadness washes over me. By the way she watched that soap, I can tell she would've loved being in love. I can tell she missed out on it.

She looks at me, reading my thoughts.

'I no upset. I have lotta love. Friend, children, and most love: Jesus.' She takes the remote and lowers the volume. 'Some people no have any love. No have family, no have friend.'

I nod, still fighting back pity. But then I ask myself why. Why, after everything I've been through, do I think that 'being in love' is so important? Most people from Tayta's generation got married out of need. They just accepted their lives and loved their husbands in the ways they could. It wasn't romantic, but it lasted. And maybe that's all we can hope for.

I settle back in my seat, feeling sorry for both of us, when Aunty Mary speaks up from beside her. 'I been in love.' She doesn't look at me; she just says it.

I stare at her in disbelief. 'With *who*?'

She puts the *kousa* down and wipes her hands. 'A boy. *Bi Libnan*.' That's all she says: *A boy in Lebanon*. I'd heard whispers growing up that she was once engaged, but it seemed to be almost a myth.

'Well, what happened?'

She swallows back a feeling, and for the first time in my life, I can see her vulnerability. 'He die.'

I frown. 'How?'

'In the street, they kill him. *Metl kalb*.' Like a dog.

Tayta doesn't react; she sits stoically beside her sister, knowing already the story she's about to tell.

'Why? What for?'

Aunty Mary gives me a twisted look. 'For money.' She huffs in disgust. 'One neighbour owe the other. And when he try to help, someone shoot him in the chest.' She points above her heart.

'By accident?'

'*Eh*. They shooting at each other, but they killing him instead.'

'*God*. Were you there?'

She steels her jaw. 'He die in my arms. I see my hands, they red. And all the people, they run.'

I look at Aunty Mary and everything about her suddenly makes sense. Her black clothes, her bad mood; the reason she never got married. *Aunty Mary has a broken heart*. A real one, from sixty years ago.

'You know this boy? I so in love. I love him more than anything. And I sleep with him.' There's a quaver in her voice and Tayta glances at her sister in surprise; not because of what she's saying, but because she's saying it to me. 'We no marry yet, but I no care. I with him every day.'

I try to imagine Aunty Mary romping around with some boy, but I've only ever known her as an old woman.

'He have nice face, and nice smile. And he love me so much; if I sad, he don't sleep.' She looks out the window at the garden, as if he were standing there among the trees. 'I remember him,' she says, and her face becomes something new. 'I remember how he dance, and how he kiss me. How we swim all day in the river and meet every night on the roof.' She's smiling now, still turned to the sun with her eyes like opals, and I can finally see it.

I can see how beautiful she used to be.

We all sit in silence. I'm staring at her the same way Tayta was staring at that stupid soap. 'And even after all this time, you still miss him?'

'Oh, yes,' she says. 'But more than anything, I miss myself.'

I look at my *tayta* and her sister; the two of them sitting side by side. One who had a husband and a family, and the other who had *one great love* but never got married. Each of them burdened by what the other is missing.

And then I think of Aunty Lou.

And I wonder if she was happy,

or was she missing something too?

Chapter 25

It's been almost nine years since my high school formal.

Nine years.

In a few weeks I'll be twenty-seven, but when I think of 'twenty-seven', I don't picture myself. I picture a grown-up, a *woman*. Someone who wears heels to lunch. 'Twenty-seven' means being confident and capable and focused. But the truth is, I felt those things more in high school than I ever have as an adult.

Sarah stands in the middle of one of Danny's spare bedrooms, gazing at herself in a floor-length mirror. I hook the buttons on the back of her halterneck and spread the hem at her feet.

'It fits perfectly.'

I'd come straight from work to help her get ready. She told me about her friends and their partners; what they're wearing and all the gossip that comes with dressing up and going out. I can't remember seeing her this happy, or even just acting her age. You only have this time once, and it's bittersweet: those fleeting few months between the school bell and womanhood, when the world wants nothing from you but to bask in your own possibilities.

I take her hand. The house is loud. I can hear Danny on the phone and their mum yelling orders from the kitchen. Sarah's friends will be arriving soon, and her aunties have come here to see her off. I know it's not her thing – walking into a room, being centre of attention – but they're waiting.

They've been waiting for this day a long time.

'Are you ready?'

She squeezes my hand.

I say, 'Sarah?'

And she nods, lifting her hem as I lead us to the lounge.

They've heard us coming; the house falls quiet. She tries to hide behind me, but I step away from the door. There's a moment – a second or two of wide-eyed suspense – and then her mum starts crying. She's crying and smiling and singing her daughter's name. All her aunties come forward, fussing and making the sign of the cross over Sarah's face.

'*Issmissalib! Aabel tsafeh arous!*' In the name of the cross! *The next bride!* '*Lelelelele!*'

Normally, I'd cringe. I'd think, *Bloody Lebs – she's barely left the house and they already want a wedding.* But I look at Sarah in her long white dress, dancing with her mum, and I see it instead as a new beginning.

'You bring your camera?' Danny comes up beside me with a plate of food. His mum spent all day preparing for Sarah's friends. There are trays of *sambousik* and *kibbeh* on a buffet table in the hall.

'Yes, boss. It's in my bag.'

He smiles. 'Good. You hungry?'

'Nah, I ate before.' I look at Sarah. 'She's so beautiful, Dan.' I lean against the doorframe, watching them dance. 'I wish it was my formal again.'

Danny looks down at me. 'If it was, would you let me take you?'

'We should've gone together the first time.'

'I know,' he says. 'We should've.'

The doorbell rings and a second wave of excitement swells through the house. I grab my camera and we funnel from the lounge room onto Danny's front lawn. Sarah's friends are waiting at the kerb in sequins and suits. I notice a boy; he's skinny and freckled, and when he shakes Danny's hand his own is trembling. Then he lines up next to Sarah so that I can take a photo of the group. I stand in front of them, camera raised, mocking Danny over my shoulder. 'That's the boy you were worried about?'

He leans in close. 'Does he have a dick?'

I roll my eyes.

'Then I'm worried.'

After a few quick snaps, Danny and I move to the footpath while Sarah takes selfies on her phone. A few years ago, the council poured a new sidewalk in Danny's street and some kid wrote 'THUG LIFE' in the wet cement. It's always struck me as ironic that this random act of vandalism was done right at Danny's door – as if it were a welcome mat and a warning all in one. Seeing it now makes me think about words; about the power of them. And how a martyred gangster rapper, dead for over twenty years, still has a foothold in the far-flung streets of Sydney's West.

I point my camera at the pavement – at Danny's Nike sneaker half covering the 'G' in THUG LIFE – and I press the shutter.

'What's that for?'

'Nothing.' I raise the lens, grinning. He tries to duck away, but I'm too quick. Then I get another of him smiling, reaching for my camera with his tatted arm.

'*Oi!* Stop!' The shutter goes again. 'You know I hate photos!'

'I can't imagine why,' I say. 'A glamour like you.'

'Oh, piss off.' He takes the camera strap from around my neck and pulls me close, turning the lens on us, and holding it high with his left hand. 'Smile, Nic.'

I feel his head leaning against mine, and even though half my face is out of frame, I decide then and there that it's my favourite photo ever.

* * *

Sarah had wanted to go in the limo with her friends, but Danny insisted on driving her to Leichhardt himself. I guess it made him feel better, seeing his sister safely to the door. He'd warned her out his window that he'd be back at nine o'clock sharp to pick her up. She'd given me a desperate look and then we'd left them, off to kill the next two hours in Bondi.

'Nine's a bit early, don't you think?'

'Well, hey,' he says, parking his car in front of the beach. 'If you can keep me busy, she might get longer.'

Bondi is one of those places that really lives up to the hype. It's big and blue and it stretches a full kilometre. A swathe of grass frames the shoreline like an amphitheatre and the cliffs on either side are stacked with multistorey apartments; homes that belong to celebrities like Hugh Jackman and James Packer. Bondi has always been a haven for the rich, and yet on the very same street there are hostels and hoarders and heritage houses. While Danny puts money in the meter, I amble along the footpath, admiring the pink sky and the panoramic view.

He joins me. 'You hungry yet?'

'Yeah, a bit.'

'Well, what do you feel like?'

'I don't know. Anything.'

He looks around, then he says, 'How about Italian?'

'Yeah, I wouldn't mind a pasta.'

'Great. Let's go.'

He guides me down a side street to a small Sicilian restaurant. There are wooden tables and dripping candles, and a chalkboard on the wall. Danny hugs the owner on our way in, some old Italian guy who says, 'You bring nice lady! She too nice for you!'

Danny waves him off. 'Yeah, yeah. Come on, we're hungry.'

'Okay, I give you the special table.'

He leads us to the back of the restaurant: a cosy corner for two.

'Do you come here a lot?' I ask Danny.

'Every now and then. I don't go out much, you know. I don't like crowded places.'

Danny always takes the chair facing out. He never sits with his back to a room or in between strangers. I watch while he studies the menu, his dark lashes veiling his gaze. He has his hands clasped together as if in prayer, his face ambered by a flickering candle.

'What can I get you?' The waiter appears beside us, pen in hand.

Danny glances up at me. 'Nic? What you feel like?'

I look away. 'I don't know; you choose.'

'You want starters?'

'I don't mind.'

He looks at the menu again. 'Okay, get us that antipasti board. It's got everything, yeah?'

The waiter says, 'Yeah, bit of everything. Any bread?'

'Maybe some bruschetta or something. You like bruschetta, Nic?'

'Yeah, I do.'

The waiter writes our order. 'And for your mains?'

Danny says, 'I'll get the chicken mushroom.' Then, 'Look, Nic, they got pink sauce. You love pink sauce.'

I look across at him. *When the hell did I tell him that?*

The waiter's waiting, so I say, 'I'll get the pink sauce, please.'

He writes it down. 'Pink sauce it is. Any drinks? Water?'

'I'll have sparkling.'

Danny nods. 'Just bring us a bottle. Thanks, mate.'

The waiter collects the menus and leaves.

I wait while Danny checks his phone, then he puts it on silent. I stare at him staring at me. 'How'd you know I like pink sauce?'

He smiles proudly. 'We were watching that cooking show on my couch. You said, "Pink sauce is the best of both worlds".'

I smile back, vaguely remembering.

'Don't worry,' he says. 'I know a lot about you.'

I laugh. 'Like what?'

He leans forward. 'Well, how deep do you wanna go?'

I try to ignore the innuendo. 'Not very.'

He grins to himself. '*Not very* ... okay. Well, I know you get scared. I know you get stuck in your own head. And I know you worry too much; you worry all the time.'

I push my hair from my face, wondering what 'deep' would've been. 'No, I don't.'

'And I know you tuck your hair behind your ear when you're lying.'

'Very funny.'

'It's true.' He grins. 'You done it since we were kids.'

The waiter returns from the kitchen with our bruschetta and antipasti. Danny lets me serve myself, then he serves me a bit more. We've just started eating when he says, 'Nic, I wanna thank you for what you done for my sister.'

'Dan—'

'No. I need to say it.' He puts his fork down. 'You helped her a lot. You being around, I know she looks up to you. And I seen the way you are with her, like she's your own. I know you care about her; I know it comes from the heart. But I know you're also doing it for me, 'cos you care about me too.'

'I do. I care about you a lot. I just want you to be okay.' He knows what I'm talking about – all the things he told me at the park. 'Have you heard anything?'

'Nah, I think it's gonna blow over.'

This surprises me. 'Why?'

'I don't know. I think if it was gonna happen it would've happened by now.' He reaches for a piece of bread. 'Anyway, work's been so busy. I gotta stay focused on that.' Danny has a thousand worries in life, and all of them bleed; his sister, his mum, his garage, Gab, the boys who work for him, his house and, now, the police. He's got all these stresses and threats, but instead of letting himself haemorrhage, he does what anyone should do with an open wound: he applies more pressure. I stare at him, wondering how he sleeps at night; hoping that he does. We eat in silence until the waiter clears our plates and our mains are brought out.

'I feel like I upset you the other day.'

Danny stops cutting his chicken. 'When?'

'At the garage, when that towie showed up.'

'You didn't upset me, Nic. Sometimes it's just hard to explain things, you know? It's hard to explain myself in a way you'd understand.' He presses his fork into a scalloped potato; a small, constrained sign of hidden feeling. 'You're the only person I've ever been at peace with. Where I can just let my guard down and rest.'

I nod. 'Me too.'

We give each other the same muted smile before he continues. 'And I want you to always think of me like that.' He pauses again, his voice low. 'Everything I done in life, I carry it. But there was never any plan. I just did what I knew at the time, whatever I could to pay the bills. And it wasn't easy, you know? A young kid, eleven years old. That's when I started this shit, working as a lookout for some fuckwit dealer.' He shakes his head at his own story. 'I was scared back then, but I wasn't gonna stop. 'Cos I was doing it for my family – for my new little sister. And for my dad.'

I look at my hands. 'Your dad was a good man, *Allah yerhamou*.'

'Yeah, he was,' says Danny. 'He was a gentleman. He would've killed me, though, if he knew what I was doing. Maybe he did, but he was too ashamed ask.'

'I don't think he was ever ashamed of you. I think he idolised you, the same way you idolised him.'

'I hope so,' he says. 'And I hope to God he doesn't know about Sarah. I hope he died, and he went to heaven, and he's never looked back.'

I let him eat a few bites of chicken before I ask him a pointless question.

'Danny?'

He looks at me. 'Mm?'

'Do you think if your dad hadn't got sick, things would've been different?'

Danny smiles to himself; it's small and self-deprecating. 'Maybe. But I was always a bit of a dickhead. I just wish I'd listened to him more.'

From there our conversation slowly lightens. We roll from one thing to another: our childhood, our friends, Chadi's car, my sister's wedding. I've almost finished my pasta when he asks me if I'm seeing anyone.

'So, any boys?' He says it like that, pretending to be busy with his plate.

'No. I'm a bit turned off, to be honest.' It's the truth, but maybe not the right thing to say.

He nods. 'Fair enough.' Then he says, 'I know it hurt, Nic. But it's over now.'

It hurt, but it's over. Sometimes, it's the simplest shit that resonates the most.

'What about you?'

He looks up at me.

'Any girls?' It's not until I say it that I realise it's the first time I've ever asked. In twenty years, he's never mentioned a girlfriend or a fling or even a crush. I know that there's been women, of course. I've heard gossip or discovered things by chance. Like at dinner with Layla the other night. Or the time that Rita told me Danny had 'two bitches' – a Vietnamese girl from Canley Heights and an Aussie from Palm Beach – and we both wondered how he did all that driving.

'Nah, no one.'

'You're a liar and a half.'

He grins. 'Come on, man, what do you want me to say?'

'The truth. I tell you.'

'No, you don't. There's heaps of shit you don't tell me.'

I raise my glass. 'Like what?'

'Like about your mate Dave.'

I stop mid-sip. 'What about him?'

'Do you like him?'

'Yeah, as a friend.'

'So, a friend like me?'

'No one's a friend like you. And how'd you know about him, anyway?'

'Scarface saw you getting into his car that night. Wanted to know why my "missus" was being picked up by another bloke.'

It annoys me he didn't say something sooner. 'Well, you could've just asked.'

'Wasn't my business.'

'So, I'm not your business, then?'

'That's not what I said.'

'Maybe you're not mine, either.'

He searches my face, then he says, 'The girls I know, they're not serious. They're not the type of girls I'd tell you about.'

'Why? Do you think I'd judge you?'

He shakes his head. 'No. I think you'd laugh.'

'So?'

'So maybe I don't want you to laugh.'

We're staring at each other, his words so loaded they sink like lead. I look at him – at his scars and his tattoos – and I pitch to him another hypothetical.

'Danny?'

'Yeah?' He pours me some water.

'If we didn't grow up together, if we only met now, do you think we'd still be friends?'

He pretends to take me seriously. 'Yeah, I reckon we would. Some people are just destined. And the fact is Nicky Naj, you like me too much.'

'Oh, really? Well, I think you like me more.'

'And why's that?'

I take a sip of water. Then I put my glass on the table, ready to play my ace. 'Well, for starters, it's a quarter past nine.'

'Fuck!' He jumps from his seat. 'Shit! Is she okay?'

'She's fine!' I laugh. 'She just messaged me.'

He calls to the waiter for the bill. I sit back in my chair, knowing I've won the hand.

Danny thanks the owner, who says to me on our way out, 'He a nice boy!' Spurred, I'm sure, by the fifty-dollar tip.

We're walking together along Campbell Parade when he sees my smug face and puts his arm around me.

I say, 'I think I want ice cream.'

'Yeah, you always want ice cream. Here, come in here, they got gelato.'

Danny drags me to a retro dessert bar and waits impatiently while I choose between thirty-five flavours. I take my time, partly because I can't decide between cookies and cream or cookie dough, and partly because Sarah has asked me to stall.

'*Ya Allah*, man. Get *any*. Get them all!'

I'm laughing and licking my cone, the two of us breathless when we finally climb into his car. He shakes his head and grins, pulling away from the kerb and speeding out of Bondi. We're almost on the Anzac Bridge when Danny looks over at me. 'You enjoying that, fatty?'

I savour my last bite. 'No.'

He laughs and puts his hand out, a gentle invitation for my own.

'My fingers are sticky.'

'So?'

I hesitate and then I reach for him. We've got the windows down and the air rushes into us, that beautiful springtime breeze that makes you feel like you're at the start of something new. I look at my polished nails against the back of his brown hand and I think, *Maybe we do go together.*

Even though we're different, maybe we're the perfect fit.

Maybe everything I ever wanted was right across the road, twenty years ago, in shorts and worn-out sneakers.

Chapter 26

Friday, 20 October. Submission day.

I wake up early and sit at my laptop. Over the past three weeks I've taken almost four hundred and fifty photos, starting from the feast day at church and ending with Sarah's formal last night. I browse through the ones from Granville and Merrylands, and the panoramic shots I took from the top of Dave's tower. There are others, too, that I've taken in between: a few from Tayta's the other day, and the storm I captured standing on the stairs of our back porch.

I favourite the ones I like, separating them into a different folder, and then I repeat the process over and over until I'm left with a workable batch. There are eighteen photos now and I take my time, slowly eliminating the final dozen. When I'm done, I sit back, scrolling through a six-chapter story told in black and white.

Photo 1
The very first photo I took.
Tayta rolling dough and smiling at the camera.

Photo 2
Badwi's shop in Merrylands. The countertop and the shelves below it; a mix of Arabic and Aussie confectionary.

Photo 3
The one that got reported: the Vote No billboard in Granville.

Photo 4
A photo of Elie from the fashion show, his back turned, with my mother's crystal clutch tucked beneath his arm.

Photo 5
The view of The Area from Dave's building.

Photo 6
My sentimental secret.
Danny's tattooed arm reaching for my camera. His face in the background, a blurred smile.

I look them over, knowing I could never show every part of myself in just six frames. But at least with these, I can show my beginnings: the city I was born in and the beauty of being both Lebanese and Australian. Of walking the line and then one day realising that there's no line at all. That even with our differences, we have all chosen *this place* – this patch of earth in the furthest corner of the world – to settle and to live, and to find our luck in the Land of Plenty.

I open my email.

Subject: Nicole Najim 2017 application

Dear Bronwyn,

Please see attached my six-photo submission.

The cursor blinks. I blink. What else is there to say? I could write her a whole letter about my life and my hopes and the journey I've been on for the last few months, but that, of course, would defeat the purpose.

It's up to the photos now.

Looking forward to hearing from you,

Nicole.

* * *

At about midday I get three messages from Danny, which immediately worries me since he never sends more than one text.

What are you doing tonight?

I want to take you for dinner.

A proper one I'll pick you up

'A proper one? What does he mean?'

'He means a date, babe.' Layla is lying across my bed in a feather-trimmed corset. She's been trying on different outfits for Monica's hens'; a last-minute panic before the party tomorrow. 'Like, he wants to come pick you up and do it proper.'

'I don't think he means it like that. Maybe it's just as a thank you for last night.'

Layla rolls her eyes. 'Last night was the thank you for last night. This is different.'

'Well, he can't come pick me up. Not with Mum keeping watch.' She's been especially vigilant lately: a twenty-four-hour surveillance of the comings and goings of her most disappointing daughter. The other night I heard her arguing with Dad, muffled shouts of my name and the slamming of a cupboard door. We haven't spoken since the fight we had, and the way things are going, I don't want to.

'Then tell him you'll meet him instead.'

Layla waits while I type, staring at me until she hears the swoop of a text.

'Relax, I sent it.'

'Good. And send him some flirty emojis, too. The tongue one or something.'

'Yeah, maybe some tit as well.'

'He's gonna try to hook up tonight, babe. Hundred per cent.'

'I think you're getting a bit carried away.'

'Babe, he's your husband, I can feel it.'

She's just had her nails done – bright purple, coffin-shaped acrylics. I watch as she holds them to the light, admiring her manicure in the afternoon sun. 'I knew he was the one for you, even when he was fucking Angie.'

'Thanks, that's really special.'

'Babe, he's a man at the end of the day. I mean they all love pussy; at least he'll know what he's doing.'

I laugh. 'You're not normal, you know that?'

'Anyway, what are you gonna wear?' She rolls onto her stomach and eyes me. '*Ooft*, not that!'

I'm holding a t-shirt dress.

'What's wrong with this?'

'Well, nothing if you're off to join a convent, babe. But you're going on a date.'

'It's not a date.'

Layla sits up. 'Are you the dumbest person I've ever met? You were with him *yesterday*. Now he wants to see you again. He wants to *pick you up* and *take you to dinner*. Like, maybe you're in denial, but believe me when I tell you, babe: it's a date.'

She's on her feet now, sorting through my wardrobe and throwing different options on my bed. One is the sequinned mini dress I wore to my sister's engagement.

'Are you serious?'

'Babe, he said somewhere proper.'

'And that means what? Black tie?'

'Well, wear some heels, at least!'

'Lay, I'm meeting him in *Greenacre*. I wouldn't wear heels to The Area even if it was New Year's Eve.'

'Fine. But if you don't show some leg, I'll fuckin' bash you.' She pulls a denim skirt from one of my shelves and pairs it with a tie-front top. 'That's classy, babe. And with the right bra, he'll wanna rip the whole thing off.'

* * *

I get to Danny's garage earlier than I expected. He said to meet him here at seven, but when I turn on to Juno Parade it's six forty-six. There are three motorbikes parked beside George's van, but when I call Danny's phone, he doesn't answer.

I wait another minute before getting out of my car to go and find him. The lot is quiet. I walk beneath the corrugated awning to the mirrored windows of his front office, unsure if he's even inside. There's a lamp on, but there's no one at the till. I put my bag down and lean against the desk, hearing muffled voices from the next room.

'Danny?' I call out.

The talking stops.

'Dan?'

I wait a moment or two, and then he comes from the back with his usual grin. 'Hey, Nicky.'

'Hey. Sorry – I'm a bit early.'

'Nah, it's okay.' He walks towards me, his eyes catching briefly on my cleavage. 'You look good.'

I smile and shy away.

He gleams at me some more. 'I missed you today.'

'Did you?'

He answers by taking me in his arms. I have to stand on my toes to reach him, but when I do, I see the warehouse roller door rising over his shoulder. There are three men in leather vests leaving the garage with George and Gab.

They're not mechanics.

'Who're they?'

He glances back. 'Mechanics.'

I push him away.

'What?'

'What do you mean what?'

'They just needed some parts for their bikes.'

'So, wait, which one is it? Are they customers or are they mechanics?'

'I don't know. Both.'

It's funny the difference a few minutes can make. If I'd got here on time, I wouldn't have seen any of this: the patched members, the secret meeting. I would've just turned up and gone to dinner. And it's always so easy to do. Because when I look at Danny, I don't see anything else. He's still that boy from Amber Way; same smile, just scarred at the lip. I watch George shake hands with one of the men. They nod and wave goodbye.

'What's Gab doing here?' I ask.

'He's helping me. He's working.'

'You think that's a good idea?'

'Nic, it's nothing.'

But I won't be lied to. Not when the truth is right in front of my face. I turn from him and take my bag.

'Hey!' He grabs my arm. 'It's *nothing*, I swear; it's just a meet.'

I feel his hand on my side, a gentle pleading. Everyone else has left the lot. There's just the low hum of a generator and some music coming from a radio on the other side of the desk.

I look at him. 'I'm worried.'

'I told you already, you worry too much.'

But I hate the way he says it; it's dismissive and it pisses me off. I push his hand away; he grabs me again.

'*What?* What are you worried about?'

'You! *This!*' I shove his chest, then I wave towards the back of the warehouse; that dark recess – a *boy's club* – only ever seen by bearded men. 'What if something happens to you? What if it's *your* car that gets shot at?'

He's not taking me seriously. 'Would you miss me?'

'*Stop it.*'

His grin gets wider. He bites his lip, then he says, 'I'd miss you.'

I try to ignore the pull in my gut. 'It's not funny; I'm really worried.'

'Don't be.' He takes my head in his hands and strokes my face. 'Everything's okay. Alright? I'm not doing anything stupid. Trust me.'

I nod now, falling again for the smell of him.

'Fuck, you're pretty,' he says.

And when I look in his eyes, I see the shadow of something painful.

'You're the only one I want, you know that?'

I don't say anything.

He leans in closer, my hands holding tight to his wrists. He breathes and then he kisses me, slowly and adoringly, and the feeling of it hurts my heart. I wrap my arms around his neck, and I kiss him back. He groans and bends to lift me, his hands on my body, bruising my thighs. I say, *'Put me on the desk,'* and his eyes turn black. He lowers me down beside the till, the both of us golden.

We kiss while he unties my top, throwing it on the floor, and then tugging at the back of my bra.

'Ayri, this fuckin' thing,' he breathes, and the two of us start to laugh. We grin against each other's teeth until it finally comes undone, and when I shrug away the straps, Danny sighs at seeing me bare for the first time.

'Fuck.'

His eyes are like embers again. He bows his head to kiss me, his heavy brown hands at the small of my waist. When he straightens and strips off his shirt, the markings on his torso are somehow bolder in the dimness, and I gaze at them as if they were new.

I want him, I want him.

I pull him back to me: I lick his tongue. He holds me closer, lying me down. There's a keyboard under my head and we shove it away. He pushes my skirt to my ribs and says, *'Tell me what you like. Fuck, I'll do anything, tell me what you like.'* I grab his jeans, he groans, *'Babe,'* and then I feel his hand at the top of my thigh, testing me. I hold his face and I breathe, and I kiss him again, arching my body while his fingers go to work.

We're not friends anymore,

we're not friends.

He's looking at me like he's woken from a dream; like he can't believe it's real, like he can't believe he's touching me. I close my eyes, ready to give myself over, when somehow through our moaning, and our ragged breathing and the deafening sound of my own pulse, I hear those haunting echoed notes, my most *hated* song, coming from the radio.

'Firestone'.

I stop moving. I think of my ex. I remember his mouth on mine and it sickens me. I try to ignore it, but all I can see – all I can conjure in my mind – is the bitter taste of someone else.

I grab Danny's wrist.

'You okay?' He stares down at me. 'Did I hurt you?'

No. *Not you.* I cover my face.

'Babe?'

'Don't call me that.'

I feel him flinch.

When I finally sit up, he's standing against the opposite wall. I wrap my arms around my body, and I look away. He stays where he is, not knowing what's going on and I couldn't tell him even if I tried.

He watches me, the top button of his jeans undone. Then he says, 'I shouldn't have touched you; it was a mistake.' There's a coldness in his voice and it riles me.

'A mistake?' I pull my bra back on. 'That's nice.'

'Well, you're not fuckin' telling me what's wrong!'

'What you said is wrong! You're making me feel like shit!'

'How! How's this turned on *me*? I'm the one should be cut!'

'*Why?*' I keep my knees together, tugging at my skirt, pulling it back in place. "Cos you didn't get what you want?' Even as I say it, I know I've gone too far.

'Are you fuckin' serious with this shit?'

'*I'm just not ready, okay?*'

He puts his hands behind his head. I can see the heat in his face. 'Don't talk to me like I'm some *low-life*. Like I was forcing you for a fuck!'

God, *why did I say that*? Of all people, *Danny*, who's been agonising over his sister for seven years. He paces once, cradling the back of his neck. 'I've never touched you. Not *ever*. You wanna take it slow, I'll take it slow. But if this is about something else' – he bites back his anger – '*someone* else, don't fuckin' come here again!'

It's the first time he's ever yelled at me and the shock of it brings me to tears. We've never been mad at each other, not like this. I know I've hurt him – *I've hurt him so bad* – but that song's still playing, and I can't get past it.

'I'm gonna go.'

He watches as I gather my things; back straight, colder than before. When I'm dressed again, I leave without looking at him. I cross the lot alone – my jaw shaking – and I feel this deep, dark panic that the two of us won't recover. That we'll never be the same.

That my truest friend tried to love me, and I fucked it all up in one night.

I've ruined it, I've ruined it.

That stupid fucking song.

He's better off without me.

He hates me.

He's gone.

Chapter 27

'Fuck, you're hopeless.' Layla sips her vodka through a penis straw. 'Like, really, babe. A song? I would've told him to turn that shit up.'

'I know, okay? I'm an idiot.'

'To say the fuckin' least, babe.' Dee is standing beside her, the two of them in matching bras and sequinned shorts. Layla insisted on bringing her to the hens', since the rest of us wouldn't know how to party, 'even if we were all on E'.

'So, has he called you?'

I shake my head. 'No.'

'Well, he's cut, babe.' Dee looks up at me, hand on hip. 'You full rejected him, and guys like that, they got a *lot* of pride.'

'I know. I probably should've messaged him, but I've been running around all day.'

We'd checked into the penthouse earlier this morning, bringing boxes of alcohol and tacky decorations. Jacqueline and I have spent the past few hours setting up the bar and the grazing table – under Elie's keen instruction – while Monica had her hair and make-up done in the master bedroom. There's another smaller suite at the opposite wing, a sunken lounge that we've filled with balloons, and a karaoke room hidden behind the marble bar.

'Well, at least we can all get drunk tonight. Try and forget about it, babe.'

I pour myself a drink, and then another for Monica. She comes from the bathroom wearing a floor-length robe made of glittery tulle and a golden crown and hides behind me.

'You okay, Mon?'

'No. I'm dying for this shit to be over.'

'Here, have some of this.' I pass her a plastic cup of wine.

'You should send him a pic, babe.' Dee again. 'A sexy one to say sorry. I mean, you're dressed for it, might as well.'

This gets Monica's attention. 'A sexy pic for who?'

'Nothing, she's just joking. I had a bit of a fight with Danny.'

'Oh, he messaged me.'

The three of us look at her. '*What?* When?'

'Late last night.'

'Well, what did he say, babe?'

Monica glances between us. 'He just asked if you got home okay. I thought your battery died or something.'

I look back at Layla.

'You really are a gronk, babe,' she says to me. 'Like, only a fuckin' gentleman would do that.'

'*Okay, guys!*' Jackie yells into a portable mic that she's taken from the karaoke room. 'It's time to get this party started!' She's wearing a corseted bodysuit – similar to mine – and has gone so far as to switch her daughter from breastmilk to baby formula for tonight's occasion. 'First, I just want to welcome everyone to Monica's Leather and Lace hens'! I know it was a bit last minute, so thank you all for coming, and for really getting on board with the theme.'

The guests have gathered around her: six of Monica's in-laws, who are dressed awkwardly in pyjama pants and leather jackets;

Nat, who spent the whole afternoon curling our hair in a light pink playsuit; Rita, who's wearing a harness bra; Yasmine in a French-lace nightie; and Elie, who's been here since midday, watching from the sunken lounge and sculling whisky in a satin shirt and a pair of velvet slippers.

'Okay, so we're going to kick this night off with a drinking game: a quiz about the groom for our beautiful bride.' Jackie extends her arm towards Monica. 'But the twist is this: if she gets an answer wrong, we *all* have to drink.'

Necessary, I think, *considering half the room are looking at each other like they're hostages.*

'I should've said no games.' Monica reluctantly takes her rosé and sits on a lone bar stool beside Jackie, who smiles pageant-style into the mic.

'Okay, Monnie, first question: Who is Luke's ultimate celebrity crush?'

The room falls quiet. 'Oh, I don't know … Bella Hadid?'

'Wrong!' Jackie raises her cup. 'He said *Margot Robbie.*'

'*Margot Robbie?* She looks nothing like me!'

Elie scoffs from the sunken lounge, 'And Bella Hadid does?'

'Well at least she's half Arab!'

The rest of us concede and drink.

'Okay, second question: What's Luke's favourite food?'

Monica touches her crown, smiling graciously at her in-laws. 'His mum's *bazella ou rez.*'

'Wrong again!' hoots Jackie. 'It's his mother's *mehshi malfouf.*'

The game goes on, and out of fifteen questions, Monica only gets eight right. By the time she staggers from her perch, the rest of the party needs a refill too. I work the bar while Jackie announces the next game: a runway competition. Everyone has to walk the length of the room showcasing their costumes, while the bridal party judges the winner. I'm about to press play on Cardi B's 'Bodak Yellow', when Elie rises from the balloon pit and commandeers the mic.

'Okay, ladies,' he slurs. 'Let's make this interesting. Best booty drop at the end of the catwalk earns you ten bonus points and a shot of Patron poured by *me*.'

What a prize.

'And to set the standard,' continues Elie, 'I'll go *first*.'

'Um, Elie?' Yasmine holds a crystal wineglass by its stem, having refused to drink '*vin*' from anything else. 'Not to spoil the fun, but I'm not really the booty-dropping type.'

Dee rolls her eyes and thrusts her cup at Layla. 'Hold my drink, babe,' she says. 'I got this.'

The next few minutes unfold like a movie. I stand beside my sisters and Layla, the four of us wide-eyed and cheering at the top of our lungs, while Elie leads the charge, striding down the runway and squatting three consecutive times like a drunk Russian. He's immediately followed by Dee, who, despite her diminutive frame, is able to twerk her little arse cheeks like a Las Vegas stripper. Everyone else fulfills the challenge with surprising levels of enthusiasm – except, of course, for Yasmine, who chooses to perform a belly dance instead. After a heated discussion, we decide the winner should be either Elie or Dee, with Dee eventually taking the points, since – as Layla so tactfully put it – 'she actually has a pussy'.

The lights are low when Jacqueline moves the party to the karaoke room. I've had four drinks so far, all sipped through a plastic penis, and I'm starting to feel the pull of a full bladder. I leave the bar to Layla and head for the ensuite with my fifth drink in hand. There's a large mirror that runs above the marble vanity, backlit by a warm yellow glow. I stare at myself a while, at my sheer black bodysuit and my bare thighs.

Maybe I should.

Maybe I should send him a pic.

I stand between the sinks with my phone raised, one hand leaning on the bench, while I subtly squeeze my cleavage. Then I stumble back to the party, scrolling for Danny's name and sending my mirror selfie, with a message that says: *miss you*.

'You okay, babe?' Layla's pouring Dee another vodka.

'I did what you said. I sent him a pic.'

Dee and Layla look impressed. 'Go you, babe! Finally you stop being frigid!'

'I'm really drunk.'

'Show us the pic; it better be good.'

I bring it up on my camera roll.

'Hot, babe. Could've done with a bit of nipple, but good enough.'

I keep my phone face down until I hear the ding of a text. Layla and Dee exchange a knowing pout, then they wait for me to turn it over.

Dave $:
Wow
Miss u to

Fuckkkkkkkk!

'What did he say, babe?'

'I sent it to Dave! I sent it to the *wrong fucking person*!'

The two of them burst out laughing. 'You really are hopeless, babe. *Haroum* Dave, he'd be fuckin' ecstatic.'

'Oh my God, *stop it*! What do I say?'

'Well, what did *he* say?'

I stare at them, realising I'm about to embarrass myself even more. 'He said "miss you too".'

They're crying with laughter now.

'Oh, babe, I can't breathe.'

'I swear, babe, same!' Dee leans her little arm on Layla, the two of them gasping for air.

'Yeah, *thanks*. This is all your fault!'

'Babe, it's *funny*, relax.' Layla takes my phone and checks the messages for herself. 'Think of it this way, babe: at least you didn't send it to your *dad*.'

Dee starts laughing again. 'Fuck, babe – true! Imagine she did.'

'Okay, enough! This is *such* a disaster. And I can't even tell him I sent it by mistake! Because who the fuck was it meant for, then?'

'Yeah, you've really fucked yourself, babe. Just leave it. Message him tomorrow; tell him you were off your tits and you can't remember a thing.'

'Yeah, babe, that's what I'd do.' Dee stops laughing long enough to speak. 'Like, I wouldn't have botched it to begin with, but at least you had a go.'

I reach around them and pour myself a double shot of tequila. 'This is an actual fucking nightmare.'

'Relax, babe, it's *nothing*.' Layla hugs me with one arm, the deep seductive beat of Beyoncé's 'Baby Boy' now emanating from the karaoke room. I slump against my cousin's shoulder, silently hating myself, when the purr of Elie's voice comes echoing through the portable mic.

'Babe, who the fuck is that?' Dee leads the way.

In the karaoke room, Elie is standing on one of the couches, singing and grinding his pelvis, while the rest of the party record him on their phones.

'See, babe?' says Layla. 'And you think you've got regrets.'

* * *

The next morning, Chadi is waiting in the lobby to pick us up. It's the first weekend he's got his licence back and we've wasted no time putting him to work. When the elevator opens, the four of us spill into the foyer: Jacqueline wearing sunglasses and sipping nauseously from a bottle of water; Monica taking deep inhalations of her puffer; Layla still in her bra; and me with my make-up down my face.

'Oh my God.' Chadi laughs. 'Youse all look munted.'

'Shut up, Chadi! Look at yourself.'

'Hey, I look good. Not bad for a Sunday morning, anyway.'

I eye him suspiciously. 'Yeah, why's that? Didn't you go out last night?'

'Nah, cuz, I went to bed early. Needed to be up on time for favourite ladies today.'

I can tell already that he wants something.

Layla rolls her eyes and limps past her brother. 'Yeah, *right*. Where's the car?'

'It's at valet, *your majesty*. Mick's waiting there, too.'

'Oh, thank God,' says Jackie. 'I'm dying to get home. I think I'm gonna vomit again.'

We all walk out to the waiting bay with Chadi carrying our bags, two on each arm. 'Here, bro, that's Jackie's.' He does a handover with Mick, who thanks him, before helping his wife into their waiting Kluger.

'Okay, *ladies*.' Chadi grins at us, enjoying the state we're in. 'Ours will be here soon. I had to drive your car, Nic.'

'Let me guess,' I say. 'Your bright blue eyesore is still at Danny's?'

'Yeah, I get it back tomorrow.'

'*Inshallah ya Rab.* Are you sure you don't want anything else? Hydraulics, maybe? Wings to make it fly?'

'Very funny, cuz. Come on, get in.'

My car appears beside us. Chadi loads our bags into the boot then the two of us sit up front, with Layla and Monica already half asleep in the back. I put my window down and Chadi drives us home, staying in the right lane and only slowing for speed cameras. We're almost in my street when he nudges me. 'Hey, Nic?'

'Yeah?'

'You mind if I borrow your car tonight?'

There it is: the reason for all this arse-kissing.

'Man, *no way*. You're getting yours tomorrow; you can wait till then.' I take my keys from the cupholder and put them in my bag.

'Oh, come on, cuz, I'm desperate!'

'*Why?* What now?'

'I got a date.'

'With who?'

'This girl – she's really hot. And she's, like, *classy* and shit.'

'Oh, well I'm sure she'll just *love* your new ride.'

'Cuz, *please*. I only need it for tonight! And then I promise I'll never ask you again.'

'That's a lie and you know it.'

'I'll clean it for you! I'll drive you around, anything you want.'

'Wow. You really are desperate.'

'Cuz, *come on*.'

We're parked in the driveway now. I stare at him, not wanting to relent, but not having a good enough reason not to. We both know full well that after last night I won't be getting out of bed until tomorrow morning. 'Okay, *fine.*' I reach into my bag for the keys. 'But no fucking in my car, and no smoking either.'

'Okay, I won't. Second base only. Third base, max.'

'Nothing that involves the expulsion of *any* bodily fluid.'

'Well, what if I need to sneeze?'

'Oh, fuck off.'

'Okay, okay! I promise I'll be good.'

The keys are in my hand. We stare at each other and then I pass them to him. He leans across the console and hugs me, but when the two of us come apart, I have this reflex to reach for him again.

'You're coming back here, yeah?'

Chadi smiles, my arm on his. 'Yeah, of course I'm coming back.'

Chapter 28

It's 3 am and I've woken in a sweat.

I can't breathe.

I can't breathe.

I check my phone; nothing. I look out my window. My car's not back.

Where's Chadi?

I call him, there's no answer. I get up and start pacing.

I call Chadi again. Still no answer.

And then my phone lights up: *Number unknown.*

I swipe and say, 'Hello?'

* * *

I'm at the hospital but I can't remember how we got here. Dad drove us but I can't remember the car ride. I woke him up – I shook him so hard – I said, 'Dad, wake up!' But I can't remember getting here.

We run through the double doors into emergency. Uncle Jimmy is on his knees; he's screaming, 'MY SON! MY SON!' Aunty Faye is groaning to God. I've never seen her in so much pain.

And Layla. Layla's not saying anything. She's just hugging herself and staring at the floor.

I reach for one of the nurses; I pull her towards me. 'Where is he? *Where's Chadi?*'

And then my aunty answers me. She wails two words and my whole world stops.

'*He's gone.*'

* * *

Danny: 4 missed calls
Danny: 4 text messages & 2 iMessages
Are you at Westmead where are you
Just tell me where you are

Rita: 3 missed calls
Rita: 3 text messages & 1 iMessage
I'm with Nat we're coming now

Elie: 10 missed calls
Elie: 10 text messages & 1 iMessage
Babe what the fuck is going on!

Yasmine: 3 missed calls
Yasmine: 3 text messages & 3 iMessages
Is it true??
Please please please call me back
Nic I'm so sorry!

Dave $: 2 missed calls
Dave $: 2 text messages & 3 iMessages
So sorry for ur loss
Here wateva u need
He was a gud friend

Chapter 29

It was in the papers the next day: NEPHEW OF CAR YARD KING KILLED IN CRASH. And that was that. I could imagine the whole of Australia reading about my cousin and not giving a fuck. To them he was just another headline, another no-good Leb. But he belonged to us; he was *mine*. They didn't mention that in the news, though. They made an example out of him. At best he was a statistic, at worst a lawbreaker.

The cops said he ran a red light, drag-racing off the M2, and got swiped by a semi. They said he died at the scene. He was on his own, coming back to my house after his date *like I'd told him to do*. I think about Chadi taking his last breath and it makes me want to tear my heart out. I should've been there. I should've been there holding his hand.

'*Allah yerhamou.*'

'Sorry for your loss.'

'*Allah yerhamou.*'

We're in the church hall at St Maroun's. We've had three nights of condolences and the funeral is tomorrow. Our immediate family are lined up along the far wall, divided according to gender. The men stand and the women sit. There're hundreds of chairs facing us and most of them are filled. People come in, they walk past us, right hand on the heart to pay respect.

'*Allah yerhamou.*'

'Sorry for your loss.'

'*Allah yerhamou.*'

Then they sit in front of our family and watch us cry. There's a framed photo of Chadi on a table; he's smiling his rakish smile and it makes me feel sick. I'll never forget the image of my car, crushed beneath the bumper of that truck. Christ Jesus, help me, I'll never forget it.

Danny comes in with George and Gab. He was here last night, and the night before that, too. I don't look up; I just stare at the floor as they pass. He tried calling me when he heard about Chadi. He must've called me twenty times. But I haven't talked to anyone. I can't stand it; all those empty words – the same ones, over and over.

'*Allah yerhamou.*'

'Sorry for your loss.'

'*Allah yerhamou.*'

I look to my right, towards my family. Aunty Faye is leaning against Layla, weak from grief. We've been giving her Valium; without it, she won't stop wailing. They sit at the head of our line because they're the closest relations to Chadi. Then it's Tayta and Chadi's aunties, my mum, then me and my sisters. We're all dressed in black, no make-up, no energy. Every now and then Tayta starts screaming and beating her chest. She swears at Chadi in Arabic, then she sobs his name; calls him *habibi, ayouni. My love, my eyes.*

When I look around the rest of the room, there are so many faces. It always amazes me the people who show up when someone dies. Yasmine and Elie are third from the back. Rita, Nat and

Aunty Houda are up front. Gary and his wife Tess sit awkwardly to the side. I can see Linda and Shivani and Dave and Dee. Even Zena is here. It's everyone we've ever met all in one place, and I can imagine Chadi sitting next to me, saying, 'Who the fuck's that?' or, 'What's *he* doing here?' I've never been without him. I've always had him in my ear or on my arm. We had our birthdays together like twins. We were christened together. We'd go to weddings and funerals just like this and we'd share it. He should be here, standing with the men, *but he's not*. I think about all the time I've spent feeling sorry for myself, being sad because I was single or stuck at work, and I'm so *ashamed*.

God has taken my cousin, *he's taken my closest friend*, and I've realised much too late that I was *never without*, that I had everything I needed, until right now.

I stand up. 'I'll be back.'

My sisters look at me. 'Are you okay?'

'I'll be back soon.'

I walk past Danny, who's seated on the outer aisle, and I touch his shoulder. I don't stop; I just walk to the door. It's a warm night, but when I finally get outside, I feel relieved. I've been sitting in that hall so long, being watched by all those eyes. I just want to be alone.

I go to the other side of the church, to an empty walkway lit by a single light, and I take my time.

I close my eyes.

I breathe deep.

I open them.

And that's when I see him. He's just standing there like a ghost, and my heart seizes up. That face; those lips, those eyes.

It's Judas.

He comes forward from the shadows and kisses my cheek. For the first time in months, I say his name aloud.

'Adam.'

He hesitates, then, '*Allah yerhamou*, Nic. I know how close you were.'

'What are you doing here?'

'I came to see you. To pay my respects.' He looks towards the hall. 'I would've gone inside, but I know I'm not welcome.'

I just stare at him. I can't believe he's here, right here in front of me.

'You okay?' he asks.

I shake my head slowly. 'Not really.'

We stand there with only a metre between us. He used to be my first call; my *only* call. Now we're strangers. I search his face, trying to find the boy I knew, but he's changed. Even his clothes are different; preppy and polished. A sign of his girlfriend's taste.

'When I saw your car on the news, I thought you were in it too.' He glances away. 'I don't know – I just needed to see you.' There's something wrong about the way he says it; something selfish.

And it wakes me.

I start to get some blood back. I can feel my heart beating in my chest. Maybe he thought he could come here and get me at my weakest, that I'd be sad and vulnerable and caught off guard – and I am. I'm dying inside … *just not for him.*

'You're not here to pay respects. You're here 'cos you got scared. You're here for *you*.'

'Is that what you think?'

'I've been waiting months for you to miss me. Now I know I'd have to die first.'

He shakes his head. 'I knew you'd be like this.'

'Like *what*? Am I supposed to be happy to see you?'

'No. But I wanted – I mean, I thought we should talk.'

'Yeah, Adam, if you haven't noticed, I'm dealing with something real here.' I gesture at the church. 'Funny that you suddenly care.'

I go to walk around him, but he grabs my arm.

'You think it was *easy* for me? You think you're the only one who got hurt?'

I almost laugh. 'Yeah, you looked real hurt, Adam. You and your new missus.' I shrug him off, not liking the feel of his grip.

'You don't know what I went through. What people have been saying about me.'

God, is he really playing victim?

'You *dumped* me, you *cheated* on me. And now what? You want me, to feel *sorry* for you?'

He clenches his jaw. 'Nic, you knew it wasn't working.'

'You didn't even *try*.' I back away. 'All that time I was fighting for us, you'd already moved on.'

'So, it's my fault? Everything that happened, it's all my fault?'

I think about the fights we used to have. About the times I'd get angry over nothing. About the calls I wouldn't answer, the games I used to play. 'I wasn't perfect. But the way you left – I would never have hurt you like that.'

'I wasn't gonna stay, Nic. I wasn't happy.'

He says it like I'd failed to please him. Like I was a worthless, replaceable thing. He's right to say he wasn't happy; I was miserable too. But the saddest part about this whole fucking story is that I would've stayed. I would've chosen my worst day with him over *anything*. And so, I look at him. I savour him one last time: his deep-set eyes, his dark lashes, the curve of his jaw. It's a face I used to worship. I hold him there and I drink him in, and then I borrow some words from my dead cousin.

'You're a *dog*, Adam. You'll never get it.'

I start to walk away, but he's angry now. 'What the *fuck* did you call me?'

And I hesitate, not because I'm scared but because I can feel *him*. I can feel Chadi standing next to me, urging me to say the word like he did that day in the car. So, I say it again. Louder. *Stronger.*

'You're a *dog*. You talk about respect, but you stabbed me in the back! I was your *partner* – your *friend* – and you stabbed me in the back!'

He comes closer and puts his finger in my face. 'You be careful what you say.'

'Or *what*? You know, you're not very threatening in that stupid cardigan.'

He huffs a laugh. 'Wow, I almost forgot this side to you.'

'Yeah, you forgot a lot, by the looks of things. Like three whole years, to be exact. Of me *helping* you, and making *excuses* for you, and dealing with all your *shit*! But she gets roses, right? You've got time for her; *you drive her places*. In your new fucking car that *I* chose!'

He squares his shoulders. He shakes his head.

'What you did, it hurt me so much.' I can feel my face start to flood. 'You *hurt* me.'

I put my hand on my heart, willing him to wake: to see me the way he used to – that one summer the year before last, when the two of us were at our best. But he can't even look at me. He can't even look me in the eye.

'You're the weakest man I've ever met,' I tell him. 'You don't love that girl; you just like what she does for you. You're a fraud.'

He's angry again. But as he steps towards me, we hear someone calling my name from up the path.

'*Nic.*'

It's Danny. He doesn't say anything else, he just stares at my ex.

I look back at Adam, realising how wrong this all is. 'My cousin just died. I gotta *bury* him tomorrow. Don't show your face here again.'

Chapter 30

Chadi's funeral causes chaos in Punchbowl.

Hundreds of people come to St Maroun's to pay their final respects. Motorbikes are stationed at every street corner and most of the mourners have to park their cars blocks away. I stand in the middle of the road, staring down at my shoes. They're suede with a pointed toe. A serious shoe, a winter shoe. A shoe you wouldn't bother with on a day that feels like summer. My sisters stand beside me, all of us quiet, all of us dressed in black. We wait for the hearse. It stops near a driveway and, when I finally raise my head to look through its long back window, everything inside me falls to my feet.

When someone young dies – someone unmarried – the Lebanese honour their short lives with a wedding procession. It's supposed to be cathartic for the parents; a way to lay to rest all the dreams they had for their child. But it only makes everything worse. The men of our family lift my cousin's body and carry his white coffin all the way down Catherine Street to St Maroun's. There're wedding drums and white roses; people throw petals at his casket. Everything is sunny and bright. Aunty Faye walks ahead of the men, wailing and clinging to Layla. The rest of us follow like bridesmaids. It's the most harrowing, heartbreaking parade, and I almost die myself just being part of it.

The older women weep loudly, grieving the end of our line. It seems that even in death, the only thing they care about is that Chadi never got married. And I know he would've hated it. He would've hated having flowers and wedding drums; he would've wanted revving cars and pallbearers wearing Bulldogs jerseys.

I watch from the kerb as his coffin passes through the gates with Uncle Jimmy up front, shouldering the weight of his son. He cries behind a pair of dark glasses, his face drawn and peppered with week-old stubble. I have one arm around Monica and with the other I hold on tight to Jackie's hand. The drumming stops at the stairs. The casket edges into the nave. Inside, the pews are filled. The men lower the coffin onto a golden bier, their necks damp with sweat. We take our seats in the front row and, for the first time in days, I find myself sitting next to Layla.

'I'm here, Lay.'

She nods and squeezes my hand. I've never seen her nails so bad. I look at her pale face and her hair that hasn't been brushed, and I know it'll be a long time – a very long time – before she's ever herself again.

The chanting starts. We stand, we sit. We stand, we sit. Father Boutros prays. He flings incense at the crowd. The choir sings the liturgy in Aramaic; it's deep and drawn out. Dozens of flower arrangements sent by different families have been placed around the altar, but Elie's overshadows the rest. It's almost two metres tall, a thicket of white roses and bright blue buttercups, and it makes me love him that little bit more for remembering Chadi's favourite colour.

We stand again. Father Boutros flings more incense, and we cross ourselves. Then he comes to the pulpit to speak.

'Death is not the end.' His voice echoes against the walls. 'We only feel it is.' He looks down at an open Bible and gathers himself. 'When Lazarus was dying, his sisters sent word to Jesus for help. But Jesus didn't go to them right away. He waited, because He wished to perform a great miracle.' Father Boutros directs his gaze towards me and Layla and the rest of the women. 'When Jesus finally arrived, Lazarus was already dead. And his sisters cried, they said, "Lord, you are too late". But they were *wrong*. Jesus had come to raise their brother, to call him from the grave and give him *new life*.'

He pauses, turning again to the congregation.

'Still, it says in John that when Jesus got to the tomb, He wept. *Why?*'

He looks around for an answer.

'Why would Jesus mourn, knowing that in just a few moments Lazarus would live?'

The church is silent.

'Because,' the priest says, 'of His *human* heart.'

I close my eyes, feeling the ache of my own.

'Christ overcame death, but still He grieved. Not because He was afraid, not because it was the end, but because He understood the pain of separation.'

He talks on, and all the while I just stare at the coffin, trying make sense of it. How can someone be alive and real, and *reachable*, and then gone? I imagine Chadi sitting with his dad, making faces at me from across the aisle. I keep getting this reflex to text him, and then my heart breaks anew, realising that he won't reply; that he'll never reply again.

I miss him. I miss my cousin.

Another priest comes to the microphone. He talks in Arabic. He mentions our family by name, our village in Lebanon, and then he prays over my cousin's body. He says that Chadi has come here today a heavenly groom, to start a new life with his beloved God. But it's of little comfort for those of us in the front row.

When they finally lift his coffin, Tayta faints in the aisle, and Aunty Faye – who up till now had been groaning in agony – lunges over the top of her towards the casket.

'*Ya ebni, ya ebni!*' she howls. *My son, my son!* '*Oum, ya mama, oum!*' *Get up, son, get up!* She screams it like it's his last chance; like his body isn't mangled beneath its pearl-white lid. There's so much yelling and panic that by the time we load Chadi's coffin into the hearse, we're loading Tayta into the back of an ambulance as well. It splits the family in two: only half of us make it to the cemetery, with most of the women either rushing to meet Tayta at the hospital or remaining behind to console Aunty Faye.

But Layla and I stay close to our dads.

We ride in a limo to Rookwood Cemetery, our car one of many in a motorcade I can only describe as presidential. Leaning against his brother, Uncle Jimmy watches on with weak knees, as they lower Chadi's body into an unmarked plot. The priest prays for mercy one last time.

There are moments in life that age you, that wake you and shape you, and the sight of my cousin's coffin resting in the earth is one of them. *He's not yours,* says the open grave. *He never was.* And I can't argue. Not with a mouth like that, with those wide, serpentine jaws that have swallowed him whole.

But when the men approach one by one to throw dirt into his grave, I start to shake.

I say, 'We can't, Dad. We can't just leave him.'
The casket is almost covered. Uncle Jimmy groans.
Layla falls to the ground, cries, 'Chadi, where you going?'
And in the distance, I see Elie.
Weeping on his own.

Chapter 31

A week after the funeral Adam gets engaged. And I feel nothing.

These days, I'm up at night over worse things.

It's the dark before dawn, and Danny's waiting for me on his porch. I'd called him at 2 am after staring at my ceiling for three hours, imagining that I'd been buried in a box. When I finally dialled his number, I hoped to God he still slept with his phone on loud.

He answered on the second ring.

It's raining softly on the path. Bruiser paces as I come through the gate, but when he sees me in the light he lies down. I don't pat him; I'm tired. I walk up the stairs to stand with Danny in the doorway.

'You okay?'

I shake my head and start crying. He pulls me inside and holds me. The house is dark and dormant, except for his monitors and his muted TV. I cling to him, shuddering with grief and the seismic waves of aftershock.

'It's okay. I'm here, Nic. I'm here.' He leads me to the couch and covers me with a heavy blanket.

I put my face in my hands and I cry it aloud: *'He's gone.'*

'I know.'

'He's gone and he's not coming back.'

'I know, Nic.' He sits next to me and rubs my shoulders.

'I should never have let him take my car!'

'Don't say that.'

But it comes again in heavy sobs. 'You were right. I said yes too much and I should've said no! I knew it that morning – when I gave him my keys, I got the worst feeling!'

'It's not your fault.'

I shake my head. 'I just wanna go back. All I wanna do is go back.'

He holds me while I cry: ugly, messy, blind. I feel his arms around me, rocking me. He reaches for the tissues and wipes my face.

When I'm done, Danny lies me down on the couch beside him. 'Just rest, Nic.'

And so, I try. But when I close my eyes I can still see my cousin, sitting next to me in the car, taking the keys from my hand. Back and forth in an endless loop. *Okay, fine.* And I pass him the keys. *Okay, fine.* And I pass him the keys. *You're coming back here, yeah?* I grab his arm. *You're coming back here, yeah?* I grab his arm.

Yeah, of course, I'm coming back.

Yeah, of course I'm coming back.

Yeah, of course I'm coming back.

God, just make it go away.

Danny reaches for another pillow. I move closer to him.

I need to forget.

I put my leg between his legs, and I coax him. He turns to me, gently stroking my waist, and I slowly feed him my tongue. When he moans and rolls on top, I sink beneath the weight of him, feeling him hesitate as I start to cry. He whispers, *'You okay?'* But I keep on kissing him. '*Fuck, I want you,*' he breathes, but when I reach for his pants, he says, 'No.'

'What's wrong?'

'Nic, I can't.'

'*Why?*' I push him away. 'Is this about the other night?'

'What? *No.* It's not …' He shakes his head. 'I can't, Nic. Not now.'

He sits at my feet with his head back, breathing through his mouth, the side of his face and his heavy limbs silhouetted by a greyish glow. I watch him with my knees up and I realise that here, *tonight*, it's too much like Sarah. Danny won't have me, *not while I'm sad.*

I crawl across the couch and take his hand. 'It's okay,' I say. 'But I still need you.'

I feel his arms around my body, drawing me closer, keeping me safe.

'I need you too. I need you more.'

And we lie back down beside each other, with my ear on his heart as it lulls me to sleep.

* * *

'FUCK! Nic, get up!' Danny shoves me away and jumps to his feet.

My eyes spring open. I hear a loud bang, then another. It sounds like the house is falling apart.

'*Ayri bil huz!*' says Danny, cursing his luck.

'OPEN UP! POLICE!'

I follow Danny's gaze to the cameras, not sure if what we're seeing is real. His entire front yard is filled with cop cars and masked men. He grabs his phone. I hear the swoop of a sent text, and then he locks it. The door splinters off its hinges.

Danny moves to stand in front of me. 'Stay on the couch and keep your hands up, okay? *Put 'em up, Nic – do it!*'

I'm shaking, I have no voice. As soon as he sees my palms, he turns back. There's another bang – just one more – and then they're rushing into the room.

'GET ON THE GROUND! GET ON THE FUCKING GROUND!'

I recoil like a trapped animal. They force Danny to the floor and hold a rifle to his head. I pull my knees to my chest with my hands still raised. I shut my eyes; I can't breathe. Someone drags me off the couch; they twist my arm and I cry out.

'*Don't fuckin' touch her!*' Danny tries to reach me, but a heavy black boot stomps him flat. They put me on the carpet, and they cuff us both. A woman spreads my legs; she pats my body and my breasts. And the only stupid thing I can think is:

Thank God Danny said no.

Thank God I'm not naked.

Thank you, God.

There're others in the house; I can hear their voices. When I crane my neck, I see four more coming down the hall.

'Clear!'

The woman lifts me; she's tall and blonde with big arms. I'm back on the couch, still cuffed. There's a man in a dark grey suit standing over Danny. He crouches beside him.

'Daniel Lahood, you're under arrest. You have the right to remain silent; you have the right to a lawyer. Anything you say or do from this point will be used as evidence. We have a search warrant for your home.' The detective shows him his ID, then he holds a piece of paper in front of Danny's face. 'Any *guns* on the premises?' He says it mockingly.

Danny glares at him but he doesn't react.

One of the cops nods towards me. 'Who's your little friend?' It makes me sick, the way he says it.

Danny ignores him. He tilts his head and talks to me in Arabic. '*Laht ouli shi.*' *Don't tell them anything.* He says it calmly, knowing already I won't, but assuring me I don't have to: that they can't make me talk, and he won't make me part of it.

I nod, but I can't stop shaking, seeing him on the floor in his own home, in a place I thought was safe. '*Danny.*' I'm being pulled towards the door. '*Danny!*'

God, I can't lose him, too.

'It's okay, Nic. You'll be okay.'

But I don't fucking care about me.

'Take her outside!'

They shove me to the porch. I'm in socks, no shoes. In the grey dawn light I see the grass is still wet. I can't remember where I left my sneakers. Next to the door? Under the couch? I want to rub my eyes but I can't. I squeeze them shut and, when I open them again, I see Bruiser being dragged across the yard at the end of a catcher's pole. They're trying to cage him but he's too strong; his teeth are bared and frothed with spit. I'm worried they'll hurt him, so I say, 'Bruise. Bruiser.' He tugs towards me. 'Sit.' And he drops his arse on the ground.

'Well, that's a good boy.' I turn to see an Asian woman in plainclothes with a holster around her waist. 'I'm Detective Tan, from Homicide.' She shows me her badge.

'What's going on?'

'You're under arrest. You're wanted for questioning.'

'What for?'

'In relation to a murder.'

I stare at her; I look away.

'You don't have to say or do anything if you don't want to. Do you understand?'

I nod yes.

She recites the rest of my rights, same as what was said to Danny, and I don't say a word. I just grit my teeth and pray to God, and when she asks me what I'm doing here, I tell her I want a lawyer.

'You'll get one at the station.'

We walk together down the stairs, me in my white ankle socks. When I get to the footpath, I look around the street. The old man across the road stands silently on his porch – the all-seeing eye of Acacia Avenue – and he shakes his head. When one of the cops tries to move him back inside, he tells them in Arabic, *Your mums are cunts.* There are other neighbours watching – the lights and the noise have woken everyone up – and they peek from behind their curtains. I duck my head, hoping to hide myself, but when I get to the fence, I see a much bigger problem. There's a Channel 7 van with a satellite dish parked across the road and a news crew waiting at the kerb: a man with a camera and a reporter in a collared shirt.

Fuck.

I stop short at the gate, hunching my shoulders and pulling the other way.

Detective Tan turns to face me. 'Is there a problem?'

She says it as if I'm not standing in cuffs, with a carpet burn under my eye.

'Yeah, there is a bit. Why are there news cameras here?'

She answers with a smile. 'Your boyfriend's in a lot of trouble.'

I don't say anything else.

She draws my hoodie over my head, and I follow her across the THUG LIFE graffiti on the footpath and into a waiting car.

Chapter 32

I'm taken to Bankstown police station.

They drive down a ramp to the back entrance, where a uniformed cop pulls me from the car and guides me across the loading dock to an open door. One of them brought my sneakers and I wear them now with the laces removed; a precautionary measure in case I decide to neck myself.

Once we're inside, I'm led along a passageway with cement walls and white lights. Up ahead, a junkie is being dragged to a cell. I watch him kick and shout, 'Suck my dick you coppa dogs! Suck my dick!'

I don't belong here.

                                        I don't belong here.

My cuffs are removed and a sergeant named Gordon reads me my rights. He calls it a 'part nine' and shows me the form. There are seventeen points and I sit quietly as he recites them aloud: my right to a lawyer; my right to contact my family; my right to medical attention; my rights if I were Aboriginal. My right to an interpreter. My right to silence. All morning my rights have been repeated, and yet I've never felt more that I have none.

'Am I being charged with something?' I ask.

Detective Tan answers me. 'We just want to ask you some questions.'

'I told you already, I want a lawyer.'

Sergeant Gordon signs the form and then he passes it to me, so I can do the same. 'Do you have your own?'

'My family does. I need to call them.'

'Alright,' he says. 'Follow me.'

He takes me to a phone on a wall. I don't know what to do. Normally I'd call my father, but I know he'll be with Uncle Jimmy, and I can't bring myself to burden them. Sergeant Gordon clears his throat. I stand there staring at the cold metal buttons, until I have enough nerve to call the one other person who can help.

'Mum?'

'Where are you, Nicole? You didn't come home. I've been calling you all morning! What the hell is going on?'

'Mum! *Mum!*' I have to shout to shut her up. 'I need you to come to Bankstown police station. And I need you to bring a lawyer.'

The rest of the call is deafening. Sergeant Gordon watches me from behind – a silent, beer-bellied shadow. I hold the phone from my ear, and when I look at him, he gives me a sympathetic nod.

After I hang up, he puts me in a holding cell. It's fitted with a bench and the walls are made of thick, clear Perspex. I spend the rest of the morning sitting there on my own, scared shitless. Not because of the cops, but because I know my mother is on her way, and she's gonna fuckin' lose it.

Finally there's a knock on my cell wall. When I look up, my dad's lawyer, Adrian, is standing at the door with Sergeant Gordon and Detective Tan. Then someone else approaches; it's the detective who arrested Danny. A sandy-haired man with blue eyes and a mouth like an old wound. He stares at me in his dark grey suit, and my heart falls to pieces. If he's here, Danny must be here too; somewhere in the station, in one of these cages.

'Nicole, are you okay?' Adrian takes my arm.

'Yeah, just thirsty.'

He looks back at the rest of the group. 'Can someone get her some water, *please*!'

Gordon toddles off and the rest of us move to an interview room. Adrian puts his briefcase on the table.

'Adrian Costas.' My lawyer introduces himself and extends his hand to Grey Suit.

'Detective Andrews.'

Neither of them sit.

'We conducted a raid this morning on the home of a murder suspect and found Miss Najim on the premises. We have reason to believe she has knowledge of a killing committed in 2012.'

'And what reason is that?'

'Her close relationship with the suspect. Certain phone records …'

'Attained *legally*, I'm sure.'

Detective Andrews shifts his stance. 'Daniel Lahood is a known criminal; he's being charged with *murder*. We know he traffics guns. If your client knows anything – anything at all – it's better she says so now, or she'll be in trouble too.'

'As you're no doubt aware, my client is grieving the death of a family member. She's in no condition to submit to an interview.' Adrian puts his hand on my shoulder. 'We won't be answering any questions, detective. This isn't procedure; it's harassment.'

Detective Tan speaks up. 'We can still hold her for another few hours.'

'On what grounds? Are you pressing any charges?'

'We need to make further inquiries.'

'You do that, detective,' Adrian says. 'But no one speaks to my client without me being present.'

I'm returned to my cell. It's all a game; moving me from room to room, watching me through plastic walls, holding me as long as they can. They're trying to wear me out, but whatever I know about Danny, I'll never give it up. Not because I'm being ballsy, but because I can't; it'd be like knifing my own reflection.

At lunchtime they bring me a Big Mac meal, which I don't eat, and then they let me use the toilet. It's in a different cell, where the walls from the waist down are covered for privacy. I duck my head and squat, hovering above a squalid bowl.

'You done?' Detective Tan calls to me from the hall.

When I emerge from the toilet, Sergeant Gordon is there too, and he tells me I'm being released.

'Your mum's upstairs,' he says. 'She's pretty upset.'

Yeah, no shit.

As we walk towards the main reception, I can hear her voice, sharp and frantic.

'WHERE'S MY DAUGHTER? I WANT TO SEE MY DAUGHTER!'

I peer at her through the small window of a closed door, while she bangs her hand on the desk, refusing to move aside for anyone else. She's dressed for the occasion in a severe-looking blazer with military-style shoulder pads and a pair of black cat-eye sunglasses that she's worn as a sort of disguise. There're other people in the waiting area; a guy in a gym singlet with a bulging black ankle monitor and a few suits, including Adrian, who's trying to placate my mother.

When I come into view, she gasps. '*Ya Allah,*' she howls. 'LOOK AT HER! I'm going to *sue* this whole department! *Do you hear me? I'm going to sue!*'

I sidle past the counter towards Adrian, just as Detective Andrews appears from the corridor beside me. When he sees my mother at the desk and how deranged she is, I can sense him starting to scheme.

God, don't.

I try to move away, but he calls out, '*Miss Najim!* I suggest you have a good, hard think about what you're doing.'

The room falls quiet.

'Hindering a police investigation is a serious offence, and your *boyfriend* – or whoever he is – is the worst of the worst. If you've played any part in his dealings, *any part at all*, you'll be sorry.'

He's already said as much to me; he knows I won't budge. He's saying it now, *again*, because he wants to scare my mum. Fear, anger, shame: anything that'll force us apart. I turn to my mother, bracing myself. But she doesn't yell. She walks over to where I'm standing and raises her winged sunglasses, looking the detective dead in the eye.

'What's your name?'

He squares himself. 'Detective Andrews.'

'Detective, I didn't move to this country from a war zone to be intimidated by bullies like you. Be *very* careful. Me and my husband, we know a lot of people. You harass my family, and *ana behrouk dinak* for the rest of your life!'

He narrows his glare. 'Is that a threat?'

'So far as *this*: if you even *breathe* in my daughter's direction again, I'll rain hell on your whole department. Don't think you've found some girl – some vulnerable, *unfortunate* girl that you can *pick on*! Now you've caught another "Leb"!'

All of us are shocked; the guy with the ankle-monitor nods to himself, impressed.

'We're not even from here!' She seizes my arm. 'We live in Kenthurst, for God's sake!'

* * *

I collect my bag and my missing shoelaces. I stuff them in my pocket and then I follow my mother from the station.

'*YALLAH!*' She crosses the road, her car chirping on approach. '*Get in.*'

I pull the door open, and we sit in silence. It's stifling, but she doesn't start the engine.

I need air.

I've gone from one prison to another, except this time I'm trapped in smaller space, preparing for a worse interrogation. The seconds tick by, I stay quiet. All of a sudden, Mum starts crying. It's not what I expected. She wraps her arms around my neck, and I start crying too.

'You *idiot*! I was so worried!'

'I know, Mum. I'm sorry.'

'I've been up all night! Are you okay?' She draws away, takes in the graze on my face, then she pulls me close again.

Sometimes in life, you find healing in the strangest places. Like on a side street in Bankstown, wearing yesterday's undies. I hold on to my mother, feeling her relief, and it adds to my own. I know she's not perfect. I know she never dresses right, and she says ugly things. I know she's rude and selectively pious; a meddler, a critic. But, whether I've liked it or not, I can't remember a time when she wasn't there. Rubbing my back when I was sick. Cooking dinner.

Taking us to school. And soccer. And dance class. Always wanting 'the best' for her daughters, 'only the best'. And always telling the truth. Even if I didn't see things the same way.

Even if it came with a flying shoe.

She strokes my hair, needing comfort herself, and I remember what Father Boutros said about love. About laying down your life for others. And I realise it's not just about men. It's about family, and friends, and even strangers. About giving love to people and expecting nothing back. It's about motherhood, and my mum, sacrificing herself every day, for someone else, *forever.*

It's a thousand degrees in this fucking car, but I hold on. I hold her tight because I know that the peace of this moment won't last.

And of course, it doesn't. She pulls away, pushes the ignition and wipes her face.

'What did I tell you? *Don't spend time with that boy!* And now look! What a *jirrseh*!'

I angle the vents and ready myself for the coming crescendo.

'No one ever listens to their mother!'

* * *

As soon as I get home I start looking online for news reports on the raid. There's a write-up about an early morning police operation in Greenacre in which *a man, 28, and a woman, 26, were taken for questioning.* That's me; that's all they said. *A woman, 26.* It's both a relief, and a coming to terms. I sit staring at my phone, and I realise that whether I feel my age or not, whether I *feel* like a grown woman or not, the fact is, *I am.*

There's not much else online – it's just the same scant details repeated on different sites – so I go and shower. I change my clothes;

I try to eat. I go through the motions of a normal afternoon, but by the evening my guts have gone. I quickly shower again, and then, with my lights off in my room, I watch the news. I watch it on every channel. They're still running stories about Salim Mehajer: what he's posted online, where he's been, his divorce proceedings. And I think, *How the fuck does he do it?* I'm a footnote in a fifty-word article and I can barely breathe.

MULTIPLE RAIDS IN SYDNEY'S WEST.

The headline spins and my heart stops.

There's footage of Bruiser barking from the back of a van, and a uniformed cop standing against a banner of blue police tape. Then I see George and Gab from behind, pinned down at Danny's garage. There're other places too: homes and shops I've never seen. Different yards and streets and people, all linked to my friend; a man I know better than anyone, but who I also know nothing about.

'The police are calling this morning's raids a crackdown on Middle Eastern crime. There are several suspects in custody, with charges ranging from money laundering and arms trafficking to homicide …'

I watch as his other life is laid out on pavements all over Sydney. It writhes and barks and bares itself in the heat, a terrifying, mutating beast.

'Strikeforce police officers have seized dozens of firearms, eleven stolen vehicles and vast amounts of cash. The alleged ringleader, twenty-eight-year-old Daniel Lahood, was arrested at his Greenacre home this morning, also charged with the 2012 murder of gangland associate –'

I fall to my bed. I can see him. He's standing with his hands behind his back. They've blurred his face, but I know it's him; the way he stands, his t-shirt, his tatts. They show a mug shot of the murder victim and then Danny again, in the loading dock at Bankstown police station. Detective Andrews talks to the media backed by bags of evidence. He says they've taken a dangerous man off the streets.

And maybe they have.

Danny is a criminal. Danny deals guns. Danny runs a crime syndicate, with cells and safehouses all over Sydney. But, as hard as I try, none of it makes me hate him. It just makes me sad, and sorry, and grateful. Because I'm seeing for the first time how deep it all ran; how dark his life must've been. And how he'd kept it all away from me.

For as long as he could,

from when we were kids,

he kept it separate from us.

I watch the rest of the report, hoping, *praying* that they keep me out of it. And you know what? *They fucking do.* I survive the whole minute without a single mention. They don't say my name, they don't even show me with my jumper draped over my head. And I take a silent, selfish moment to thank God that I haven't embarrassed my dad.

I can hear my mum in the next room watching the same report, waiting to see how ruined I am. When the anchor rolls to the next story, she yells '*Ya Rab!*', relieved to be cleared of an unfixable scandal.

I turn the TV off, I'm exhausted.

There's a numbness in my arms and in the cavities of my chest. I breathe out, willing myself to accept the gaping spaces.

My cousin's dead.

Danny's in jail.

I try to make sense of the loss. I think back; a month, two months, a year.

It all fell away so fast.

I wish I could've known.

I would've spent my time much better, with the men I loved the most.

* * *

Fri 03/11/2017 8:09PM

Dear Nicole,

Thank you for your application. We are pleased to inform you that you have been accepted into Bronwyn Farley's mentorship program for Semester 1 of 2018. Please see attached information package and enrolment form.

Congratulations!

The Bronwyn Farley School of Photography

And then a personal note:

Nicole – the photos you submitted were some of the best I've received in a while. Your story was simply told, but so insightful.

You have an eye for the truths around you and, more than that, you have shown me in your work that you have an honesty and an understanding about yourself.

Looking forward to meeting you,

BF

Chapter 33

I haven't heard from Danny; no one has. I called Sarah after I watched the news; she said her uncles were over. There was yelling and crying in the background. It sounded like another house in mourning, another life lost.

My lawyer told me to keep to myself. He said the cops didn't have proof of hinderance, but they might try to use me later as a way to weaken Danny. Because they know I mean something to him. They know we're close enough that I slept at his house. They know his pit bull does what I say. They'd have photos and phone logs and all types of shit, and while none of that proves anything, it's enough to know that the man they've locked up – the person at the centre of their whole case – really gives a fuck about me.

It's been a week since I received my acceptance email from Bronwyn, but I haven't told anyone about it. Mainly because the two people I'd most want to tell are gone. It hurt me just to read that email; to think of all the photos I took and the memories hidden within them. Everything feels haunted; everything is seen through the long-range lens of hindsight and loss. I remember sitting with Chadi in Granville. I remember him looking at his watch and saying I only had three weeks to get my photos together. And the thought of it makes me shake. Because even though we had no idea at the time, Chadi only had three weeks, too.

With Danny, I'd had some warning at least; I was prepared for the possibility that he would be taken away. But the death of my cousin – the *loss* of him – eclipses everything.

* * *

'I can't believe tonight would've been my *laylieh*.' Monica sits beside me, while Jackie nurses Ava on the other lounge.

'I know.'

'I can't believe he's not here. I just can't believe it.' She holds tight to a used tissue, her face still damp.

I look out to the yard, to where her marquee would've been. Monica and Luke had to cancel the wedding. The Maronite church has a forty-day mourning period, which means that for the next month or so no one in our family can do anything except sit around and be sad.

And it suits us just fine.

'You know what I can't believe?' says Jackie, looking at me. 'That you bloody got arrested.' She shakes her head while she burps Ava. 'Jesus, what a shocker. And you of all people.'

Monica shakes her head too. 'Does Dad know yet?'

'I think so.'

We never actually spoke about it, but the morning after everything happened, I woke to find him sleeping on the chair beside my bed. When he finally stirred and looked at me, he said, 'Don't worry, Nic. I won't let anything happen to you.' And then we both fell asleep for another hour.

'Well, I hope Danny's okay,' says Jackie. 'I heard Gab got out; maybe Danny will too.'

I look at her. 'Sorry, what?'

'Didn't you know?'

'*No.*'

'Oh. Yeah, Rita told me yesterday. Reckons she heard it at the salon.'

Of course. I swipe my phone and call Rita on speaker.

'Hey, Nic.'

'Hey, mate, I'm with Jackie – she just told me Gab got out?'

'Yeah, he did. That idiot with the eyebrows reckons he's on home detention. She heard his aunty telling Houda at the salon. Apparently he's back at his mum's and he's been really upset.'

'Did anyone else get out? Did George?'

'Nah, just Gab. Makes sense, I guess. They were saying since he's only been out for a month, he couldn't have got up to much.'

But I know that's bullshit. Gab was always with Danny; I even saw him at that meeting in the garage that night.

You have an eye for the truths around you.

'Alright, I'll call you later.'

I hang up the phone, frowning. This isn't the first time Gab's had the benefit of an early release. When I look at Monica, I see my own cynicism reflected in her dark features.

'I think it stinks,' she says.

'Me too.'

'Well, what are you gonna do about it?' Jacqueline stares at us. 'Carry out street justice?' She's still tapping Ava on the back.

'No, but –'

'You're not a gangster, Nic. These boys, they're all fucked. And I know you care about Danny, but none of this shit is your problem. Let them sort it out between themselves.' She puts Ava in a bouncing bassinette. 'You're the only one of us that still has these ties to our old neighbourhood. And maybe it's time you cut them off. You don't belong there anymore. Maybe you think you do, but you don't. Danny and Gab and all those boys, they're different now. The best thing you can do is stay away.'

It's the same sound advice that I'd got from my lawyer. And up until a minute ago I would've agreed. All this time I've felt like an outsider, never at home in The Area the way I used to be. I've stood by silently while the men in my life made a mess of things, somehow thinking they had the right.

But they don't.

You have an honesty and an understanding about yourself.

I couldn't save my cousin. He's buried now; there's nothing I can do. But I won't make the same mistake with Danny. I won't let him ruin his life and my life, too.

I look at the sky outside, slowly fading to dusk. And I realise that, after all this time, I'm still the middle link. Same as when we were kids, with my house between Danny's and Gab's, at the top of our street. I think about Danny; about the look on his face when they cuffed us on the ground.

And I can't leave him there.

'Monnie, do you mind if I borrow your car?'

I have to go back to where it all began.

I have to go back to the start.

Chapter 34

I pull up to the kerb at Amber Way. I haven't been back here since we moved.

Most of the houses have changed, but there's still those familiar three, right at the end of the cul-de-sac: Danny's house, my house and Gab's. We all sold up except for Gab's mum. I can see her porch lit up and her blinds pulled down. I sit in the dark, gripping the wheel to stop my hands from shaking. Being here strips me to my core: to a time and a place where I had everything and everyone, and my world was only three blocks wide.

I know Gab's house is being watched. There's a car parked across his driveway: an unmarked Holden with a monstrous antenna. I look at my Nav as if I'm lost, and then I do a U-turn out of the cul-de-sac and drive to the local reserve behind our old houses.

We used to jump Gab's fence to get here instead of walking around the block. When I think about those days, I only remember summer. It feels like the nineties was just a decade of Decembers: of hot nights and choral cicadas. Of dancing across black tar, barefoot, firewalking to my friends' houses. Of bindies, and dandelions, and warm water running through the hose, turning cold and crisp. I loved those years. They were so simple.

But it's late now.

There's a chill in the air, a ghost-like stillness all around. I stand in the dark, wondering what to do. I know if they catch me, I'm fucked. They'll charge me, they'll noose my neck with accusations. But when I think about Danny being locked up, I feel less and less like I've got something to lose.

So, I walk. I cross the reserve to the back of Gab's yard. The grass is long and wet, and it licks at my ankles with every step. I don't know if he's there, but there's a floodlight homing me forward. I creep closer, until my hands are touching the fence. And when I peer through the wooden slats, I see exactly what I came for. He's sitting under the washing line with a bottle of Chivas and a cigarette. Just as he goes to ash it, I call his name.

'Gab.'

He freezes up. 'Gab, it's Nic.'

He stands and walks to where I'm waiting, one of his hands now pressed against mine, with only the fence between us. He peers through the crack, searching for my face in the shadows.

'Nic?' He's drunk.

'Yeah.'

'Nic, you gotta go. Get outta here.' His breath hangs hot.

'What did you do?'

He shakes his head, then he hides behind one of the slats. 'Nothing, Nic. Just go.'

I can see him start to move away, so I speak up. 'They got Danny, Gab.'

He comes back, defensive. 'I don't know nothin' 'bout that.'

'Yes, you do.'

I can see his face again; he's squeezing his eyes shut.

'They took our friend, Gab; they took him away.'

'They had him already.'

It's the closest I'll get to a confession, and I know I haven't got long. I think back to those summers, to the three of us together. I need to say something that'll bring him back. *Something true.* I need to remind him of who we are; of who he was.

'You remember when we were kids, we'd play here at the park?'

He nods; he's tired. I can see the glass bottle, hanging at his side.

'Remember that ranger came after us?'

God, it was scary. We were chased by an angry old man in a high-vis vest. Danny and Gab gave me a leg up, but then the two of them got trapped, stuck on the wrong side of the fence. I remember watching them, pressed against the wood like I am right now. 'It was you, Gab. You graffitied the swing set.'

I can hear his breathing; I can smell the booze.

'But Danny copped the blame. 'Cos Danny wouldn't dob.'

He lets out a staggered sigh.

Then I say it, calm as I can. 'You dobbed on Danny.'

He sniggers in the dark. 'Poor Danny. Always pussy-whipped over you.'

God, he doesn't get it.

I go again, this time really saying his name. 'You *ratted*, you flipped on *Danny.*'

He goes quiet. He doesn't even breathe. I'm waiting, wondering if he'll speak. Then he whispers, 'I couldn't stay there no more. Couldn't take more time.'

I come closer. 'So, what? You put your friend there instead?'

'Go away.' There's a break in his voice; the bottle slips from his hand.

'Gab, you've gotta take it back.'

'GO AWAY!'

A door swings open behind him. Someone shouts, '*Oi!*'

I turn and start running to my car – across the grass, through the trees – hoping I've said enough.

There's a heaviness in my chest and my throat is tight. I keep running; I'm running for my life. What we started here, the three of us, that innocent friendship – it's over.

I get to the end of the park, feeling it's smaller somehow. And even though I'm gone, even though I'll never come back, I can still hear Gab, sobbing through the fence.

'Go away.'

Chapter 35

Rookwood Cemetery sprawls out over a whole suburb. It's the largest necropolis in the Southern Hemisphere, and it's right here in Sydney's West. Over a million people have been buried or cremated at Rookwood, which means that almost every wog who ever lived in this town is laid to rest in this place. It's divided into denominations; you've got the Italians in the Roman Catholic section with their big mausoleums, and the Greeks and the Russians in the Orthodox plots. There're the Muslim graves with Arabic headstones, and the Jews with their six-pointed stars. I walk between the rows, looking at photos and flowers and burning candles. I can't believe we all end up here. Our worries, our fears, our dreams; everything we hold in our hearts gets buried in dirt.

I find Chadi with all the other Lebanese, in the same section as Aunty Lou. I take a moment at her tombstone and then I go find my cousin. His grave is fresh, marked only with a white wooden cross. I haven't been back since the burial, but I can tell Aunty Faye's been here. The mound on his grave has been clawed at. She must've tried digging him up.

I smooth the dirt, then I sit at his feet, and I cry.

'Cuz, I miss you.' I put my hands on his grave and I say it again: '*I miss you.*' There's no one around so I talk to him out loud. 'I wish you were here. So much shit has happened; I really need you.'

I take the set of keys from my pocket and put it on his grave. 'Your car's finally finished. I've been driving it around 'cos mine's gone. I bet you're laughing at me, now that I'm stuck with it.' I sniff and wipe my face. 'Anyway, I brought you the spares, in case you wanna go for a cruise sometime.'

I stare at the dirt until I can't anymore; until my eyes fill to the brim, and I'm blinded. I lay my hands on the earth and I sob it out. 'You said you'd come back. You hugged me and you said you'd come back.'

It was a lie, and I hate him for it. I try to remember that day; I try to remember his face and his hands, and the way he said those words. Before, I wanted to forget. I wanted the memory of it erased, because it hurt too much, and it felt too real. Now all I want is to keep him clear in my mind. But when I close my eyes, the sharper details – the exact colour of his shirt, the few freckles he had on his face – they're already starting to fade.

I sit there, praying in the hot sun. And when I'm done, I go back to his stupid blue car and I cry some more. If it were up to me, I wouldn't move. I'd put the seat back and stay here for the rest of the day, just knowing he's close. But I promised Layla we'd go for lunch. She called me last night and insisted on it – the one person I can't say no to.

I start the car and drive along a narrow lane, passing hundreds of granite graves. When I get to the main gate I stop, as if I'm stuck on the border of two worlds. Everything behind me rests. This new day, the rushing traffic – it means nothing to the dead.

But I rejoin it. I take my foot from the brake and ease around the bend, back to the land of the living.

And it's loud.

There're trucks and horns, and the thrum of bass. I follow the highway past Greenacre until I get to Canterbury Road. I'm waiting to turn at the lights when a call comes through on my phone. I look at the blue-lit dash; it's a private number. I let it ring and then I answer.

'*Hello. You are receiving a call from Goulburn Correctional Centre. This call will be recorded and may be monitored. If you do not wish to receive this call, please hang up now.*'

There's some static and then the sound of Danny's voice. 'Hey, Nicky.'

'Dan!'

'We got a story for our kids, huh?' He's smiling, I can hear it.

'You're a dick! I've been so worried; I got scared you wouldn't call.'

'I know, I'm sorry. I've been dying to hear your voice, but I never get the phone. All I been talking with are fuckin' lawyers.'

'Are you okay? Are they getting you out?'

He goes quiet, then he says, 'They will. It'll be a while, but I'm not worried.' He never is. 'How about you – are you okay?'

'Yeah.' The light goes green, I turn left.

Danny lowers his voice. 'I'm sorry, Nic. I can't get it out of my head, the way they grabbed you. The whole time they were charging me, I didn't care. I kept thinking about you and if you were scared.'

'It's alright; I'm alright. I was more worried about my mum.'

I meant it as a joke, but he sighs. 'Fuck, she must hate me.' Then he says, 'It's your birthday today.'

I say nothing. I've been dreading it; wanting it to pass without mention.

'I know it hurts, Nic. I wish I was with you. That's the only thing that's killing me.'

My throat tightens. I take a slow turn into a side street and park by the kerb. When I close my eyes, the tears spill over. 'I've never had one without him. I just miss him so much.'

When we were kids, Chadi would say our birthdays were only 'one sleep' apart. Now, for the rest of my life, we'll always be only one sleep apart.

Danny breathes down the phone. 'Fuck, I'm sorry. I just wish I was there.'

We sit for a while, then I say, 'I want to come see you soon.'

'No.'

I lean on the wheel. 'Why not?'

'What do you mean why not? Imagine your parents find out.'

'They won't.'

He kisses his teeth. 'It's too far.'

'I don't care, I like driving. And I got a new ride.'

'*Nic.*'

'*Danny.* Are you really going to say no to me on my birthday?'

There's some thinking; some static. 'Fuck, alright,' he says. 'But no cleavage.'

I roll my eyes. 'That was *one time.*'

His voice becomes playful. '*Man*, I couldn't *wait* to get you on that desk.'

'*Stop it.*' I laugh. 'Don't they listen to this shit?'

'Fuck 'em.' There's a grin in his voice. 'Tell me what you're wearing.'

I'm smiling, but it fades. I think back to that night at his office – how I walked out, and how we might've lost our only chance.

'You okay, Nic?'

I can't speak.

He says softly, 'What's wrong?'

I sniff and breathe, my voice breaks. 'I shouldn't have left that night. I don't know what gets in my head. It was so dumb and now you're gone. I just feel like I ruined it.'

'Nic, you haven't ruined anything, okay? Me and you, it's not your fault.' Then he says, 'Come up next week. There's some things I gotta tell you.'

I go quiet. 'What thi—'

Click.

The call ends. And I realise I'll have to get used to it.

It's all we've got now: *six minutes.* We used to sit on his couch for hours and now I'm racing against the clock, trying to pour my heart out in the same time it takes to boil an egg. The screen's gone back to the map and all I can do is wait. He could call again today, or tomorrow, or in a week. And there's nothing I can do. I think about the last thing he said, and I wonder what he wants to say.

He never tells me too much, only what he has to.

Always choosing his moment.

He's smart like that.

Chapter 36

Goulburn Correctional Centre is a two-hour drive from Sydney. When I called to book my visit, the woman on the phone told me I had to be there by 8 am. She said they're very strict on time, so I set my alarm for five, and left my house at dawn.

The roads are clear, and the sky is a glowing pink. I'm getting used to driving Chadi's car, even though the engine sounds like a jet, and there's a half-pack of condoms in the glove box. I think when people die, we start seeing them in a different way; as not being *human* anymore. And maybe they're not. But Chadi was never a saint. He was a boy like any other – fun and dumb and flawed – and I loved him for it.

The freeway feels endless. I try to prepare myself for seeing Danny, but everything I know about prison comes from the movies. And this isn't a movie. It's a supermax jail, built in the middle of the bush, for serial killers and paedophiles and terrorists.

When I finally get to Goulburn, there's a black-and-white sign that says VISITORS CAR PARK. I roll past the gate and reverse into a space, with my bumper backed to the grass. The wilderness thrums around me; a blistering thirty-six degrees, as if the town itself were a pit stop on the way to hell.

And I guess for some it might be.

I crane my neck to see a red-bricked tower with a burly guard, watching the grounds below. He's holding a rifle that looks as if it could shoot down a plane. My stomach drops. I get out of my car and walk to the visitors' entrance. It's a demountable office surrounded by gates and uniformed staff with sniffer dogs. Once I'm inside, a woman with a taser tells me to take off all my jewellery and put my valuables in a locker. I don't have much and I was careful to dress down. I've got my hair pulled back in a ponytail, and I'm still wearing black for my cousin.

There's a machine that exchanges cash for tokens and we're told to buy a few. It's the only 'money' we can bring to the jail. I join the queue and wait, checking out the other visitors. Some are what you'd expect: a young mum with an eyebrow ring and three screaming kids, a few bearded Lebs and a white guy wearing a death metal tee. But then there are others. I see an older couple, well-dressed with tired eyes, and a disabled teen accompanied by a carer. It's the strangest group I've ever been a part of.

Once I've bought my tokens, an officer gives me a form to fill out. I write down all my details, including the make and registration of the vehicle I drove here. BULDOG.

When I'm done, I'm directed to a window where a woman takes my form and checks the information I've written against the details on my driver's licence. My eyes and my fingers are scanned, then she slides my paperwork and my ID back to me. I think it's over, but it's not. I'm taken to another building, where I'm told to remove my shoes and then I'm ushered between three different security checks – a body scan in a glass box, a metal detector and then a hand-held wand. The form I filled out follows me through each step, until I'm told to present it at another window. The man behind the counter goes over all my details, before looking at me quizzically. '*Buldog*?'

I cringe. 'Yeah.'

He slides the papers back to me. 'You must be a Doggies fan. They didn't do too well this year.'

I nod. 'I know, they're shit.'

He smiles and points me in the direction of the toilet. 'You better go now, 'cos you can't go later.'

I do what he says.

After a while, the guards lead us through a metal door into a glass-walled room. Only a few of us are allowed to enter at a time – it's me, the Lebs, the older couple, and the guy in the Slipknot tee. Our eyes and fingers are scanned again, and once the whole group's been rechecked, we're moved to the next room for a final wanding.

It's only now – after an hour of processing – that we arrive at the last station: a waiting area with a vending machine. The other visitors start buying snacks and, under the supervision of several guards, they empty their chips and chocolate onto paper plates. It's all we're allowed to bring for the men inside. When I reach the front of the queue, I realise I have no idea what I should get Danny. I'm starting to panic when I see those shiny red wrappers – our childhood favourite – tucked at the end of the bottom row.

I put in all my tokens and buy as many KitKats as I can.

There's a guard at the entrance of the visiting area. He says, 'No touching. You get a kiss hello and a kiss goodbye. That's it.'

I step through the door into a large concrete room. There are stools and round tables, all of them bolted to the floor. I keep walking, I'm shaking. I've got both hands clutching my paper plate and I don't know where to go.

'Table one.' A female guard points to the far corner.

And I see Danny.

He's standing at the wall in a white jumpsuit. I rush to him, dropping the KitKats on the table and jumping into his arms. He hugs me tight; I'm crying. I grab his face and I kiss him. He holds my wrists for a moment, and then he pushes me away.

'Nic, we can't.' He shakes his head. 'They'll tell you to leave.'

I look around; the guards are watching us. I say, 'I'm sorry – I just miss you.'

'I know, Nic, I know.' He leads the way to the table. 'Come.'

I wipe my face. We sit side by side as he drags the paper plate between us. He takes a KitKat and snaps it in half, then he says, 'Just like old times.'

'Not really.'

Danny slides the plate towards me. 'You okay?'

I take a KitKat for myself. Then I glance at the guards and the other inmates. 'I don't know. Are you?'

'*Nic*,' he scoffs. That's all he says, but the meaning is clear: in this place, in any place, he holds his own. 'How's your family, your sisters?'

'Yeah, they're good. Monica moved her wedding. I think this time next year.'

'It'll still be hard. I hope it's nice for her, though.'

'Me too.'

'What else has been happening? How's your photos?'

'Yeah, good. I got into a course.'

He beams at me. '*You did?* That's so good, Nic. *Mabrouk*.'

I smile back at him, trying not to cry. 'Have you made any friends?'

He laughs. 'Friends? Yeah, sure – we get together, watch the footy.'

'Shut up.'

We stare at each other a while, then he lowers his voice and says in Arabic, 'Did you hear about Gab? Just say yes or no.'

My hands go numb. Gab overdosed last week. They found him in the park, sitting on the swings with a needle in his arm. He might not make it.

I tuck my hair behind my ear. 'No.'

Danny shakes his head. 'I told you before I know when you're lying.'

'What do you want me to say?'

He sighs and touches my finger. A guard moves towards us. He pulls his hand away.

'Sarah said you been checking on her,' he says. 'Calling her and that.'

'Yeah, all the time.'

'Thanks, Nic. I mean it. You being there; it takes a lot of stress off me.'

'I know.' I stare at him now, relaxing enough to take him in. His beard and his hair have been trimmed, and he's put on size. 'You're looking good.'

He smiles, showing off his prison scrubs. 'Well, I knew you were coming so I wore something special.'

There's a little lock at the back of his neck; I felt it when I hugged him. 'What's that?'

He reaches for it. 'It's to lock the zip. You know – in case you try to slip me a knife.'

Just looking at it chokes me. I remember what he said to me at his garage that day, about living without rules. And now the pitiful, ironic reality of where it's got him.

'How long, Danny? And no more jokes.'

He hears the anger in my voice; he won't look at me. He breaks off another piece of KitKat. 'I don't know.' He's silent for a moment, then he says, 'I won't go to trial for another year. A year at least.'

I cradle my head in my hands, both palms pressed to my temples. 'I just want us to leave. I want you come with me now and I'll drive us home.'

He looks at me, his eyes like open wounds. 'You know how hard it is to sit here and see you like that? And I can't even touch you. I can't even be a man and touch you.' He shakes his head and draws away. 'That's why I let you come here, to this fucking ugly place. 'Cos you needed to see it; you needed to see how fucked it is.'

'What are you saying?'

'I'm saying I can't be anything real to you. Not anymore.'

'Is this your way of telling me to piss off?'

'*Nic.*'

'Do you think I'd just forget about you? Is that what you'd do to me?'

He puts his head down. 'I don't want you waiting, okay? If you wait, you'll waste your life.'

'You're my best friend, Danny. Before anything else, that's who you are. *Ana w'inta ma fina net farak.' Me and you, we can't be broken.* 'Even now, even with you locked up in here.'

He stays silent; a minute's worth that feels like a month. Then he says, 'Nicky, remember when we first met?'

I don't answer, I can't think. We would have been kids; four years old, maybe five.

'You were wearing a yellow dress, and you smiled at me.' He reaches across the table, our fingers almost touching. 'We were at a birthday party; you had your face painted. A purple flower on your right cheek. You were just a baby, Nic. We both were. But I been in love with you a long time. I had so many chances,' he says. 'So many windows over the past few years, but I wasn't brave enough.'

It's hard for me to see him that way – as someone who was afraid – because in my eyes, he's never faltered.

'You been my whole world for so long. Any chance I got to be close to you, I took it, even when we were kids. Even if it was just a walk to the park. And I waited for a sign, you know? Some small sign that you wanted me – a touch or something – but you never did. I guess maybe you were waiting on me, too.'

Danny looks down at our hands on the table. 'I wish I married you,' he says. 'I wish I did the right things. I wish we had a house and a baby, and I could watch movies with you every night.' He smiles to himself at the thought of it. 'But when you moved away, I became someone else, and I couldn't see an out. I thought I was doing the right thing. I thought that dickhead would be better for you.' He stops and flexes his jaw. 'I should've stepped up, but I didn't. You deserve someone better than me – someone *good*. A man who can give you a life, and some kids, and a nice wedding. Someone you can be proud of, and not have people talk.'

His hopes for me, they make me feel small. Months ago, those were the things I wanted. I used to cry to him all the time about not being married. But now I'm on a different path. One with some perspective. I think back to before Adam; back before Danny did his first shady deal. And if I could, I'd turn the clock to save us both. I think about us as kids, how happy we were, and I shake my head.

'No,' I say. 'The person I really deserved was you.'

We stay like that for the next few hours, not really speaking. The two of us coming to terms. I know he's not getting out. I know it deep in my gut; a dark cavern, lit only by the smallest ember of denial. And I know he knows it too. That maybe what we were is all we'll ever be. Just a couple of kids from Amber Way.

Two best friends.

With a fence between us.

Chapter 37

The SOLD sign went up on Tayta's front lawn yesterday. I stand on her driveway and stare at it, at the word in bold, and the grinning face of some oily agent with fake white teeth. I didn't think it would hurt this much; after everything I've been through, I thought I'd be numb. But it makes my lungs feel like lead.

Not just because I'm losing a home, but because I see it as a sign of defeat.

Tayta has given up.

She lost her purpose the day Chadi died: her hope that our name and her husband's legacy might live on in this house.

In her mind now, there is no point keeping it.

I climb the stairs to her front door and let myself in. The stove is cold. There are no simmering pots, no welcoming aroma. I can hear the TV, so I turn from the kitchen, stopping short at what I see across the room. Tayta's shrine has a new photo. My cousin smiles at me from a silver frame placed beside the picture of Aunty Lou, and it's the second time today that I feel my heart sink.

When I get to the lounge, I'm surprised to find Tayta sitting in Jidou's chair, taking comfort in its worn-out arms. I've never seen her sit there in my life.

'Hi, Tayta.'

'*Ayni.*'

I bend to kiss her, and she holds me close.

'It's okay, Tayta,' I say. 'I'm here.'

She nods into my neck, her breathing shallow. 'I sad.'

'I know. Me too.'

We pull apart and I sit beside her.

'You friend, he nice man. When he come here and meet with the builder, I no think they say yes. But they do – they pay a lot.'

She's talking about Dave. He had offered to help with the negotiations, and so I let him. I watched as he stood on the porch and pressured the agent, knowing that a property like this – so pivotal to the whole development – should be sold for much more than the million they'd offered. In the end, Tayta's three-bedroom, red-brick house broke property sales records in Bankstown.

I say, 'Yeah, he is nice. He was Chadi's friend, too.' Then I take her hand. 'Tayta, are you sure you want to live with Aunty Mary? You can always come stay with us; you know we'd love to have you.'

'*Khalili albik,*' she says. 'I sure. I have friend here, I have church. What I'm gonna do in you place? I get bored.'

'True,' I say. 'I get bored, too.'

She sniffs and I turn away, the two of us watching the TV. We sit in silence while the four o'clock news runs a teaser: a triumphant rainbow rally to celebrate the Yes Vote victory. I'm half-expecting Tayta to make some doomsday prediction, or to pray out loud, but today she doesn't bother. She just sighs wearily while the anchor segues to a moving map of Sydney's West. Out of the whole of Australia, the highest No Vote result came from here, at almost seventy-four per cent. I stare at the image on the screen, at The Area coloured red while the rest of the country shimmers blue, as if it were its own sovereign enclave.

'You know the world,' says Tayta, still watching the report, 'it no stop for no one. Not for you, not for me, not for Chadi. It always keep moving; every day, something new.'

I nod silently.

'That life,' she says. 'You never know what coming. The things that happen, even in my dream I can't imagine.'

'Well, I never thought you'd sell this house.'

'*Eh.*' She nods. 'But I move before. When you dad was born, I move *country*. In Lebanon I have house and friend and all my family. But we very poor. And so I pray to God to go to Australia. I pray with all my heart. Because I want the education for my children. I want them to go to the university and to have good job. And that no easy, Nicole. Coming here, no money, no language. But I *pray*, I *pray*, I *pray*.'

'You're right,' I say. 'That was a much bigger move than this.'

'*Eh*, twenty-three day on the ship. And when I come to this country, I have nothing. All I do is work and make home for my children. Never I think I lose my daughter. *Never* I think I bury Chadi.'

'I know, Tayta. It's very hard.'

'Mm.' She nods. 'But God never leave. Everything in life, it go. But *Allah hadik.' God is beside you.* 'He no watching you from above; He see your life from next to you. And He remember it all.' She says it with an unexpected joyfulness. 'When you think about you day, about the people you see, you never imagine God. But He was there too. When you eating, when you shopping. Always there. He the only one that never leave you alone.' She puts her hand to her chest. '*Ana*, I old now, Nicole. In a few year, I almost eighty.

I marry, I have baby, I have lots of thing. But they no here now. They gone.'

I look out the window at her garden; at a day my cousin will never see. 'Nothing seems real anymore. Do you feel that way sometimes?'

That we're standing on a spinning rock, being watched by another world.

'*Eh*,' says Tayta. 'But it is. Today is today; we no go back. All we can do, we move on.'

'I've never been good at that – at letting people go.'

She sighs. 'Listen, Nicole. Sometime life, it like this house. You happy, but the people around you – you neighbour – they move. And they no coming back. If you stay, *you miss them more*. And you live alone. And everywhere around you, empty house.'

I nod. 'Yeah, I know.'

'But you can move, too. You can find new home, and new neighbour. And maybe you be happy there; maybe it better for you.'

She rests her head back and I look at the walls, knowing they won't be standing for much longer. I think about life; about love and loss, and how neither can exist without the other. I think about the weight of them, the balance. The relentless pull of the world, and all the people that get left behind.

And I think, *What if I can't?* 'What if I can't be happy?'

Tayta keeps her eyes closed, her face peaceful in the setting sun. 'You will be,' she says. 'Life funny like that.'

* * *

Later that afternoon, I get in my blue car and start the long drive home to Kenthurst. It made me sad to leave her, and the feeling of it follows me to a set of lights on Rookwood Road. I think about my cousin buried somewhere to my right, and for a moment it's hard to breathe.

Seconds pass. The light stays red.

I put my windows down and that's when I notice the driver beside me. He's in a white HiLux with a Bulldogs flag hanging from his rear-view.

'*Go the Doggies!*' he yells, and he honks his horn.

I sit staring at him, and then I do what Chadi would do. I smile and I honk back.

'*Onya, Doggies!*' he yells, this time with his fist in the air, as the lights go green.

I watch him drive off and I think, *What a fucking maniac*. And then despite it all, I start to laugh. I laugh out loud, and then I cry like a kid.

And by the time I get to the freeway, I think,

Tayta might be right.

Acknowledgements

Thank You God. Only You and I truly know the journey we've been on for the past few years. Thank You for never leaving me. Thank You for always guiding me with a gentle hand. My best friend, my closest companion. Thank You for making my dream come true.

To my parents – thank you for everything you've done for me; for always supporting me and letting me be myself, and for raising me to love books! My life has been blessed because of all the sacrifices you've made. I wouldn't have been able to write this story without the time and space that you gave me. I love you Mum and Dad.

Thank you Tayta for being brave enough to migrate from Lebanon all those years ago, and for being the best *tayta* in the world. And thank you to my sisters, Tina and Vic for being my partners in life and for all the laughs, I love you both.

Vic – you read this story in its absolute worst version, over four years ago. You were one of the first people to see the potential in it, and to tell me to keep going. Thanks, sis.

To my cousin/brother George Sarkis – thank you for reading this book a million times. Thank you for sitting with me and agonising over single words for hours on end. Thank you for believing I'd get it published from the start.

To my friend Christine Khoury – there's no mate like you. You took this dream of mine on, like it was your own. I'll never forget all the help you've given me, from reading drafts, to staging zoom sessions so I could practice my pitch. Also, thank you for taking the photo that's been used as my official headshot – if anyone knows me, they'll know that this was no small task!

Now for the business end – ULTIMO PRESS! Alex Craig, James Kellow, Robert Watkins, Katherine Rajwar, Alisa Ahmed, Emily Cook and Brigid Mullane – I couldn't have asked for a better team. Many publishers talk about diversity, but Ultimo walks the walk. Thank you for giving writers like me a platform to tell stories that deserve to be heard. I can honestly say that *Something Blue* found the perfect home at Ultimo. I especially want to thank my hero and publisher Alex Craig, who discovered my book and believed in it right away. I've been so blessed to have you as a mentor, thank you for championing my work and for all your time and attention. A special thanks also to the amazing Katherine Rajwar for being so passionate about promoting this book, and for listening to me rant about Kanye West, twice. A big thank you to my brilliant editing team: Alisa Ahmed, Ali Lavau and Rebecca Hamilton – your feedback has been invaluable, and equally so your kind words! Thank you all!

To George Saad, who designed my dream cover – you are a stunning talent, thank you!

Last, but definitely not least, thank you to all my friends and family who have supported me over the years – my cousins, my best friends, and the Lebanese community at large. It has been the enduring honour and privilege of my life to be born in Sydney, and to be a part of a community like ours: vibrant, faithful, and proud!

I hope this story brings you joy and pays homage to The West in the ways that it should.

Alex Sarkis was born and raised in Sydney's West to Lebanese immigrant parents. In her early twenties she began writing stories of her own. Her main source of inspiration has always been the wild and wonderful landscape of her hometown, her family's heritage, and the pride she feels in being an Australian. *Something Blue* is her debut novel.